ANNIE'S AUTUMN ESCAPE

Debbie Viggiano

For the lovely and much-treasured Mother Bryant

Chapter One

'Annie, darling,' said my husband. 'Leave that for a minute. Come and sit down. There's something I need to tell you.'

'One moment,' I replied, as two slices of wholemeal, slightly burnt around the edges, shot out of the toaster and catapulted across the worktop. I scooped them onto the breadboard and, just like every morning, began spreading on the butter. 'Be a love and get the marmalade out of the cupboard.'

Keith was sitting at the kitchen table, an expectant look upon his face. In another five minutes I would look back at this moment and realise his expression was nothing to do with patiently waiting for breakfast. A lot can happen in five minutes, as I was about to find out.

'I don't want marmalade,' he said.

'But you always have marmalade,' I countered.

We always had marmalade. That's how it was. We were creatures of habit.

As my husband hadn't moved from the table, I fetched the marmalade myself. Women do these things when men don't. Females are programmed to run on autopilot. Invariably, by the time most men have lumbered their way out of a chair, scratched crotches, smacked lips, and looked vaguely at a row of kitchen cupboards wondering which one housed the marmalade, the efficient wife would have likely done the online weekly shopping in the interim.

'Here,' I said, setting the toast with its marmalade topping in front of him. 'Oh.' I looked at the table in surprise. Something was missing from our habitual routine. 'You haven't made the tea.'

Keith *always* made the morning tea. While I tended to the toast, he was the one who boiled the kettle and took charge of the PG Tips. As I said, we were creatures of habit.

'This morning I don't want tea.'

I peered at him. Was my husband coming down with something?

'But we always have a cup of tea with our toast and marmalade.'

'Annie, will you please sit–'

'Yes, yes.' I waved an impatient hand. 'I will in a minute. Sorry, but I can't eat toast without a cuppa. It's too dry.'

Keith sighed as I picked up the kettle. There was plenty of water within. I flicked the switch and began pulling mugs from the overhead cupboard.

Over the whine of the kettle, he repeated, 'I don't want tea.'

I turned to look at him. 'What's up with you?'

'I want a change.'

'Okay, I'll make you a coffee.'

Ignoring his eye roll, I reached into the same cupboard

that was home to the marmalade and withdrew a jar of instant. Keith was now quietly sighing. It was something he'd been doing a lot of lately. It was faintly annoying. But then again, we all sighed. I did it myself sometimes. I sighed when I picked up his pants. I sighed when finding a pair of festering size nine socks under the bed. I sighed when rescuing sodden towels from the bathroom floor and I sighed as they were refolded over the heated rail.

Keith was now drumming his fingers. That was something I never did on account of them always being occupied and far too busy to drum. Our daughter might have long flown the nest, but I still worked, still had a home to run, and – as any female will attest – a woman's work is never done.

'Annie, please leave the coffee. I don't want that either.'

'I've done it now,' I said, bringing both mugs over.

I placed them on the table, pulled out a chair and flopped down heavily. *Oooph!* Picking up a slice of toast, I took a huge bite. Mm.

I loved the weekends, and this particular Saturday morning in the first week of a golden September was no exception. There was no work to think about. Instead, just moments to savour. Steaming tea. Hot toast with all the melted butter running into the marmalade. Except it was a bit congealed now. The warmth had been lost while overseeing the tea and coffee. Strange how Keith hadn't made it. I couldn't remember the last time he'd not tended to the teas. Probably when he had been in bed with that virus.

'Annie?'

'Yes, darling. What is it you want to tell me?'

I smiled benignly at my husband of thirty-five years. He was still a decent looking guy. Okay, he no longer made my heart flutter but that wasn't his fault. It was probably down to my menopause.

I was no longer interested in "things". Hadn't been for a while. Romantically "things" had petered out months ago. I couldn't even remember when we'd last made love. Oh, wait. Yes, I could. It had been painful. He'd repeatedly jabbed his erection between my legs, but that area had been as unyielding as a nun in a chastity belt. In that moment – bizarrely – I'd recalled reading an article in the papers about an elderly actress who'd gleefully told her reader she was "still moist". That moment with Keith had absolutely not been "moist". More… dry and completely shrivelled up. I'd been left wondering how the actress – with endless toy boy lovers – was achieving the elusive slide-and-glide factor that so evaded me.

Keith had eventually given up and – sore and chaffed – I'd felt nothing but relief. We'd hugged instead. And that's what we'd done ever since. I'd presumed the once glorious slide-and-glide intimacy between us was now that of sliding and gliding into the autumn years of our lives.

'…not easy.'

'What's not easy?'

'Why aren't you listening to me?'

'Sorry, I was miles away.'

4

'Evidently. Annie, this is important. I need you to hear what I'm saying. Not gaze out the window and mentally drift off.'

'I'm all ears,' I assured, reaching for my tea.

Whatever Keith had to say, I wished he'd get on with it. I wanted to ring our daughter this morning. Talk to Carly about her growing bump. Maybe go shopping together for some more tiny sleepsuits. It was too exciting! Our first grandchild. In another three months Carly and husband Ryan would be the brand-new parents of Baby Charlotte. How joyful. Although it wouldn't have mattered if Charlotte had been a Charles instead. We were just ecstatic that everything was going well and–

'Annie!' Keith's voice was sharper now. 'It really is most galling when you don't pay attention.'

'Sorry, I was just thinking about Carly and–'

'I'm trying to tell you something important.'

'You have my full attention,' I promised.

Oh my goodness. I'd never seen Keith looking like this before. Everything about him seemed to be at bursting point. It must be something momentous. A real whopper of a surprise. Oh *wow*. I had a sudden sneaking feeling what this was about.

My next birthday was a big one. In fact, it was a horrendous one. It carried a zero. Not forty – which had been faint-making. Not fifty – which, metaphorically, had seen me reaching for the smelling salts. But sixty. How the heck could I be coming up to sixty when the *essence* inside me still felt twenty? Mind you, the mirror bore testament to the fact that I was decades past twenty, no matter how young the heart felt. The mirror and I weren't friends. These days it was rarely looked at unless tweezing a hair from the chin.

'…and it's going to come as a surprise.'

I knew it! I just KNEW Keith was on the verge of exploding with this secret. How thrilling! A tiny part of my heart began to sing. My birthday was in two weeks' time, so he'd probably been plotting behind the scenes for a while. What had he been planning? A swanky meal out? No, no, of course not, Annie. This was a BIG birthday. Therefore, my husband was hugging a BIG surprise. And then I gasped as another thought occurred.

A couple of years ago, when Keith had been approaching sixty himself, he'd mentioned going to the Maldives. Experiencing the holiday of a lifetime. After all, it was now, at this stage of our lives, that we finally had some dosh to spend on ourselves. The mortgage had been paid off. There was money in the bank. But then Covid had come along. The travel industry had been in uproar, and the Maldives had been put on hold. But now… well now things were normal! And *another* sixtieth birthday was looming. Mine! I looked at my husband with shining eyes.

'I think I know what you're going to say,' I beamed.

'Do you?'

'The surprise. Is it the Maldives?'

'Er–'

'Ah, okay. Is it New York?' That was fine. It was on our Bucket List.

'No, it's–'

'Oh. My. God.' I clutched my heart. 'Australia. Am I right or am I right?'

'None of those. Annie, I'm leaving you.'

Chapter Two

It's funny how you can happily bumble through life, thinking everything is perfectly peachy.

Splurge on baby gear – tick.

Check out new coffee shop with my besties, Bella and Caz – tick.

Spend fortunes at garden centre unconcerned about bank balance – tick.

But while getting on with such things and grumbling about minor nuisances – like the postman being late or running out of loo rolls – behind the scenes something stellar had been stealthily creeping about. Unobserved. Invisible. Completely undetected, but slyly waiting for the right moment to reveal itself.

In many ways, married life had gotten so much easier. The only real anxiety in the last couple of years had been our parents. Last year my in-laws had passed away and Keith had been devastated. They'd left a tidy inheritance which had added to his distress. "They had more money at the end of their lives than at any other time, and what did they do? Hoard it! Why didn't they spend it? Go on a cruise or something. Instead, they sat watching telly from morning to night. *We're* not doing that, Annie. You can't take the filthy lucre with you, so we're going to spend it."

I'd been delighted and initially treated myself to a new pair of jeans. But after that, I'd realised there was nothing I really wanted. Keith hadn't exactly indulged either. He loved gardening and his only splurge had been at the garden centre. In the last few months, he'd spent hours there, mulling over perennials and plants with eyebrow-raising names. When I'd told Caz and Bella that my husband had come home with *Sticky Willy* and *Cockhold Herb,* they'd snorted down their noses. Even so, Keith had done a good job in the garden, and the flowerbeds looked amazing – as did our new bank balance.

Keith's bereavement grief had eased when Carly and Ryan had ecstatically announced their baby news. Life was an eternal cycle. As the old left, the new came in. And on, and on.

My own parents were frail and doddery, and Mum had dementia, but both were still clinging to independence. Refusing help. A source of endless worry. But dealing with these things together – whilst approaching our own autumn years – had become our own personal "new normal". What was absolutely, categorically *not* normal, was listening to my husband of thirty-five years calmly announcing he was off.

I stared at him. Eyes wide. Silent. Inside my head there was a cacophony of screaming. Outside my head the only noise was the steady tick-tock, tick-tock of the kitchen clock. This couldn't be true. I must have misheard.

'What did you say?' I whispered.

9

Keith leant across the table and enfolded my hands – so suddenly cold – within his. They were warm. Large, caring, capable hands. Hands that had held mine the first time he'd said, "I love you." Hands that had squeezed mine when I'd said, "I do". Hands that had wiped our respective tears when our sleeping son had been born. Hands that I'd crushed when pushing Carly into the world. We'd even promised that – when it was time to leave this planet – the one who was going would have their hand held by the other until it was all over. How ironic. Keith was now holding my hand, telling me he was leaving my world, except this experience was surely far worse than dying.

'I can't do this anymore, darling.'

The endearment was tender, the preceding words brutal.

'W-Why?' I stuttered.

He didn't reply. Just looked at me. Sad. His face oh so sad.

'D-Did I do something wrong?'

I cast about for clues. Looked around the kitchen table as if to find the answer propped against the salt and pepper pots. Oh God. I'd made him a drink that he'd not wanted.

'Was it… the coffee?'

An almost imperceptible shake of the head. No. Not the coffee. Stupid question.

'You haven't done anything wrong, Annie.'

Another gentle squeeze of my hand.

I stared at him in confusion. So… if *I* hadn't done anything wrong, then…

'Have *you* done something wrong?'

My words were barely audible.

This was ridiculous. Of *course* Keith hadn't done anything wrong! He was a law-abiding sixty-two-year-old man. He'd been in the same job, completely and thoroughly resolute, for nearly forty years. In any family crisis, his voice had always been the one of reason... like when Carly, teenage and hormonal, had ranted and raved; or the family cat had got run over; or when my mother – in the grip of a dementia frenzy – had spitefully said I wasn't her daughter.

'Yes,' he confirmed. 'I've done something wrong.'

My brow puckered.

'So... you want to leave me because' – I fought for clarity – 'of a *wrongness*.'

'That's about the gist of it.'

It still didn't make sense.

'Did you break the law?' I ventured.

Had Keith driven his car too fast? Been pulled over by a policeman? Behaved in a very un-Keith-like way and punched Ploddy on the nose and was now going to jail? Was it that sort of *wrongness?*

'Annie, let me get you a brandy.'

'It's half past eight in the morning,' I muttered.

'You're in shock.'

A glass of golden liquid materialised in front of me. I sipped obediently welcoming the burn at the back of my throat as it blazed a hot trail down my oesophagus.

Keith paused. Chose his moment carefully. Waited

11

until colour had returned to my ashen face. And then, unflinchingly, he told me why he was leaving.

'I've met someone else.'

He remained unflinching when the brandy – in one swift and sudden movement – hit him squarely in the face and dripped pretty, golden puddles across the kitchen table.

Chapter Three

'Who?' I demanded. 'Who have you met?'

Keith silently reached for the dishcloth draped over the back of a chair. He wiped the brandy from his face, then dried the table.

I stared at him with wild eyes. I didn't want to observe my husband – yes, *my* husband, he wasn't available to anyone else – calmly mopping up. I wanted answers to *this* mess. The one of *his* making. I snatched the towel from his hand.

'I'm talking to you!'

Keith put up his hands. A gesture of surrender. 'Someone else. I have met another woman.'

'I heard that bit. I want to know her name.'

'Why? What purpose does it serve?'

'What purp–?'

I broke off and glared at this man sitting so familiarly by my side. He looked like Keith. He sounded like Keith. But the words coming from his mouth belonged to an alien.

My voice was suddenly shrill. 'Because I can't get my head around what you're telling me. Right now, I feel like I'm in a bad dream. Where on earth would you get the time or the opportunity to meet another woman? And anyway' – I pointed out – 'it's not like you even frequent the sort of places to pick up another woman.'

Keith rarely went to the pub. And whilst he wasn't quite at a time of his life where he had a burning desire to play Bingo, you certainly wouldn't find him queuing for entry into a London club like *Tiger Tiger*. Even if he were up for it, the bouncers would possibly object. After all, Keith thought garage music was something to play while tinkering under the bonnet of his car.

'Her name doesn't matter.'

'It does to me.'

And then my hand flew to my mouth as a thought occurred.

'Oh God. Do I know her? Is that why you're reluctant to tell me?'

I suddenly felt horribly sick. Was it a pal?

Mentally, I went through a list of our mutual friends.

Graham and Callie. Could it be Callie? Nah, Keith had always said Callie bore a striking resemblance to Bob, her border collie. She certainly had Bob's halitosis. It couldn't be her.

Paul and Sue. Could it be Sue? Surely not. Sue was so tall she made a giraffe look like a dwarf. Whilst Keith was no shortie, I couldn't see him craning his neck to fondly nibble her ear.

Derek and Clare. Could it be Clare? She had ankles that neatly folded over her Marks and Spencer shoes and bore a striking resemblance to Boris Johnson. No, not

Clare.

That left Colin and Bella, and Andrew and Caz. Bella and Caz were my best friends. But it couldn't be either of them. They might periodically moan like blazes about their husbands, but they wouldn't leave them.

Would they?

Suddenly I didn't know. I wasn't sure of anything. If someone had asked me five minutes and ten seconds ago if my husband of thirty-five years was off to pastures new, I'd have looked at them as if they'd spoken in tongues.

'No, you don't know her.'

'Please, Keith. I want details. Put me out of my misery.'

'Darling,' he said softly. 'I don't want to hurt you.'

I couldn't comprehend his words. My husband was still using the most affectionate term of endearment – in my opinion – but at the same time he was killing me. A slow suffocation.

My hand reached for my throat and began to claw. Suddenly I couldn't breathe. I was choking. My tonsils had unhooked themselves from my pharynx and were now blocking a vital airway.

Keith was off his chair in a trice, pulling me up, wrapping his arms around me.

'You're having a panic attack. It's okay. *You're* okay. I'm here.'

For now.

The unspoken words seemed to hover in the air between us.

I clung to him. His familiar body. Arms like a welcoming haven. My rock. Except the rock had shifted. Now it was hurting me. I sucked in a lungful of air and pushed him away.

'Just tell me her bloody name,' I wheezed.

'Pippa Kipling.'

Chapter Four

'Her name is Pippa Kipling,' I sobbed.

It was Sunday morning. A whole twenty-four hours had passed since Keith had delivered his bombshell.

I was in Bella's kitchen, weeping all over her fashionably distressed table. Caz was sitting alongside, patting me on the back, like a mother soothing a child who'd cut its knee. But in my case, it was my heart that was lacerated.

Keith had since packed a bag and gone. I had no idea of his whereabouts. No forwarding address. Nothing had been discussed. There had been no mention of divorce. No talk of when he'd be back for more clothes. No indication of when we'd need to divide up the contents of the marital home before putting it on the market. Right now, I was in Limbo Land.

I'd spent the entirety of yesterday under the duvet, hugging Keith's pillow, sobbing until my sinuses were so swollen, I could no longer smell the faint trace of him on the bed linen.

The realisation that Friday night had been the last time in my life that he'd lain by my side, felt like a gaping wound. Was I now destined to spend the rest of my days sleeping alone, emotionally bleeding into the mattress?

I'd cried until exhausted and slept the day away, awaking at random times. Half past three in the afternoon to relieve a burgeoning bladder. Twenty past nine in the evening, ravenous but unable to eat. Two o'clock in the morning, dehydrated and with a pounding headache. Finally, just before six this morning. My head had thumped worse than any hangover, but my rumbling stomach had demanded nourishment.

As I'd stood in the kitchen waiting for the kettle to boil, I'd messaged Caz and Bella via our group WhatsApp thread.

Girls. Keith has left me. I haven't told anyone else, not even Carly xx

An hour later, Bella had been the first to read the message. My mobile had erupted within seconds.

'Annie, darling. What the bloody hell has happened?'

'Oh, Belles.' I'd put down my tea and tried to stem a fresh flow of tears. 'Keith told me he has met someone else, then he gathered some belongings and left.'

'What… just now?'

Bella had sounded as befuddled as I'd still felt.

'No. Yesterday.'

'YESTERDAY?' she'd shrieked. 'Why the hell didn't you tell us immediately?'

'I couldn't think straight. Couldn't function.'

'Stay right there, lady.'

Ten minutes later she'd screeched to a halt outside my house, likely causing net curtains to violently twitch.

18

Within seconds I'd been bundled into her car and driven away at top speed.

By the time we'd roared into Bella's road, Caz had been parked on the driveway in her ancient Polo. Their respective husbands were none the wiser about my personal drama. Colin had apparently left at dawn to go fishing and Andrew had been uninterested in Caz erupting out of bed crying, "Belles and Annie urgently need to see me." He'd pulled the duvet over his head, determined to have his Sunday morning lie-in.

And now, here we were. Three friends together, one of whom was shrieking and gasping in Bella's recently extended kitchen. The room could have been straight out the pages of a showroom catalogue. Despite the early hour, my friends were as glossy as this splendid kitchen, whereas I looked as shabby as the old cabinets that had been dumped in a skip. And then it dawned on me.

'I've been recycled,' I gasped in horror.

'I think you mean *replaced*,' said Bella.

'Is Keith's mistress a younger woman?' asked Caz.

'I don't know.' I reached for the roll of kitchen towel on Bella's table. Ripping off two sheets, I trumpeted noisily. 'All I know is her name. Pippa Kipling.'

'Pippa Kipling?' said Bella, looking blank. 'Never heard of her.'

'Maybe she's new to the village,' suggested Caz.

Little Waterlow was our stomping ground and Caz, Bella and I had known each other ever since meeting at the village primary school on our respective kids' first day in the classroom some twenty-five years ago. We'd shared everything together. From the *Terrible Twos* to the *Downright Bloody Awful Teens*. From having a crush on the new PE teacher to avoiding school committees. From sharing the minutiae of arguments with our husbands to… well, this new territory of one of them doing a bunk.

Bella had once said we were like *The Three Musketeers*. Colin had countered that we were more like *The Witches of Eastwick*. He'd joked that our weekly coffee catchups were really a smokescreen for a secret coven. He'd warned that we should watch what we discussed in case it came true. But we'd never talked about the possibility of our husbands having affairs or checked out a woman called Pippa Kipling. Indeed, the only Kipling in our midst had been the brand of cakes regularly bought and consumed when we got together.

Caz produced her phone and began tapping. 'Let's see if she's on Facebook.'

My stomach contracted. Any second now, Caz might well unearth my nemesis.

'So you haven't told anyone apart from us?' said Bella, as we waited for Caz's findings.

'No.' I shook my head. 'How on earth am I going to tell Carly that her dad has gone off with another woman?'

'Don't say anything for now,' Bella advised. 'It might be a mid-life crisis.'

'Isn't Keith a bit old for one of those?' I asked.

'Perhaps he's a late developer,' Caz suggested, not taking her eyes off the phone screen as she scrolled. 'It's not that long ago that Keith lost his parents. Perhaps it unhinged him. Grief can do strange things. Maybe he needs to find himself, or something.'

'What, by shacking up with another woman?' Bella rolled her eyes. She caught my look of distress. 'Sorry, Annie. That was insensitive. I just meant...' she shrugged helplessly.

'That Keith is behaving like a knob.' I gave her a watery smile.

'Exactly.' She squeezed my hand. 'He'll be back in six months' time with his tail between his legs.'

'Along with a worn-out dick,' Caz muttered.

I let out a strangled sob. How had this happened?

'Found her!' Caz let out a squawk of triumph. 'Oh crap.'

'What?' Bella and I chorused.

Caz pursed her lips. 'Annie, you'd better brace yourself.'

Chapter Five

Suddenly I was shaking. Caz had found Pippa Kipling on Facebook. Now there was a profile picture to put with the name.

'Why must I brace myself?' I quavered.

'Because' – Caz gave me a sympathetic look – 'she's quite a bit younger than us.'

'Younger?' I whispered.

Why was I so surprised? Had I really thought that my husband would exchange his fifty-nine-year-old wife for a fifty-nine-year-old lover? Of course not!

'Dolly Bird younger?' asked Bella.

'No, but' – Caz made a see-saw motion with one hand – 'forty-two. Forty-three.'

I closed my eyes and pinched the bridge of my nose. Whatever Pippa's specific age, she was approximately twenty years younger than Keith. For heaven's sake, he was old enough to be her father. And Pippa was potentially only a dozen years older than our daughter.

Oh my goodness. How would Carly feel having such a youthful stepmother? No, stop that, Annie. Keith hasn't even divorced you yet, never mind remarried. Don't go there.

'Her account information is limited,' said Caz. 'There

are private settings in place but... let me see... I *can* tell you she lives in Meopham and works at Silver Birch Garden Centre.'

'SILVER BIRCH GARDEN CENTRE?' I shrieked, making both women jump. 'That explains why Keith couldn't wait to beetle off there. He'd visit the place every weekend and often during the week too. So instead of checking out bedding plants, he was actually bedding Pippa Kipling.'

'Let me see.' Bella grabbed the phone off Caz.

'Is she pretty?' I asked.

Bella pulled a face. 'If you like that sort of thing.'

I lunged forward and snatched the phone. Peered at it.

'Clearly my husband does.'

My eyes swam, blurring the image of a fresh-faced brunette with honey-blonde highlights. I blinked rapidly and my vision cleared enough to note hazel eyes with a fan of faint lines at the sides. Pippa also had a wide forehead and generous mouth. Suddenly I felt bitter.

'I bet she's still moist.'

'Moist?' Caz frowned.

'Yes. You know.' I jerked my head. 'Down there.'

Bella snorted. 'Sorry, Annie.' She snorted again. 'I've never heard it put so, um... succinctly.'

Suddenly I felt extremely put out.

'It's not flipping fair. If we'd been able to have sex, then none of this might have happened.'

There was suddenly a highly charged silence in Bella's kitchen. Whilst we talked about pretty much everything,

23

we'd never told each other what went on in the bedroom. Well, not in my case. I was a private person.

Caz was the first to speak.

'Have you not been sleeping together?'

'Sleeping together, yes. Getting the sheets into a tangle, no.'

Bella and Caz exchanged a look.

'So... when did you last do it?' asked Bella.

I shrugged. 'I dunno. Ages ago.'

'Years ago?' Caz was looking worried.

'No.' I shook my head. 'But... well... months ago. Long enough for Keith's willy to perk up at a forty-something still wafting pheromones. Don't look at me like that, girls, and please don't tell me you both still behave like rabbits with Colin and Andrew?'

'Well, not like rabbits, no,' said Bella.

'But certainly once a week,' put in Caz.

'Once a *week*?' I gasped. 'So... so... is there something physically wrong with me? Should I see a sex therapist? Or a gynaecologist? Ask him or her to shine a light between my legs to see if I still have all my bits and pieces?'

'Annie, it's the menopause. It happens to all women. One day you look at your husband and while your brain is thinking, "I want you", the body is saying, "One moment, girlfriend, I'm not sure I can get on board here." But it doesn't have to be like that.'

'How?'

'You've heard of hormone replacement therapy. Why didn't you try it?'

'Because I like to be natural,' I protested.

'Of course,' Caz soothed. 'But sometimes the body needs a little help. What about some alternative herbal jollop?'

'The thought never entered my head. I just presumed...' I trailed off.

'I know,' said Bella. 'It's unfair that Mother Nature lets men continue to father children even into their eighties, while women are left redundant in that department. Nonetheless, help is at hand. It's not too late for you to go on HRT. Talk to your GP.'

'Even better, see an endocrinologist,' Caz advised. 'They take a snapshot of your blood and give you bio-identical hormones.'

'Is that what you did?' I asked.

'Yes,' Caz nodded. 'And whilst I'm not a sex maniac by any stretch of the imagination, when Andrew waggles his eyebrows, my body does manage to splutter into life and generally a nice time is had by all.'

I handed back the phone – and Pippa Kipling's image – to Caz. I'd seen enough.

'And to think I'd initially thought Keith was revving up to tell me about a surprise birthday present to somewhere exotic.' I heaved a sigh. 'Anyway, thanks for the advice, ladies, but it's not particularly helpful. What's the point of going on HRT and waking up one's libido? First, I no longer have a man to be sexy with and, second, I don't *look* sexy. Who the heck is going to give me the eye and say, "Whoa, check out the sassy sixty-year-old over

25

there!"

Caz gave me a wicked look. 'Maybe it's time to change.'

'And also' – Bella was looking thoughtful – 'maybe Annie should metaphorically stick two fingers up at Keith and take herself off somewhere wonderful to celebrate her big birthday. In fact, why don't the three of us have a girly holiday?'

'You cannot be serious,' I said.

'Never more so,' said Caz. 'I'm on board. Andrew won't mind.'

'Nor will Colin,' said Bella. 'Right. Where do you want to go, Annie?'

'W-Where...?'

I gaped at these two wonderful women. My besties. There for me through thick and thin.

'Yes, where?' Caz prompted. 'If I were a genie and giving away free wishes – Keith excluded – what would you ask for?'

'Well, I'd... I'd like to go to a waterpark and behave like a kid. Ride a camel in the desert. Watch a spectacular sunset. Dance like nobody is watching.' Suddenly I felt rebellious. 'Shop until I drop and get spectacularly drunk with a hunk.'

'Attagirl,' said Caz, slapping her thigh.

'I know just the place,' said Bella, looking like she'd glimpsed the Holy Grail.

'Margate?' I feebly joked.

'Dubai.'

Chapter Six

'Dubai,' I repeated. It came out as a sigh. 'That's... far away.' The furthest I'd ever been from home was Greece.

Caz was once again tapping her phone's screen.

'From Heathrow Airport, Dubai is almost three and a half thousand miles away.'

My stomach contracted. Could I really travel that far from Keith? The thought filled me with terror. But could I go that far to escape Pippa Kipling? Definitely. Suddenly the thought of packing a bag and sodding off was immensely appealing.

'How soon can we go?'

'According to my info here' – Caz tapped her screen – 'it's still warm.'

'Warm sounds good,' said Bella.

'By that, I mean stinking hot,' Caz clarified. 'I think we need to do this properly, girls. Also' – her eyes lasered into mine – 'if you're serious about getting drunk with a hunk, you need to do something about how you're looking.'

'Caz!' I gulped. 'Haven't I been wounded enough in the last twenty-four hours?'

'Sorry, sweetie, but we're your best friends. We can say these things.'

'Hey, leave me out of it,' Bella protested.

'No. Honesty is the best policy.' Caz was adamant. 'You've told me so many times that Annie could knock years off herself just by doing something with her hair.'

'Have you?' I gasped, giving Bella an injured look.

Her shoulders sagged. 'Yes. Sorry, Annie. While it's nice to be natural, it doesn't always do one favours. You have gorgeous long hair but all that salt-and-pepper is beyond aging. Apart from anything else, the lack of colour washes you out.'

'Right,' I said, folding my arms across my chest. A defensive gesture. 'So maybe if I'd gone on HRT and dyed my hair, my husband wouldn't have left me. Is that what you're both saying?'

'Don't get chippy.' Caz waggled a finger. 'This is nothing to do with Keith but everything to do with Dubai. If you want to go there and do the things you just said, you need to look the part. Dubai is glamorous.'

'And I'm not.'

'No, darling.' Bella leant across and squeezed my shoulder. 'But there's nothing to say you can't be.'

I let my folded arms drop into my lap.

'You're right. I've let myself go.'

'Only a teensy bit,' said Caz kindly.

'But it's all fixable,' Bella assured. 'Apart from anything else, your confidence is in pieces and – after looking at Ms Kipling's profile pic – your self-esteem is probably a bit wobbly too. It's time to spoil yourself.'

'Abso–flipping–lutely,' I said fiercely. 'And anyway, I

know I look bloody awful.'

Blimey, where had that bit of backbone come from?

Bella and Caz were only fifteen months younger than me but – on a good day – they could easily pass as fifteen years younger. But my friends were no stranger to the hair salon with their highlights, lowlights, and several shades in between.

I'd mainly opted to grow old gracefully because of Keith's attitude to aging. He'd always poked fun at Bella and Caz bleaching their hair and teeth, but at least I now knew their secret weapon on why their sex drive hadn't keeled over and their chin wasn't growing a goatee. It also explained why Caz, earlier this year, had taken up pole fitness while Bella, giggling girlishly, had bought both leotard and ribboned pumps from eBay and signed up for ballet classes at the village hall. Keith had hooted, and I'd dutifully laughed along with him. But so much for Keith mocking my friends, for what had he done? Gone off with a woman who had a head full of highlights and a forehead that, thanks to Botox, was smoother than the slippery slope my marriage had skidded down.

Suddenly I realised there had been "signs" with Keith. I'd just been too complacent to notice. He'd thrown away his old-fashioned jeans and taken to wearing skinnies, then shaved his head to 'hide' a widening bald patch. Under my nose his sap had been rising, but I'd failed to recognise it.

'You know, girls, I've been dreading my upcoming birthday. Everyone says "Naughty Forty" and "Nifty Fifty". But what do they say about sixty? It's a completely new season in one's life. The autumn years.'

'Annie, stop being negative,' said Caz. 'It's not about how old you are, it's about how you *feel*. Change how you *feel*. It's time to be "Sexy Sixty".'

'Ha bloody ha,' I sighed. 'Nobody is sexy at sixty.'

'I think several *Loose Women* might let rip with rude words if they heard that,' said Bella.

'Listen, Annie' – Caz regarded me earnestly – 'if you live to be one hundred, you have another forty years to go. You might as well enjoy yourself. For the first time in your life, money isn't an object. The mortgage is paid off, Carly has long flown the nest, and there's money in the bank. Are you going to die lonely and embittered with a bulging bank balance?'

'Keith more or less said the same thing after his parents died. But we've never got around to spending any of his inheritance.'

'Well maybe you should take action, before he blows the lot on Pippa Kipling,' Bella pointed out. 'If Keith is on a marital break, that means you are too.'

'Blimey. I never thought of it like that.'

'I propose we go to Dubai the beginning of October,' said Caz. 'That gives Annie time to get on top of her hormones, visit a hairdresser, and do some wardrobe shopping. Dubai is blingy. Even the buildings are blingy.'

'You're kidding,' I blinked. 'How can a building be blingy?'

Caz tapped her phone screen again. 'Look.' She showed me a picture of a skyscraper at night that appeared to be glittering. 'Sparkle Towers. Part of a multi-building complex at Dubai Marina. We'll make a note to go there.'

Despite my misery over Keith, I felt a tiny flicker of something. Hope. A glimpse of an immediate future that, whilst new and unnerving, provided baby steps in helping me to adjust. Something to focus on. A distraction. A starting point. A goal. Okay, going on a break with my girlfriends wasn't going to fix my life in the long term, but it would give me a breathing space to recalibrate and take stock.

I felt a sharp pang that I wasn't planning this incredible travel destination with my husband. However, I was lucky to have two girlfriends so willing to thoroughly support me. And they were right. Money wasn't an object. As such.

I, personally, didn't have the funds to pay for Dubai. My working life had wound down in the last couple of years. From full-time personal assistant commuting to London to part-time virtual secretarial services from the study at home. Copy typing, proof reading, editing. Nothing mind-blowing. I was my own boss, which was great. But the income ebbed and flowed.

The joint account was something else. It was like a gun. Fully loaded. Ready to be emptied. But hopefully not by blasted Pippa Kipling. However, the bulk of the balance belonged to Keith. Inheritance money. I couldn't just help myself. I'd need to talk to him first. Also, ringing him would give me an excuse to hear his voice.

I just hoped, when I rang his number, Pippa Kipling wouldn't answer on his behalf.

Chapter Seven

Walking into a silent house – after Bella had dropped me home – felt most odd.

My emotions were all over the place. I felt like I'd been on a rollercoaster and been mangled on the descent.

CRASH! There went the heart. Little pieces everywhere.

WHOOSH! An adrenalin rush, images of Dubai and blingy thingies.

WALLOP! Realising your hair shade is *Worzel Gummidge Grey.*

BANG! Take HRT or grow a beard like Del Boy's Uncle Albert.

WHAM! Pippa Kipling. Observe then scream, rant and rave.

SCREECH! Rollercoaster performs emergency stop leaving one gasping for breath and wondering where to stagger off to next. Home? Travel shop? Gynae? Or Google Pippa Kipling's name, find her address, drive to her house, and scream through the letterbox, 'YOU ARE A BITCH!'

What would Pippa's neighbours make of that?

Ethyl-two-doors-down: I knew that Pippa woman was up to no good.

Beryl-across-the-road: Indeed. The visiting bald guy isn't her husband.

That brought me up short. Did Pippa Kipling have a husband? Presumably she was divorced. Unless she had an amazingly amenable spouse prepared to share her. I had a sudden vision of Keith in bed with Pippa and... and... Larry?

Keith: Sorry about this, mate. Could you budge up a bit?

Larry: Sure. I know this isn't ideal, but my back can't take the sofa.

Pippa: Well, isn't this nice!

And what about the children? Did she have kids? If so, at her age they'd likely be teenagers. Would Keith be up for moving into her place with a couple of sulky all-knowing teens on either side of their mum's bedroom walls?

Kayleigh: Bleurgh. Mum has a lover.

Kyle: Disgusting. She's forty-two. Totally past it.

Kayleigh: And the grandpa is sixty-two. I think I'm going to throw up.

No. She couldn't have kids. Unless Kayleigh and Kyle were living with Larry. Or, unless everyone was just so thoroughly modern that nobody gave a hoot about lovers, husbands, and kids all under one roof.

Keith: (to Larry) I'm just popping upstairs with Pippa for, er...

Larry: Sure, you carry on, matey.

Kayleigh: Will you be long, Keith? Dad never was.

Shall I put the kettle on?

Kyle: Or would everyone like a G&T?

Pippa: Well, isn't this nice!

And never mind what was going on in Pippa's house and what the neighbours thought, what would *my* neighbours think? There was definitely an element of nosiness in my road. Little Waterlow was a tiny rural dot on the map of Kent and had a typical village mentality. Gossip was a pastime. It wouldn't take long for everyone to know that Keith had left me. And whilst it shouldn't have mattered what anybody thought, I couldn't help feeling ashamed.

Mrs Busybody: You okay, Annie?

Me: (fixed smile) Never better.

Mrs Busybody: Only I saw Keith in Tesco with another woman.

Me: Ah, rumbled! Yes, he met someone else and we've "consciously uncoupled".

Mrs Busybody: It's better for your mental health to be consciously outraged.

Me: You're right. I hope his knob turns green and falls off.

Mrs Busybody: Mind if I tell the whole street?

Me: About his knob falling off, or that he's left me?

Mrs Busybody: Both.

Me: Sure. Saves me the trouble.

I stomped into the kitchen, slung my handbag and keys on the table and then slumped down on a chair. One way or another, in the last twenty-four hours this room was seeing a lot of emoting. It surely wasn't good energy. Perhaps I should ring up a *feng shui* guru and do something about it.

Guru: Can I help?

Me: I think I need smudging.

Guru: Have you checked your chakras?

Me: No, and don't roll your third eye at me.

I put my head in my hands. Was I going mad? Possibly. But right now, I needed to ring Keith. Ask if it was okay to spend some money. I reached for my handbag and grabbed my mobile, but before I could make the call, it erupted in my hands making me jump. A quick look at the display revealed that Carly was calling. I took a deep breath, gathered my wits and made sure to answer with a jaunty tone.

'Darling! How are you?'

'Mum,' my daughter squawked. 'What the heck is going on between you and Dad?'

Chapter Eight

For a moment I was too stunned to answer.

'Mum? Are you there?'

'Yes,' I croaked.

'Then talk to me!'

'Yes,' I said again.

'Can you answer my question?'

Carly sounded shrill. A sure sign she was upset. Not good, especially when six months' pregnant.

'Er...' – I felt like I was feeling my way through the dark and such reply should be cautious – 'what makes you think there's a problem between me and Dad?'

'Oh for heaven's sake, Mum. I'm thirty. Not flipping three. You don't need to protect me.'

'How did you find out?' I whispered.

'Not in the best of ways. Ryan and I decided to visit the local garden centre, buy some shrubs, and then go to its café for a cuppa, and what did we see?'

'I don't know. What did you see?' I suddenly felt like I was in some sort of ridiculous knock-knock joke, waiting for Carly to deliver the punchline.

'I saw my father outside the café chatting to a woman dressed in garden centre uniform. Her name badge spelt

Pippa. At first, I thought Dad was asking this woman for some sort of assistance, like where to find the compost or something. I was all set to sneak up behind him, put my hands over his eyes and trill, "Surprise!" but instead I was the one left surprised. Suddenly Dad's gazing into this woman's eyes like she's the best thing since Miracle Grow, then she stands on her tiptoes and gives him a kiss full on the mouth.'

I made a strangled noise.

'God, sorry, Mum. I should have been more sensitive telling you this. Ryan often tells me off for lack of tact.'

'It's okay,' I warbled.

'No, it's *not* okay.'

I sensed Carly raking her hair.

'Did Dad see you?' I asked.

'Oh, yes,' she spat. 'I made sure he did. I left Ryan standing by the winter pansies with his mouth hanging open, then marched over to this woman and said, "I can see your name is Pippa but who the bloody hell *are* you?". She looked at my swollen belly and for one glorious moment I could see the horror in her eyes, especially when Dad said, "Darling, whatever are you doing here?". She rounded on Dad and said, "Is there something you haven't told me, Keith?".'

Despite the awfulness of what Carly was relaying, a part of me felt spitefully thrilled. Good. Let this woman have a scare, however short-lived. She'd stolen my husband.

'Dad then did some hasty explaining. He apologised profusely. Said this wasn't how he'd wanted me to find out.

The woman slipped away leaving him to talk to me. He told me you knew about Pippa. So how long has my father been having an affair?'

'I honestly don't know. I only found out yesterday.'

'What? Didn't you suspect anything?'

'No. Nothing. It sounds ridiculous, but... I didn't. It's all been... terribly sudden. A horrible surprise. I'm still' – I struggled to find the right word – 'processing.'

'Processing?' Carly shrieked. 'Stuff that, Mum. You need to get round to that garden centre and chuck a few plants about, then drag Dad home all the while telling him to stop making a damn fool of himself.'

'Carly, I can't do that. If Dad doesn't want to be with me, I can't force him to stay – as much as it hurts. You know that saying. If you love someone, set them free. If they come back, they're yours, and if they don't then they never were.'

'Don't spout that poppycock at me, Mum. You've been married for thirty-five frigging years. Of *course* Dad is yours.'

I took a huge shuddery breath. 'Darling, please. Don't rant. You've had a shock. We've *both* had a shock. Can we just let things settle for a bit? It's my fault this has happened.'

'What *are* you talking about?'

I was hardly going to tell my daughter that her mother's sex drive had disappeared down the sink along with the washing up water leaving her red-blooded father sexually frustrated. For surely that was why Keith had wandered down the path of temptation and ended up tickling Pippa's lilies and stroking her sweet peas. Possibly Carly might have worked this out for herself, along with incredulity that her father was still sexually active. No one wants to think about their parents doing it, whatever their age. Taboo!

'I'm talking about' – my voice was placating – 'the fact that I've been complacent. Like not bothering with my appearance anymore. Certainly not since giving up commuting and working from home.'

'And?' Carly sounded incensed. 'I never had my own mother down for being a pleaser.'

'A pleaser?' I gasped.

'Yes! So what if you stopped colouring your hair? So what if you abandoned make-up? You have envious bone structure, fantastic skin, and you've kept your figure. You look like an unkempt version of Julia Roberts.'

'Thank you, darling. I'll take that as some sort of compliment. But I can't help thinking...'

I trailed off. Keith wasn't shallow. It went much deeper. It basically all boiled down to sex. Or, rather, the lack of it. The absence of intimacy had led to a gradual distancing between us as husband and wife. Cuddles were nice but hardly intimate – unless under the duvet and completely starkers. And once, that was exactly what Keith and I had done. But, bit by bit, it had petered out. A quick, fleeting hug while in a bobbly cardi and baggy trousers before hastening off to do something else. It wasn't the same thing.

'Anyway' – I rushed on – 'I'm sure everything will sort itself out. In time.'

'What's that supposed to mean?' Carly demanded. 'You surely aren't thinking about forgiving Dad and having him back, are you?'

'Darling, he's only just gone. I don't think he's going to want to come back for some time. If at all,' I added.

But her question had also brought me up short. Of *course* I'd have Keith back. Wouldn't I?

I heard Carly sigh at the other end of the phone. A huge release of breath.

'Do you know, I had a horrible inkling about this, but didn't want to worry you.'

I frowned. 'You suspected my marriage was in crisis?' I gave a hollow laugh. 'That's strange because I was completely clueless until yesterday morning.'

'Confession time. I've been to the garden centre before and seen Dad there. It was a while ago. We bumped into each other, and he looked... all sparkly-eyed. And he had a spring in his step. We had a coffee there, and this woman passed by. I knew she worked there because she was wearing a dark green top with the garden centre's logo on it. And as she sauntered past, she and Dad exchanged a look. It was...'

'Tell me.'

'Maybe I shouldn't,' she muttered.

'I want to know.' My voice was suddenly harsh. I wanted details. So far, information had been scant.

'They gave each other this really gooey-eyed look.'

Gooey-eyed. Right. Good to know. I'd like to look gooey-eyed at something – even if it were only a flaming chocolate cake.

'After that, my female intuition was on red alert.'

'I wish you'd told me.'

'I couldn't, Mum. But it prompted me to call Dad on his mobile and ask if everything was okay between the two of you.'

'Oh my goodness, Carly.'

'I know. Sorry.'

'And what did Dad say?'

'He said everything was fine. But he sounded guarded.'

I took a deep breath and then exhaled noisily.

'Listen. You questioned him with the best of intentions. But whatever has happened, we both still–'

'Mum, I'm a bit old for the "we both still love you" pep talk.'

'But we do,' I protested.

'I know that, and before you say it, I will endeavour not to let my relationship with Dad be affected. But the truth of the matter is, I'm mad at him. *Really* mad.'

'Yeah,' I nodded. 'I can identify with that. I'm mad too. But more than anything, I'm just incredibly sad.'

'It's your birthday soon. A big birthday.'

'Don't remind me.'

'This is such a rotten thing to happen. More than ever, right now you need to spoil yourself.'

'Ah, I am. I can promise you that. Hand on heart.'

'Oh?'

'I'm going away with Caz and Bella.'

For the first time in our conversation, I sensed Carly relaxing slightly.

'Good. A spa break will be wonderful.'

'It's a bit more than that, darling.' I paused for a moment, letting some anticipation build. Then, 'I'm going to Dubai!'

'Flaming Nora, Mum. Well, good for you. Just don't go falling in love with a handsome Emirati with smouldering eyes and a wicked smile.'

'As if,' I hooted.

Nobody had a holiday romance at sixty. Did they?

Chapter Nine

After Carly and I had ended our call, I didn't miss a beat, and instantly rang Keith.

As the line connected, I suddenly felt a bit wobbly. Interesting. Since when had telephoning my husband ever given me the jitters? Never. Until now.

I now knew from Carly that, despite it being Sunday, Pippa was at work. Whilst it might be joyful working in such a lovely flowery setting, she would be on the garden centre's rota covering weekends and bank holidays. Was Keith still there too, shadowing his lady love? Or had he holed up in the café with the Sunday Papers, one eye scanning the sports section while the other fondly regarded Pippa's backside as she bent over pots of geraniums and dahlias?

I tried not to gnash my teeth as the phone continued to ring. Was my husband going to avoid speaking to me?

'Hello, Annie,' said Keith.

He sounded cautious. Also, slightly breathless. Had he distanced himself from Pippa to speak without being overheard?

'Hi,' I said.

'Is everything okay?'

'Fabulous. Wonderful. Never better. You?'

'Sorry, that was a stupid question.'

'I've just been talking to Carly.'

'Ah. So you know what happened.'

'Yes.'

'Are you phoning to put a flea in my ear? If so, I'll quite understand.'

I closed my eyes for a moment. Counted to five. It was no good letting rip, despite every part of me clamouring to do just that. It would resolve nothing.

Somewhere in the back of my head I heard my inner voice pipe up.

Don't get mad. Get even.

My eyes widened as a realisation dawned. Pippa was at the garden centre. Why not take a trip there? Yes, indeed. Just stroll in. Handbag swinging jauntily from my shoulder.

'Heyyy, Pippa!'

'Sorry, do I know you?'

'I'm Keith's wife. Annie. You met our daughter this morning, so I thought' – big grin – *'it was time you met me too. ISN'T THIS NICE!'*

'Are you there, Annie?'

'Sorry. I... yes. Look, it's about the joint account.'

'What about it?'

'Well, Caz and Bella have asked me to go away with them for my birthday, but I don't have any savings to pay for–'

'So take it from our joint account.'

'But it's quite a lot of money. It's not a day trip to

Brighton with fish and chips on the beach. It's a week in Dubai.'

Silence. To fill it, I attempted flippant banter.

'I thought I'd make a start on our Bucket List without you.'

More silence.

Terrific. Not. I could see where this was going. Bye-bye, Dubai.

'I think that's a good idea,' he said eventually.

I sat up straight. 'Pardon?'

'I want you to go, Annie. It's my present to you. And take as much spending money as you like. I've heard they do some crazily impressive fake handbags over there. All illegal of course. Get yourself something nice. And don't scrimp on the excursions. You'll probably want to buy some new clothes too. That's fine. Go berserk. It's meant to be a magical place and I want you to have a perfect time with Caz and Bella.'

I suddenly had a vast lump in my throat. It should be me and Keith doing this. Not me, Caz, and Bella, as much as I loved my besties.

'Thank you. That's... very generous.' *Salving a guilty conscience.*

'It's your money as much as mine.'

'Hardly. The bulk of it is from your mum and dad's house sale.'

'We'll sort out finances another time. For now, enjoy.'

I should have left it there but a chunk of me – the bitter part – rushed to the surface and my mouth was suddenly spitting out unchecked words.

'And how does Pippa feel about her *boyfriend* – the reference seemed utterly ludicrous on a man of sixty-two – 'splurging money on his wife?'

Keith didn't rise.

'It's nothing to do with Pippa. I must go. Bye, Annie.'

And I was left sitting at the kitchen table, alone, holding a disconnected phone, wishing with all my heart that things really weren't this way.

Chapter Ten

When Monday arrived, I wanted to keep busy.

There was no husband to chat to over breakfast. Suddenly, marmalade on toast didn't seem the right thing to eat. It had been a routine, along with the morning brew.

On a whim, I checked the larder. A box of porridge oats was hiding at the back of the cupboard. Was it still in date? Happily, yes. From now on, I'd start work after consuming a different breakfast. And two fingers up to tea. Time to switch to coffee.

From nowhere came the memory of a book I'd once read. It had been about breaking the habit of being oneself. Perhaps it was time to do just that. In fact, I'd make a start just as soon as I'd finished today's secretarial jobs. There was only one thing in today's diary entry. Copy-typing a local writer's spidery handwritten draft chapters. There weren't too many. When finished, I'd drive into town. Hit the shops. Get on that starting line to becoming a whole new me. Whoever that was.

In between tapping away at the keyboard, several texts were exchanged with Caz and Bella about dates for Dubai. Early October seemed to be the most sensible time as that was when the temperature was bearable – thirty degrees rather than a sweltering forty.

I also mentally earmarked that a conversation needed to be had with my parents about my new marital status. I gulped. What exactly was that? Divorcee-to-be? Estranged wife? Newly separated? Single?

Should I even continue to use my married surname? I was officially Mrs Anne Rosewood. Somewhere along the way an '*i*' had crept in. *Annie* sounded less formal than *Anne*. That's who I'd been for the last thirty-five years – Annie Rosewood.

Maybe I should adopt *Ms* instead of *Mrs.* I tried it for size, addressing my reflection in the computer screen.

'Hello. I'm *Ms* Annie Rosewood.'

It sounded alien. Perhaps I should go back to my unmarried name?

'Hi, there. I'm Miss Evans.'

That sounded even more strange. It had been decades since anybody had referred to me as Anne Evans. Childhood memories of school days rushed to the surface of my mind. "Anne! Stop talking!" and "Anne Evans, go to the headmistress's office now!" No, I wasn't Anne Evans.

My mobile rang. Unknown number. Possibly a new client. As I answered the call, I automatically informed the caller to whom they were talking.

'Hello, Annie Rosewood speaking.'

Resolved. Annie Rosewood I would remain.

By three o'clock, I was done with work. Time to start that transformation! Bluewater Shopping Mall beckoned. I could have ventured into Little Waterlow or visited one of the larger surrounding villages, but skincare and fashion weren't in abundance locally. It was more this season's must-have wellies and matching Barbour jackets, or fruity salves to stop lips from chapping.

Starting up the car, I drove along meandering lanes that eventually widened from single track – where you hoped and prayed to avoid a tractor coming from the opposite direction – to country roads where at least one could squash their vehicle into a hedge in order to pass another, scratching paintwork in the process. Soon I was on the A2, speeding towards glass-fronted shops and cosmetic counters with lights brighter than a theatre spotlight.

Forty minutes later, I was stationed by a glossy make-up island that artfully displayed skincare products with price tags higher than my electricity bill.

'How much?' I squeaked to the pretty young girl behind the counter.

'It's expensive,' she acknowledged. '*But* it gives sun protection, firms the jawline, plumps up the cheeks, smooths the neck and gives long-lasting moisture hydration.'

'Haven't you a brand that knocks off half a century and only costs a fiver?'

The girl gave a twittery laugh then leant in, as if to confide.

'No. But I know a man who can do that.'

'A man?'

I had visions of a male healer garbed in flowing white robes rubbing moisturiser across my forehead. Jesus?

"Annie, I've been hailed as a miracle worker, but on this occasion, I admit defeat."

The girl looked conspiratorial and moved in closer.

'My mum went and saw that guy off the telly. You know the one? He gave her an eye lift.'

I now had a mental image of my eyeballs being lifted out of their sockets and gently placed on my forehead.

'It's more affordable than you might think,' she added.

However, I didn't think Keith would appreciate having his inheritance squandered on plastic surgery. Instead, I left with an expensive face cream that promised to *restore and replenish*. Bring it on.

Keith had told me to buy new clothes, so I did. There were bargains to be had in many of the shops with sales on summer stock that needed shifting. I bought a couple of one-piece swimsuits with high cut legs – ensuring slim thighs were showcased rather than a knackered navel area – and several dresses that nodded towards glitz. Caz and Bella had emphasised that Dubai was "blingy".

Last night we'd had a Zoom get-together and discussed the cast of *TOWIE* who'd once visited Dubai. It had been noted that everything about the women was extended. In other words, eyelashes, hair, nails. Hemlines too. But down, rather than up. Theirs had swished across the ground. No shoe-string straps on dresses either. Apparently, that was frowned upon. As was flashing of underwear. No Rhianna-style matching bra and pants under a transparent dress. Well, not at our age, that was certain.

I went home with three cocktail dresses, a full-length

evening dress and lots and lots of blingy costume jewellery. I'd pass on hair extensions, but nearer the time would get some eyelashes and maybe some long nails. The latter all the better to claw Pippa Kipling.

Meow.

Chapter Eleven

I spent the rest of the week keeping as busy as possible.

The nights were horrendous. Laying on the right side of the bed meant acknowledging the left area was empty. In the end I shoved Keith's pillows in the back of the wardrobe and changed my sleeping position to the centre of the mattress. On the upside I could starfish out without a disgruntled voice saying, "For heaven's sake, Annie, move over."

During the day I made sure every minute was filled. If I wasn't working in the study, then I was filling the desk diary with appointments. Not just with clients, but personal things too. Like making a date to visit a hairdresser. Ditto a beauty salon who boasted their electrolysis services would fry chin hairs to oblivion.

I also went online and, with the curtains drawn against the outside world, attempted some yoga and body-firming exercises as shown on *YouTube*. I wasn't sure when – if ever – my body would bend and flex the way it used to, but I was determined to give it my best shot. And maybe one day I'd be able to lift my leg up and give Pippa Kipling a Charlie's-Angels-style karate chop. *Hi-yaaa!*

I also pencilled in an appointment to see my GP to

discuss hormone replacement therapy. In between all this, I regularly popped in on Carly for coffee which kept both of us upbeat because we were so excited about "Charlotte Bump".

I telephoned my parents daily and looked in on them a couple of times to cook their dinner. It was beyond Mum's capabilities to put a proper meal on the table and Dad was very laissez-faire. A pile of salad leaves and boiled eggs was a common meal. Dad would relieve the boredom by occasionally swapping the boiled eggs for a tin of salmon.

My parents refused to accept any form of care assistance. Mum was adamant she didn't have dementia and Dad didn't dare aggravate her by having any outside help – or "interference" as my mother preferred to call it. It was only in the last six months that Mum had been persuaded to have a cleaning lady, although that wasn't without its problems.

On Sunday afternoon I once again drove over to my parents' place, this time to take them out for a roast lunch. It gave Dad some much needed respite and a change of scenery. I had also made the decision to finally update them about Keith leaving. I'd harboured hope that he might have come home before the new week was out, but regrettably that idea had shrivelled and died.

'Yoohoo,' I trilled, letting myself in.

'In here, darling,' Dad called from the kitchen.

'Hello,' I said, stooping to deposit kisses on floury cheeks. 'How are you both? Oh, you're not dressed, Mum.'

'I am,' Mum protested.

Dad and I exchanged a look.

'She's being a little difficult today, dear,' he murmured.

'I heard that, Michael Evans. Don't you start on me. You're in enough trouble as it is.'

I pulled out a chair and sat down. Thankfully, I hadn't booked a table at Little Waterlow's local pub, The Angel, so being late wasn't an issue.

'You look upset, Mum,' I said, bracing myself for a tirade of nonsense.

'You'd be upset if you were me,' she said indignantly.

'What's Dad done now?'

Mum stuck out her chin. A petulant gesture. I was reminded of why old age was sometimes referred to as "second childhood".

'Your father's been flirting. Again.'

'Ah,' I nodded. This was familiar territory. Apparently, these days my father had the hots for all women. On one occasion this had even included the postman on account of him having a blond man-bun. 'Who has Dad been fluttering his eyelashes at this time?'

'The young strumpet that visits here.'

'You mean your cleaning lady, Alison?'

'Cleaning lady my arse.'

'Mum!' I chided. The dementia had not only robbed my mother of her faculties, but also finesse.

'That's no cleaning lady,' Mum continued. 'All she does is flick her duster about. The rest of the time she's wobbling her bosoms and giving your father come-hither looks.'

'Mum, do you have any idea how ridiculous you sound? Alison is in her twenties. Dad is nearly ninety.'

'She's after his money.'

'Oh for–'

'And she steals things.'

'No, she doesn't.'

'She's taken my red trousers.'

'Mum, you have the build of a sparrow. Do you really think Alison – even if she wanted your trousers – would get them over her thighs?'

'She could have them altered.' Mum's chin jutted further. She was definitely feisty today.

'Never mind Alison. How about you get dressed so we can go out for lunch?'

'I want to wear this.'

'But it's a nightdress.'

'It's pretty and I like it. Anyway, I don't have any clothes. Alison has stolen everything.'

'Mum, you have loads of clothes. Alison would need about six suitcases to take away your stuff.'

'That's where you're wrong. She's clever, see? She rolls everything into tiny bundles and pops them in her handbag.'

'Well, how about we go out and buy you some more clothes then, hm?' I coaxed, getting up.

'What are you talking about, Annie?' My mother's cloudy blue eyes momentarily cleared. 'I have a whole wardrobe of clothes upstairs. I don't need anything new.'

I sat back down again. Lunch wouldn't be happening any time soon.

'Would you like a coffee, darling?' said Dad. 'You look tired.'

'That would be lovely.'

As my father made to get up, I leapt to my feet.

'I'll do it. You stay there.'

The truth was that my dear old dad would take about fifteen minutes to make the coffee. By the time he'd creaked his body upright, staggered across the kitchen, picked up the kettle as if it were a weightlifter's bar bell – arm all the while shaking violently – I could have made for the entire street.

My eyes pricked with tears as I remembered how capable my parents had once been. Dad, fit and strong. Mum, so practical.

I opened cupboards, removed mugs, darted to the fridge, fetched milk, boiled the kettle, and put drinks on the table for the three of us before perching once again.

'Plans for lunch aside, there's another reason for my visit,' I told my parents. 'I have some bad news.'

Mum put away her jutting chin and Dad immediately looked concerned.

'Is Carly okay, dear?' he asked.

'Who's Carly?' said Mum.

'Your granddaughter, and everything is fine with her, Dad. No, it's something else. It's Keith.'

'Who's Keith?' said Mum.

'My husband.' I took a deep breath, mustering

56

patience. 'I didn't tell either of you straight away because I didn't want to cause worry.'

'What's happened?' said Dad, his craggy brow furrowing.

'Keith packed his things last Saturday morning. He's left me.'

'What?' Dad gasped. 'Why?'

'Why don't you listen, you silly old fool,' berated Mum. 'He's left her because he's died.'

'Dorothy, will you please settle down,' Dad implored. 'Annie, darling.' His gnarled hand reached for mine. 'Where has he gone?'

'Not to Heaven, that's for sure,' muttered Mum, her lips pursing. 'I remember him now. I never liked the man.'

'Yes, you did,' I protested. 'You thought the world of Keith, and he of you.' I looked at Dad. 'He's left me for another woman. Her name is Pippa Kipling.'

'Who's Pippa Kipling?' said Mum.

I tried not to gnash my teeth. 'The woman who is now with my husband.'

Mum frowned. 'Is she dead too?'

I couldn't be bothered to engage and took a sip of coffee. In a few more seconds Mum wouldn't even remember that I'd ignored her.

'I'm so sorry, Annie.' Dad squeezed my hand. 'You should have said so last week. Do you want me to ring Keith up? Have a word with him, man to man?'

'Thanks, Dad, but no. He must work through this himself. But the truth is, I think he's already done that. I

57

suspect he's been contemplating this for a while. Unfortunately, I didn't see it coming. Guess I took my eye off the ball.'

'What ball?' said Mum, looking around the kitchen for a mid-air flying object.

'I feel bad,' said Dad. 'Maybe it's our fault. You should have spent more time looking after him than coming over here and seeing to us.'

'Don't be silly.' Now it was me squeezing his hand. 'It's nobody's fault. Anyway, Keith has gone, and that's that.'

'So when's the funeral?' said Mum.

I took another sip of coffee and didn't answer.

'Now that you're a widow, you should get in touch with Malcolm,' prattled Mum.

'Who?'

'That nice boy you met at college. He was a catch.'

'That was forty-four years ago. Anyway, I'm not looking for another husband.'

'Suit yourself,' she shrugged. 'Be a dear and put the television on.'

'Mum, that's the microwave.'

'I'm here for you, darling,' said Dad. His benign expression momentarily changed. 'I might be a bit doddery' – his cheeks were turning pink with anger – 'but if I saw Keith right now, I'd be tempted to sort him out.'

'Walking sticks at dawn?' I smiled sadly. 'I guess there's no fool like an old fool.

'Who's a fool?' demanded Mum.

Chapter Twelve

I left my parents feeling slightly frazzled, as was always the case after a conversation involving gibberish. I had no idea how my father coped with my mother twenty-four-seven. When I'd once asked him, he'd shrugged and calmly said, "She's my girl. I love her."

On the short drive home, Caz rang.

'Where are you?' she squawked.

'In the car. I was meant to be taking the parents out, but Mum was having none of it.'

'So are you free right now?'

'Yes.'

'Good. Turn around and get yourself over to The Angel. Bella is on her way too. Both our husbands are busy. One is washing his car, the other is watching football, so us girls can have lunch. Plus I have news.'

The Angel was a pub Keith and I had frequented many times throughout our marriage. Landlady Cathy was on first name terms with the pair of us, as indeed with all her locals. She was a pleasant lady with a ready smile. She was also one of the biggest gossips in Little Waterlow.

A part of me was relieved that I wasn't in The Angel's restaurant with Mum and Dad minus Keith because I know Cathy would have asked about his whereabouts. I was still coming to terms with my husband's departure, and until I *had* made my peace with the situation, I didn't want to make up excuses about Keith's absence. But walking into Cathy's pub with Bella and Caz – minus Colin and Andrew – to all intents and purposes we were three women indulging in a girly lunch and chit-chat.

Fifteen minutes later we were kissing each other hello and, armed with a glass of Prosecco apiece, were perusing menus at a table in a tucked-away corner.

'This is so good,' I said, sipping appreciatively. 'Also, much welcomed. I was starting to feel like I'd disappeared down one of Alice's rabbit holes.'

'Was Mother Evans in fine fettle?' Caz enquired with a grin.

'Just a bit.' I sipped again. 'She's started to forget people's names. I dread the day she doesn't recognise her loved ones.'

'How's your dad coping?' asked Bella sympathetically.

'Brilliantly. Somehow, he just goes with the flow. I wish I had an ounce of his tolerance. I always turn up at their place mentally saying, "Be patient. Be kind." And I always leave thinking, "You failed again, Annie."'

'Don't beat yourself up,' said Caz. 'I think you're flipping marvellous if that's any consolation. When Andrew's mother went gaga, I used to end up silently screaming. He wanted her to come and live with us, but I flatly refused. Shirley was a nightmare. Up all through the night watching telly. Making breakfast at three in the morning. Then she took to ringing neighbours' doorbells in the early hours asking if anyone had seen her husband. My father-in-law had died years before. It was when Shirley started wandering and getting lost that Andrew realised she needed full-time care. The nursing home cost a fortune, but the staff were angels. Ah, heads up. Cathy's coming over to take our orders.'

I immediately pasted a ready smile on my face.

'Aye, aye,' Cathy beamed. 'Three ladies out to lunch without their hubbies.'

'Absolutely,' giggled Bella. 'We're rebelling. They're at home with pinnies on, pushing vacuum cleaners and slaving over hot irons. Colin is always saying that his home is his castle, so I told him he could jolly well have a go at cleaning it.'

'My old mum once gave me some sound advice before I married my Frank,' said Cathy. 'She said, "Think before you walk down the aisle to say *I do*. Ask yourself why you want to take home the whole pig when all you want is a bit of sausage."'

She laughed uproariously and we chortled along with her. Yes, all good fun giggling about our spouses with Cathy none the wiser about where Keith was putting his pepperoni.

We all decided to order The Angel's roast beef and Yorkshire pud. As Cathy disappeared with her notepad, Caz foraged in her handbag. Whipped out a travel brochure.

'Look, ladies.' She held the mag aloft like a taxi driver holding a placard at an airport. 'Dubai. The best value for money is the Blue Jade Hotel at Jumeirah Beach. It's currently offering seven nights for the price of six. Want to see what it looks like?' She opened the brochure to a marked page, then pushed it across the table. 'We can get a triple room with an ensuite. There's a vast mirror in the bathroom so we won't have to jostle for space when glamming up and putting our lippy on.'

'Looks great,' I agreed.

'Oooh, I'm so excited,' said Bella, hugging herself.

'However, the only availability that suits us is the first Saturday in the month. That will be' – Caz checked the dates – '2nd October. It's a little earlier than I would've liked. The temperature can still top the late thirties, but they have air-conditioning everywhere. It looks like the swimming pool is semi-shaded plus there's plenty of sun parasols.'

'Let's go for it,' said Bella.

'Go for what?' said Cathy, returning to our table. She was bearing three roast dinners, a plate in each hand and one balancing on her forearm.

'Away,' Caz explained. 'It's Annie's sixtieth this month, so we're celebrating on a grand scale with a girls-only holiday.'

'Good for you, lovelies,' said Cathy, setting the plates down. 'But how will your husbands manage without you?'

'Last time I went away without Colin' – Bella laughed – 'he ate cornflakes for the duration. He was too helpless and hopeless to cook anything.'

'Better send your men over to my pub,' said Cathy.

'I'll keep them fed and watered.'

'We'll be sure to tell them,' said Caz. 'The last thing we want is for them to fade away and…'

She trailed off as her attention visibly fragmented. Her eyes registered shock as she focussed on something – or some*one* – behind me.

I turned to look, as did Bella and Cathy, and gasped. Directly in front of us, Frank – Cathy's husband – was showing my husband to a table. On Keith's arm was a woman. She had a mane of highlighted hair which swished about as – like an excited racehorse – she tossed her head this way and that. Her free hand constantly touched the silky tendrils, repeatedly flicking them about. It was a wonder her neck wasn't covered in whip marks. Pippa Kipling wasn't working at the garden centre today. She was out for Sunday lunch with *my* hubby.

'Well,' said Cathy dryly. 'Looks like you won't have to worry about one of them while you're away.' She tore her eyes away and looked at me. 'I'd say your Keith already has someone to look after him.'

Chapter Thirteen

I felt my face flame with embarrassment. How dare Keith stroll into Little Waterlow with Pippa. Why the heck couldn't they go to a restaurant in Meopham? Better still, why didn't the pair of them sod off to Mars?

My shoulders slumped. But then again, why should they *not* have lunch in Little Waterlow. Who was I to dictate where my husband and his new partner dined, or lived, or worked? I couldn't control what places they chose to frequent. Instead, it would have to be me making changes. Like moving house. Preferably far away. Maybe to the coast. That's where all the old ducks went.

Yes, good idea, Annie. Check out Devon. And maybe err on the side of caution. Perhaps buy one of those warden-controlled apartments – even though I didn't yet need an electrically operated stairlift or a cord in each room for emergency assistance. However, my fast-approaching big birthday meant I would qualify for "assisted living". How depressing was that?

But right now, all I wanted was to shrivel up like a dying leaf and let the ground consume me.

Pippa was far more glamorous than her Facebook profile pic. I stared in both horror and fascination. My brain took a snapshot of her, then filed the image away. Later, when home, I would get it out, pore over it, study it. Preferably with a crate of wine inside me. In time villagers would gossip and say, "There goes Annie Rosewood. The local drunk. No wonder her husband left her."

I gulped. I wasn't a sot. But currently I could see how easy it might be to drown one's sorrows. And boy, did I feel sorrowful.

Keith and Pippa were now sitting down. Hastily I looked away. The last thing I wanted was either of them becoming aware of eyes upon them. It would be too awful for words if Pippa looked up and caught me spying, while Keith said, "Oh no. I'm so sorry, sweetheart. I had no idea my estranged wife would also be here. Is she making you feel uncomfortable? We can go elsewhere if you like?" And then Pippa saying, "No, Keith. It's fine. It's you I feel sorry for. Fancy being married for thirty-five years to that frump. No wonder you left her."

Never had I felt so humiliated. Not at Cathy finding out about my personal life in such a public way, but to have the spotlight shone on me here, where local people knew me and would – possibly right now – be making comparisons between Pippa and myself. The glaringly obvious age difference. The glossiness. One woman like a full-blown rose. The other, wilted with fading petals.

'Oh hell,' Caz whispered. 'Keith is looking this way.'

I thanked God in his heaven that my back was to them. I hunched over my plate, staring at the cooling beef and

Yorkshire pudding, my hair falling forward to hide burning cheeks. Tears threatened.

'Are you okay, Annie?' asked Bella.

'Not really.'

I wanted to make a run for it. To flee the restaurant. Yodel, "Must dash, Cathy, please send on the bill." But getting up now would mean drawing attention to myself.

Cathy leant forward and gave my shoulder a quick squeeze.

'You stay right there, lovely.'

'What's happening?' I whispered, after Cathy had moved away.

'She's walking over to Keith and Pippa's table,' said Caz. 'They're now on the receiving end of a professional smile but also a pair of steely eyes. She's talking to them. Now she's gesturing at our table. I suspect Cathy is explaining that they've inadvertently walked into an embarrassing situation. Keith appears to be nodding understandingly. Uh-oh. Pippa looks put out. Her hair flicking has gone into overdrive. She's starting to look outraged. Change that to furious. Change that to eyeball-popping livid. Oh dear. Oh-dear-oh-dear-oh-dear.'

'What?' I hissed.

'Fasten your seat belt, Annie. Pippa Kipling has leapt to her feet and is heading this way.'

Chapter Fourteen

'Omigod!' I gasped.

'Wait… phew. Keith to the rescue. No need to panic,' Caz assured. 'He leapt up and caught hold of Pippa's arm. Now he's yanking her back. I must say, she's not so attractive when angry. Give it another couple of years and I can see her in hair curlers accessorised with a rolling pin. Andy Capp's wife springs to mind.'

I could now hear raised voices behind me. The Angel was a large pub with a good-sized restaurant. The hum and buzz of chattering drinkers and diners diminished as a fracas broke out by Table Eight.

'I've never been so insulted in all my life,' Pippa was shrieking. 'How *dare* you suggest we eat somewhere else just because my partner's ex happens to be here too. It's discrimination, that's what it is. Do you hear that everyone? I'M BEING DISCRIMINATED AGAINST! I've a good mind to sue you. Meanwhile you can take your crummy pub and stick it up your backside – it's certainly big enough.'

'Flaming Nora,' breathed Caz. 'Cathy looks like she's about to explode. Fancy calling her prized pub "crummy".'

'Or her backside big,' added Bella.

Cathy was now raising her own voice.

'You're BARRED! And as for you, Keith Rosewood,

it's obvious you've lost the plot taking up with this harpy.'

'You COW!' screeched Pippa.

'OUT!' Cathy boomed.

'They're leaving,' said Caz. 'Keith looks mortified. Pippa has already stalked off. Keith is making placating noises to Cathy. She looks tight-lipped but is nodding. He's putting up a hand in apology to everyone. Now he's hastening after Pippa. Well, it looks like the pair of them won't be coming here again.'

'I don't think I will be either,' I muttered.

That warden-assisted flat in Devon was looking increasingly attractive.

'The show's over,' said Cathy to the dining room. 'Carry on.'

Ah yes. Keep calm and carry on. Easier said than done.

Cathy was suddenly back by our table.

'Annie, I'm so sorry about that. I thought discreetly asking the pair of them to come back another time wouldn't be an issue. Keith was fine about it, but she was something else.'

I nodded, unable to speak.

'You make sure you have a flipping fantastic time in Dubai, lovely.' She leant over and patted my hand. 'Go bloomin' bananas.'

I swallowed. Found my voice.

'I'm not sure you *can* go bananas over there.'

'Course you can. Where there's a will there's a way. And today's lunch is on me. Call it an early birthday present. I can't rewind the last five minutes, but hopefully it softens the experience. Also, a bottle of champers on the house for you ladies to share. Frank! Over here. Champagne for Annie, Bella, and Caz.'

'Be right there,' said Frank, giving a thumbs up.

'Right, I'd better get back to my customers. Keep that pecker up, lovely.'

'Thank you,' I mumbled. Currently my pecker was nowhere in sight.

'Aww,' said Caz, as Cathy moved away. 'She might come across as hard, but on the inside Cathy is as soft as a caramel chocolate.'

'Yes,' I agreed. But I also knew that Cathy and her patrons would be gossiping about this public spat for weeks.

To the left of our table was Mabel and Fred Plaistow, hard-core Little Waterlow residents. Their roots went back four generations. I could only imagine what they were currently saying to each other. "Blimey, Fred. Who would have guessed the Rosewoods would ever go their separate ways? I thought they were a life-long double act, like us." And Fred gloomily picking up his Guinness without commenting, earning a sharp look from Mabel. "Don't you go getting any fancy ideas in your head."

Just beyond Mabel and Fred were newlyweds Daisy and Seth Kingston. Daisy had had her own fair share of public humiliation. She was looking at Seth and saying something. Possibly: "At last! From now on everyone will talk about Annie and Keith, rather than my first husband going off with his best man's sister."

'Stop it, Annie,' said Caz.

I flinched. 'Stop what?'

'Wondering what everyone is saying. The conversation has moved on, and ours needs to as well. So, let's get back to that travel brochure and decide when to jet off to the Emirates.'

'If you can get tickets for this evening, I'll go now,' I said with feeling.

'No.' Caz wagged a finger. 'We need to prepare. I haven't even bought any sparkly clothes yet.'

'I have,' I said.

'What did you buy?' said Bella, clapping her hands like an excited schoolgirl.

'Blingy stuff. Like Caz suggested. Shimmery cocktail dresses and a long evening gown.'

'Sounds fab.' Caz gave a nod of approval. 'Even better, here comes our champagne.'

'Hello, ladies,' said Frank, setting down a tray with three flutes and an ice-bucket containing a bottle of fizz. 'Enjoy.'

'We will,' Caz assured. 'Girls, raise your glasses. Here's to shopping, glamour, bling, and fun in Dubai.'

Our glasses clinked.

'And here's to new beginnings for Annie,' said Bella.

Our glasses clinked again.

'And here's to being sixty,' I said. 'Because guess what? I'm going to make sure it's flipping fabulous.'

'Attagirl,' said Caz.

And as our glasses clinked again, I realised I meant it.

Chapter Fifteen

After hoovering up the champagne, it had been a while before the three of us could drive.

Long after our meal, and when nearly all the other diners had left, Caz, Bella and I had remained at our table, drinking coffee, working our way through The Angel's cheeseboard, and even doing some online holiday shopping together.

The spotlight of public embarrassment had gradually faded and by the time I was on my third frothy cappuccino, jaw and facial muscles had slowly unclenched.

Now, finally back home, I'd barely kicked off my shoes when there came the sound of an engine ticking over. Peering through the hallway's side window, I was surprised to see Carly pulling up on the drive. Moments later, she was heaving her baby bulk out of the car. I opened the front door.

'Darling! How lovely. But whatever are you doing here?'

'I've come to see if you're all right,' she puffed, waddling into the hallway.

'Of course I'm okay.' My tone was light, but I felt guarded. 'You didn't need to drive over here to ask me that.' I shut the door after her. 'A phone call would have saved the journey.'

'I tried calling, but your mobile kept going to voicemail.'

'Ah. I was at The Angel. The signal isn't great at that end of the village.' I went through to the kitchen, Carly following behind. 'I was having lunch with Caz and Bella. We did some online holiday shopping while there, even though the signal was iffy. Let's hope our purchases turn up.' I gave her a bright smile. 'Coffee?' I picked up the kettle. 'I've drunk so much of the stuff this afternoon I probably won't sleep tonight.'

'Yes, please,' Carly nodded. 'And stop gabbling. Whenever you talk at a hundred miles per hour, it's always a dead giveaway that you're upset.'

I put the kettle down and looked at my daughter.

'Okay. Spill the beans. What have you heard?'

'I was at home with my feet up and having a major chocolate craving. Ryan said he'd nip out to the corner shop for me. So off he went. While queuing to pay, he found himself standing unnoticed behind Fred Plaistow who was gossiping like an old biddy to Rishaan Patel. Ryan was shocked to hear the subject matter was you and Dad. Fred told Rishaan that, earlier, he'd been at The Angel and seen Dad with another woman who, upon realising you were also there, went bonkers. According to Fred, Dad's floozie is called Harpy, and she marched over to you and threw wine in your face. You retaliated by leaping up and pulling her extensions out. Fred said there

73

was hair everywhere. Then Cathy waded in to break up the fight, and Harpy insulted her by saying her pub was crumbling and should be reported to Watchdog. To add insult to injury, Harpy told Cathy that her bum was so big she must be stealing food from patrons' plates. Apparently, Cathy then frog-marched Dad and his fancy woman off the premises, and you shouted, "Good riddance," before pelting them both with bread rolls.'

I shut my eyes, clung on to the worktop, and counted to ten. The joys of living in a tiny village, especially with bored pensioners like Fred Plaistow who had dodgy hearing aids and a penchant for embroidering the truth.

'When I'm back from Dubai, I'm moving far away.'

'Don't be silly, Mum.' Carly pulled out a chair and sat down. 'You can't do that. You wouldn't see your granddaughter every day. Anyway, you know what they say. Today's news is tomorrow's fish and chip wrapping.'

'Except in Little Waterlow they seem to endlessly recycle the wrapping. You do realise that by the time this story has been told and retold, it will bear absolutely no truth to what really happened. Pippa won't be thrilled to hear she's been renamed Harpy. On the other hand, at least it means she remains anonymous. No chance for me. How unfair is that?'

'Very. Are we having that coffee?'

'I guess.' I picked up the kettle and held it under the tap.

'Do you have any cake?'

'No, sorry.' Plugging the kettle in, I looked in the

74

biscuit tin. 'There's some chocolate digestives. Any good?'

'Yes, please. Oh, and some peanut butter. I can't seem to get enough of the stuff. It's going on everything at the moment. This morning, I even put it on my toast and jam.'

'How revolting.'

'The Americans do it. Except they call it peanut butter and jelly.'

'Sounds bizarre.'

'Only to us. I once read that the average American child will eat fifteen hundred PB&J sandwiches before graduating from high school. That's one of the useless facts I've recently gleaned while sitting on my bum doing nothing. Anyway, enough of that. Is *any* of Fred Plaistow's story true?'

'Only the absolute bones of it. Cathy took it upon herself to have a quiet word with your dad. She pointed out that I was there too, and to perhaps slip away and go elsewhere to avoid any awkwardness. Pippa took offence and, yes, she did make a scene. She shouted about discrimination, insulted Cathy, and then flounced off. Your dad looked mortified. I did feel a teeny bit sorry for him.'

'Well, don't,' said Carly fiercely. 'Seems like Dad's bitten off more than he can chew. She sounds like a total nutter.'

I made the coffee and set the mugs on the table along with the chocolate biscuits, peanut butter and a knife. Carly spun the lid off the pot and immediately got to work.

'Mm, divine,' she said, spraying crumbs everywhere.

I sat down beside her. 'Rather you than me.'

Carly chomped for a moment. Swallowing, she said, 'Dad wants me to meet her properly.'

I stared at my daughter. 'Oh.'

'He's invited me and Ryan over to her house for dinner one night.'

'Right. Well, I guess that's a good idea.' I wasn't sure if I was trying to convince Carly or myself. 'It's best to be friendly and not have any bad feeling.'

'You're too nice, Mum. I don't want to shake hands with the woman who split up my parents.'

'Darling, listen to me, please. If it hadn't been her, it would have been someone else. The fact is…'

I trailed off. What were the facts? Well, that Keith hadn't been happy. He'd had a wandering eye. He'd got bored. All of those things and maybe more.

'The fact is he's gone.'

There was no denying that.

Carly washed her biscuit down with a sip of coffee before replying.

'I've told him I'll think about it.'

'Yes, do that. But it's better in the long run to try and get on with Pippa, for your dad's sake if nothing else.'

'I wish I were like you, Mum. Laid back.'

'Ha, I'm not so sure about that. If I confessed that I enjoyed listening to Fred's version of events, would you tell me off? I quite like the idea of pulling Pippa's hair out.' I gave Carly a rueful smile. 'I wonder if she really does have extensions?'

She grimaced. 'It wouldn't surprise me. I suspect

everything about her is fake, including how she feels about Dad.'

I tried not to raise my eyebrows. 'What makes you say that?'

Carly rubbed some crumbs from her hands.

'Dad might look okay for his age, but he's a lot older than her. Realistically, she could pull someone much younger. So why Dad? She works at a garden centre, but I can't see the wages paying a mortgage, bills *and* supporting her high-maintenance overall look. I know I'm hypothesising but maybe she targeted Dad – and any other male in his age category for that matter. Perhaps Pippa struck up conversation, batted her eyelash extensions whilst doing a bit of casual digging, then thought, "Oooh, bingo! A homeowner. There's bound to be lots of equity at this guy's age." And you know what Dad's like. He tells everyone his business. Then' – Carly rubbed her fingers together and mimed sniffing the air – 'maybe Pippa got wind of Dad's inheritance from Nanny and Grandad's estate.'

'Oh come on, darling. Your imagination is running away with you. Dad's inheritance is from the sale of a modest bungalow. He's hardly Jeff Bezos. You're accusing the woman of being a gold digger without even knowing her.'

'Yes, I am,' Carly agreed. 'And I'll bet I'm right. Time will tell. Oh. There's no more peanut butter.' She peered at the empty jar in dismay.

'I'll make sure supplies are replenished for your next

visit,' I grinned.

Carly heaved herself to her feet. 'I'm not sure how much of me is baby, or weight gained from stuffing my face. I can't seem to stop eating.'

'It will come off when Charlotte is born, especially if you manage to breastfeed. If I remember, it's a massive calorie burner.'

'In which case I'll give it my best shot. Sounds better than diet clubs and exercise boot camps.'

She kissed me on the cheek, and we hugged as best we could with Charlotte Bump between us. After I'd waved her off, I decided to have an early bath and relax in my PJs. There was no one to see. Nowhere to go.

Ten minutes later, I was about to hop into a deep tub of foaming bubbles when the doorbell rang. For a moment I dithered whether to answer, but the bell rang again, this time more urgently.

Winding a towel around my torso, I crept downstairs and peered through the spy hole. Then gasped. This was someone I hadn't expected to see.

My husband.

Chapter Sixteen

I opened the door and, clutching my towel awkwardly, looked at Keith.

'Um, sorry. I'm not dressed.'

'Ah. I didn't like to use my key.'

I blanched at the thought. 'No. Er…' – I scanned the driveway – 'are you alone?'

'Yes, of course.'

'I was about to get in the bath.' This was weird, talking to my husband on his own doorstep. 'Without sounding rude, what do you want?'

'To apologise.'

I realised he was hiding something behind his back. A hand whipped forward, and my face was instantly immersed in a vast bouquet.

'O-Oh.' For a moment I wrestled with both flowers and bath towel. 'What are these for?'

'As I said, to say sorry. About what happened at The Angel. You must have been mortified.'

'Yes. I won't lie. It was humiliating. Still, at least Little Waterlow's gossiping grapevine is now in full flow. It lets me off the hook about answering any awkward questions if I pop into Daisy's floristry or Chloe's café or any other local shop. I guess Pippa did me a favour in some respects. Our grubby marital laundry is now available for everyone to comment upon.'

At that moment I spotted Fred Plaistow creaking past with his dog. Oh no. He caught me looking. He touched the flat cap on his head in a gesture of acknowledgement.

'Is he trying to woo you back, lass?' he called out.

A wicked part of me reared up out of nowhere.

'Ha! Yes, but I've told Keith it's going to take more than flowers to win me over.'

There. Let Fred spread *that* little gem around Little Waterlow, and have it filter back to the diabolical Pippa Kipling.

'What did you tell him that for?' Keith was looking aghast.

'Just humouring Fred,' I said innocently.

My husband peered anxiously after the pensioner. Fred suddenly had a spring in his step, no doubt anticipating more juicy gossip to share with wife Mabel. Between the two of them, rumours would soon be circulating.

'Well, I must say these flowers are stunning.' I pretended to sniff them. 'Are they from Pippa too?'

'Don't be silly,' he muttered.

'No, I thought not. I hope she's apologised to *you* though. After all, it must have been almost as embarrassing for you as it was for me. There you were, minding your own business, all set for a pleasant afternoon with your new lady, only to have her spectacularly let you down in public. I can't imagine Cathy welcoming either of you back after

80

being told her pub is crummy and her backside bigger than Pippa's mouth.'

Don't bitch about Pippa, Annie. Be the bigger person.

'I will send Cathy some flowers too.'

'Perhaps Pippa should be the one to do that. After all, it was her who was rude.'

Keith gave a strangled laugh. 'Unlikely. Pippa isn't someone who backs down. She's quite... opinionated. Always right about everything and never takes no for an answer.'

Was it my imagination or did my husband sound disillusioned? Bitter, even? Like someone who had invested in bullion only to discover it was nickel with gold plating. Could it be that the sparkles and glitter were already wearing off in his new relationship?

'Does Pippa know you're here?' I asked.

My husband studied his shoes for a moment.

'No. She doesn't. I'm supposedly at Carly's.'

'You're using our daughter as an alibi?' I raised my eyebrows. 'Whatever next?'

'Well, thanks to that bit of banter with Fred, it won't be long before Pips finds out my true whereabouts.'

Pips? All the better to spit out. Oh, stop the catty thoughts, Annie.

'Is it such a big deal you're here?'

'Yes! She'll know I've lied.'

'And that would never do, eh?' I said, my tone hardening.

I wondered how many times *I'd* been lied to in recent

months. "Just popping over to the garden centre, darling. We're out of weed killer." Then Keith setting off in his trendy skinny jeans. A sweater from Marks and Sparks slung around his shoulders. Doing his best to channel a bald version of David Gandy as he drove off. *Wham!* blaring from a buzzed-down window. *Rake me up before you hoe hoe*. My lip began to curl unattractively.

'Do you fancy a coffee?' Keith blurted.

'No, thanks. As I said, I've run a bath.' I indicated my towel garb.

'I could always scrub your back.' Keith gave a half laugh.

My mouth dropped open. Was he flirting?

'Sorry,' he apologised. 'I don't know why I said that.'

'Me neither,' I muttered.

'I'm just… not in too much of a hurry to go home.'

Home. The word was like a dagger. Keith regarded Pippa's house as his home. Not this one – along with the doorstep upon which he was standing – where he'd lived for nearly all our married life. That hurt.

'Why aren't you bothered about getting back to her?' Curiosity got the better of me.

'Pips wants to pin me down and have a chat about making some changes to the house. She has some grand ideas.' Keith began to tick them off on his fingers. 'A conservatory. Landscaping the garden. A new kitchen. Extending the bathroom and having a steam area. Oh, and making one of the bedrooms into a cinema room. Truth be told, I'm not interested.'

Oh my goodness. Was Carly right about Pippa being a gold digger?

'She must be earning great money at the garden centre,' I said lightly.

'Er, no. Not really. She's hoping I'll fund it.'

'Is she now,' I murmured. 'Well thanks for the flowers but my bath is getting cold, and so am I.'

'Yeah, sorry. Don't want you catching a chill. Right then, I'll be off. See you another time.'

Keith leant in and for a moment I thought he was going to kiss me good-bye. I took a step back, and he immediately recovered himself.

Old habits. Hard to break.

Chapter Seventeen

I quickly arranged the flowers in a vase, then returned to the bathroom in a pensive mood.

So Pippa Kipling not only had a firework temper but had also set her intention on Keith funding expensive home alterations. Well, well, well.

I had a sudden urge to gossip like Fred Plaistow. Abandoning the cooling bath, I found my mobile and tapped out a message to Carly.

Think you were right about Pippa being a gold digger. Watch this space.

And then I deleted it. No, I didn't want to involve Carly in what her father was doing with his money. It was none of our business. And much as I had no love for my husband's new partner, if he was going to spend the rest of his life with her, it was vital that Carly had a decent relationship with Pippa. I'd save the chinwagging for Bella and Caz. But not right now. I put the mobile down.

Topping up the bath with more hot water, I sank below the bubbles. Sighing deeply, I closed my eyes and retrieved that mental snapshot taken earlier at The Angel.

Pippa was glam. A younger model. The one who'd superseded me. Seeing Pippa in the flesh, I realised we were both about the same height and build. We had the same length hair too. But that was where the similarities ended. She was glossy. I wasn't.

But maybe you could be? said my inner voice.

I had an appointment with the hairdresser in the morning. In my handbag, safely folded away, was an article I'd found in an old magazine. It talked about how the right cut could define a jawline, enhance cheekbones, and knock off a good number of years. There were sixty styles to choose from. I'd homed in on that figure. Sixty. It matched my upcoming age. I'd taken it as a sign of synchronicity from the universe to follow through on a restyle.

I hadn't told Bella and Caz my plans, preferring to surprise them. To actually see their reaction. Gauge whether I was doing the right thing attempting to reinvent myself at sixty, or whether I was behaving like my husband.

In other words, being a silly old fool.

Chapter Eighteen

'Hello!' my hair stylist beamed. All six foot four inches of him.

I was gowned-up and sitting in a chair facing a well-lit mirror. My stomach was letting me know that the body was feeling like an apprehensive patient about to go into Theatre for a life-saving operation.

'Hi,' I said, nervously addressing Jason's reflection in the mirror. He had the looks of a film star and physique of a footballer.

'I don't think I've had the pleasure of getting my hands on your hair before.'

'No,' I twittered. 'I usually have my hair trimmed locally.'

'And where, may I ask, is that?' He picked up some strands of hair and peered intensely.

'Little Waterlow.'

'Sounds very rustic.'

'A village in Kent. Blink and you'll miss it.'

'I'm sure it's delightful. Just like you.'

I turned pink with pleasure. The charm was likely well-rehearsed and regularly trotted out to every new client that entered this plush London salon, but I didn't care. I was here and going to make the most of every moment.

'So I'm guessing you didn't zoom up here via Ebbsfleet International and negotiate the tube just to have your split ends removed.'

'Er, no.'

'Let me guess.' Jason put a finger to his chin and adopted a theatrical pose. 'Getting divorced. Washing that man right out of your hair.' He caught my expression. 'Bingo. Honestly, sweetie, you aren't the first delightful lady to frequent this place hugging a sob story, and you won't be the last. So!' He regarded me speculatively via the vast hanging mirror. 'Are we going for the big chop?'

'No!' I squeaked, feeling slightly panicky. Please don't let Jason be a scissor-wielding fiend intent on giving a pixie crop. I pulled the saved magazine from my handbag. 'It says here' − I pointed − 'that I could look up to twenty years younger.'

'Darling heart. Let's be realistic. One decade, not two.'

'I'll take that,' I breathed, eyes shining. 'But I'd like to keep it long. Other than that, do what you like.'

'Wonderful,' Jason purred. 'Let's have colour and lots of it. I want plenty of drama.'

'Steady, I've had enough of that lately.'

'Then brace yourself for more,' Jason warned. 'You will only leave this salon when there is *volume*.' He brought his hands up like a conductor gathering his orchestra. 'Shape.' Down went the hands. 'Bounce.' He brought them up again, moving one hand as if to hush a noisy trumpet, the other to urge on a dozen violinists.

'When you move, your hair shall move with you, and when you turn, it will ripple. In a breeze, every strand will lift and swish. You, my lovely, are going to turn heads.'

I was captivated. Enthralled. Which was just as well because there wasn't going to be much change from three hundred pounds for this experience.

Half an hour later, my head was rapidly gaining tin foils.

'So this husband of yours,' said Jason conversationally, as he lathered on lilac-coloured goo. 'What happened?'

'Oh, the usual,' I said lightly. 'Keith traded me in for a younger model.'

'And how are you coping?'

'Ha ha!' I laughed uneasily. 'Does your salon offer counselling too?'

'But of course.' He looked at me in the mirror. His face was deadly serious. 'It's all part of the service. There's absolutely nothing I've not heard, believe me. The most extreme tale was one of my customers taking the ultimate revenge on her philandering husband. She murdered him.'

'You're kidding,' I gasped.

Jason made a criss-cross sign over his heart.

'Totally true. Promise. She laced his tea with copious amounts of eyedrops. The liquid contains tetrahydrozoline. She nearly got away with it too! It only came to light because her husband was an organ donor and high amounts of the chemical were found in his blood samples.'

'Geez.' I regarded his reflection in shock. 'Was she remorseful about what she'd done?'

Jason considered. 'No. More… put out. She told me all this over the phone. She'd called to say she wouldn't be able to make her appointment on account of being arrested. After the trial she dropped me a line to say she wouldn't be getting her roots done for a little while. Twenty years, to be precise.'

'Heck, that's a long stretch.'

'She was quite young. In her early thirties. When she's released, she'll still have a good amount of life left to live. Don't think I'd ever let her make me a cuppa though,' he chuckled. 'I think the best confession I ever heard was from a nineties Reality celebrity who was milked financially dry by her first husband. They subsequently divorced and she made sure her second husband was both ancient and wealthy.'

My ears pricked up. 'Don't tell me. She set about spending his money on her heart's desires.'

'I think she was all set to, but unfortunately her husband was tighter than the proverbial duck's bottom. He wouldn't give her a penny. He was so mean, he made her promise that when he died, all his money would be cremated with him. He wanted to take it into the afterlife, so to speak. Anyway, he eventually died. At the funeral, the undertakers went to seal the casket and she said, "Wait. I have something to put inside for my husband's journey." She tucked a wooden cashbox alongside her husband's body. Her friend was aghast and said, "Please don't tell me you honoured his wishes." And my client replied, "I'm a Christian, so keep my promises. However, I transferred all his money into my account and then wrote a cheque. If he can cash it, he can spend it." Straight up.' Jason folded the final foil into my hair. 'All done. I'm going to ask you to move over to this side of the salon. You need to go under the heat lamp. Meanwhile, cup of tea?'

'That would be lovely.'

'With or without eye drops?' he teased.

Three hours later, Jason had fulfilled his promise. I left the salon with hair that swished, rippled and moved. I almost didn't recognise myself. And whilst I wasn't vain enough to think I was turning heads, it certainly *felt* like it.

With a spring in my step, I hailed a black cab. An hour ago, while under the heat lamp, my surgery had telephoned explaining that my GP wouldn't see me to discuss hormone replacement therapy because I was now too old to take it. "Too old?" I'd gasped. "I'm fifty-nine, not flaming ninety-nine." Apparently, HRT was to help menopause symptoms, which I didn't have. Undeterred, I'd hit Google and found an endocrinologist who'd just happened to have a last-minute cancellation.

'Where to, love?' asked the cabbie.

'Harley Street.'

Chapter Nineteen

'Many post-menopausal women have this problem,' said Miss Walter sympathetically.

'What, husbands leaving to get their satisfaction elsewhere? Sorry, that sounded bitter. I'm a little out of sorts.'

'I can't rectify the absent husband, only the hormonal system. A blood sample will give a snapshot of your oestrogen levels – which will likely be on the floor – but then we can start gently dripping in some bioidenticals. You'll realise, over time, that your skin is looking better, energy levels have improved, and – if the husband deigns to return – even finding yourself in the mood for sex. That said, I would also recommend product assistance.'

'Product?' I looked blankly at Miss Walter. I'd left Jason's hair salon with a 'hair product'. Was there 'product' for one's nether regions? Apparently so.

'You wouldn't go to bed at night without face cream, would you?' said Miss Walter cosily. 'Well, this is the same. One application before lights out.'

'Thank you,' I said faintly.

I left Miss Walter's consulting room clutching a private prescription.

As I headed back to Ebbsfleet International, there were two further appointments to oversee, and both were at the same address. A private house in West Malling. Not too close to home. The lovely Lindy was going to work some final magic.

It was early evening before I was back in Little Waterlow. Letting myself into the house, I caught sight of my reflection in the hall mirror. What a transformation.

'Hello, stranger,' I whispered. 'I haven't seen you for ages. About ten years to be precise. How are you doing?'

I tucked a strand of newly coloured hair behind one ear admiring the new nails in the process, and then examined my lustrous lashes. My reflection gave a cheeky wink.

'I'm doing surprisingly well,' said the woman in the mirror.

Grinning, I took myself off to the kitchen to make a cup of tea. I hadn't felt this – what was the word? – *light* in ages. The joint account was also lighter. But Keith had told me to use it, so I had. And best to indulge myself now, before Pippa Kipling had her way with it.

All that was left to think about now, was making a few phone calls to family and friends. This Saturday heralded an important date in the diary. My big birthday. And one thing was for sure. I wasn't celebrating turning sixty alone.

Chapter Twenty

'Happy birthday!' sang Carly, coming into the hallway. Ryan was bringing up the rear, arms full of gaily coloured bottles that clanked alarmingly.

'Thank you, darling,' I smiled, ready to embrace my daughter. But she took a step back at the last second and my arms hugged air. Carly's mouth fell open and she stared incredulously at me.

'Oh my goodness!' she exclaimed. 'You've gone and reinvented yourself.'

'Don't be silly,' I giggled. 'It's only a new hair-do.'

'And lashes.' She glanced at my hands. 'And nails. And *what* a dress you're wearing. Hugging all the right places, too. Very flattering.'

'I bought it for Dubai but decided to wear it this evening for my…' I trailed off. I'd almost said *party*. But such a word conjured up images of a heaving crowd and loud music. Instead, I'd opted for finger foods and background jazz. '*Soirée*,' I finished.

'Oooh, that's a fancy word,' Carly grinned. 'Well, whatever this evening is, you certainly look the part. And when I have my figure back, I'll borrow that dress for a date night and wow Ryan all over again.'

'A date night,' said Ryan pensively. 'I can't remember the last time we had one of those.'

'Cheeky.' Carly nudged him in the ribs. 'It's not my fault I'm too knackered to stay out after nine o'clock on a Saturday night. In fact, I seem to remember I ended up in this condition because we stayed *in.*'

'Too much information in front of your mum, sweetie.' He winked at me. 'Shall I put these in the kitchen, Annie?' He nodded at the bottles.

'Yes, please. Be a love and pop them in the ice buckets. I've set them out on the worktop.' I turned back to Carly and this time gave her a proper hug. 'And yes. Of course you can have this dress when I'm back from Dubai. It's highly unlikely it will ever be worn again.'

'Thanks, Mum,' she beamed. 'Heads up. I can hear a car on the drive. No, two cars. More guests presumably. I'll go and help Ryan and play waitress.'

'Thanks, sweetheart.'

I smiled as she waddled off to the kitchen. Seconds later I was greeting Bella and Colin, and Caz and Andrew, who'd all arrived at the same time.

'Happy birthday!' Caz and Bella shrieked in unison. Then they both stopped dead in their tracks. Caz was gaping and Bella was making *squeeee* noises.

'Look at you,' she finally gasped. 'Wow.'

'You look totally amazing,' said Caz. 'I know you're nursing a broken heart, but you'd never know it. You look gorgeous, darling.'

'Thank you,' I beamed, just as Colin and Andrew came

over the threshold. Both men did some noisy wolf whistles.

'If I weren't a happily married man' – Colin winked – 'I'd claim you for myself, Annie.'

'He'd have to see me off first,' Andrew bantered. 'Looking sensational at sixty, sweetheart.'

'I must say, I'm loving all these compliments. Come on in and we'll get stuck into the champagne.'

Half an hour later, the merriment was interrupted by the doorbell. This time it was my parents.

'Sorry we're late,' said Dad apologetically. 'The usual.' He subtly jerked his head at Mum who was bringing up the rear.

'I hope you're not blaming me for any tardiness, Michael Evans,' said Mum bossily.

'No, dear.'

'If we're late, it's your fault.'

'Yes, dear.'

'Glad we've sorted that out.'

'Let me look at you, Annie. Good heavens. I don't know what you've done to yourself.' My father looked baffled. 'I'm an old man and your mother tells me I'm not observant. But whatever it is, you look lovely, dear.'

'Thanks, Dad.' I smiled at his clumsy compliment, while relieving him of walking stick and coat. 'Go on through. I'll help Mum sort herself out.'

'Thank you, dear.'

As my father toddled off in anticipation of a drink plus male company and sensible conversation, I steered my mother into the hallway and shut the door after her.

'Whatever are you all glammed up for?' she asked, looking me up and down.

'Because it's my birthday. We're celebrating, Mum. Sixty years ago today, you gave birth to me. Isn't that amazing?'

'Whatever are you talking about?' She looked thunderous. 'I'm not sixty years old myself, so you can't possibly be that ancient. Nice dress,' she acknowledged. 'I love sequins but isn't it a bit over the top for Keith's wake?'

'Mum, I just told you. It's my birth–'

'Your father reminded me this was a formal occasion. That's why I'm wearing black. However, I thought I'd brighten things up with this pretty coat.'

'Right.'

My mother was attired in her own inimitable style. Black trousers. Matching blouse and shoes. But she'd topped the whole thing off with her floral dressing gown.

'Shall I take your, er, coat?' I suggested, extending one hand.

'Absolutely not.' She slapped my wrist away and tightened the dressing gown around her midriff. 'Someone might steal it.'

'Nobody will steal it, Mum.'

'You're right – because I'm not going to give them the chance. Now where's that hapless husband of mine? He's losing his memory, you know. Earlier on he said it was your sixtieth.'

'It is.'

'Don't be silly. You don't look a day over forty.' And with that my mother pushed her way past me, leaving me aghast at her gibberish. But for once, she'd left me delighted. I looked at my reflection in the hall mirror.

'Did you hear what she just said?' I whispered to the sparkly-eyed woman gazing back at me. 'Apparently you look forty!'

I was about to hasten after Mum – she took a lot of laughing off these days – but the doorbell rang again. All my guests were now here. Perplexed, I answered the door, and immediately the breath whooshed out of me.

'Keith.'

'Annie, sorry I'm so late calling by. I couldn't… earlier… it was difficult…'

'You don't need to explain,' I said gently. 'I'm not your keeper.'

'No.' He shrugged. 'However, I couldn't let today go by without giving you a gift.' He held out a small beribboned box.

'Oh! But you've already given me a present. I'm off to Dubai with Bella and Caz next weekend, plus I dipped into the joint account yesterday for, er, a few things.' It was one thing to splurge on hair, lashes and nails, but the endocrinologist's bill had left me reeling.

'Not a problem – I told you that. Anyway, I wanted you to have a keepsake for your sixtieth. Open it.'

'Okay.'

I tore at the wrapping and opened a reputable jeweller's box. Inside was an exquisite gold chain and sapphire heart.

'To match your eyes,' he said.

'It's beautiful. Thank you.'

'Let me help you put it on.'

I turned and allowed him to move my hair, trying not to shiver as familiar warm hands briefly touched my neck.

'Here's a birthday card.'

Keith produced an envelope from his jacket's inner pocket. Not too big. The right size to squirrel away and not risk being seen by one's partner.

I took it without saying anything and ripped along the seal, then withdrew an elegantly understated card.

To My Wife on her Birthday

So I was still his wife? Well, for now. I read the handwritten message within.

Darling Annie. Happy 60th. With all my love. Always. Keith xxx

Hardly gushing words. But definitely affectionate. And utterly confusing. What was going on here? Such mixed messages. Still a wife, but not living with me. Still a darling, but not *his* darling.

I felt flustered. First, Keith turning up. Second, an expensive gift. Third, written endearments.

'Look, do you want to come in?'

'Um...' he hesitated. 'The cars outside tell me you have guests. I don't want to intrude.'

'Don't be silly. Carly and Ryan are here. I hardly think your own daughter is going to protest at your presence. And Caz and Andrew, and Bella and Colin will be perfectly pleasant.'

'Well, if you're sure.'

Keith stepped inside looking… what exactly? Hopeful? I tried to read his mood and general vibe. He seemed… happy. Yes, happy to be invited to join in. Genuinely pleased to be here. I wondered why that was? I also wondered why he wasn't at "home" with the delectable *Pips* on a Saturday night.

As he made to go into the lounge, I caught his arm.

'Just to give you fair warning.'

'Oh?' Alarm flashed across my husband's face.

'Mum and Dad are here too. Mum seems to have it in her head that you recently died.'

For a moment Keith's eyes twinkled and we exchanged a look. Humour. Mutual understanding. He was aware how Mother Evans had been for the last couple of years.

'Okay, I'll brace myself.'

He grinned, and for a moment it was as if nothing had gone wrong between us. As if the recent past had been erased.

'And can I just take this moment, Annie, to say that you look absolutely gorgeous. You remind me of someone.'

'The hairdresser jokingly called me Julia Roberts.'

'You do seem to be channelling her,' Keith agreed. 'But actually, I think…'

'Yes?'

'You look like the woman I married.'

That shook me. For a moment I felt unable to speak.

'As opposed to the woman you left,' I said lightly.

'Sorry, that was crass of me. I meant…'

'I know what you meant,' I said quietly. 'I'm still that woman.'

He nodded. 'You look incredibly beautiful and carefree. I took you for granted, Annie. That was wrong of me.'

Okay, now things were getting seriously weird.

'It's fine. That was then. This is now. Shall we?'

I indicated the lounge door, and Keith moved off, leaving me clutching my wits and his card. I put the empty envelope and card on the hall's console table, along with the jewellery box, then followed him in.

Everybody greeted Keith as if it were perfectly normal for him to be there, although I caught an enquiring look from Caz, and then Bella. Slightly raised eyebrows. Facial expressions that conveyed, "Are things changing here? Is there something you haven't told us?"

I gave them both a discreet shake of the head.

Carly hugged her father while Ryan got him a beer, and then Andrew, Colin and Dad pumped Keith's hand. Meanwhile, I opened my cards, laughing at the messages within.

Bella: *I regret to inform you your fifties have expired.*

Caz: *Sixty! Time to iron the birthday suit.*

Carly: *Dear Mum. You're not bad for an old bird.*

Dad (and on behalf of Mum): *Our child of the sixties is turning 60.*

'Thank you everyone,' I grinned.

'Just a minute,' Mum spluttered, catching sight of Keith. 'Whatever is HE doing here?'

'Now then, Mum.' I adopted a placating voice. 'Keith has come to say hello and help me celebrate.'

'But he died. What is this, the resurrection?'

Bella tittered nervously.

'For heaven's sake, Mum. I've repeatedly told you that Keith never died. I said he'd left me. Now can we just drop the subject?'

I gave her one of my special looks. One that said I didn't want to discuss the whole "he left me for another woman" topic in front of an audience. But Mother Evans was having none of it. She gave Keith a considering look.

'I suppose you've been kicked out, eh?'

Keith flushed. 'Er...'

'I knew it,' Mum crowed. 'Good old St Peter. He's booted you out of Heaven. It's good to know the saints and angels are still picky about who they let in.'

Chapter Twenty-One

'Come on, this way,' Caz urged, as the three of us hauled ourselves out of the minicab. 'Thank God I didn't agree to Andrew driving us to Heathrow. He'd have totally lost his temper in that horrendous traffic jam. We're going to have to get a wiggle on, girls. Keep up.'

Extending the handles on our suitcases, Bella and I scampered after Caz, ducking between cars, coaches, and minibuses, all of which were swooping for kerbside positions for passenger drop-offs. Frustrated drivers were everywhere, trying not to get caught out by officious-looking airport stewards.

'Oooh, look!' I exclaimed in excitement, pointing with my free hand, and nearly dropping my passport in the process.

An overhead sign said *Welcome to Terminal 3*.

Suddenly we were plunging into a huge crowd of travellers and dodging what seemed like a million suitcases. The airport carried that vibe of energy, always so palpable in such places. Hellos... goodbyes... new beginnings... business meetings... holidays. Some people were hugging each other in delight, overjoyed to be seeing one another again. Others were in tears, not wanting to let loved ones go. Chatter filled the air in a buzz of different languages. We were now submerged in a human soup that repeatedly came together before breaking up and peeling off in all directions.

Despite getting up at the crack of dawn, I could feel myself fizzing and popping with anticipation. Carly had given me a number of pep talks in the days since my party, culminating in a lecture yesterday afternoon about the perils of being a newly-single woman abroad.

'Don't accept drinks from strangers.'

'I won't.'

'Stick with Caz and Belles at all times.'

'I will.'

'Don't have unprotected sex.'

'Carly!' I'd gasped aloud. Since when had our roles reversed? 'For heaven's sake. I'm sixty, not sixteen.'

'Yeah, but looking somewhere in between,' she'd grinned. 'And although you didn't *ask* to be let off the marital leash, the fact is that you *are* footloose and fancy-free and no longer looking like a gran-to-be.'

'I promise I won't come home in the same condition as you,' I'd joked.

'I'm more worried about an STD,' she'd muttered.

'What was that?' I'd asked sharply.

'Nothing,' she'd trilled. 'Just... look after yourself.'

Keith had telephoned me late last night just as I was trying to squeeze another pair of sparkly sandals into my case.

'Hello,' I'd said, surprised to hear from him.

'Um, I can't talk for long.'

'Are you on a timer?' I'd joked.

'Er...'

I'd rocked back on my heels, sparkly sandals momentarily forgotten. What was going on with my husband? He'd left me for another woman but indulged me with lavish gifts. Now I was on the receiving end of a seemingly secret telephone call. It was almost as if *I* were the other woman.

'Keith?'

'Yeah. Er, Pippa's in the shower.'

'What's that got to do with me?'

'Nothing. I just don't want her knowing I'm calling you.'

'And why *are* you calling me?'

There'd been a moment's hesitation. Then, 'To wish you a happy holiday and to have a terrific time in Dubai. I'm very aware that it's a place that was on our Bucket List.'

'Well, now you can look forward to going there some day with *Pips*.'

I'd tried and possibly failed not to sound bitter.

'I don't wish to travel with Pippa. I want...'

He'd abruptly stopped, leaving unspoken words hanging in the air. What had he been about to say? *I want to go with you.* Oh, don't be so ridiculous, Annie. If that was how the man felt, then he'd never have gone off with another woman in the first place.

'Have a great time, sweetheart.'

Another endearment. Not quite the same as "darling" but – in my book – a fairly close second.

'Thanks. I'm sure I will. Meanwhile, could you do me a favour? While I'm away keep an eye on Carly, please. If there's so much as a whiff of anything not being right – anything at all – phone or text or FaceTime or all three at once, and I'll be on the next plane.'

'Of course, but I'm sure there won't be any need to worry. Our daughter will be fine. *Is* fine. Anyway, be sure to send me lots of pictures.'

I raised my eyebrows. Was it the done thing to send one's estranged husband a photographic diary of what you were up to?

Here's me staying sober on Bubble Milk Tea!

Me again on a camel – think it had the hump, ha ha!

Another one of me, this time getting swept off my feet by a sheikh, woohoo!

'Er, I'll put them on Facebook for everyone to see.'

'Great idea. And, um, when you're back, Annie–'

I caught the hesitancy in his voice. A reluctance to say something. But nonetheless it needed saying. Or discussing. Uh-oh. My stomach clenched.

'Yes?'

'I'd like us to have a talk.'

Right. The official heave-ho. To date I'd been thoroughly spoilt. A trip to Dubai. Access to the joint account. Exquisite jewellery. I realised now that such tactics had been a softener. Keith was preparing to broach the subject of solicitors. Soon it would be time to legally dismantle the marriage of Mr and Mrs Rosewood.

I'd taken a steadying breath, then slipped off my wedding and engagement bands. It was ridiculous that I'd continued to wear them. Why? Clearly I'd been harbouring false hopes about remaining Mrs Rosewood.

'Sure,' I'd lightly replied.

'I must go.'

His call had then abruptly ended. Presumably *Pips* had chosen that moment to step out the shower, long legs wet with water droplets, but nonetheless ready to wrap around my husband's hips and–

'This way,' said Caz, fragmenting my thoughts.

'Shouldn't we stop and read the overhead thingy?' puffed Bella, as we shot past an illuminated flight information board.

'Already have,' Caz assured.

'I didn't see it,' Bella grumbled.

'Because you're too vain to wear glasses. You should get your eyeballs sorted out, Belles. Contact lenses have been around for decades.'

'I need a wee,' I complained, as Caz shepherded us at speed past a public loo.

'You'll have to hold on for a bit. Let's get shot of these suitcases and go through Security. Then you can relieve your bladder while I find a bar and order double G&Ts all round.'

'It's ten in the morning,' Bella protested.

'And we're on holiday!' retorted Caz. 'Now keep moving.'

'I really *do* need a wee,' I protested.

'Practice your pelvic floors.' Caz was unrelenting. 'Now come *on,* girls!'

'This is so exciting,' said Bella, catching hold of my arm and pulling me along with her as we hastened after Caz. 'I feel like we're in that programme.'

'Which one?'

'You know. *Sex in the City.*'

I rolled my eyes as we bowled after Caz. 'More like *Sex in the Sixties.*'

Chapter Twenty-Two

I'd barely emptied my bladder and gulped down my double gin when Caz was once again marshalling us towards the Boarding Gate.

'I wanted to buy a book,' grumbled Bella, as she and I were frogmarched past WH Smith.

'Didn't you pack your kindle?' said Caz in exasperation.

'I don't have one. I prefer paperbacks. There's nothing like holding a physical book in your hand, flipping through the pages, *smelling* the print—'

'And bunging up your handbag, or weighing down your suitcase, not forgetting pages being hard to read when your sun cream explodes, or even worse, pages coming unglued when splashed with pool water.'

'You can borrow my kindle,' I said, as we once again rummaged in handbags for passports and boarding passes. 'I have about a zillion unread books you can choose from.'

'Won't you want to read it?'

'Not all the time because…'

My mouth dried up. Through the floor-to-ceiling windows, I'd caught sight of our plane. It was a double decker. How the heck was that going to get off the ground?

'What's up?' said Caz, giving me a prod to keep moving.

'Nothing.'

'You've gone a funny colour,' said Bella. 'Putty grey.'

Caz linked an arm through mine as we bounced along the jet bridge to the aircraft's open door. 'Are you getting cold feet?'

'No. It's more… worrying about this thing falling out of the sky. That is, if it can even *climb* into the sky in the first place.'

'Of course it can, silly,' said Caz adopting her best teacher-talking-to-a-schoolchild voice. 'This is the Emirates Airlines' coveted Airbus.'

As we stepped within, my legs nearly buckled.

'*How* many seats in one row?' I bleated.

'Come on,' Caz cajoled. 'In a bit, Belles and I will ply you with more G&Ts. Soon you'll be flying without the aircraft.'

'Right,' I croaked. 'Oh God.' I abruptly stopped, sending the people behind cannoning into my backside.

'What now?' said Caz.

'Booze is illegal. We've cocked up, girls. We should have gone to Jamaica and sat on a beach drinking rum all day. Is it too late to change flights?'

'Yes,' said Caz, steering me along the aisle. 'And of *course* we can have a drink. It's fine, just so long as you don't drunkenly stagger about in public. I promise that tourists can drink in approved venues.'

'Sure?' I clutched my handbag to my chest, glancing about nervously.

Caz had been wrong. This wasn't an Airbus. It was a hotel. A bloody great horizontal skyscraper with staircases to suites. *Suites!* Who the heck reserved a suite for a flight? Perhaps it was full of sheikhs wiling away a few hours counting their oilwells and money.

'Here's our row.' Caz pointed to four seats. 'What a shame we're in a middle aisle and not by a window.'

'Good,' I said with feeling. 'The last thing I wanted was to see the ground rushing up if the plane went into freefall.

I flopped down in my own seat, dumping my handbag on the empty seat beside me and miserably fondled my mobile. Was there a signal? Maybe I should message Carly. What if things went wrong on this flight? What would I write? I closed my eyes and considered.

I love you so much. Have a wonderful life with Ryan and Baby Charlotte.

Then there was Dad and Mum.

The flight to Dubai has turned into a trip to Heaven. No, Mum, I can't see Keith either.

Oh good grief. Keith! He'd have to be included.

Sorry not to have made it back for the chat you wanted, but at least you don't have to go through the expense of divorce. Please leave my share of the house to Carly. If I find out Pippa has used it to add to her list of home improvements, rest assured I will not be a happy ghost and shall return to haunt you.

But then again, if I haunted Keith and Pippa, I might risk visiting at an inopportune moment. I closed my eyes. The last thing I wanted was to see the duvet going up and down, up and down, up and–'

'Excuse me,' said a voice. 'Your handbag is on my seat.'

My eyes snapped open. My brain made a nano-second judgement of the person hovering in the aisle. Male. Tall. Mid to late forties. Good physique. Very Gerard Butler in his heyday. Definitely attractive enough to snog. Not that sixty-year-old women *did* snogging. Or did they? Well, some must do. Like Madonna. Exactly how old was the pop star? I'm sure Carly had mentioned her being sixty-three. *And* my daughter had gossiped that the icon was dating a guy of twenty-seven. Talk about stamina. Madonna. Not the guy. But then again, Madonna did major workouts every single day. She could swing her feet around her head and was so flexible she could probably kiss her own–

'The handbag?' said the man.

'Sorry.' I snatched it up.

He didn't say thank you. Instead, he did a sort of half-grimace, which presumably was meant to be a smile, but instead made him look as if he had bowel problems.

I gave him a sympathetic look. 'Are you a nervous passenger too?'

'No. I'm tired. And grumpy. So please don't feel obliged to make small talk throughout the flight, because I'm not up for it. Okay?'

111

Wow. Rude. I was just about to give a starchy response, like reassuring I wouldn't speak to him if he were the last human on Planet Earth, when I realised that this in itself could be classed as conversation.

Instead I made sure my lips were glued together and volleyed back a look of my own. Oh yes. If he could look like he had bowel problems, then so could I.

Chapter Twenty-Three

An hour after take-off, with another couple of gins under my belt, I was feeling more relaxed – which was good. Not so great was the diuretic effect of the alcohol.

'Belles,' I whispered, giving her a nudge for good measure.

She tore her eyes away from the in-flight entertainment and whipped off her headset.

'What?'

'I need the loo.'

'Well off you go. You don't need my permission.'

'I know, but I feel awkward asking this guy to move. Could you do it for me?'

She looked at me incredulously, as well she might. 'Why can't you ask him?'

'He told me not to make conversation.'

'You're not. You're asking him to shift.'

'Yeah, but he specifically told me he was tired and didn't want to be disturbed.'

'Too bad. It's an occupational hazard of anyone in an aisle seat that sooner or later they're going to have to get up for the person sitting next to them.'

'But he's a stroppy sort.'

'Then tell him you forgot to wear your incontinence knickers and if he doesn't move, you'll pee all over him. Now let me get back to my film. Oh look,' she tutted. 'I've missed a crucial bit.'

'But Belles, you don't under—'

She rolled her eyes and rammed on her headset, blocking out my words.

'Belles! Can you hear me? BELLES!'

'I think the whole aircraft can hear you,' said an irate voice to my right. 'Not that I was eavesdropping, but if you really forgot to put on your incontinence pants, I don't want to be responsible for any sort of flooding.'

I turned and glared at Gerard Butler.

'I thought you didn't want to make conversation?'

'I don't. But asking me to move so you can relieve yourself is a tiny bit acceptable.'

'Is that so?' I said disdainfully. 'Because I really wouldn't want to put you to any trouble.'

'You're putting me to more trouble by yakking and not getting on with it.' He undid his seat belt. 'I simply want to sleep without interruption. So go use the bathroom, then let me kip in peace.'

He got up and effortlessly swung his body into the aisle. I undid my own seat belt and stood up like a hunched-over cotton picker. A pocket of turbulence knocked me off balance and I came down awkwardly on the armrest between our seats.

'Ouch,' I squeaked. Oh terrific. A bruised fanny.

'Any time this year,' Gerard huffed.

'I'm trying my best,' I hissed.

'Definitely trying,' he mumbled.

'I heard that.' Okay. Getting confrontational.

'You were meant to.'

Right. Even more confrontational.

'Has anyone ever told you that you're really rather rude?'

'Yes. My ex-wife. Has anyone ever told you the same?'

'I won't bother answering that question, but I pity your ex-wife.'

'Please don't. She took me to the cleaners.'

'Maybe she wanted compensation for suffering years of rudeness.'

'You're a fine one to talk. You're not exactly Mrs Politeness yourself. But maybe you're no longer a Mrs. Where, exactly, *is* your husband?' He put one hand to his eyes, as if scanning the horizon. 'Oh, wait. You don't seem to have one. I wonder why that is?'

'How DARE you!' I said, attracting some attention from the passengers seated around us. 'I'll have you know that my husband–'

'Was nagged to death?'

'Annie, darling,' said Caz, suddenly materialising by my side. My friend had either used her enviable fitness skills to vault over Bella and two empty seats or had zoomed around the entire mid-cabin section to assume the role of in-flight police officer. 'Let's not get into trouble before we've even arrived in Dubai, hm? So sorry.' She flashed a charming smile at Gerard. 'My friend has been under immense strain recently.' And then, out of the corner of her mouth, 'Her husband left her.'

My index finger shot up and began waggling. 'Don't say it,' I warned Gerard.

'Say what?' he said innocently.

'My husband left me because I was a nag.'

'I'm so sorry to hear that but, then again, why am I not surprised?'

'Oooh, you arrogant–'

'Enough!' Caz barked. 'To the bathroom. Now.'

She linked her arm through mine and propelled me forward.

'Did you hear what he just said?' I was aware that my face was working, and I seemed to be opening and closing my mouth like a hyperventilating goldfish.

'How on earth did you end up scrapping with him in the first place?'

'Because Belles wouldn't ask the guy to move on my behalf.'

Caz looked perplexed. 'Why didn't you simply ask him yourself?'

'You don't understand,' I wailed, suddenly feeling close to tears.

'Look, use the loo, and I'll get you another G&T to calm you down.'

'Are you trying to give me a drink problem?'

'Noooo,' she soothed. 'I simply think you're a little overwrought. The last few weeks have caught up with you.' And with that, she pushed me inside the plushest airline restroom I'd ever clapped eyes on.

Flipping heck. I boggled at my surroundings. Now I knew why Carly and her friends always took selfies in posh toilets. EasyJet eat your heart out.

When I came out, Caz had gone. I returned to my seat and Gerard gave me a withering look.

'I suppose you want me to move again?'

I smiled sweetly. 'If it's not too much trouble.'

I squeezed back into my seat and Bella silently handed me a gin and tonic.

'Is that wise?' Gerard nodded at my drink.

'No, it's Hendrick's,' I quipped.

He tutted. 'You'll be wanting the loo again in five minutes. Unless, of course, you've put on your incontinence pants to avoid troubling me again.'

'Trust me, I won't be asking you to move for the remainder of the flight.'

Needless to say I'd regrettably had to ask Gerard to let me out again exactly five minutes after finishing my drink. And then twenty minutes after that, I'd been overcome with the urge to stretch my legs. Then I'd needed to get into the overhead locker.

'Literally?' Gerard had asked sarcastically. 'I'm more than happy to give you a leg-up and lock you in it.'

Then I'd busied myself with a crossword, tapping my pen against my teeth, and promptly dropped the biro which had rolled under Gerard's chair.

And then, when I'd needed yet another wee break and Gerard had been fast asleep, I'd attempted shimmying over him, only for another bit of turbulence to send me flopping down awkwardly on his lap.

'Jesus,' he'd wheezed. I had a nasty feeling I'd squashed his crown jewels.

'Sorry,' I'd twittered. 'I seem to have fallen for you.' I'd caught the horrified look on his face. 'Joking,' I'd assured. 'An accident.'

'Oh God. Please don't tell me you've finally wet yourself.'

I hadn't bothered to reply and instead given him my haughtiest look.

When the plane finally landed at Dubai International Airport and taxied to a standstill, he unfastened his seat belt but, before standing up, turned to me.

'I wish I could say it has been a pleasure sitting next to you, but it wasn't.'

'Absolutely mutual.' I glared at him. 'And I hope never to see you again.'

'Absolutely mutual,' he parroted.

What a horrible, *horrible* man.

Chapter Twenty-Four

Dubai was three hours ahead of England. By the time we'd collected our luggage and been transported to the Blue Jade Hotel at Jumeirah Beach, it was gone 10 o'clock at night.

As we pushed our way through the heavy glass revolving doors and stepped into the brightly lit interior, the three of us gasped aloud.

'Wow, plush or what?' said Bella.

'Look at the pillars everywhere,' Caz marvelled. 'They're holding up a ceiling that gives the illusion of being several hundred miles away.'

Vast chandeliers glittered and sparkled everywhere.

'Oh, look. Restaurant to the left,' I pointed. 'If we hurry, we should still be able to grab some dinner.' The last meal on the plane had been some time ago.

Bella made a moaning noise. 'I'm starving.'

'Reception first,' said Caz, taking charge.

We wheeled our suitcases over and were relieved to find nobody else queuing. Suddenly some shrieks of excitement rent the air. Turning, we saw a gaggle of *Towie* types tripping past.

Caz hadn't been joking about bling. As the glossy beauties clicked-clacked past us on impossibly high heels, I noted their stilettos. Their shoes were smothered in fake jewels. My eyes swept over their elegant long dresses. All were sparkly. The women had long shiny hair that – as stylist Jason had said – *moved* with them. Every single one of them had vast eyelash extensions that made my own look quite non-descript.

'Perhaps that will be us tomorrow night,' I grinned.

'Hope so,' said Bella.

Meanwhile, Caz was being greeted by a smiley receptionist.

'Good evening, ladies.'

'Hello!' Caz beamed. 'We're checking in.'

Five minutes later, the receptionist wasn't so smiley. Neither were we.

'I'm *so* sorry, Madam,' she said to Caz. 'There seems to have been a booking error.'

'Not possible,' said Caz, looking and sounding like Monica from *Friends.* 'I did the booking myself. *Efficiency* is my middle name.'

'Sincere apologies, Madam. I have no idea what's happened, but there is no triple room. There must have been a computer error. But, rest assured, this is the Blue Jade Hotel and we will try not to let you down.'

'Try?' Caz spluttered. 'We've already paid our money. And a lot of it.'

'And we're starving,' I put in, as I watched – ahead – a lone server preparing to shut the restaurant for the night.

'Okay, ladies,' said the receptionist. 'I have a suggestion. First, go to the restaurant. Second, I will liaise with the manager. This matter will be fully resolved when you have finished your meal.'

Trying not to feel despondent, we drooped off to the restaurant telling ourselves the booking error was just a blip.

'Quite a big blip though,' grumbled Bella.

'Look on the bright side,' I said, trying to muster up some cheer. 'They'll probably upgrade us by way of apology.'

'Oh my goodness, you're right,' said Caz, tired eyes suddenly sparkling.

'So let's have some late dinner and relax while things are sorted out,' I suggested. 'Mm. The food looks delicious. Oh. Wait! Hey' – I called to the server who was stacking food trays on a stainless-steel trolley – 'you can't take that back to the kitchen.'

He turned and regarded us in surprise.

'I'm sorry, Madam, but the restaurant is now closed.'

'No, no, no.' Caz tore at her hair. She was morphing into Monica with every passing second. 'Speak to the receptionist.'

'Why?'

'She said we could have our dinner here.'

'But the restaurant is closed.'

'She said it would stay open for us.'

'But the restaurant closes at ten o'clock. It is now ten past the hour.'

'Speak to the receptionist!' Caz insisted.

'The receptionist has nothing to do with the restaurant.

If you want food, go to your rooms and ring for Room Service. Housekeeping will bring up a tray.'

'But we don't have a room.'

'Then apologies, ladies, but you should not be in this hotel. I will have to ask you to leave.'

'No, you don't understand.' Bella chimed in. 'You really *must* talk to the receptionist. There's been a mess-up about our booking. We're tired and hungry. It's been a long day and we just want something to eat. You have the food right there on the trolley.' She pointed. 'It's no biggie to let us help ourselves.'

'Biggie?' The server frowned. 'I don't know this word.'

'Big deal,' Caz clarified.

'There is no need for rudeness, Madam. Please, I cannot help you. I do not want to be sacked. The restaurant is closed.'

'Okay, enough of this nonsense,' I said, pushing in front of Caz and Bella.

Something had boiled to the surface in me and suddenly I wasn't... quite myself. Whether it was the loss of my marriage, Pippa Kipling humiliating me at The Angel, a long flight with a cranky companion, or now the blip in our hotel booking, all I knew was this server's refusal to give us food was the last straw.

I snatched a banana from a steel tray and pointed it at the server.

'Put your hands in the air and step away from the food trolley.'

'Annie,' Caz whispered, paling. 'I don't think you

should do that in Dubai.'

I ignored her and held on to the banana, pointing it at the server's heart.

'Listen carefully. Nobody will get hurt if everyone does as I say. Belles, grab some plates. Caz, get the cutlery. And you' – I waggled the banana at the server – 'will not disturb us. Do you understand?'

At that moment the receptionist appeared. 'Is everything okay over here?'

'Yes,' I trilled, whipping my hands behind my back.

'No,' cried the server, pulling off his apron and throwing it down on the trolley. 'I have just been totally intimidated by a banana.'

The receptionist looked confused. 'We can address any fruit issues later. Meanwhile' – she turned to us – 'please enjoy your meal and come back to Reception when you've finished. I have spoken to the manager and we have a proposal regarding the accommodation issue.'

'Excellent,' I purred, pulling out a chair and ignoring the server's dark looks. 'Do you know, ladies, I have a feeling we're going to strike lucky. I can't wait to see our upgrade.'

Chapter Twenty-Five

'You cannot be serious,' said Bella, who was now doing a plausible impression of John McEnroe.

It was nearly two in the morning and things had gone from bad to worse.

'If I had some toys in a pram, I'd be tempted to throw them everywhere,' said Caz.

'Where's that banana?' I growled. 'I'm going to terrorise the manager.'

'Ladies,' said the receptionist. 'I appreciate these rooms aren't ideal—'

'Rooms?' said Caz, looking outraged. 'They are two cupboards with bunkbeds.'

'And an en-suite shower room,' the receptionist quavered.

'I thought you were going to upgrade us,' said Bella, her lip wobbling.

'Unfortunately the hotel is full. Likewise, our sister hotel.'

'What about a brother hotel?' I suggested.

'I'm not sure I understand,' said the receptionist. 'Everything in the area is fully booked. Now lockdowns are over, and things are normal, everyone has gone berserk travelling to places like Dubai, wanting sunshine and a happy holiday.'

'Yes, that's what *we* wanted,' said Bella, a tear now rolling down her cheek. 'A happy holiday, but it's turned into a disaster.'

'Please, Madam. Don't be upset. The manager apologises for you having these two staff overflow bedrooms. They are in Basement One and completely out the way of the other staff who are on a different floor. At least you won't be disturbed. I would also ask' – she took a deep breath – 'that you do not discuss this with anyone here for, er, legal reasons. The manager is most emphatic about that. To make up for your distress and... all difficulties on both sides' – her body language was nervous and fluttery although I had no idea why – 'this hotel wishes to pay for all your excursions, drinks, meals' – she flung her arms wide – 'everything. Anything. It is our pleasure to make you happy again.'

Wow. Generous.

I sighed. 'Look, girls. It is what it is, and I don't know about either of you, but I'm knackered and just want my bed.'

'Annie's right,' said Caz. 'And as this trip is meant to be her birthday celebration, I elect that she has one of the cupboards – I mean rooms – for herself. Bella and I will share.'

'Really?' I said, my spirits rising a smidgen.

Bella's shoulders sagged. 'I suppose. C'mon. Let's just get some sleep. I'm exhausted.

125

'Thank you for being so understanding,' the receptionist twittered. 'The air-conditioning is on. There are plenty of clean towels and toiletries in the bathroom. Come to Reception tomorrow and we will sort out a driver for your excursions. Meanwhile, sleep well, ladies.'

The receptionist took herself off and Bella, Caz and I stood in the harshly lit corridor devoid of any glitz. It was very different to the opulence upstairs.

'I guess we're lucky not to be out on the streets.' I gave them both a hug. 'Thank you for letting me have one of the cupboards for myself. I really appreciate that.'

'You're welcome,' said Bella. 'I guess one day we'll laugh about this.'

'That day is currently far in the future,' said Caz firmly. 'Night, Annie.'

'Goodnight, lovelies.'

Letting myself into the cupboard room, I peered about. There was nowhere to hang up anything. I'd have to shove my luggage under the bottom bunk. The staff here must literally live out of a suitcase. There wasn't even a window. I tried not to focus on that, for fear of being overwhelmed by claustrophobia.

I turned up the air-con, instantly feeling comforted by its mechanical squeaks and rattles as it sucked in cool air, making the room feel less of a prison cell. Opposite the bunks, set in the centre of the wall, was a narrow door. I stuck my head around it and took in the tiniest shower room in the world.

Telling myself the place was at least clean and the

lower bunk's mattress felt reasonably comfortable, I found my nightdress and climbed into bed.

Seconds later, I whipped off the nightie. Despite the air-con, it was too warm to wear anything. Best to sleep in pants. I'd bought new undies especially for the holiday after having visions of Caz and Bella hooting at my old faithfuls in Sock Grey. Even my knickers were blingy. Today's choice was midnight blue smothered in tiny "diamonds". They'd likely eventually fall off in the wash, but for now even my bum was dressed for Dubai. Tossing my nightdress into the overhead bunk, I climbed back into bed.

I plumped up the pillows, pulled up the sheet, then reached out to the wall-mounted mini-fluorescent light to one side of the bunk. A second later and my cell was plunged into darkness. For a moment I thought longingly of my lovely bedroom in England which, by comparison, was positively vast. At least things couldn't get any worse.

I closed my eyes. Ten seconds later, they pinged open again. What was that noise? My ears strained to hear. Was there somebody lurking in the corridor, outside my room? There came another sound. Tap-tap. Tap-tap-tap. It sounded like someone was tampering with the room's lock. Oh my God. Someone was trying to get into this room! That was when I realised things could not only get worse, but also reach nightmarish proportions.

The door swung open, and the corridor's light revealed a man's silhouette. Hell's bells. Was it the restaurant server? Had he come to wreak revenge? I tried to scream but no sound was forthcoming.

'What do you want?' I croaked.

'What fresh hell is this?' said a horribly familiar voice.

Panicking, I reached for the bedside light and flicked it on. A pair of furious eyes met mine. It was him. The man on the plane. Gerard Butler!

Chapter Twenty-Six

'Is this a bad joke?' Gerard was looking angrier by the second.

'What are you doing here?' I demanded, my voice making a miraculous comeback. I clutched the bedsheet about my cleavage, fervently wishing I'd kept the nightdress on.

'Apparently this is my room,' he said, dragging his suitcase in and shutting the door behind him.

'It most certainly is not,' I protested, not liking the fact that I was now in this tiny prison cell with a guy I didn't know from Adam. 'This is *my* room.'

'I've been informed that the hotel's computer system had a meltdown and' – he parked his suitcase at the far end – 'four reservations didn't register. Mine was one of them. Let me guess, you and your gal pals are the other three. So where are they?' He peered under the bunk.

'Next door. What are you doing?' I squeaked, as Gerard began peeling off his shirt.

'Going to bed.'

'Not here you're not,' I spluttered.'

'Listen, lady' – Gerard was now revealing the sort of six-pack I'd only ever seen on male models – 'I went straight from the airport to an urgent late-night business meeting which went on and on and on. Nor was I at my freshest thanks to an airline passenger who was like a jack-in-the-box wanting to get up every five minutes–'

'That's an exaggeration,' I protested.

'And now that I've bagged the contract and have new business to stop debt collectors knocking on my door, I'm going to grab some sleep and, tomorrow, start enjoying a well-deserved break.'

'Not here. Do you understand? You are NOT sleeping with me.'

'Thank God for that, because you're really not my type.'

My mouth dropped open. 'I see you're as rude as ever.'

'If you don't like this situation, join your girlies next door and sleep on their floor.'

'I'm not disturbing them at this hour,' I snapped. 'Why can't you sleep in the corridor?'

'Why can't you?' he volleyed back.

I narrowed my eyes. 'Pass me the phone. I'm going to ring Reception.'

'There isn't one. In case you hadn't noticed, there are no niceties or frills in this so-called room. Can I make a suggestion?'

'What?' I glared.

'That for now we put up and shut up. It's either this – admittedly intolerable – situation or kipping at the airport while waiting for a flight home. Now if you don't mind, I want some sleep.'

And with that, he kicked off his shoes, stripped off his trousers and climbed into the top bunk. I caught a glimpse of a perky designer-clad butt and then he disappeared out of sight.

'I don't believe this is happening,' I shrieked, completely losing my cool.

Holding tightly on to my sheet, I climbed out of my bunk ready for a full-blown confrontation. A bundled-up nightdress instantly landed on my head. Gerard rolled on to his side, presenting me with his back. I prodded his bare shoulder.

'I'm talking to you.'

'Don't do that,' he growled, shrugging off my proddy finger.

'I'm going to count to ten, and if you don't leave, I shall scream very loudly.'

There was a moment's silence.

'One,' I began.

'Two,' he said.

'Three.'

'Four.'

'This isn't funny, you know.'

'Shall I say *five* or will you?'

'Six,' I snapped.

'What happened to five?'

'*You* said five. Six.'

'You've already said six.'

'SEVEN,' I said raising my voice.

'EIGHT.'

'I'm warning you.' My tone was ominous. 'Nine...
TEN.'

Now what?

'What happened to the scream?' he goaded.

'ARGH!' I bellowed. And then again. 'ARGH....
ARGHGHGHGH!'

Suddenly there was a hammering of fists on the door. I
yanked it open, and Caz and Bella fell into the room.

'Whatever is the matter?' gasped Caz.

I stood there, chest heaving, unable to speak having
now made my throat sore, and instead pointed to the upper
bunk.

'What the...?' Caz gaped in astonishment.

'A *man*,' said Bella stupidly.

'I do believe I am,' said Gerard, sitting up.

I noticed Caz and Bella's eyes automatically sweep over
Gerard's broad chest. It was sprinkled with just the right
amount of dark hair. Oh Lord, were Bella's pupils dilating?

'I wish I could say it was lovely to see you again,
ladies,' he drawled. 'But it really isn't. The Blue Jade have
royally fluffed up and here we all are. So, what shall we do?
Have a midnight feast, Enid Blyton-style — even though it's
way past the witching hour? I might be able to produce
some of Emirates Airlines' finest packets of peanuts from
my suitcase, and a bottle of Duty-Free plonk. Would you
like to fetch your toothbrush mugs?'

Gerard swung a pair of well-muscled legs over the edge
of the bunk's safety rail. Without bothering to use the
ladder, he landed on the floor, towering over the three of

us. I cringed away, trying to melt into the wall – and promptly fell backwards into the shower room.

'*Aaaaaaah!*' I screeched, flinging my arms wide for something to break my fall. My bedsheet promptly fell to the floor, and my exposed and unsupported breasts seemed to go in two different directions as I clawed at the shower curtain. A second later and the entire rail came off the ceiling. I went down, banging my back painfully on the toilet bowl before being engulfed in heap of vinyl.

'Oh God,' gasped Caz.

'Ow,' I bleated, fighting off the shower curtain and metal pole. 'Ow, ow, ow.'

Suddenly strong hands were pulling me up.

'I'm not looking,' said Gerard, averting his gaze. 'I hope you tell Reception it was you who did this, and not me. I'm not paying damages.'

'For goodness' sake cover yourself up,' said Caz, scooping my nightdress off the floor and chucking it at me.

'Right,' said Bella, looking bemused. 'I'm so tired I don't know if this is really happening or whether I'm dreaming.'

'Oh it's definitely a nightmare,' I growled, pulling the hateful nightdress over my head. Why hadn't I worn the wretched thing in the first place? 'I've a good mind to tell the management exactly what–'

'Get into bed,' Caz ordered.

'No, I'm–'

'GET INTO BED!' she bellowed. Not for nothing had she raised her children with a rod of iron. 'And YOU' –

133

she jabbed a finger at Gerard – 'if you touch one hair on my friend's head, you will have me to contend with. Do I make myself clear?'

'Perfectly. Goodnight.'

'I don't believe it,' I whimpered, as Caz ushered Bella out, shutting the door behind her.

'Right, can we now get some sleep?'

And with that Gerard leant one arm over the side of the bunk and snapped off the side light. Suddenly the room was plunged into darkness.

I lay there, sheet up to my chin, sweating profusely, telling myself I'd never sleep a wink.

Chapter Twenty-Seven

I was awoken by the bedside light flicking on.

As the harsh glare seeped between the tiny spaces of my – modest – eyelash extensions, I groaned and turned away, facing the wall.

'Is it okay with you if I use what's left of the bathroom?' said the horribly familiar voice.

'Go ahead,' I mumbled.

Seconds later came the sound of Gerard peeing. Terrific. If I could hear him, that meant he'd also be able to hear me. And what about when it came to doing a Number Two? I really didn't want to listen to–

Oh marvellous. Gerard was now doing exactly that. Seconds later came the sound of vigorous flushing. Now the shower was going on. Without a curtain rail, no doubt the floor would get soaked. The patter of running water signalled my bladder that it was time to be emptied.

Gingerly getting out of bed, I winced. My back was likely sporting a fabulous bruise from last night's close encounter with the toilet bowl. I found my mobile and peered at the screen. It was a little after nine in the morning.

Letting myself out of the cupboard room and into the

corridor, I knocked on Caz and Bella's door.

'Are you awake?' I called.

Bella greeted me, bug-eyed.

'I'm not sure.' She blinked owlishly. 'What time is it?'

'Time for breakfast. Although in these rooms, when the light is off, it's hard to know whether it's day or night. Listen, Belles, can I use your bathroom? My unexpected roommate is in ours and has been doing the works.'

'Ewww.' She pulled a face.

Caz suddenly appeared behind Bella. In the harsh corridor light, her face looked as creased as a bedsheet.

'Is it time to get up?' she said, yawning.

'Yes.'

'How's it going with Mr Sex On Legs?'

I pulled a face. 'At least he didn't snore. That's probably the only good thing I can say about him. The guy is a total neanderthal. Think... caveman in designer underpants.'

'Er–' Bella gave me a look and widened her eyes meaningfully.

I jumped as a voice behind me said, 'The caveman has vacated the bathroom.'

Turning, I regarded my tormentor.

'Good to hear. Have you left it fragrant and fit for purpose?'

'Yes, and I hope you'll do the same. If not, you can borrow my deodorant. It makes an excellent room freshener. A quick squirt under each armpit and then one in the toilet bowl. Works every time.'

Caz let out a titter of amusement.

'That won't be necessary,' I replied.

'Ah, of course. You're one of those.'

My eyes narrowed. 'What's that supposed to mean?'

'A woman who poops roses.'

'Do you have to be so vulgar?'

'What's vulgar about roses?' said Gerard innocently. 'See you later, ladies.'

And with that he sauntered off trailing a hint of evocative aftershave.

'Mm, I like that pong.' Caz wrinkled her nose appreciatively.

'And I like him,' said Bella impishly. 'If I weren't a happily married woman, I'd be fluttering my eyelashes at him. Lucky you, Annie, sharing a cupboard room with him.'

'Are you mad?' I said incredulously.

'You've got to admit' – Caz agreed – 'he's quite a hunk.'

My eyebrows almost catapulted off my forehead.

'Okay, you've both clearly taken leave of your senses. Anyway, I don't think anybody says "hunk" anymore. Carly would say "hot".'

'He was certainly hot last night, standing there in his undies,' said Bella. 'I had a major menopausal heatwave afterwards, and I haven't had one of those for yonks.'

'What's his name?' said Caz.

'Haven't a clue.'

'He wasn't wearing a wedding ring either,' said Bella.

'Just think, Annie. Theoretically you're single. Maybe you and he might get friendly and—'

'Trust me, never in a million years. Anyway, I'm way older than him. At least I can sleep at night knowing he's not lusting after my body.'

'I wouldn't be too sure about that,' Bella giggled. 'You certainly gave him an eyeful last night. Lucky you that they still bounce so well.'

Chapter Twenty-Eight

Half an hour later, the three of us left the dark, air-conditioned interior of our cupboard rooms and took the lift to the Ground Floor.

As we stepped out into the vast foyer, it was like entering a different world. Colourful plants and exotic floral arrangements artfully placed throughout the area instantly lifted one's mood. Bright sunshiny light was spilling in through vast windows filling one's soul with a sense of hopeful anticipation. From here it was possible to see numerous palm trees huddled together, like a group of gossiping women. The bluest of skies contrasted gloriously with the greenery and was showcasing a vast golden orb never seen in an English autumn.

'Ooooh, look.' Bella's eyes rounded with delight. 'There's the swimming pool. I can almost hear it calling to me.'

'Sorry, but a cooked breakfast is calling louder,' said Caz, taking charge. 'Follow me, ladies.'

My eyes scanned the restaurant ahead and I silently prayed we would avoid last night's server. The area was open plan, comprising the foyer and Reception, a sit-soft waiting area, atrium and then a walk-through auditorium directly leading to the restaurant. From here, the diner looked busy. I could see one empty table, but it wouldn't stay that way for long.

At that moment, last night's Towie girls stepped out of another lift and headed towards the dining area. They'd be wanting to nab that table too.

'Quick!' I hissed.

As if hearing me, the Towie girls immediately had the same idea. Suddenly there were was a commotion as we all began sprinting at the same time.

'Hang on to your handbags' – I roared – 'and MOVE!'

Caz, Bella and I pelted across the marble floor, flip-flops slapping, bingo wings flapping, and shot past the Towie girls who were only defeated because of their six-inch wedged footwear no doubt designed to lengthen legs when they paraded poolside.

I streaked ahead of Caz and Bella and grabbed the table. I was about to give a triumphant grin when I caught sight of last night's server. He was behind the counter ladling out baked beans with a couple of other staff doling out eggs and sausages. As if sensing my eyes upon him, he looked up and glared at me. I slunk down on the table's bench seat just as someone else slid in next to me.

'Sorry, but this table is t–'

'Room for one?' said Gerard. He set a mug of coffee down in front of him.

'Are you kidding?' I scowled.

'No. I left my table for two minutes to get another coffee and four old ducks came along and took it. I could hardly tell them to quack off.'

'So, instead, you thought you'd come over here and ruffle my feathers.'

'Helloooo,' trilled Caz and Bella in unison. They sat down opposite Gerard and me.

'My goodness, it's a bit chaotic in here,' said Bella. She looked at me in admiration. 'Well done for grabbing the table.'

'I saw you running,' said Gerard, giving me a sideways look. 'Quite impressive. I bet you used to enter and win the parents' races on your kids' sports day.'

'She did,' Caz beamed. 'And I don't mind telling you, it was serious stuff. Some of the parents used to *train* for it. Can you believe it?'

Gerard raised an eyebrow. 'Train? Did you do that?'

'No, of course not,' I said, my face doing a giveaway flush.

I'd never told Caz and Bella, but as sports day had loomed, I'd been up and out of the door before Carly was even awake, jogging around the block, finishing off with lunges and squats in the back garden. Keith had thought I was bonkers. But there was something about taking part in the race that was irresistible, plus it had made Carly proud when I'd pounded over the finishing line and, later, been awarded a rosette with *1st* printed upon it.

'Well, certainly a good effort,' said Gerard.

Was he being condescending?

'You sound like a PE teacher.'

'In which case I'll grade you. Somewhere between

OMG and WTF.'

Okay, he *was* being condescending.

'Well don't let us stop you drinking your coffee and getting on with your day,' I said through gritted teeth.

'I won't,' Gerard replied, draining his cup. 'And can I suggest that when you get your breakfast, one of you stays back to keep this table from being taken.'

'I'll get your breakfast,' said Bella to me. 'Full English?'

'Please,' I said gratefully. I wanted to avoid the server who was still casting dark looks my way.

'Good choice that you're the one to mind the table,' said Gerard, looking at me again.

'Oh,' said Caz, looking slightly put out. 'I always thought that I was the one who looked the most authoritative.'

'You do,' Gerard assured. 'But your friend is better at impersonating a cross Rottweiler.'

'How dare you,' I protested. 'At least I don't look like a smug pug.' I turned to Caz and Bella. 'I was hoping to avoid the server, but I'll take my chances.'

'I'll come with you,' said Bella. 'Look after the table, Caz.'

As I walked away, I heard Gerard address Caz.

'What happened with the server?'

'Ah. My friend upset him. She went berserk with a banana.'

Oh for heaven's sake. I stalked up to the breakfast counter, Bella scampering after me. Grabbing plates, we stood in the queue. There were only two people in front of us. The server immediately spotted me. I contemplated. Maybe it was best to make our peace with each other. After all, there were many more mealtimes to get through in the days ahead.

I gave him my best grovelling smile. He stuck his nose in the air and looked away.

Okay, Annie. Be pleasant. Pretend all is well.

The people in front moved on and suddenly it was my turn to be served.

'Good morning,' I said in my best Theresa May voice. Actually, she hadn't been too good on placating the opposition, had she? 'Good morning,' I repeated, in my best Margaret Thatcher voice. Although Margaret Thatcher hadn't endeared herself to many people either. Perhaps I needed to be more approachable. More *Lorraine*. 'Good morning,' I said again, this time in my best Glaswegian accent, making sure my eyes twinkled with just the right amount of mischief. 'I do hope we have moved on from last night's little misunderstanding.'

The server noted it was just me and Bella in the queue and then, with his own eyes conveying a suitable number of twinkles too, he leant forward, as if to confide.

'Mrs Lady. I'm busy right now. Let me ignore you some other time.'

Chapter Twenty-Nine

Okay, so the server and I were never going to be besties. Fine.

I returned to our breakfast table pleased to note that the *other* never-going-to-be-a-bestie had gone.

'Why were you talking to the server in a Scottish accent?' asked Bella, setting her plate down and sliding along the bench seat.

'What have you been doing now?' said Caz, looking incredulous.

'Nothing,' I muttered. 'Just trying to befriend the server. It backfired.'

'Hardly surprising,' said Bella. 'You visibly morphed into Nicola Sturgeon. She's terrifying.'

'Annie, try and stay out of trouble for five minutes, eh?' said Caz, standing up. 'I'm going to get my own breakfast. Back in a minute.'

'Honestly' − I protested − 'anyone would think I'm some sort of juvenile delinquent.'

'You're sixty, sweetie. Hardly juvenile.'

'Don't remind me.' I rolled my eyes.

'So what's the deal with you and Mr Sexy?'

I stabbed a sausage with my fork. 'Are you referring to

my annoying roommate?'

'Yes, of course. Sparks seem to be flying between the two of you.'

My fork froze mid-air. Wobbled violently. 'Sparks?'

'Yes. You know.' Bella popped some fried egg in her mouth and chewed thoughtfully. 'Chemistry.'

'Hardly. The vibe between us is more like' – I pondered – 'the police stopping me for having sodium chloride and a nine-volt in my car, and me pleading a salt and battery. In other words, he brings out the worst in me.'

'Have you asked him his name yet?'

'No, and I have no intention of doing so. I'm not interested in knowing anything about him.'

'Hm.'

'What's that supposed to mean?'

'You're protesting an awful lot, Annie.'

'And your whacky suppositions are giving me indigestion, Belles. Now let's change the subject.'

'Change what subject?' said Caz, depositing a fully loaded plate. She slid in beside Bella.

'Annie's roommate,' said Bella to Caz. 'Do *you* know his name?'

'Nope. Never thought to ask. It's probably something really dreamy to match his looks.' Caz popped a tomato in her mouth and considered. 'He reminds me of Gerard Butler.'

I visibly flinched.

'Ha!' she crowed. 'You agree!'

I shrugged carelessly. 'Admittedly my first impression

of him was thinking that he looked a bit like the film star. But now I've got to know him, he's more like Blakey from *On the Buses*.'

'You're definitely showing your age remembering that old sit-com, darling,' Caz grinned. 'I have a feeling, Annie, that he likes you.'

'And I have a feeling that jet lag has addled your brain. I'd like to change the subject. What shall we do after breakfast?'

'Sunbathing,' said Bella without hesitation. 'Last night's sleep wasn't exactly restful. I want to lather myself in sun cream and lie horizontal on one of those inviting loungers.' She nodded at the palm trees surrounding the pool beyond the window. 'Oooh, look at their figures,' she said enviously, as the Towie girls – now outside – removed their sundresses to reveal itsy-bitsy bikinis.

'What I'd give to have a body like that again,' said Caz wistfully. 'No cellulite. No mum tum.'

'No stretchmarks,' Bella added.

'Let's face it, girls.' I gave Caz and Bella a frank look. 'They have youth. Now let's fetch our sensible all-in-one swimsuits and celebrate not yet having varicose veins.'

Chapter Thirty

Half an hour later, the three of us were lathered in sun cream and stretched out on loungers.

The weather was incredible. I was secretly thrilled to hear that, back home, the UK was enduring thunderstorms and set for a week of low temperatures and downpours.

Bella had appropriated my kindle, so I spent a pleasant hour reading the newspapers online via my mobile and exchanging WhatsApp messages with Carly. I also sent her a picture text of the turquoise pool.

OMG, it looks amazing, she replied.

I'll send you a snap of the bedroom later. You'll be gobsmacked!

Keith also texted me.

Hope the holiday is going well. Give my love to Caz and Bella. Looking forward to seeing you when you're back and hearing all about Dubai.

My heart sank. Keith getting in touch was giving me mixed feelings. On the one hand it was lovely. It made me feel like he still cared. But in addition, his message carried a sub-text. A reminder that, once home, a conversation was to be had. And we both knew what about.

I read his words again and felt a pang of loss. It was a bit like being in a gorgeous Designer shop with an assistant dangling a must-have dress in front of you... a garment made of exquisite fabric and in the perfect size... but then having it snatched away and told, "Sorry, apparently someone else has put a deposit down and it's no longer available."

Pippa Kipling had claimed my husband. No matter how much it hurt, I needed to accept this. To move on. Easily said. Not so effortless to carry out.

A shriek of surprise came from the pool followed by a few more squeals and squawks. The Towie girls were easing themselves into the water. From their open mouths and wide eyes, they were experiencing that initial freezing sensation against sun-scorched flesh. Now they were giggling and splashing each other. One of them was doing jiggly little bounces, hopping from one foot to the other. The girl squealed with each bob but, unlike her friends, didn't venture further out and stayed close to the side. Her bust was hugely enhanced, and I watched in fascination as her bikini struggled to contain two bouncing balls. She'd attracted the attention of every man on a lounger and – oh hello – Gerard was now zipping past doing a flashy front crawl.

I studied him behind my very dark sunglasses, confident he couldn't see my gaze upon him. I could have been looking anywhere. For example, at those colourful climbing flowers exploding over the far wall... or the waiter passing by asking if anyone wanted a drink... or even that elderly couple over there, veiny arms wrapped around each other as they slowly made their way back to their sunbeds.

There was no denying that Gerard was an accomplished swimmer. His muscles were impressive too. I noted how they flexed as he powered past the Towie girls who were now nudging each other and conferring. I wondered what they were saying. Possibly, "Wow, look at him. He might be in his forties and miles older than us, but he's still a looker. Shall I flirt with him, or will you? Or shall we *all* flirt with him?"

Perhaps that was indeed the mutual decision because suddenly they were all sticking out their chests and bouncing energetically. Any minute now and the one with the enhancement was going to black her eyes.

Gerard had reached the end of the pool. Strong hands touched the sides as he hauled himself up, then … oh, I see, not to stand up and walk off, but rather to sit and preen like the handsome peacock that he was. The Towie girls didn't seem to be disguising their admiration.

He threw back his head, raked hands through his hair to squeeze out the chlorine, all the while a mini waterfall running off his body and puddling around him. How unfair that men seemed to get better looking as they grew older. More… distinguished. Keith had partnered up with a woman some twenty years younger than himself, and now Gerard was going to take his pick of these beauties, all who were years younger than him.

I inwardly groaned. Please God that he didn't want to bring one of them back to our cupboard room. The thought made me suddenly go a bit hot. I could see it now.

Me returning after a night out with Caz and Bella. The three of us saying goodnight in the corridor. Letting myself into the cupboard room only to find the bunk bed rhythmically creaking. Then a pair of eyes peering over the safety rail.

Gerard: *Ah, you're back.*

Me: *You're so observant. Will you be long?*

Gerard: *Don't know. I can keep going for hours.*

Me: *Could you make it minutes. I'll wait in the bathroom.*

Gerard: *You'll be waiting a long time. I've already told you. You're not my type.*

Me: *You're so funny. Not.*

And then, upon going into the bathroom, discovering the rest of the Towie girls crammed in there, apparently awaiting their turn with Gerard.

'Are you all right, Annie?' said Bella, peering at me over her sunglasses.

I tore my eyes away from Bust Enhancement Girl who was now frolicking around Gerard's legs and giving him cute little splashes with her hands.

'Yes, of course,' I said distractedly. 'Just a bit hot. I think I'll have a swim.'

I stood up and moved to the water's edge. Suddenly I was aware of being scrutinised by two American guys to the right. One was bald, with skinny legs and a stomach that flopped like exhausted knicker elastic. The other was pot-bellied and covered in the sort of tattoos that looked like a child had gone berserk with a biro. Neither were attractive, but I was nonetheless secretly thrilled to have them check me out... until they started to loudly discuss me.

'She ain't bad,' drawled Skinny Legs.

'Take it or leave it,' said Tattoo Man dismissively.

I froze, rooted to the spot.

'Well I wouldn't say no,' drawled Skinny Legs.

'I would.'

'Why?'

'Too old.'

Too old? It was too much. Too raw. Too personal. First a husband who'd dumped me – admittedly as gently as possible – for a younger woman. Second, watching middle-aged Gerard effortlessly attract young girls. Now these two plebs loudly dismissing me as no longer "doable". That I was past my Sell By Date. That I should be scrapped like an old rusty car. Tossed aside like Grandma's bloomers. Binned like last week's stale bread. Overlooked like... like... my face worked as I tried and failed to come up with further analogies. Just who the *hell* did they think they were?

Furious, I marched over to them and leant in.

'What makes either of you think you'd even be in with a chance?'

And with that I executed a perfect dive into the swimming pool – hopefully splashing them in the process – then flipped on to my back and did my own flashy swim moves across the pool.

Eat your heart out Mr Skinny Legs and Tattoo Man.

Oh yes. I might be sixty. But I bet I can still swim faster than you two plonkers. And yes, I had also entered the parents' swimming race at school. And won. And of *course* I'd trained for it. You have no *idea* how competitive playground mothers can be.

Reaching the other end of the pool, I spotted Gerard and the Towie girls looking at me. In fact, Gerard was openly staring, and the girls seemed to be gobsmacked. I felt a frisson of triumph. I might be about to become a grandma, but I could still shift. No one would be catching me using a walking stick or mobility scooter any time soon. So, ha bloody ha to you, Gerard. You weren't the only show-off in Dubai!

Ignoring them all, I disappeared underwater, performed a perfect somersault, neatly changed direction, kicked off, whooshed back to the surface, and once again set off for a second length of backstroke, arms whirring like windmills. In that moment I felt empowered. Like an Olympic swimmer. Look at me go!

Back to the starting point, I paused alongside Caz and Bella, absolutely buzzing. Everyone's eyes were upon me. Ha! Stuff you, Keith. You too, Gerard. And two fingers up to Mr Skinny Legs and Tattoo Man. I felt like bursting into song. Morphing into Helen Reddy. Belting out the first few lines of *I Am Woman.* I continued to pause poolside, milking the moment.

'Annie,' Caz urgently hissed. 'For God's sake cover up. You've fallen out of your swimsuit.'

Chapter Thirty-One

I checked my reflection in the cupboard room's tiny bathroom mirror.

Today's sunshine had already turned my skin to the colour of honey, although my face looked a little red – possibly from major embarrassment over the boob fiasco – but at least the colour provided an illusion of glowing health.

Slicking some coral gloss over my lips, I then smoothed out a slight crease in the fabric of my halter-neck dress. The material went all the way down to the ankles but was super-feminine and trendy. I'd found it in *Monsoon.* It had practically screamed from its hanger on the rail, "I'M PERFECT FOR DUBAI SO BUY ME!"

I heard a step in the corridor. Suddenly the door opened, and Gerard walked in.

'Could you knock in future?' I said primly. 'I might have been undressed.'

He affected surprise. 'Since when did that bother you?'

'I beg your pardon?'

'You're often in a state of undress. From draping yourself in a sheet and swapping it for a shower curtain, to swanning round in an open-fronted swimsuit. Or did you accidentally put your costume on back-to-front?'

'How dare you.' I could feel my flushed face deepening

to the colour of lobster, no doubt clashing violently with my lipstick.

Gerard grinned wickedly. He'd caught the sun and was several shades darker than me. He was one of those enviable types who only had to be kissed by the rays to turn the colour of toffee.

'It's good to see you've finally mastered this country's dress code.' He nodded at my attire. 'Off anywhere nice?'

'As it happens, yes. After dinner, my friends and I are heading to Downtown Dubai. We're visiting the fountains.'

'Enjoy. Just refrain from jumping in and doing the backstroke. It wouldn't do to get arrested in this place.'

I glared at him. 'Unlikely. And talking of inappropriate behaviour, can we have a quick conversation about bedroom protocol.'

'Bedroom protocol?' Gerard affected a frown. 'Are you going to moan at me about the festering socks under your bunk?'

'No. It's about the possibility of returning to this room later and discovering you have an unexpected visitor.'

'I promise that all my visitors are expected.'

I gritted my teeth. 'I'm talking about interruption.'

'Oh God, there's nothing worse. Don't worry. I'll put a *Do Not Disturb* sign over the door handle.'

'Will you stop being flippant,' I howled. 'I do not want to come back here, tired and wanting my bed, to find you in a compromising situation with one of the Tow–' I caught myself – 'one of your new lady friends.'

'Ah.' Gerard's eyes widened theatrically. 'You want me to go to *her* room instead.'

'That's it.' I gave him a glacial smile.

'Message received and understood.'

'Thank you.' I made to slide past him, but he didn't move.

'Before you go, Madam…'

'Yes?'

'Can I point out that bedroom protocol works both ways.'

'What do you mean?'

'Likewise, I don't want to return to this room to find you displaying your wares with any of the gentlemen from around the pool.'

'Don't be ridiculous.' I gave Gerard a withering look.

'On the contrary. You see, I overheard those two Americans discussing you earlier.'

My face reddened even further. At this rate I'd be making a lobster look anaemic.

'What about them?' I spat.

'Just to confirm that, following your spectacular swimming display, both gentlemen said they would.'

I opened my mouth to say something, then thought better of it. Pulling myself up to my full height and gathering as much dignity as I could muster, my stomach practically touched my backbone as I squeezed past him.

'Enjoy the fountain display,' Gerard called after me.

I paused. Turned. 'Rest assured I will. And just remember. No shenanigans, Mr Butler.'

155

Chapter Thirty-Two

Dinner promised to be a far more civilised affair than breakfast.

First, my surly server wasn't on duty. That was a huge relief and instantly made for a relaxing vibe. Second, unlike this morning, there was no marathon to run in order to secure a table.

Caz, being the uber-efficient one, had reserved a table for the evening and booked for the entire week ahead.

Unlike the breakfast area – which had a posh café atmosphere – the hotel's second restaurant generated an air of reverence. As we walked in, the carpet was so thick I was at risk of pegging my heels. Tables were laid with crisp white linen, polished silver cutlery, and sparkling crystal glasses. The lighting was ambient, and diners were speaking in hushed tones.

The maître'd' ushered us in with much bowing and scraping. We'd barely sat down when napkins were flicked open and laid across our laps, and vast tasselled menus placed before us.

'Have you seen the cocktails?' whispered Bella.

Caz put on her reading glasses and peered at the print. 'Good heavens. I'd have thought Dubai would have been too prudish to print this.'

'Me too,' said Bella. 'I was expecting something far more basic.'

'Mm,' Caz agreed. 'Pink drink, blue drink, orange drink.'

They giggled as I delved into my evening bag for my own specs.

'Shall we indulge, or stick to wine?' asked Caz.

'I'm up for a cocktail.' Bella giggled naughtily. 'It's a good thing Andrew isn't here. He'd turn purple if I named my choice.'

'What about you, Annie?' asked Caz.

'Hang on a sec.' I was still rummaging in my evening bag. 'Oh bother. I've left my reading glasses in the cupboard room.'

'Borrow mine.' Caz whipped off her specs and passed them over.

But as I peered through the lenses, everything blurred.

'Thanks, sweetie, but they're no good. I'll just have to hold the menu away from me.' I extended one arm until the word "Cocktails" swam into view but struggled to make out what was listed under the heading. My arm stretched further still. 'Ah, yes. I see them. Oh!'

'Ladies?' said a waiter appearing from nowhere. He inclined his head.

'We're having cocktails,' said Caz authoritatively.

'The name, Madam?'

'Er...' – Caz flushed slightly – 'this one, please.' She pointed.

'And for you?' said the waiter, addressing Bella.

She hesitated, then opted to copy Caz. 'I'd like this one.' Bella pointed with a manicured fingernail.

The waiter turned to me. 'Madam?'

Just as I was squinting at the menu, Gerard walked in. The Towie girls were flocked around him, like seagulls eyeballing a lone juicy fish. My concentration fragmented. Instantly there came a sense of foreboding.

Uh-oh. What were the chances of finding a *Do Not Disturb* sign hanging off the door later tonight? But… wait. Gerard had promised he wouldn't have visitors and would go to their room instead. But then again… what if he didn't fancy an orgy with *all* the Towie girls and instead wanted a straightforward private coupling with just one individual. He couldn't very well say, "Now then, my lovelies, can the rest of you clear off so me and Diamante here can have the place to ourselves for a few hours." There would be girly mayhem. I instantly imagined Diamante tugging on Gerard's arm and giving him a sly wink. "Can't we go to your room, Squirrel Nutkin?" And then Gerard looking awkward. "It's tricky, Angel Bunnykins. You see, I've been forced to share a cupboard room with an ancient harridan who talks about *bedroom protocol* and probably hasn't had sex since 1999. We wouldn't want to give her a stroke." And Diamante roaring with laughter, and saying, "The only thing I want to stroke is—"

'Madam?' the waiter prompted.

'Oh, er, yes, sorry. I'll have…'

'Good evening, ladies,' said Gerard.

He'd broken away from the Towie girls to come over and speak to us. Bella and Caz were suddenly all smiles and – oh for goodness' sake – giving him adoring looks. Had he mesmerised them too? What was the matter with everyone?

'Are you having a good evening?' he enquired politely. 'Oooh, cocktails.'

'Two of us have chosen,' Caz simpered. 'We're just waiting for our friend to make up her mind.'

'Let me see.' Gerard read aloud from the menu. '*Hanky Panky.*' He cast an enquiring look in my direction. 'I think our earlier chat about bedroom protocol rules that one out. *Frozen Pink Panties.* A definite possibility for all ice maidens but, wait, this one is perfect–'

'I'll have *Sex on the Beach*,' I said to the waiter, interrupting Gerard's wind up.

'Really?' Gerard feigned surprise. 'Personally, I'd have thought *Slippery Nipple* was sooo more you.'

I glared at him. 'Don't let me hold you up, Mr Butler. Your harem is looking most put out.'

He grinned and winked. 'Laters.'

'Oh my goodness,' said Bella, picking up the menu and fanning herself. 'He is so hot.'

'Don't tell Andrew but' – Caz gave an impish look – 'I wouldn't mind sharing some *Sex on the Beach* with that guy. What do you think, Annie?'

'I think' – I scowled, turning my attention to the dinner menu – 'that the sun has befuddled your brains.'

Chapter Thirty-Three

The Blue Jade Hotel were fulfilling their promise to look after us.

Immediately after dinner, we made our way to Reception. The manager himself led us through the shiny revolving doors and introduced us to Ahmed, our personal chauffeur.

'On behalf of the Blue Jade, may I wish you a wonderful evening.' He opened the rear door to the spotless Mercedes and held it wide as we clambered in. 'Buy what you like and enjoy. Keep all receipts and you will be instantly reimbursed.'

'Careful' – Caz paused to waggle a playful finger – 'or we might instruct Ahmed to take as to the marina and purchase a yacht.'

'Ha ha,' laughed the manager.

'She's not kidding,' said Bella, keeping a straight face.

'Ha ha,' laughed the manager again, this time looking twitchy. 'This is the great British sense of humour, yes?'

The drive to Downtown Dubai had me agog. First, everything was so clean. I scanned the streets, buildings, and overhead signage looking for graffiti. There was none. Nor was there any rubbish. The kerbs and gutters were

160

completely free of litter. Neither an empty coffee carton nor a squashed blob of chewing gum marred the walkways.

'It's too sterile looking,' whispered Bella.

'I don't agree.' I shook my head. 'It looks smart. Glossy. Cared for. I love it.'

'What happens if you drop litter?' said Caz to Ahmed.

He raised his eyebrows in an expression that begged the question *why would you even WANT to drop litter?*

'Not advisable, Mrs Caz. You cannot even leave a cigarette butt on the ground without getting a huge fine.'

'What's law enforcement like here?' asked Bella.

'Strict.' Ahmed answered without hesitation. 'I'm sure you ladies are very polite, but for those who swear...' He trailed off.

'What?' Caz prompted.

Everyone uttered the odd expletive now and again, didn't they? Why, I'd let rip with several oaths earlier when alone in my cupboard room. I'd painfully stubbed my toe on the corner of the bunk bed and for a while the air had turned blue.

Ahmed continued. 'Saying a bad word carries a potential two-year jail sentence.'

Caz, Bella and I nudged each other while exchanging horrified looks. Caz made a facial expression that silently conveyed, "For God's sake don't drop a verbal bollock in Dubai."

'I'm sure your travel agent gave you some basic advice,' Ahmed continued. 'Like men and women being prohibited from publicly displaying affection. This country is very strict about such things. In a hotel, you cannot share a room with your husband unless you show a marriage certificate.'

'Interesting,' I muttered, arching an eyebrow at Bella and Caz. What would the police make of me sleeping in a cupboard room with a man whose name I didn't even know? No wonder everything had been so hush-hush with us bundled off to the basement, out of sight, and a nervous manager and fluttery receptionist offering the sun, moon, and stars by way of recompense.

'What happens to thieves?' asked Bella. 'Not that we steal,' she hastily added.

'Just remember.' Ahmed looked grave. 'Dubai is a beautiful country, but it has laws that carry the death penalty.'

I gulped and made a mental note. Monitor both alcohol and expletives, and do not under any circumstances tell anyone about Gerard Butler in your bunk bed. Perhaps I should pin him down for another chat about *bedroom protocol*. Part Two. Do not get caught corridor creeping.

I gazed at the scenery beyond the window. The architecture here was so different. In the United Kingdom, our cities contained a mishmash of structures. Some of London's streets had elegant buildings from bygone eras. London also had some amazing contemporary structures. But the old and the new didn't always sit well together. Indeed, some offices simply looked like concrete-and-metal eyesores. But here, buildings totally complimented each other.

Caz and Bella thought everything looked too brand new and consequently soulless, whereas the cityscape blew me away. It was like being on the giant set of a sci-fi film. I gazed in awe at a horizon of turrets and towers, half expecting a spacecraft to swoop through the sky.

Modern features flowed seamlessly with a blend of towering skyscrapers, each sporting innovated and exposed-glass walls. There were stepped ascending spirals and subtle nods to gorgeous traditional Arabic motifs. Eye-popping style was on every corner, from hotels sporting a wave-shaped design to another replicating prayer hands.

I was quietly excited that, this evening, the three of us would glimpse the world's tallest tower alongside space-age blocks that defied gravity.

As we cruised along the freeway, intermittent bridges looped artistically overhead. Not a whiff of *Spaghetti Junction* here. Not only were the bridges artistically lit, but their colours repeatedly changed too.

'Mood lighting,' I gasped, as the side of a sweeping bridge changed from neon blue to soft lilac. 'That's incredible.'

Ahmed shrugged. He'd never known any different and was unmoved by his surroundings.

Fifteen minutes later we were in Downtown Dubai.

'Enjoy the dancing fountains,' he said, as we spilt out of the car. He'd already given us a bit of info about it. 'Don't forget, the evening shows are every thirty minutes. You have my mobile number. Text me when you're ready to return to the Blue Jade.'

163

We thanked him, then made our way through an orderly crowd at the foot of the Dubai Mall.

As we wandered, I noticed with a pang that many of the people were coupled up. And loved up. Even though nobody was holding hands or publicly kissing, there were plenty of dewy-eyed looks going on between young men and women. There was an air of anticipation and, judging from the crowd's excited chatter, we knew our timing was perfect for the next display.

'Look!' gasped Caz.

The Burj Khalifa – a building so impossibly tall it looked like its peak was knocking on Heaven's door – had been transformed by over a million LED lights. Suddenly the entire façade had become a screen.

'The world's biggest television,' said Bella in awe.

The sky was black now. Everywhere, buildings glittered and sparkled, flashing on and off, then twinkling in an electrical pattern. It reminded me of fairy lights on Christmas trees, or London's Oxford Street in December, except an Arabian version and on a far grander scale. It was mesmerising.

We were now on the Dubai Fountain Boardwalk, casually strolling along a floating platform and getting even closer to the spectacle.

Suddenly, music filled the air. Powerful water jets – strategically laid over an area the size of two football pitches – burst into life. Thousands of gallons of water whooshed upwards. I craned my neck to gauge the height. Wow, the plumes had to be reaching some four hundred feet before arcing over. Each one – and there were many – were colourfully illuminated.

The jets began to sway, twirl, twist, and pulse in time to a deafening melody that echoed around the entire area. The notes were so emotionally stirring I could feel the small hairs on my neck beginning to rise. Who sang this? It was enchanting.

As my eyes roved around the thirty-acre lake set between the Dubai Mall, Souk Al Bahar, and the Burj Khalifa, I greedily drank in the atmosphere. The music was now vibrating within my whole body. It felt like every internal organ was humming along. The haunting strains combined with the ever-changing lights and fountain choreography were both breathtaking and incredibly moving. Unable to resist, my body began to sway in time to the beat.

From nowhere, came a memory. Keith and I listening to this same beautiful song. A female opera singer. What was her name? I could see Keith's face as he pretended to sing along in a falsetto voice. Oh, yes. The magnificent Sarah Brightman. And then another memory of me splitting my sides with laughter as I joined in with Keith. My brain continued to track back in time. Keith putting his arms around me and impulsively whisking me around the living room in a parody of ballroom dancing as Sarah warbled away.

Now the male accompaniment was taking his turn. I closed my eyes, remembering Keith making out he was the handsome Andrea Bocelli, trying and failing to mime along to the Italian tenor's incredible voice.

What was the song called? Ah, wait... Sarah was now singing the title. That was it. *Time to Say Good-bye*.

I froze. Why did everything seem to come back to saying good-bye to Keith? Time to say good-bye to my marriage. Time to say good-bye to my husband.

There, amongst the crowd, I suddenly felt so alone. The writhing fountains became a blur as my own eyes filled with water. Shit. I was on the verge of breaking down in public. And judging from the chuggy breaths building up in my chest, the outward display might be as eye-catching as the dancing fountains.

Caz and Bella were enthralled with the show, and the music was drowning out any chance of letting them know that I needed to get away – now!

Ahead were glass doors to the largest shopping mall in the world. Hopefully, I wouldn't get lost. But if I could just get inside... find a female rest room... hide in a cubicle until the wave of grief had subsided. I'd text Caz from the sanctuary of a loo. Make out that I'd needed to urgently spend a penny. Let her and Bella know that I'd only be five minutes. Although I had a horrible feeling that the tears now running down my cheeks was going to take a while to stem. I couldn't wait a moment longer. Desperate to be elsewhere, I turned and stumbled blindly through the crowd.

Straight into Gerard Butler.

Chapter Thirty-Four

Horrified, I barged past Gerard, mumbled a strangled apology, and took off at speed towards the inner sanctuary of the shopping mall.

I had no idea if he'd clocked my tear-stained face, or even realised that the overwrought female who'd nearly knocked him over bore a striking resemblance to his detested roommate.

Inside the mall, I was instantly immersed in a wave of cool air-conditioning. Disorientated, I peered around. Good heavens. The place was like Bluewater on steroids. Spotting a sign, I hastened towards it.

Pushing through the heavy door, I was immediately greeted by a lady wearing a pretty *shayla* over her hair. She pretended not to notice my distress and instead discreetly ushered me into a cubicle. Oh no. Did Dubai have assistants in all their loos? I just wanted to bawl in peace.

I grabbed a wad of toilet paper and buried my face within, emitting several muffled squawks and shrieks. At least my tears were being instantly mopped up. Heaven knows what it was doing to my carefully applied make-up. Likely wreaking havoc.

A faint ping came from the depths of my handbag. Leaning against the cubicle door, I took a shaky breath, and found my phone. A text from Bella.

Where are you, Annie? We're worried you've been kidnapped by a sheikh looking to expand his grandad's harem! xx

Despite the ludicrousness of that last sentence, I couldn't help but smile. Trust darling Belles to have a rampant imagination. I'd have to come clean about my disappearance. Anyway, my wrecked eye make-up would bear testament to the truth.

I'm in the loo. Sorry. The song… it made me think of Keith. Had a meltdown. Sorting myself out. Won't be long xx

I blew my nose, lobbed the tissue into the toilet bowl and flushed. As I cautiously exited the cubicle, the assistant gave me a curious look. She smiled tentatively and brandished an expensive looking bottle. Oh. I see. A human soap dispenser.

As I washed my hands, she pointed to her face and then mine. It was then that I looked in the mirror.

Shreds of toilet tissue were hanging off my eyelids, like mini party poppers stuck to a damp ceiling. Eyeshadow had smudged everywhere, and lipstick was smeared over my chin. Great.

I nodded my thanks to the lady, then set about soaping the whole lot off. Moments later a soft paper towel was pressed into my hands, followed by another bottle offering. This time it was thick and creamy hand lotion. She indicated I rub some of the moisturiser on to my cheeks, and I did so. What a thoughtful soul.

I surveyed my scrubbed face in the mirror. Red rimmed roadmaps gazed back at me. I looked like a conjunctivitis victim. Oh well. I extracted the coral lipstick from my handbag. Moments later, my mouth and eyes matched perfectly.

Smiling my gratitude, I tipped the loo attendant, then made my way back to the fountains feeling a smidgen better. Caz and Bella had moved on, but after a few more exchanges of texts, we were reunited in a restaurant called *Gia*.

'All the way to Dubai to sit in an Italian restaurant,' I feebly joked.

'Never mind that, Annie,' said Caz, her face serious. 'Are you okay?'

'I am now. Honest. Sorry for worrying you both, but the music was loud. You wouldn't have heard what I was saying so…' I shrugged helplessly.

'It's okay.' Bella patted my hand. '*You're* okay. That's all that matters. It's only to be expected to have moments where your emotions are ambushed. You're still mourning the loss of your marriage.'

'Thanks for understanding, girls.' I picked up the menu, eager to move on from the matter. 'Are we really eating here? I'm still immovable after dinner at the hotel. We'll go home the size of the Burj Khalifa if we eat two meals in one night.'

'Let's have coffee and ice-cream,' Caz suggested.

'That sounds lovely,' Bella agreed. 'Something nice and sweet. Lots of caramel, chocolate, and oodles of gooey stuff. Sugar is always wonderful for soothing an upset.'

'Okay. Comfort eating be damned.' I turned my attention to the Dessert Menu and winced. 'Have you seen these *prices*?'

'Don't forget' – Caz reminded – 'the Blue Jade are paying. And flipping right too after that muddle-up. My toes were visibly curling when Ahmed told us that men and women shouldn't share–'

'Don't say it.' I put up a hand to cut Caz off. 'I have no idea what trouble we'd be in – or the Blue Jade – if it all came to light.'

Minutes later we were in gelato heaven and mulling over life – and our marriages.

'I just didn't see it coming,' I lamented. 'In hindsight the warning signs were there, but I was oblivious.'

'I once suspected Andrew of having an affair,' said Caz.

'What?' squeaked Bella and I in unison.

'It was years ago.' Caz shrugged, looking faintly embarrassed. 'One of his female colleagues had a soft spot for him. Jackie. There was a works 'do' and spouses were invited. Jackie was all over Andrew like prickly heat rash, but he did nothing to stop her. I suppose he was flattered, but his lack of protest fuelled my suspicions of something going on. She dragged Andrew onto the dance floor for a smooch. After three consecutive slow numbers, I'd had enough. I picked up Andrew's untouched pint of beer, marched over and flung it.'

'Oh God!' Bella squeaked.

'That's what I said.' Caz looked bashful. 'Because my

170

aim was badly off. I soaked another woman in mid-snog with her guy.'

'What happened?' I gasped.

'This other woman – thankfully nothing to do with Andrew's work – was drenched. Her hairdo was instantly wrecked. One of her false eyelashes was sticking to her cheek like a wet spider. But before I had a chance to apologise, she turned on the guy and spat, "You told me you were divorced." And suddenly the pair of them were having a blazing row in the middle of the dance floor. I went smartly into reverse. Anyway, I was more interested in the woman who *was* after my husband. I confronted her just as Chris de Burgh was yodelling the last line to *Lady in Red.* Jackie admitted she fancied Andrew but promised she hadn't bedded him. Andrew was aghast. He was a bit worse for wear but quickly sobered up. Too quickly as it happened because he upchucked all over Jackie's shoes. She went berserk and then said I was welcome to him. It was all a bit embarrassing to be honest.'

'Oh Lord.' Bella was wide-eyed. 'Did you ever have to see her again?'

'No. Thankfully, she left the firm soon afterwards, and everybody else was too sloshed to take in what had happened. I know Andrew was thrilled by the attention, but I sometimes wonder what might have happened if I hadn't seen her off.' Caz sighed and for a moment looked pensive. 'Men can be such fools when their ego is stroked.'

'No more than us, surely?' said Bella. 'I mean, I'd be secretly delighted if Annie's heavenly roommate paid me some attention.'

'Shh,' I said, looking nervously about.

'But you wouldn't act upon it, would you?' asked Caz.

'No, of course not.' Bella shook her head. 'But catching someone's interest gives such a lift.'

'Do either of you still get wolf whistles?' asked Caz, looking wistful.

'Ha!' Bella snorted at the very idea. 'The last time I heard a toot was about five years ago. I looked up to see a lorry driver hanging out of his cab window. His front teeth were missing and he was wearing a grubby vest that strained over his belly. Hardly Pierce Brosnan. But I guess you have to take your thrills where you can.'

I tried to remember when anyone had flirted with me. Probably back in the Eighties when walking to the office via Fleet Street. Those were the days.

'Do you remember how annoyed we used to get if the lads on building sites shouted out?' I laughed. 'I always used to stick my nose in the air. Now I'd have to pay someone to make cheeky banter and drop a wink.'

'I wouldn't be too sure of that,' said Bella cosily. 'I'm convinced your roommate is a tiny bit smitten.'

'Belles, he really isn't.'

'He definitely looks at you with interest,' said Caz.

'Because he enjoys winding me up,' I retorted, remembering Gerard's earlier cocktail quip. Suggesting I choose a *Slippery Nipple* was a reminder about my full frontal in the pool. 'He is the most infuriating person. Anyway, I think he's working his way through those young girls he's taken to hanging around with.'

'I don't agree,' said Caz. 'I think he's just being friendly with them. After all, he's old enough to be their father.'

'Since when did that ever put a man off,' I said witheringly. Keith was definitely old enough to be Pippa Kipling's father – albeit an early starter.

'I suspect one of the young girls might have a crush on him,' said Bella. 'The one with the massive boobies.'

'I honestly doubt it's reciprocated,' said Caz. 'His eyes always seem to be on Annie.'

I shook my head. 'Any thrills he's getting from me are purely from sparring. I'm probably old enough to be *his* mother.'

'No you're not,' Bella tutted. 'Stop doing yourself down. Have you seen yourself lately?'

'Yes, about half an hour ago in the shopping mall restroom, looking a total fright.'

'You've been looking *fabulous* since Keith left,' Caz insisted. 'Anyway, I have a cunning plan.'

'Oh yes?' I said warily. 'What cunning plan is this?'

'Well' – Caz leant in closer – 'before time marches on any further and we're reaching for walking sticks, this could be our last chance *ever* to go…'

She trailed off dramatically, her eyes darting from Bella to me.

'Where?' we chorused.

'Clubbing!'

Chapter Thirty-Five

'I am not going clubbing,' I repeated for the umpteenth time.

It was after midnight. The three of us were now sitting together in the rear of Ahmed's limousine and heading back to the Blue Jade Hotel.

'It might be fun,' said Bella carefully, not wanting to get on the wrong side of Caz. She was leaving me to be the adamant one and protest on her behalf. The wily moo.

'Seriously, what part of being sixty and doing the Birdie Dance is fun?' I huffed.

'*Darl*-ing.' Caz rolled her eyes. 'No one does the Birdie Dance these days.'

'My Great Aunty Mabel can do the Birdie Dance,' said Bella. 'She did it at Cousin Lily's wedding.'

'Yes, that would have been when you were in your twenties,' Caz tutted. 'I'm telling you, these days it's completely different.'

'Voguing?' I queried.

'Madonna did that,' said Bella excitedly. 'I can remember trying to copy her.' She began to demonstrate, raising her arms and making lines of symmetry around her face – and promptly elbowed Caz in the cheek.

'Stop that.' Caz slapped Bella's arm away. 'No, not the Birdie Dance and not Voguing. I'm talking about twerking.'

'Twerk–?' I stared at Caz in disbelief. 'Have you totally lost the plot?'

'No.'

'Yes.'

'No! I am simply saying we could give it a go.'

'Listen to me. When I bounce up and down the only thing that twerks is my jawline. I am not getting on a dance floor in Dubai and doing *that*.'

'Oh come *on*,' she wheedled.

'No.'

'Please.'

'No.'

'Pretty please.'

'For heaven's sake, you sound like Carly when she was fifteen. Do you even know how to twerk?'

'I might,' said Caz nonchalantly, studying her fingernails.

'Don't tell me. You've been having lessons. I don't believe it! First pole fitness. Then burlesque. Then aerial hoop. Now flipping twerking. What's with you?'

'I'll teach you,' she clapped her hands in delight. 'It's really easy. First step–'

'First step' – I interrupted – 'is to reconsider.'

'We'll discuss it later.' She gave me a meaningful look and inclined her head. I caught on and spotted Ahmed looking at us via the rear-view mirror. If his eyes bulged any further, they'd be in danger of popping right out of his head.

When I finally crept into my cupboard room, Gerard was already in his bunk. His rhythmic breathing confirmed sleep had already claimed him. He'd left the bedside light on for which I was grateful. I tiptoed into the bathroom, taking care not to disturb him. The last thing I wanted was questions about me slamming into him at the fountains earlier. It had happened so quickly that I was confident he hadn't realised it was me, but nonetheless I was keen to avoid any risk of the subject cropping up.

Five minutes later I clicked off the light and almost immediately found myself gravitating towards sleep. My mind drifted down a dark tunnel. Bliss. I sighed with contentment and continued to float in inky darkness.

But... wait. Ahead, the blackness was being interrupted by streaks of colour. I hastened towards the phenomenon. Bright lights in rainbow colours. But in the middle of this neon spectrum was a large black vertical rectangle. It took me a moment to realise that I was standing before a door, and the colours were light spilling around its frame.

Perplexed, I dithered. Then, carefully, I put my fingertips upon it and gently pushed. As the door swung inward, throbbing music assaulted my eardrums. I recognised the song. *Blurred Lines* and... omigod... a dance floor. I was in some sort of night club. And there was Caz! She was dancing and sizzling-it-up with Gerard. In one hand she was holding a giant foam palm tree. The trunk was emblazoned with the words *I love Dubai*. She saw me looking, waved, then stuck her tongue out... and out... and out a bit more and... good heavens, she was emulating Miley Cyrus. Now she was leaping about and... uh-oh... prodding Gerard in an iffy place with the foam palm tree and... argh!... twerking against his crotch!

'Caz, stop!' I called over the music. 'For heaven's sake you'll get us all arrested.'

'Don't be silly,' she protested. 'We're simply having fun.' She beckoned me with the foam palm tree. 'Come on over and join in.'

'I'm out of practice,' I protested.

'For what?' asked Gerard.

'Doing it. I can't remember the last time...'

I trailed off. Had it been at Bella's barbecue just before lockdown? When we'd all got tipsy, and I'd self-consciously hopped from one foot to the other in time to The Beach Boys? Yes. Most probably. The impromptu jig with Keith and *Time to Say Good-bye* didn't properly count.

Gerard was now looking at me speculatively.

'I could teach you,' he murmured.

'Teach me to *twerk*?' My voice was incredulous.

Suddenly I was squinting, and it was nothing to do with rainbow lights. Now there was only a harsh glare.

'W-What's going on?' I stammered.

'Are you okay?' Suddenly I was looking into the upside-down face of my roommate as he peered over the bunk's safety rail.

'You've woken me up!' I protested, squinting

attractively.

'Correction, Madam. It was *you* who woke *me* up.'

I opened my mouth and shut it again. Oh Lord. I'd been dreaming. *And* sleep talking. How embarrassing. This was all Caz's fault.

'I... I... I'm sorry,' I finished lamely.

He peered at me. 'Good heavens. An apology. This must be a first. Say it again and I'll record it on my phone for posterity.'

'Why are you so utterly annoying?'

'Because you hauled me out of a lovely dream wanting to know if I could twerk.'

'I can't help what my subconscious gets up to while I'm asleep,' I snapped.

'The mind boggles. Well as long as you don't sleepwalk and try any strange moves in the sink.'

'The sink?' I frowned.

'Tap dancing.' His face was expressionless.

'Very funny. Not.' I glared at him. 'Goodnight, Mr Butler.'

'Goodnight, Madam.'

He reached for the switch and the room was once again plunged into darkness.

Chapter Thirty-Six

'What shall we do later?' asked Bella.

The three of us were stretched out on our loungers and enjoying the hot Emirati sun. It was blissful. I could have stayed by the pool all day but, after visiting Downtown Dubai yesterday, I was keen to return and preferably before nightfall. I wanted to check out the half-mile-high skyscraper, *Burj Khalifa*.

'I think—' began Caz.

Shrieks and splashes distracted the three of us. On the other side of the pool, like a sheikh with his harem, was Gerard Butler and the Towie girls. Several of the women had jumped into the water. The one with the big boobies had refrained and was rubbing sun lotion into Gerard's shoulders. The two American guys were watching enviously.

I looked away. 'You were saying?' I prompted Caz.

'The shopping mall is something to be experienced. Not that we can afford anything, but I'd love to check out all those Designer shops. Louis Vuitton... Christian Louboutin... Armani.'

'What, no Primark?' Bella pretended to be outraged.

'Doesn't it have an aquarium?' I said, suddenly excited.

'I'm sure I read somewhere that there's this vast underwater–'

'Good morning, ladies,' said a voice I was starting to dread.

'Hello,' said Bella, giving Gerard a dinky wave.

'Hi,' Caz grinned. 'Are you enjoying yourself?'

I gave her one of my special looks. One that conveyed:

What a stupid question. He's pressing youthful flesh and experiencing how Hugh Heffner must have felt with his bunny brigade.

Caz gave me one of her own in return:

What's your problem with this guy?

Gerard grinned back. His teeth seemed to be gleaming more than ever. Surely it wasn't normal to have choppers that white. They were probably bleached. Or maybe false, I thought uncharitably. No, Annie. Gerard isn't old enough to have false teeth. But you are.

My mouth drooped as I remembered the horrible gap hiding right at the back of my mouth. A few months ago, I'd lost a molar. Since then my dentist had been pressing me to have an implant. However, I'd gone all squeamish at the thought of bone being drilled for the placement of a titanium screw. The dentist had suggested an alternative. Making a "piece". Basically, a denture. *Quelle horreur!* But what was the alternative? There wasn't one.

Actually, that wasn't entirely true. The third option was to do nothing. Put up with a gap. But it wasn't ideal. Chewing on that side was currently compromised. And what to do if another tooth eventually had to be pulled?

And then another? End up with gums like a newborn? How utterly depressing. My thoughts fragmented. Gerard was addressing Caz.

'Thanks for asking. I'm having a better time than expected.'

Ha! Of course he was. All he needed was Hugh Heffner's burgundy smoking jacket and velvet slippers. Admittedly he was younger and better looking than HH, but he still had a horribly smug smile.

'We're loving it too,' Bella simpered.

'Have you been in yet?' Gerard indicated the pool.

'No. Maybe in a little while,' Caz replied.

'What about you, Madam?' Gerard turned to me. 'What will you be doing today? A spot of synchronised swimming?'

My eyes narrowed.

'Are you making fun of me?'

Gerard's eyes widened. 'Me? Good gracious no. I just know how keen you are on unusual dancing.'

'Really?' said Caz, looking at me incredulously.

'Didn't you know?' said Gerard, totally deadpan. 'She woke me up last night asking if I could twerk.'

'You dark horse,' said Bella, giving me a sly look.

'I can twerk,' Caz informed Gerard. 'I've had lessons and I'm going to teach my friends.'

'And she wants us to go clubbing,' said Bella, squeaking slightly.

'Is that so?' said Gerard, giving me a speculative look. 'Do let me know when. Something tells me it's a night not to be missed.'

I scowled at him. 'Your many girlfriends might have something to say about that.' I nodded in the direction of the shrieking women. 'They're yoo-hooing for you to join them.'

Only the one with the big boobies remained poolside. She looked most put out at Gerard chatting to the three of us.

'They're not my girlfriends,' he said mildly.

'I think that one over there might like to be,' said Caz, discreetly indicating the sulking blonde.

'That's Celine.'

Right. Not Diamante.

'And you're right,' Gerard continued. 'She says she likes older men.'

My lip curled attractively. 'How charming. So, you're a Sugar Daddy. Congratulations.'

Gerard threw back his head and laughed.

'Celine is a lovely girl and extremely easy on the eye. But I like my women a little more...'

He paused to consider. Suddenly I was curious. A little more what? Flat chested? Less blonde? More geeky?

'Older,' he finished, looking me directly in the eye. 'The older woman knows who she is, and she's classy. She has everything to flaunt but chooses not to.'

His eyes seemed to be boring into mine and I could feel myself getting inexplicably flustered. Why was he looking at me like that? As if... as if he were referring to *me*. I mean, he couldn't be. Could he?

'Unless she has a wardrobe malfunction,' he winked.

And with that Gerard sauntered off leaving me feeling hot, bothered and out of sorts.

Chapter Thirty-Seven

'I'm sure he fancies you,' said Bella.

'I'll second that,' said Caz. 'Did you see the way he was looking at you?' She waggled her eyebrows. 'Scorching! And what's all this about you waking him up in the middle of the night and asking him to twerk?'

'Nothing,' I said crossly. 'Apparently I was sleep talking – no thanks to you.'

'Stop being so grumpy. And anyway, how can that be my fault?' Caz protested.

'Because you were the one who brought up the subject.'

'Twerking?'

The two Americans looked our way and began nudging each other.

'Shh,' I hissed. 'Can we just drop the subject?'

'For now.' Caz flopped back on her lounger with a smirk. 'Meanwhile, when we see Ahmed later, we'll ask his advice on which are the best clubs around here.'

Oh God. I wasn't engaging in the topic.

'I'm going for a swim.'

I stood up smartly, ignoring Caz calling me back. The two Americans were once again nudging each other, possibly hoping for another full frontal. I glared at them, checked my swimsuit, then executed a decent dive and broke into a speedy front crawl.

As I ploughed through the water, somebody powered past me. Reaching the other end of the pool and swiping the chlorine from my eyes, I spotted Gerard next to me.

'Beat you!' he crowed.

'I wasn't aware it was a race.'

'Weren't you?' He raised his eyebrows. 'In which case, I challenge you to one.'

'No thanks.'

'Why ever not?'

'Because I'm on holiday and relaxing.'

'Correction. If you live in the present moment, you'll realise you're on holiday and *swimming*.'

'Actually, I'm listening to you talking nonsense.'

'*Actually*' – he mimicked – 'you're catching your breath.'

'*Actually*' – I mimicked back – 'I'm simply… pausing.'

'Pausing, eh?' He grinned. 'So you're not experiencing a hammering heart and waiting for your galloping pulse to return to normal?'

No. That had been *before* I'd dived in.

'If you want company, why don't you ask Celine to swim with you?'

'Because she needs water wings and is too self-conscious to wear them.'

I didn't know whether he was winding me up or being serious.

'Then ask one of the other girls.'

'Can't. They either have their noses in *Grazia* or want to discuss nail polish. Such riveting conversation. I've never had children, but these girls are giving me a crash course in what it must be like to have an adult daughter. Their talk is all about the benefit of lip filler or whether one should have their eyebrows tattooed.'

'Not all daughters make banal conversation,' I protested.

'Are you speaking from experience?'

'Yes. My daughter Carly is wonderful, as are our chats.'

'What do the two of you discuss? Don't tell me. Heavy subjects. World peace. Who will win the next election. Whether global warming really exists or if it's all down to chem trails.'

'Sometimes.' Never. But I wasn't going to tell him that. 'More recently our conversation has been about babies. She's pregnant with her first child.'

Gerard raised his eyebrows. 'You're a grandmother-to-be. You don't look old enough.'

I was so thrown by his comment, for a moment I couldn't speak.

'Thanks,' I said eventually.

'I guess that's why you don't want to accept my race challenge.'

I frowned. 'You've lost me.'

'It's psychological. Soon you'll be a grandma. Therefore, you're already thinking like one. Telling yourself you're too old to race the likes of me because you'd lose.'

'I'm thinking no such thing.' My eyes flashed.

'Oh I see.' He nodded knowingly. 'You're simply worried about losing.'

'Listen, Mr Butler' – I gave him my haughtiest look – 'if I *wanted* to beat you at front crawl, then I would, okay? I certainly don't have to race you to know that.'

'And I put it to you, Madam, that your words are nothing more than posturing.'

'Posturing?' I spluttered. God this man was so infuriating. 'Okay. Challenge accepted.' I glared at him. 'One length. And may the best man win.'

'That'll definitely be me then, because you're a woman.'

'Could you, just for one moment, stop being so–'

'Readysteadygo!' he gabbled, before taking off.

'Hey, that's cheating,' I called after him. 'I wasn't ready.'

Oh for God's sake. Annoyance flashed through me as I gave chase. My arms whipped through the water, feet emulating flippers as my head turned to the side, sucking in great lungfuls of air so I could keep my head down longer and make up for Gerard's two-second head start.

Why was I doing this? Why had I allowed myself to be goaded? And all because winning was all. I felt like I was back in a parents' race at one of Carly's swimming galas. Whether the edge of a pool or a painted line on a field, I'd always been like a greyhound after a fluffy.

'Tie!' said Gerard, as our hands touched the side at the

same time.

'Hardly,' I protested. 'You started before I was ready. Technically, I won that race.'

We were standing in the shallow end alongside Caz and Bella's sun loungers. Caz peered at us both.

'It looked like a tie to us, Annie,' said Caz. 'Sorry, darling.'

'The judges agree,' said Gerard gleefully.

I put my hands on my hips. 'Well I don't. So we'll do it again.'

'Fine by me.'

And with that Gerard once again took off without me being ready.

'Quick, Annie, or you'll lose,' Bella urged.

'But—'

Argh.

I shot off, once again ploughing through the water at speeds I hadn't achieved since Carly's last gala race. On that occasion I'd almost met my match. A parent had been filming on the side. I'd demanded they replay their video in slow motion to determine the nano-second moment of whose hand had touched down first. Thankfully, it had been mine. I'd walked off triumphantly clutching a cheap plastic medal. Too ludicrous for words. But somehow, I just couldn't help it.

'Tie!' said Gerard again.

'You are a total cheat!' I declared furiously. 'Are you going to race properly under starter's orders?'

'Uh-oh,' said Gerard, looking delighted. 'My

roommate is getting angry.'

'Shhh.' I glanced about nervously. 'Nobody is supposed to know about–'

'Third and final time. Do you accept the challenge, Madam?'

'I do, Mr Butler.'

His eyes twinkled with mischief. 'In which case' – he glanced over at Celine who gave a dinky wave – 'let me call upon an impartial person to start this race.'

'Fine by me.'

I tried not to feel sour as Celine unfolded long legs and, chest wobbling alarmingly, sashayed over. There was also another emotion running through me. One I didn't like – and certainly didn't want to acknowledge. A sense of possessiveness. This was *my* race with Gerard Butler, and I didn't want anyone else muscling in.

'Are you ready?' she said breathily.

I gazed at Celine incredulously. Okay. She was trying to channel Marilyn Monroe. Well, good for her.

'Are you steady?' she giggled, making lots of little catchy noises in her throat. Oh for goodness sake, was she for real?

'G–'

I was off before she'd finished saying "Go". Irritation about Celine whooshed through me. Interesting. Why was I letting a gorgeous, nubile, fan of Gerard irk me? I had no idea. Nor was I going to dwell upon it. Instead, I used the emotion to propel me further, pushing that little bit harder, going that littler bit faster and... yessss!

I turned to Gerard, and this time it was *my* face that was smug.

'I think the matter is now settled. I'm a faster swimmer than you.'

Whereupon my tormentor winked and said, 'I know how much winning means to you. I intentionally let you have that race.'

As he hauled himself out of the pool, I gazed after him in disbelief.

Celine wiggled over. 'You're such a gentleman, darling,' she giggled, sticking out her chest before linking an arm through his. She shrieked girlishly as the cold water running off his body touched her skin.

Returning to my sun lounger, I suddenly felt inexplicably miserable.

'Well done, sweetie,' said Bella, clapping her hands together and applauding me.

'I think we should toast your swimming success with a poolside cocktail,' said Caz.

'Sounds good,' I agreed. Perhaps a shot of this and that mixed with the other would sweeten me up.

A few minutes later, full of rum and gin, I was feeling wonderfully mellow. The sun beat against my eyelids, making them incredibly heavy. I'd close them. Just for a moment.

I must have nodded off because suddenly warm hands were shaking me awake.

'W–Whassup?' I said blearily.

Gerard's face swam into focus. He was now wearing a

towelling robe in readiness for leaving the pool area.

'Whilst your gal pals are snoozing so prettily, I thought it prudent to give you some friendly advice. Don't fall asleep on your back after drinking cocktails in the sun. You were snoring and making a terrible racket.'

'I do not snore,' I said irritably.

A quick glance around the pool revealed all eyes upon me, hands covering mouths, shoulders shaking, and the two Americans guys were practically doubled over with mirth.

'Regrettably, Madam, that wasn't the case.' He adopted the grave tones of a BBC newsreader. 'This afternoon, a guest of the Blue Jade Hotel snored not just for England, but for the entire United Arab Emirates. I'll be back tomorrow to report further on this phenomenon. In the meantime, I wish you a very pleasant afternoon.'

He slung a damp towel over his shoulder and once again sauntered off leaving me gnashing my teeth as I stared after him.

Chapter Thirty-Eight

When I returned to the room, there was no sign of Gerard.

The only indication that he'd been in before me was a dark curly chest hair nestling in the shower tray and a whiff of aftershave that lingered in the air.

I sniffed appreciatively. Nice pong. And then I scowled. I didn't want to approve of whatever scent my roommate was splashing all over. No doubt Celine would cover herself in it later when she planted frantic little kisses all over him. The thought of her lips on his neck made me grimace. Now why was that? I couldn't care less if she snogged Gerard.

I stomped into the bathroom, rinsed out my swimsuit, had a shower, and then debated what to wear. Shoving a pair of Gerard's flip-flops to one side, I pulled out my suitcase from under the bunk, all the while telling myself to stop being grumpy. At least the aftershave aroma still permeating the air wasn't the same as that which my estranged husband wore, otherwise I'd have been even crankier.

I had a sudden vision of Pippa Kipling pressing her lips into Keith's. In an instant, my mood changed from grouchy to melancholy. For goodness' sake, Annie. Get a flipping grip. Just tell yourself that all men are a pain in the whatsits, then let the emotion go. Meanwhile, get dressed and sort out your face!

Half an hour later, I was outside the hotel with Caz and Bella. Ahmed's black limousine glided to a halt and the three of us piled in. I was thankful the hotel had provided another driver for Gerard. Certainly, nobody had suggested we share Ahmed.

I wondered if the Towie girls were taking advantage of my roommate's free travel pass. Probably. Perhaps Celine was, right now, sitting next to Gerard in a Mercedes with blacked-out windows. Maybe snuggled into his armpit. Looking up at him with adoration. Eyes dilating to the size of a sheikh's oilwell as her body leant against his. Making hushed sexy conversation. "Gerard, darling... *(breathy-breathy)*... we're not allowed to have a snoggy-kiss-kiss in public... *(breathy-hic-hic)*... but the moment we're alone together... *(gaspy-gasp)*... I'm going to push you down and–"

'Annie?' Caz gave me a sharp prod. 'Stop daydreaming and open the door. We're here.'

'Sorry,' I said, blinking. What went on in my imagination? I seemed to have been obsessing about Gerard and Celine. Why? It wasn't like I fancied him or something. Heaven forbid. The guy might exude oodles of charm to the Towie girls, and I knew Bella and Caz were secretly smitten, but he was far too overconfident for my liking. He'd probably made love to more women than James Bond.

As I clambered out of the car, I tried to imagine Gerard leaning in and kissing me. The very thought made my brain go *ewwww* and my heart go—

Whoosh!

'Ngggh,' I gasped.

'What?' said Caz. 'Are you all right, Annie?'

She grabbed hold of me as I wobbled violently and stared, shell-shocked, at the towering skyscrapers around us.

'Yes,' I squeaked faintly. 'Just a bit hot.'

Why had my body reacted like that? Maybe it was simply the Emirati sunshine. On the other hand, perhaps I should test the theory. Only to reassure myself. I'd think of Gerard again. But not kissing. Something else. Something less... obvious. Like Caz and Bella being in the swimming pool. Me on a lounger, trying and failing to rub sun cream into an awkward spot. Gerard conveniently passing by and – no banter or twinkling eyes – offering his assistance. "Here, let me help you." So far, so good. Gerard picking up the bottle of sun cream. Me disinterested but polite. "Thank you, Mr Butler. Marvellous weather, what?" Hang on, I seemed to have morphed into a different era. Okay. Rewind. "Thank you, Mr Butler. I need the cream here." Then pointing to the area between my shoulder blades. His hands touching my skin and...

Whoosh!

Noooo. Dear God, please—

Wait. I was in the United Arab Emirates. I needed to change heavenly hotlines. Okay. Try again.

Dear Allah. My name is Annie Rosewood and I'm here

in Dubai to forget all about my estranged husband. I've met this guy and – please don't tell the authorities – but I'm sharing a room with him. I absolutely promise nothing is happening between us. Cross my heart and hope to die. Well, not die, nothing dramatic, please. Anyway. I thought I couldn't stand him. But now–

'Come on.' Caz scattered my thoughts. 'Let's head toward the shopping mall. It will be cool in there and you can get steady on your pins.'

'Give me your handbag,' said Bella, fussing about.

'I'm not an invalid,' I protested.

'You've had a funny turn,' said Caz sternly.

Yes. I'd one of those all right. Except there was nothing funny about it. *I* might not fancy Gerard Butler, but my *body* was begging to differ. How DARE it let me down like this.

The girls frogmarched me into the building complex. As the air-con softly enveloped us, my pounding heart rate went down a notch.

'Phew, that's better,' I said brightly. 'It was probably my body adjusting to the hormonal jollop that Miss Walter recently prescribed. Let's go back outside.'

'No need,' said Caz, sweeping me onward. 'Ahmed said the entrance to The Burj's viewing decks are in the mall, next to Bloomingdales.'

'Oooh, Bloomingdales.' Bella was now looking like a child who'd been told Father Christmas was waiting to see her. 'We simply have to go there.'

'And we will. After we've been up the tower,' said

Caz.

'Right.' Bella's smile quickly faded.

Was it my imagination or was she starting to look a bit green?

By the time we'd bought our tickets and were queuing for one of the lifts, I was completely distracted and buzzing with excitement.

'It says here' — I read from my mobile's screen — 'that the elevator goes at thirty-six kilometres per hour. Whoop!' I grinned. 'Better hang on to our stomachs, girls.'

'Indeed,' Bella muttered, suddenly swaying like a belly dancer.

'Oh no. First Annie. Now you,' said Caz. 'Have you drunk enough water today?'

'Yes,' she assured. 'I'm perfectly hydrated. It's... something else.' She looked shifty.

'Well what is it then?' I prompted.

The queue shuffled forward. We were seconds away from the embarkation area.

'Now probably isn't the best time to tell you that I'm not good at heights.'

I boggled at her. 'You don't like heights?'

'Don't keep mentioning the word.' She screwed up her eyes and began fanning herself with her ticket. 'I need to overcome the problem. Be my own master.'

'Blimey,' said Caz. 'Nothing like throwing yourself in at the deep end. How high is The Burj, Annie?'

'Er, not too bad, really. In the grand scheme of things.'

'What do you mean, *in the grand scheme of things?*'

said Bella.

'Um, well, you know.' I shrugged. 'It's higher than Asda, but not as tall as…' I trailed off trying to think of comparisons that would make Bella feel better.

'The moon?' she prompted.

'Y-e-s,' I answered, making a see-saw motion with one hand. 'That's quite a good comparison.'

'How high?' she demanded. 'Tell me. I want to know.'

I stared at my phone in dismay. 'It says here it's just over half a mile high.'

Bella's eyes bulged just as one of the elevators arrived. Its doors sprang open.

'This way, please, ladies,' said an assistant.

We trundled forward, cramming into the lift along with what seemed like a thousand other people. Boy, they really liked to squish you in. In that moment I knew exactly how one of John West's sardines felt.

'Wowww,' said an American boy to his dad. 'This tower is twice as tall as the Empire State Building.'

'Awesome,' his dad replied. 'I read that if you laid the tower's pieces end to end, it would stretch over a quarter of the way around the world.'

'What floor are we getting off at, Dad?'

'Number 124, son.'

'GET ME OUT OF HERE,' screeched Bella, just as the lift operator was about to push the button.

'Are you okay, Madam?' he enquired solicitously.

'HELPHELPHELPHELP,' Bella burbled.

'That means "help" in English,' I informed the wide-eyed operator.

Bella catapulted through the still-open doors, tripped, and collapsed in a heap on the floor.

People waiting in the queue were now staring. They gasped at the prostrate woman in European clothes. Caz fought her way out and leant over Bella.

'It's okay,' she said to no one in particular. 'Just a little panic attack. Come on, Belles. You're fine. Annie, you carry on. I'm not bothered about seeing the aerial views. I'll take her to Bloomingdales and wait for you there.'

'Oh, I'm not sure…' I dithered, one foot in the elevator, one foot out.

'Well I am,' said Caz firmly. 'Now go. You're holding everyone up!'

Obediently, I reversed back within the recess. As the lift door started to close, I caught a last glimpse of Caz administering to Bella.

'Breathe! That's it. In. Out. I said OUT!'

As the lift shot upwards, the interior lighting changed. Soft music began to play. Soothing Arabian notes. The walls had changed into a light show depicting a velvety black sky full of sparkling white stars. I felt as though I'd stepped into a rocket that was powering through the universe. And when the lift doors opened, for a moment I thought I'd landed in Heaven. For standing there, in all his twinkly eyed, devil-may-care glory, was Gerard Butler.

Chapter Thirty-Nine

'We meet again,' said Gerard, giving his familiar wicked grin.

I felt my stomach lurch which was nothing to do with the lift's catapult ride.

'Hello,' I said stiffly.

You do not fancy him. You do not fancy him. You do not fancy him.

'All alone?' he enquired.

'My friends are waiting in Bloomingdales. The height of this building gave one of them vertigo while she was still on the ground floor.'

'Shame.'

'And you?'

I looked around for the Towie girls and, more particularly, Celine.

'I'm on my own too. The girls have gone shopping. Apparently, there is a "must have" make-up brand to be bought here that doesn't retail in the UK. I would have thought if you'd seen one lipstick, you'd seen them all. But then again, I'm just a regular guy, so what would I know about pink having a hundred different shade names?'

'Quite. Personally, I'd just buy the lipstick at Boots.'

'You sound like a sensible lady.'

'I am.'

Unless my foolish imagination wanders off down an inappropriate path.

'I've already looked around, but I'm not in any hurry to return to the girls. Would you like me to keep you company?' he smiled. 'I'm also pretty clued up on this place and can give you some free tourist info.'

'Oh, have you been here before?'

'No. Earlier I eavesdropped on a tour guide.' He laughed.

I considered. Something within me had shifted. Instinctively I wanted to put distance between us – as if Gerard were a dangerous desert cat. The previous scathing words that had so easily tripped off my lips now seemed to be wedged in my oesophagus making me feel like a tongue-tied teenager. It was one thing to be sharing a cupboard room where he was in the top bunk and out of sight. It was quite another to be walking around together, his arm accidentally brushing against mine and...

'*Eeeep.*'

'Sorry?'

'Nothing. Static shock.'

On the other hand, it was ridiculously thrilling to be alongside this handsome man and have him all to myself.

'Well' – I kept my tone casual – 'that would be nice, if you're not in any hurry to rush off to Celine.'

As I uttered her name, my lip involuntarily curled which seemed to instantly amuse Gerard.

'Come on, then,' he said. 'Let's go this way. I'll take you to the observation deck. It's a nifty outdoor terrace.'

We moved through groups of tourists, gathered in their cliques, all jabbering away in a number of different languages. I stuck close to Gerard. The area was smaller than I'd imagined, but it was still easy to get separated by a throng of continually moving people. Most were snapping away with their cameras or mobile phones.

'Did you know' – Gerard guided me by the elbow which instantly sent another zinger up my spine – 'that Tom Cruise filmed a scene here for *Mission Impossible 4.* Have you ever watched any of his films?'

'Yes, years ago. But I can't specifically remember the one you're talking about. I can't even recall the name of the character he plays.'

'Ethan Hunt.' Gerard pulled out his mobile and tapped the screen. 'I'll see if I can find a video on YouTube where Ethan has to reach the 130th floor of the tower, then ditch the elevator to outwit his enemy.'

While Gerard searched for the appropriate film clip, I gazed at the panorama of Dubai's evolving skyline. From here everything looked so ridiculously tiny. Even the skyscrapers had morphed into bog-standard buildings.

My eyes narrowed to focus on specific structures. Ahead was the city's oval-shaped opera house. It was the centrepiece of a new district designed to encourage pedestrian traffic. Over there was the water desalinisation plant. I'd heard that without it, the country would run out of water in four days. Directly below was downtown Dubai and the shopping mall… the fountains… Sheikh Mohamed Bin Rashid Boulevard… a number of hotels and private residences stretching off into the horizon… and the bridge that connected the Dubai Mall and Souk Al Bahar to numerous café's, bars, and restaurants.

'*Eeeep*,' I squeaked again, as Gerard touched my arm.

'Another static shock?'

'Yes,' I mumbled.

'Here's the clip.'

I watched as Mr Cruise, wearing what looked like a thin harness, launched himself through a window, swung wide of the building, then gracefully whirled in a loop, feet landing squarely against the Burj's sides as – now hanging sideways – he ran part of the circumference before changing direction and then – like Spiderman – abseiled down the side of the building.

'What a stunt,' said Gerard in admiration.

'Rather him than me,' I said with feeling.

Gerard slipped the phone back in his pocket and pointed in another direction. 'See over there? You can sample Arabic coffee at *Café Bateel*, or enjoy an Arabic breakfast at *Social House* or even indulge in shisha and Arabic tea under the stars at *Shakespeare & Co.*'

'You make it sound enchanting.'

'It is. There is magic all around' – he gave me an unfathomable look – 'and a genie willing to grant your every wish.'

I had no idea if he was being serious or winding me up. Presumably the latter. After all, there were no flying carpets or mysterious looking lamps handily laying around.

We moved on. From this viewpoint there was… wow… nothing. Just desert. It seemed to stretch on and on, the horizon melting into endless nothingness. Such a sharp contrast to the city views.

'The design of the Burj' – Gerard continued – 'embodies the Spider Lily. It's a regional desert flower that apparently inspired the architect's vision.'

I stared ahead, enthralled. There was something about the sun beating down on the sand and creating a shimmering haze that was both bleak but also enticing. I nodded at the space.

'Can you go into it?'

'Certainly. Celine and the girls have persuaded me to join them on a trip and do some Dune Bashing. Will you be giving it a whirl?'

'Probably,' I said airily. 'There's no point in coming to a place like this and not doing a spot of… er… that.' I had no idea what he was talking about.

'Have a word with Reception. After all, the hotel is paying for everything,' he pointed out. 'Tell them you want to book a Safari Adventure.'

'Okay, I will. It sounds… fun.'

I was all for hopping into a Land Cruiser and pottering through the desert. I had an idea it might get a bit boring after a while. After all, there was only so much sand you could see. But I was sure Caz and Bella would be up for it and – as Gerard had said – the Blue Jade were picking up all tabs. We might as well make the most of every opportunity.

Gerard's phone pinged, and he checked his screen.

'Time for me to go.'

'Oh.' I suddenly felt deflated.

'Celine has finished her shopping. Apparently, the rest of the girls have scattered to all corners of the mall and left her on her tod. She wants to meet for something to eat and show off all the scented candles she's bought.'

'You can get that sort of thing back home.'

'But not from *The White Barn Store.*' Gerard waggled a reproachful finger. 'And I can guarantee the scent will be raved about and pitched as something never smelt before, even though you and I know both know that you can probably buy something similar in John Lewis.' He laughed. 'Are you staying up here a bit longer?'

'Yes, I'll have another walk around.'

'In which case I'll see you later. With a bit of luck, I'll be back in our room just in time to catch you attractively slathering on your night cream.'

He was back to winding me up. And that was fine. It was more familiar territory. I could cope with that. Whereas the constant electric shocks he'd given me had been another matter.

As Gerard walked towards one of the elevators, I felt a huge sense of relief.

And also disappointment.

Chapter Forty

'You missed a treat,' I said to Bella and Caz.

The three of us were standing outside Bloomingdales.

'Yes, we saw your roommate about twenty minutes ago,' said Caz slyly. 'He and his girlies tripped past us. He waved and said he'd bumped into you at the top of the tower.'

'I'm not talking about *him*,' I retorted. 'I'm referring to the Burj's views. They were staggering.'

'Don't let Caz wind you up,' said Bella, patting my hand. 'Although I must say, your roommate is almost as scrumptious as this store. While you were at the tower, we had a good old nosy around, and now we're ready for some coffee and cake. What about you, Annie?'

'Definitely. How amazing to find a Bloomingdales in Dubai. I'd assumed it was exclusive to the States.'

'Apparently it's the brand's first ever location outside the USA,' said Caz, leading the way. 'We checked their *Home* section earlier, and rather naughtily sent picture texts to Colin and Andrew telling them we were restyling our front rooms. They're probably having a fit believing we've arranged the shipping of new sofas and sideboards.' She chuckled. 'I do like teasing my husband.

He falls for it so easily.'

'Here we are,' said Bella, standing outside Bloomingdale's Magnolia Bakery. We walked in and immediately exclaimed in delight at shelves laden with cupcakes, cookies, freshly baked desserts and – we gasped aloud – stunning wedding cake samples.

'Go and find a table,' said Caz. 'I'll get our order.'

'Keep the receipt,' I prompted.

'Thanks for reminding me. Flaming Nora. Since when did three cappuccinos and cupcakes come to forty quid?' she gasped. 'You know, I'm almost glad the Blue Jade did mess up otherwise I think I'd already be in my overdraft.'

Once we were settled, I casually mentioned the desert trip that Gerard had talked about.

'Sounds rather fun, don't you think?'

'Driving over endless sand?' Bella looked unimpressed. 'What exactly is there to see?'

'I don't know. Maybe nothing. I suppose that's the point. Being a tiny person in a huge expanse of nothingness.'

'I'm not sure about it.' Bella looked worried. 'What if the Land Cruiser ran out of fuel? We could be stuck out in the desert for days with no Wi-Fi signal… the sun beating down on us… nothing to drink… hallucinating… running towards waterfalls which turn out to be mirages… falling to our knees in despair and–'

'Belles, for goodness' sake get a grip,' Caz tutted. 'Look.' She thrust her phone screen at Bella. 'I've just tapped *desert trip* into a search engine. It's a properly organised tour and might be a good laugh. There's a desert feast, belly dancing, and you can even ride a camel.'

'The Dubai equivalent of sitting on a donkey at Broadstairs Beach.' I gave Bella's hand a reassuring squeeze. 'Happier now?'

She nodded. 'Yes, that sounds more like it. I don't like stepping out of my comfort zone.'

'Me neither,' I assured.

'It will be fine,' Caz promised. 'A bit of gentle entertainment.'

Chapter Forty-One

'WHAT HAVE YOU SIGNED US UP FOR?' screeched Bella, as the Toyota Land Cruiser hurtled towards a towering wall of sand.

I didn't answer for two reasons. First, I was too busy hanging on to both a grab rail and my bouncing bosoms. Second, fear had shrivelled my vocal cords.

A quick glance at Caz revealed she was in a similar situation with her lower arm flung firmly across her bust while the other – skin stretched over white knuckles – clung to a second grab rail. However, unlike me, Caz wasn't taking this torture quietly and was making the sort of embarrassing noise that sounded like she was having energetic sex.

'Ooooooh,' she moaned, as the Cruiser scaled the dune. 'Ahhhhh,' she exhaled at the peak. For a split second the vehicle hovered, momentarily giving the illusion that it was about to go into freefall. 'OOOOOOOH,' she yodelled as the four-by-four shot over the edge.

A second later and we were slamming down, slipping from side to side as the driver wrestled with the wheel. Billions of grains of sand sprayed up the sides of the passenger doors.

'Oh-oh-oh-OHHH,' Caz groaned as we careered towards another towering mound.

'This is why it's called *dune bashing*,' yelled the driver.

'I'll bash these two when this vehicle stops,' Bella exhorted. She glared at Caz and me. 'Go for a jaunt in the desert, you both said. Enjoy a gentle drive. Be part of Mother Nature's wonder and–'

She broke off as the Land Cruiser again violently zig-zagged. For a horrible moment I thought we were going to flip right over.

'Don't be scared,' the driver assured. 'This vehicle is fitted with roll bars.'

'So good to know,' I croaked – hoping none of us would.

I had a fleeting moment of wondering what the headlines would be if the worst happened and we were squashed to death between the Land Cruiser and a dune.

BRITISH TOURISTS SAND-WICHED!

Up until this moment, Tuesday had been relaxing. The three of us had snoozed on our loungers, enjoyed refreshments, and then had a dip in the pool. We'd almost had the place to ourselves. There had been no sign of Gerard and the Towie girls, or the Americans.

'Hold on tight,' the driver warned, as we soared over another dune. I closed my eyes as all four tyres were momentarily suspended mid-air.

'I'M GONNA KILL YOOOOO!' Bella wailed.

'Me?' yelped the driver.

'MY GIRLFRIENDS,' Bella clarified.

I cleared my throat. Tried to speak. Nothing came out.

'One, two, three. Testing,' I muttered.

'WHAT?' Bella yelled.

'I said' – I cleared my throat again – 'ARGHHHH,' I screamed as the Cruiser thumped back on the ground.

'Bloody HELL,' Caz winced. 'That was my EAR you just fog-horned into.'

'What is the matter, ladies?' asked our driver as he once again grappled with the wheel. 'This is good fun. Relax. Chill. Enjoy!'

And that was another problem in this current madness. Our driver. Earlier, he'd introduced himself with a quiet voice and mild demeanour. He was barely five feet tall on his tiptoes, which completed the illusion of docility.

Before setting off, tyre pressure had been adjusted to aid grip. We'd felt safe. In good hands. Tootling off on completely flat land (apparently the dunes were "further in"), he'd gone on to point out groups of Arabian Sand Gazelles and named the sparse vegetation on the outskirts. *Rimth* that the Bedouin used for firewood, *Al Ara* that sprouted woolly flowers and was used for cushions and camel saddles, and evergreen *Toothbrush* trees.

We'd hung on to his every word, including when the topic had switched to his personal life, and how he'd come to Dubai for work, married a good woman who metaphorically wore the trousers, and how much he doted on his kiddies. We'd been duped into believing the man was a pussycat. But as the landscape had shifted, a miniature lion had emerged.

As we'd paused briefly to survey – in puzzlement on our part – endless steep walls of sand, our guide had morphed from passive family man to testosterone-filled nutter. His dainty size four shoe had slammed down on the accelerator, aggressively revving the engine, and causing frissons of alarm. Caz, Bella, and I had exchanged anxious looks.

Other vehicles had lined up alongside our Land Cruiser and, for a few seconds, it had felt as if we'd been on the starting line of a Grand Prix race. Nervously, I'd glanced at the four-by-four to our left. It contained the Towie girls, giggling and whooping. I'd then peeked at the vehicle to the right and locked eyes with Gerard.

'Okay?' he'd mouthed.

I'd given a brief nod by way of response.

Celine had been sitting next to him looking proprietorial. She'd regarded me coolly and then leant across Gerard, blocking any further eye meet.

Suddenly the air had been filled with screaming engines and we'd become the passengers of Lewis Hamilton, Max Verstappen and Daniel Ricciardo. But instead of Silverstone stretched out before us, it was the Margham Desert.

As we flew over another impossibly high dune, I felt like I was on a looping roller coaster. Our driver let out a squeal of rage as Gerard's vehicle shot past us. I had a fleeting glimpse of Celine looking like her stomach might be saying hello to her tonsils. I knew exactly how she felt. Just when I thought I couldn't take another moment of being tossed about, the driver slammed on the brakes.

'We are here,' he calmly announced, returning to pussycat mode.

Caz, Bella and I gazed around in confusion. Ahead was an open tent. It looked like a bar. Men wearing the traditional white *kandura* dress with red-checked *shemags* on their heads were serving refreshments. Was I hallucinating? Was this one of the mirages Belles had feared we might fall foul of?

'Flaming Nora,' said Caz, shakily clambering out. 'I hope there's a large G&T in that tent.'

'I'm afraid not,' our driver apologised. 'Orange juice. But you can recover by stretching your legs and walking about. Afterwards, settle down on one of the dune's peaks. Get your camera at the ready. We shall watch the sun going down. I promise it will be a dramatic sunset, the likes of which you'll have never witnessed.'

'I'll catch you up, girls,' I said to Caz and Bella. 'I just need to...' – I jerked my head at a nearby dune – 'collapse.'

They nodded understandingly and staggered off to the tent, hanging on to each other like disorientated survivors in a disaster movie.

I teetered over to a mound and slumped down. Thank goodness the dune bashing was now over and done with.

Inhaling shakily, I let my mind wander to Keith. I had a feeling that he wouldn't have enjoyed racing over the dunes either. I felt my mood suddenly drop. It would have been so nice to have had him here right now, sitting by my side, laughing off this queasy moment together. Him saying, "Phew! At least we can cross *that* off The Bucket List." Me leaning into his shoulder and agreeing. "Now we can lose ourselves in a spectacular sunset." Instead, it was going to be a sunset for one.

I glanced over at Caz and Bella. They were hoovering up orange juice in the tent and chatting to some of the Towie girls. Their gesturing hands and body language suggested they were regurgitating the dune ride and comparing horror notes.

A breeze played around my shoulders, lifting my hair. A rash of goosebumps broke out on my bare arms. I hugged my knees to my chest, absorbing the desert's energy. Miles and miles of striated sand. Desert winds were constantly lifting and shifting the tiny grains into a seamless corrugation of ridges and grooves. The pattern wasn't dissimilar to rippling water. I found my mobile and took a picture.

The sun was now directly ahead, low, and vast, hanging like an enormous eyeball-searing white star. Shadows were lengthening and the rapidly changing light was turning the golden sand to a shade of dark brown. I shivered again. The temperature was rapidly dropping.

Someone flopped down beside me. I turned, expecting to see Caz or Bella, and was surprised to see Gerard.

'Here.' He handed me an orange juice.

'Thanks.'

I took the plastic cup, horribly aware of his proximity and the heat emanating from his body. The contrast between the cooling desert and the radiator-like warmth next to me made me want to snuggle into him – but obviously that wasn't an option.

For a moment, we silently sipped our drinks, watching the white sun transform into a ball haloed with orange.

'What did you think of the dune bashing?' he eventually said.

'Honestly?' I gave him a sidelong look. 'Terrifying. But I'm glad I did it.'

'Well done for being brave.'

'And you?'

'Loved it.'

'And… um… did Celine enjoy it?' Why was I asking this question?

'Nope. She made a big fuss and kept shrieking' – he adopted an accent – '"Oh my gawd, oh my gawd, I fink I'm gonna die."'

Ah. So she'd stopped channelling Marilyn Monroe.

'Look,' he pointed. 'The sun is setting.' He reached for his phone to take a picture. 'Quick. Start snapping.'

For a moment we didn't say anything as we clicked away.

'Let me take a pic of the two of us watching it,' he said casually, leaning into me.

I didn't dare say anything as his arm went around my shoulder and his head inclined towards mine. Instead, heart thumping, I mimicked his body language. Leant in. Looked at the camera lens.

'Smile,' he instructed. 'Lovely.' He showed me the captured image and I was both pleasantly surprised and somewhat shocked. Pleasantly surprised because it was a terrifically flattering photograph, thanks to the lighting. And shocked because the image looked like that of a couple. A man and a woman, together. Even more startling was how "right" that couple looked together.

'Not so good of me, but brilliant of you,' he said softly.

I was very aware of his arm still around me. The chills going up and down my spine were nothing to do with the cool desert breeze but everything to do with his touch.

He turned and smiled. For a moment – cliché that it is – I felt like we were suddenly in our own little bubble full of Arabian magic. And then a squawk rent the air and the bubble popped.

'Oh *there* you are, darling,' said a voice that was once again back to emulating Marilyn Monroe. 'You're a very naughty boy escaping me. I thought we were going to watch the sun go down together.' Celine pouted prettily before turning to me. 'I think your friends are looking for you,' she said pointedly.

Chapter Forty-Two

Gerard ignored Celine and turned to me.

'Give me your number and I'll send you the picture.'

As he tapped the digits into his phone, I couldn't help noticing the daggers Celine was giving me.

'Time for the next adventure,' called one of the guides. 'Ladies and gentlemen, please return to your assigned vehicles.'

By the time Caz, Bella and I had belted and buckled up inside our Land Cruiser, we were in much better spirits.

'On reflection' – Bella was laid back now the dune bashing bit was over – 'that was rather good fun. I've sent some picture texts to Colin and just *know* he's going to be wildly jealous when he looks at them.'

'Glad you've recovered your humour,' said Caz, patting Bella on the knee. 'And what about our Annie?' She looked at me speculatively. 'You seemed to be getting very cosy with a certain someone back on that dune.' She arched an eyebrow.

'He was just being friendly,' I shrugged.

'Belles wanted us to sit with you both, but I stopped her because it looked like the two of you were having a romantic moment.'

'You wouldn't have been interrupting anything,' I said emphatically. Even to my ears, the words sounded fake.

'Then why are you looking shiftier than the sand dunes?' asked Bella.

'I am not!'

'I don't think it's a coincidence' – Bella continued – 'that Celine suddenly spotted the two of you with your heads together and zoomed over faster than one of these Land Cruisers.'

'She has nothing to be concerned about.'

'Hmm,' said Caz, eyes beady. 'Would it be fair to say that a thaw has taken place between you and Mr Hot Guy?'

'A small thaw,' I agreed. 'We're talking tiny. Hang on. Why are the two of you nudging each other and exchanging furtive looks?'

'Nothing!' they trilled.

I shook my head in exasperation and stared out the side window. The desert was now in complete darkness. Only the bobbing headlights of the four-by-fours were visible as we rumbled across the terrain.

A little while later, we were approaching a Bedouin-style camp via a dune valley. The vehicles drove into a picturesque courtyard overlooked by a traditional-style watchtower. I was astonished to see, despite being out in the middle of nowhere, paved walkways lined with flower beds and ambient lighting which led to several *qarya* – clusters of colourful tented areas for eating, smoking shisha, partaking in henna painting, and watching belly dancing.

The three of us made a beeline to the restroom

facilities which were as grand as any five star hotel in a travel brochure.

'Isn't this amazing?' beamed Bella, standing before a lavish mirror and touching up her lipstick. Her humour was now fully restored.

'Yes, although that light display outside slightly spoils the pretence of authenticity,' said Caz. As we left the restroom, she pointed out an illuminated block of giant letters announcing *Arabian Nights* in neon pink and blue.

'Hm, a bit tacky I suppose,' I laughed. 'But I still love it.'

We were now passing a roped-off area containing a group of camels, their legs folded beneath them as they rested.

'Oooh, look!' I stopped to admire them. 'We can't go home without getting on these beautiful creatures and having a trek across the desert.'

Bella whipped out her mobile and took a picture of them.

'This is the bit of the excursion which is like a donkey ride at Broadstairs.'

'I guess,' Caz shrugged.

'In which case' – Bella continued – 'your hopes to trek across the desert, Annie, might be somewhat limited. I rather suspect we might be shambling around in a large circle on a lead rein.'

'That's fine by me,' said Caz. 'Come on. Let's get in the queue.

Fifteen minutes later, Bella's gung-ho evaporated.

'I'm no longer sure about this,' she said fretfully.

'Why?' I asked.

'They're a bit whiffy to say the least.' She wrinkled her nose. 'And do you think they're dangerous?'

'They can't help being whiffy,' I protested. 'And I wouldn't have thought they were dangerous, otherwise tourists wouldn't be riding them.'

'Then why are they muzzled?' she asked.

It was true. Every camel was wearing a brightly coloured gag.

'Maybe it's to stop them spitting,' I said. 'Anyway, we're here now, and you're not bottling out, Belles. At least camels don't soar half a mile into the sky or hurtle over sand dunes.'

'Thank the Lord,' she replied, putting her palms together as if in prayer.

'Here we go,' said Caz as the queue shuffled forward. 'Our turn.'

'Only two on a camel,' said the master, ushering Caz and Bella to his left. 'You, Mrs Lady, to the right. You wait for someone to partner you.'

I stood by my camel, feeling a bit like Annie-No-Mates. The animal gazed back at me placidly. Nervously, I gave his neck a quick pat. His coat was soft and woolly, but also very smelly. Too late, I realised the pong had transferred to my hand.

'Madam,' said a voice. 'The universe has conspired to push us together again.'

I turned to see Gerard behind me. There seemed to be

no getting away from him this evening.

'We've watched the sun set' – he continued – 'and now we're going to hug a camel together. We'll be setting tongues wagging at this rate,' he mocked.

'Not when you have the lovely Celine so constantly by your side.'

'No sign of her right now,' he pointed out.

'Did the glue come unstuck or did you peel her off?'

Oooh, steady Annie. That sounded a little bitchy.

Gerard laughed. 'She declined.'

'Why?'

He affected the same accent as when we'd been sitting on the dunes.

'I ain't gettin' on one of them fings. They stink!'

I laughed. 'She's right. They do.'

'They're not that bad,' Gerard protested. 'Anyway, I had an ulterior motive.'

'Oh?'

'I wanted to share this experience with you.'

My heart skipped a few beats and for a moment I didn't know what to say.

'Whatever for?' I eventually said.

'Because you're such fun to wind up.'

Which took the wind right out of my billowing Bedouin sails.

'Ready, Mrs Lady and Mister Sir?' said the master in heavily accented English. We swung our legs over the still sitting camel and settled into the saddle. 'Hold on here,' he pointed. 'Lean right back when the camel's bottom rises.'

He patted his torso by way of indication. 'You're safe. My camel is on a rein, see?'

I gasped as the animal began to awkwardly rise, leaning back as far as I could and subsequently finding myself spooning into Gerard who'd opted to sit behind me. The camel grunted and groaned as it shifted on to its front legs, and I found myself grunting and groaning with it.

'Are you in pain, Madam?' Gerard teased. His breath was warm on my neck, instantly sending zingers up and down my spine. I reminded myself that he was likely getting a vicarious thrill out of my discomfort, and mentally told the zingers to zing off.

Many years ago, I'd enjoyed riding horses. Naïvely, I'd expected a camel to be a similar experience. It wasn't. Its gait was most odd. Completely irregular, and totally herky-jerky.

'Relax,' said Gerard, lightly touching the top of my arm and sending another mini explosion up my spine. 'Let your body swing back and forth.'

'Are you always such a know-it-all,' I said, over my shoulder.

'Only sometimes,' he laughed.

I was right about one thing. It was indeed the Dubai equivalent of a donkey-on-a-beach ride. The camels shuffled around the makeshift pegged-off paddock. As soon as they'd completed the circuit, every single one of them sank back to the ground groaning loudly. It was like listening to a bunch of old men sighing with relief as they collapsed into favourite armchairs.

'Do you want a picture?' said the handler, coming over.

'Sure,' said Gerard.

And once again we stood side by side, leaning into each other, as the master captured another shot of the two of us.

'Thank you, Madam,' said Gerard, as we headed out of the paddock. 'Enjoy the feast and belly dancing entertainment.'

'I will, Mr Butler.'

And then he was gone, Celine having quickly reclaimed him. She wasn't impressed with the camel reek that had rubbed off on Gerard.

'Poo, darling.' Her words floated over on the night air. 'You blinkin' stink.'

Chapter Forty-Three

The feast took place with us sitting cross-legged at low candlelit tables. We were outside and under the stars while fire eaters, *tanoura* and belly dancers entertained us. It was colourful, noisy, amusing, and screamingly commercial.

As dancer after dancer came to the centre of the floor and showed off their torso-driven slides, shimmies, twists, and undulations, I suddenly found myself yawning.

Caz spotted me and promptly did the same thing.

'Why is yawning so infectious?' she said.

'Dunno,' said Bella, trying and failing to stifle one of her own. 'Let's head back.'

'I can't believe how tired I suddenly feel,' I said, clamping a hand over my mouth.

'Well we need to change this attitude if we're going clubbing,' said Caz. 'It will be a much later night than this one.'

'I am NOT going clubbing,' I said emphatically. I'd rather hoped she'd forgotten about that. 'What shall we do tomorrow?' Hopefully a change of subject would distract Caz.

'I fancy going to Jumeirah Beach,' said Bella.

'Sounds good,' Caz agreed. 'What about we do the

beach in the morning and then some shopping in the afternoon? I'd like to buy one of those fabulous fake handbags you hear so much about. Ahmed was telling me' – she lowered her voice – 'that he knows someone who knows someone who knows someone *else* who has a secret warehouse.'

'Oooh, I do love a bit of furtiveness.' I rubbed my hands together in anticipation.

'Yeah, but that really must be the name of the game.' Caz gave Bella and me a serious look. 'It's big business here, but very much a hidden one. It's illegal to sell fake goods.'

Bella looked anxious. 'Could we get slung in prison if caught?'

'I don't think so. Ahmed told me that it's a bit of a crazy law in that it's illegal to have the goods inside your premises in order to sell them, but when you're buying it's totally legal. However, I'm not so sure about taking fake products home. We might have to bury them in the bottom of our suitcases.'

'Blimey.' I blew out my cheeks. 'It's all a bit Secret Squirrel.'

'Or Morocco Mole,' Bella pointed out. 'Given that we're in Dubai.'

Caz's brow furrowed. 'Hardly, Belles. Morocco is two thousand miles away. Anyway, let's get back to our cupboard rooms and get a good night's sleep. I think I might dream of a Chanel handbag tonight.'

I nodded and agreed, although privately I suspected I'd

be dreaming of something else... a spectacular desert sunset and a man who increasingly made my spine tingle.

Chapter Forty-Four

The following morning Gerard and I made for the bathroom at the same time.

'Ladies first,' I quickly said.

'I don't think so, Madam. As a female, you'll be in there for at least half an hour, whereas I will only be half a minute.'

'Nonsense.'

'Okay, a small exaggeration on my part. Three minutes max. Thirty seconds to clean the teeth. Fifteen seconds to empty the bladder. Forty-five seconds to…'

My hand shot up like a traffic cop. 'Too much information.'

'…and ninety seconds to impersonate Tom Jones whilst singing in the shower. You, on the other hand, take three minutes simply rubbing in a face cream that promises to smooth, flatten, lift, tone, and knock off thirty years.'

I glared at him. 'How do you know my face cream promises to do all those things?'

'Confession time. You left the pot on the side of the sink. I borrowed some.'

'How *dare* you.' I was outraged. 'Do you know how much that tiny pot cost?'

'No doubt an arm and several legs. Why waste your money on something that doesn't work?'

'Cheers for that. There's nothing like being reminded how ancient one looks.'

'I didn't say you looked ancient. I *s-a-i-d* the face cream doesn't work. Proven by *moi.* It didn't make me look any younger.'

'I'm telling you now, Mr Butler, keep your paws off my face cream.'

'In which case, Madam, keep your hands off my expensive deodorant.'

I blinked, suddenly wrongfooted.

'You told me I could use it as' – I reddened – 'a room freshener. And anyway, my face cream probably cost twenty times the price of your deodorant.'

'Don't bank on it.' Gerard wagged a finger, his face deadpan. 'It's from Waitrose, not Aldi. Now, if you'll excuse me.' He made to move past. 'I could have been in and out by now if you hadn't held me up wanting to debate the merits of being ripped off all because' – he posted quotation marks in the air – "you're worth it".'

I opened my mouth to protest, but then shut it again. Oh, let him have the bathroom. While he was proving his three-minute point, I'd get back into bed and relax, go on Facebook, and upload yesterday's snapshots of the Arabian Adventure.

'Fine,' I shrugged. 'Go ahead.'

A moment later and Gerard was singing *Sex Bomb* in the shower. I rolled my eyes and settled down to tap-tap my way through every picture thumbnail. I couldn't be bothered to edit them. It didn't matter if was blinking in the shot of me with Caz and Bella next to the Land Cruiser – or the Land *Bruiser* as we'd renamed it on account of some sore spots.

I was suddenly distracted by Gerard's rousing chorus.

Sex bomb, sex bomb, with your face cream
And you can give it to me when I need to be
slippery slippery, gimme gimme gimme
Baby you can lather it on (ooh)...

The door opened and he walked out with a towel slung around his hips.

'All yours,' he said, eyes twinkling mischievously.

I blinked. What was all mine? Him? Or the bathroom?

The bathroom, Annie. Obviously.

'Thank you,' I said stiffly.

Hastily, I finished uploading the pictures, then shut myself in the tiny cubicle and got on with cleaning my teeth.

'Laters,' Gerard called out.

I didn't answer on account of having a mouthful of foam. A moment later and the door banged shut. Hurrah. Alone at last. It wasn't easy sharing this space with a strange man. Now he was gone, I could titivate in peace.

This morning I was off to Jumeirah Beach with the girls but, before going, there were things that needed to be done. Like checking my bikini line. There was nothing worse than trying to pull off a high-legged swimsuit with a stray pube letting one down. Although – I pinched the skin at the top of my legs – the crepe might be more of a horror show.

Sighing, I wiggled into a new swimsuit, then overlaid it with a long floaty beach dress. Perhaps I should try and emulate Celine – ha, fat chance – and wear wedged heels to lengthen the leg and distract from the skin crepe. I sighed again. Own it, Annie. You're sixty, and no Celine.

I picked up my pot of expensive face cream. Shame it didn't work on thighs.

Chapter Forty-Five

Ahmed dropped us at Jumeirah Beach, suggesting we text after we'd had our fill of sunshine. Afterwards he'd take us to "his contact" in Al Karama.

Getting out of the limo, the three of us looked around in delight. There was the beach – white sand no less. Ahmed had told us that it stretched for more than fifteen miles along Dubai's Persian Gulf coast. He'd verbally painted an amazing picture, describing how the shoreline extended from the Jumeriah Mosque in the north to Palm Jumeirah in the south, and how it included a string of private sections as well as public beaches like this one.

'What's that funny looking structure?' asked Bella, as we crossed the road and walked onto the sand.

'Which one?' I said, peering about. There were buildings everywhere. It was strange to see a beach with such a prolific city backdrop.

'There.' She pointed to what looked like an enormous boat sail.

Caz gave a low whistle. 'That, my dear Belles, is the world's most iconic and luxurious hotel. *Burj Al Arab.*'

'It looks like it's leaning.'

'Probably an illusion,' I said.

The beach was exceptionally clean, with plenty of lifeguards and – glancing around – toilet facilities. Hurrah. I wasn't one for doing a wee in the sea. Also, it would be good to change out of a damp cozzy before going on to Al Karama. However, there didn't seem to be any places selling coffee or cold drinks. Thank goodness we'd had the foresight to ask the hotel for a packed lunch.

Soon we were stretched out on our towels. Caz had managed to acquire a *Daily Mail* and was doing the crossword. Bella had finished with my kindle and was now engrossed in Sudoku puzzles. With a sense of delicious anticipation, I opened a newly downloaded romantic comedy by one of my favourite authors. I sighed happily. The perfect beach read on a perfect beach.

I suddenly realised I'd had no intrusive thoughts about Keith for a while. Progress! Right now, I was in a happy place. Okay, it was only temporary. But that was fine. The real world of autumn rain, damp days, and switching on the central heating was currently suspended. As were letters from Keith's solicitor and me getting round to appointing a legal representative. For now, everything was on hold. I knew these things *would* happen. Eventually. There was no point trying to pretend otherwise. But in this wonderful present moment it was just the sunshine. The warm breeze. Lapping water. Sounds of anonymous revellers. I sighed again. This time with pleasure.

My phone let out a ping. Putting down my kindle, I glanced at the screen. A message from Carly. My heart gave a flutter of anxiety. I didn't like being so far away from my pregnant daughter, even though she wasn't yet due. I clicked on her message.

Lovely pictures on Facebook. Must confess I was slightly gobsmacked. Please take care, Mum. Remember our chat. Protection! Xxx

I smiled indulgently. My goodness, who was the parent here, and who was the child?

Thank you, darling. The Arabian Nights jaunt was such fun. Yes, I was gobsmacked too. Bouncing over those dunes was something else. I didn't think I'd be brave enough! Don't worry about protection. Was wearing a seat belt. And today I have on a large straw hat. No sunburn! Xxx

Carly replied almost immediately.

Never mind the belt and hat. I'm talking about the socks Xxx

I frowned. Had pregnancy hormones befuddled her brain?

Too hot for socks. Going bare. Xxx

I'd barely pressed send when Carly pinged another text.

I can't believe I'm having this conversation with my mother!

rolling eyes emoji

Yes, she was clearly hormonal.

Agree! Try not to worry. I'm being careful, okay! Xxx

I slung the phone back in my tote bag and picked up my kindle. Now then. Where was I? I'd only read the first paragraph when the phone pinged again.

'You're popular,' said Caz, looking at me over the rim

of her sunglasses.

'It's Carly. She's worrying, bless her. Wants to make sure her old mum isn't forgetting the Factor Thirty.'

But this time it was a text from Keith. I felt my stomach flip unpleasantly. What did he want? Please don't let him be suggesting solicitors yet. Not while on holiday.

I dithered. Should I ignore his message? But then again, I didn't want to annoy him. So far, he'd been incredibly kind and amenable. Obviously, a guilty conscience was behind his motives, but even so. Sighing, I picked up the phone.

Hello, Annie. Regarding your photographs. Wow. Speechless.

Ah. He too had seen my Arabian Nights pics on Facebook. He hadn't put any kisses after his message. That was a first. Oh well. It was inevitable he'd switch to "cutting out the affection" sooner or later. Ex-spouses could be friendly. Of *course* they could. But should they be exchanging kisses? Whether texted or otherwise? Probably not. Perhaps, when the divorce certificate had been stamped and the dust had settled, we could one day resume such signoffs. Meanwhile, I'd take care not to automatically end my text with some of those little crosses. I tapped out a reply.

Thought I was too set in my ways. It just goes to show it's never too late to do the unthinkable!

There. Perfectly polite. But no kisses. Now go away, Keith. Stop reminding me that you're there, and I'm here, and you're with Pippa Kipling, and I'm with no one.

I picked up my kindle again.

Ping… ping… pinggggg.

Three texts, all hot on the heels of each other.

Trying not to feel exasperated at my beach read being constantly interrupted, I once again checked the messages. Again, Keith.

Gobsmacked…

And rather hurt actually…

Didn't have you down for moving on so quickly…

Moving on? What on earth was he talking about? But before I could give the matter further consideration, the phone startled me by ringing in my hand. The caller display said *Mum and Dad*.

My heart instantly lurched as fear clattered through me like a high-speed train with no brakes. Was everything all right? Had Dad fallen over? Had Mum wandered off and forgotten who she was and where she lived? Even worse, had one of them died? Oh God, oh God, oh God. My fingers, greasy with sun cream, fumbled to answer the call.

'Hello?' I said breathlessly.

'Annie?'

'Dad! Is everything okay?'

'Yes, we're fine. It's you I'm worried about. I've been on Facebook and, well, I saw your photographs.'

'That's nice,' I said.

My poor father. If only he could have some lovely days out, like me, and get some respite from Mum.

I immediately felt guilty for being at Jumeirah Beach and silently moaning about not reading my kindle in peace.

234

And then another bucket of guilt washed over me. I shouldn't have come to Dubai. I should have gone to Center Parcs instead. Taken Mum and Dad with me. Okay, it would have been hell trying to persuade Mum to partake in any sort of break, but I should have made the effort for my father's sake.

My mind wandered back to the previous year. Keith and I had taken my parents to Cornwall. The trip had been challenging to say the least. At the time there had been restrictions because of the virus. Activities like swimming, or relaxing in the hot tub, had had to be pre-booked. We'd missed out on all our slots because Mum had refused to comply. She'd packed eight different swimsuits and been unable to decide which one to wear. The fact that seven of them were as old as the hills and no longer fitted was neither here nor there. When I'd tried to cajole her into the costume that *did* fit, she'd become agitated and told me to clear off. I'd wanted to scream.

'Annie, darling, I'm glad you're having a nice break but–'

Anxiety churned in my stomach. 'But what, Dad?'

But Annie come home?

But I can't cope with your mother?

But I'm not feeling well?

'But I think it's too soon for you to be parading a new man.'

For a moment I stared at the blue horizon trying to work out what my father was talking about. Parading a new man?

'The picture of you in the desert,' he continued. 'It's absolutely lovely of you, darling. And the gentleman looks very handsome. But I'm worrying about my daughter. You may be sixty, but you're still my little girl. Do you understand?'

The penny dropped. Hell. I'd accidentally posted the sunset picture of me and Gerard. In the background I heard Mum squawk.

'Give me that handset.'

'Yes, dear.'

I could envisage my hen-pecked father handing over the phone to his wife who – despite her atrocious memory – hadn't forgotten that she was the one who wore the trousers.

'What's all this about a new man, Annie? It's outrageous behaviour. You've only just buried your husband.'

Chapter Forty-Six

'Is everything all right, Annie?' said Caz, putting down her Daily Mail. 'I can hear Mother Evans fog-horning from here.'

I was holding the phone away from my ear while my mother ranted. What would the neighbours say… my name would be mud… *her* name would be mud… it would be NippleGate all over again.

'Nipplegate?' said Bella, stifling a giggle. 'I can't imagine your old mum once watching Justin Timberlake and Janet Jackson singing together.'

'She's lost the plot,' I said, still holding the phone in mid-air. 'I'm amazed my mother even remembers the year 2004.'

I put the phone back to my ear.

'Sorry, Mum, but I have to go. Sending lots of love.'

I now realised why Carly had made that comment about "protection". She thought I was having a holiday fling. Ditto Keith. I quickly tapped out a message to the pair of them.

Man in pic just happened to be on same excursion. Don't even know his name!

And then I felt annoyed. Why was I justifying myself?

Especially to Keith! Pot, kettle, black. Who the *hell* did he think he was? What a flipping cheek.

I could feel anger rising faster than that pot and kettle coming to the boil. I picked up my kindle, read the same paragraph without absorbing any of the storyline, then chucked it down again on my towel.

'I'm going for a dip.'

'Good idea,' said Caz, who'd been quietly watching me. 'You look like you're going to explode into a thousand pieces. Go and swim up and down the coast a few times and get it all out of your system.

'I shall.'

Twirling my hair into a top knot to avoid it getting wet, I stomped off to the water's edge. The last time I'd swum in the sea had been last summer on that never-to-be-forgotten Cornish holiday. Even though England had been in the middle of a heatwave, the sea had been freezing thanks to cold streams from the Atlantic Ocean. The water had been so bone-numbingly cold, that after two minutes I'd not been able to feel my feet, and after five my entire body had started to lose sensation. Here, however, the water was as warm as a lover's kiss, and I immersed myself without hesitation.

For a while I launched into a full-throttled breaststroke – no front crawl on account of salty water stinging eyes – then moved further out and trod water. I was still silently seething at Keith's message. Why did my estranged husband think it was okay for him to have an affair – hang on, backspace, backspace – for him to *leave me* for another woman, but then express shock and... what had he said?... oh yes... *hurt*... at me apparently moving on so quickly. Really, Keith? REALLY?

I set off again, my movements still jerky with anger. And what if I *did* meet someone else at some point? What if I *did* have "a fling"? What if I did exactly what Keith had done? Locked eyes with someone who made my heart pump erratically. Turned my legs to liquid. What then? Should I write letters to my various family members, explaining and apologising?

Dear Carly, you're my daughter and I love you. I also love Mr [fill in the blank] and am cautiously stepping back into a relationship. And yes, we are using protection. I hope you can be pleased for me. Love Mum xx

Now Keith.

Keith. You are a hypocrite, and my private life is none of your business. Yours sincerely, Annie. (Please note lack of kisses.)

Now my mother.

Dear Mum. Sorry about NippleGate. I have been on eBay and bought a packet of starburst-shaped shields. Love Annie xx

I turned around to swim back towards Caz and Bella and crashed straight into another swimmer. For a moment I floundered and nearly swallowed seawater.

'Is there no getting away from you?' said Gerard in mock outrage.

'What are you doing here?' I spluttered.

'Having a swim. You?'

I narrowed my eyes. 'Are you following me?'

'And why would I want to follow you, Madam?'

'I don't know. I don't know anything anymore. All I know, Mr Butler, is that I'm fed up. In the space of three minutes, I've had as many family members texting and phoning to tell *me* – a grown woman no less…'

'Outrageous – fancy not realising you were a grown up.'

'Not to have sex without socks…'

'What about shoes?'

'Not to move on…'

'What about move in?'

'And never to let Justin Timberlake take advantage of me.'

'What about George Clooney?'

'You don't understand.'

'You're right, I have absolutely no idea what you're ranting about. Is it some sort of modern-day problem in the world of women in their late forties?'

'Late forties?' I gasped, gawping at him.

'Oh dear. Have I said the wrong thing again? I guess we're back to the face cream that doesn't work. I should have said "late thirties", right?' He adopted a pained expression and looked to the heavens. 'Dear Lord. I have dropped a clanger about the smoothness of this woman's cheeks. Forgive me Father, for I have skinned.'

'It's no big deal,' I said guardedly.

Oh my flipping GOD. Gerard Butler thought I was in my late forties! If I hadn't been treading water, I'd have jumped up and run around in excited circles. Me! Sixty-year-old Annie Rosewood. Previously *Frump of the Year*. Winner of *Frump of the Year Award* 2018, 2019, and 2020!

'Are we friends again, Madam?'

'I… yes.'

'And just to let you know, I might have been following you a teensy bit.'

I stared at him for a moment. 'Why?'

'Because I was desperate to have a mini break from Celine. She's a sweet girl, but there's only so many conversations I can have about' – he affected the accent again – 'me mum and me dad and me bruvver and me pink rabbit.'

I frowned. 'Rabbits aren't pink.'

'Um… let's change the subject. We're going to Al Karama later. Celine wants to buy six million handbags, despite having five million of the same languishing in dust covers back home.'

'We're going to Al Karama too.'

'In which case, I will likely see you there. Meanwhile, shall we?'

'Shall we what?' I stared at him blankly, my heart still singing over the late forties comment.

'Enjoy having a swim together, of course.'

Chapter Forty-Seven

As we bobbed along, I felt a rush of conflicting emotions. Flustered. Thrilled. Anxious. Soothed. On edge. At ease. In other words, totally discombobulated.

My body felt as if it were flashing in and out of reality. One minute I was human, seemingly solid, and experiencing a rush of agitation. The next, it was if my body had deconstructed and melted into nothing, leaving me completely at peace and in harmony with my surroundings.

I suddenly spotted Celine standing at the water's edge. She was paddling up to her ankles and searching the waves for Gerard. Due to her not being able to swim, it was unlikely she'd venture out any further. It was all too easy to unexpectedly get out of one's depth in the ocean. In my peripheral vision, I saw her body stiffen. She'd located Gerard and spotted the two of us together.

We swam on, circumnavigating around a young family who were playing with a brightly coloured inflatable ball, then meandered around several other small groups of people. Some were treading water and yakking in a language I couldn't identify, while others were simply doing what we were. Swimming companionably together.

We circled a larger group, venturing out into deeper waters.

As Gerard and I kept pace with each other, my previous outrage at Keith's texts simply melted away. Suddenly I felt ridiculously happy.

'Feeling better?' Gerard enquired.

'As it happens, yes, I am.'

'Thought so.'

'How could you tell?'

'You've stopped hacking through the water as if giving someone a karate chop.'

'Oh, I see. Yes, I was feeling a bit like that earlier. Not that I would ever slap anyone. I'm not a violent person.'

'That's good to know. Especially as we're sharing a room. For a moment there, you gave me a frisson of anxiety.'

'You're safe. I only take revenge in my head.'

'And can I be so nosy as to ask who rattled you?'

'I suppose so. It was my family. Carly – my daughter – got the wrong end of the stick about... er... something. As did my mother. But she has dementia and gets muddled over everything. Mum has it in her head that my husband died and I'm behaving like a merry widow.'

'And are you?'

'No,' I tutted. 'Nor is my husband dead. He's with someone else.' I said the words with a shrug in my tone. 'And it's because he's with someone else that I suddenly became incensed about him getting the wrong idea about... er... something.'

'It all sounds very mysterious. What exactly is this "something"?'

'Just... something.'

'Or is it some*one*?'

I hesitated for a moment. Then, 'Yes. Someone. Look, I might as well tell you − ridiculous as it sounds − I posted the pictures of yesterday's desert trip to my Facebook page but failed to properly check them.'

Gerard let out a gasp of horror. 'You really did that? You didn't forensically examine every single snap − like Celine and the girls − before adding filters or doing a spot of photoshopping?'

'I don't do filters or photoshopping.'

Mainly on account of not knowing how. But I wasn't going to tell him that.

'And your family were outraged because you hadn't airbrushed your photographs?'

Despite his grave tone, I knew he was teasing.

'There was a bit of a... *reaction* because one of the photographs' − oh hell − 'was of me and you.' There. I'd said it. I could feel my face reddening and was glad we were in the water and looking ahead. I didn't want Gerard observing my embarrassment. 'They put two and two together and came up with the proverbial five.'

'Good heavens. How ridiculous.'

'Well, yes, obviously. There's no comparison between Celine and myself.'

'You're right. Zero competition, because Celine isn't a patch on you.'

For a moment I wasn't sure I'd heard him correctly.

'You don't need to pretend-flatter me, Mr Butler.'

'I was trying to pay you a compliment, Madam, but in future I shall keep them to myself. So, your family saw the picture of us and weren't happy.'

'To be fair, my daughter wasn't *un*happy. She simply misread the image and reacted out of concern. She seems to think I'm terribly naïve, and vulnerable for getting my heart broken.'

'And your husband?'

'As I said, he's with someone else, so I'm not sure why the snap put his nose out of joint.'

'Perhaps he wants you back.'

'Hardly. He's already made it perfectly clear that when I'm home it's time for a serious talk. In other words, formalising our separation.'

'The D word.'

I nodded. 'Yes. Divorce. I never thought it would happen to us.'

'None of us do, otherwise we'd never get married. We all hope to grow old with our partners, but sometimes circumstances dictate otherwise.'

'I gather you're speaking from experience.'

'Yup. You're talking to a member of The D Club. But life goes on, and all those other hackneyed phrases.'

Before I could reply, a faint – and indignant – voice floated our way.

'Can... you... hear... me?'

We paused and turned to see Celine shading her eyes

245

against the sun. She'd moved along the shore, keeping pace with us, and was now cupping her hands around her mouth to make an impromptu tannoy.

'I SAID... CAN... YOOOO... HEEEEAR... MEEEEE?'

Gerard gave Celine a thumbs up, before giving me a conspiratorial grin.

'I think the whole of Dubai just heard her. I'd better go back and dry off. It's time to visit Al Karama. Catch you later.'

'Yes,' I said, trying not to feel deflated at no longer having his company.

He made to swim away but then paused, treading water.

'What are you doing this evening?'

'I... I'm not sure.'

That was a strange question. Why should my whereabouts be of interest to him?

'Celine and the girls are dragging me off to a club. You and your girlfriends should come along too. Let your hair down.'

'A club? At my age?'

Gerard gave me one of his twinkly-eyed mischievous looks.

'What are you? Ninety? Ask your driver about the secret club on the top floor of a well-known hotel.'

'Isn't it simpler to tell me its name?'

'If I knew it, I would. But I don't. There are plenty of advertised clubs out here. They post amazing pictures of their bar, the dance floor, the DJ, and claim they're buzzing with activity, whereas they're mostly empty and have been bypassed. I've been informed that this secret club is the place where it all happens. I have a feeling your twerking buddy might like it.' He winked. 'Laters.'

Chapter Forty-Eight

I remained in the sea for a little while longer, treading water in its dark blue depths, relishing the sensation of being weightless, of semi-floating in the gentle waves whilst admiring the distant cityscape against the sandy shoreline. What a place. What a country. I loved it.

Feeling my nose inexplicably tickle, I scratched it and was surprised to see my fingertips looking like shrivelled prunes. Heaven knows how long I'd been swimming. Perhaps it was time to head back.

'At last,' said Caz, as I plonked myself down on my beach towel. 'You were gone for so long we thought you'd headed off to Qatar.'

'I was enjoying myself. It's gorgeous in.'

I tipped my face up to the sun, enjoying the warmth of its rays drying my body.

'It's gorgeous out, too,' Bella giggled. 'Your roommate came over to see us.'

'Did he?' I said casually.

'Now don't get stroppy,' said Caz, giving me a warning look. 'But he tipped us off about a secret nightclub. I said we were up for it. *All* of us,' she added. 'So no protests about going out clubbing this evening, because you're going. It's been decided. The Executive Board collaborated while you were swimming, and the majority motion was carried.'

I shrugged. 'You win.'

'Well really!' Caz blew out her cheeks. 'I wasn't expecting you to cave in just like that.' She clicked her tongue. 'What a relief that I don't have to persuade, cajole or coerce you.'

'Truly, it's fine,' I grinned. 'Although heaven knows what Carly will say when she discovers her sixty-year-old mother is visiting a nightclub.'

'She'll tell everyone she has a cool mum,' Bella assured.

'Ha, I don't know about that.' I rolled my eyes. 'Anyway, let's do it. After all, what's the worst thing that can happen?'

'We get sore feet from dancing,' Bella pointed out.

Later, I would recall this conversation with a wry smile because Bella's prediction about sore feet being the worst thing that could happen was not only wrong, it was also *waaaaaay* off beam.

'Shall we call Ahmed?' said Caz. 'If we're going out tonight, I quite fancy heading off to Al Karama now so that we have plenty of time for glamming up later. Also, it might be a good idea to squeeze in a nap after we've finished shopping.'

'A nap?' I said incredulously.

Caz gave me a look. 'Annie, we won't be going out until midnight – and who knows what time we'll return to the hotel.'

'You're winding me up, yes?'

Her expression told me she wasn't.

'Right,' I said faintly.

An hour later, after consuming our packed lunch and now fully dry from swimming, we found ourselves in one of the older parts of Dubai.

Ahmed informed us that the name of the area was inspired by the Arabic word *karama* meaning "dignity". He dropped as off at Zaa'beel Street, the main thoroughfare of the central area which gave way to numerous commercial units. As we set off on foot, working our way into the inner streets, I suddenly felt like I'd been transported to London's East End.

These narrow thoroughfares were more like that of a marketplace. As we wandered along, I kept wanting to stop and gaze. There were thrift and souvenir shops. Colourful souqs with displays of herbs and spices laid out in vast ceramic bowls. Clothing shops with mannequins dressed in tunics that were smothered in beading and embellishments. There was even a utensil souq which might have been this particular street's answer to *Lakeland*.

It also seemed as if every other building belonged to a jeweller. All were near identical with illuminated windows full of elaborate necklaces. Brightly coloured gold was twisted into intricate designs. Nearly all were encrusted with gems fit for an Arabian princess. Glass shelves displayed jewelled bracelets, arm bangles, and dangly earrings that looked so heavy I'd have fretted about my earlobes meeting my shoulders.

However, none of these were our intended destination. We kept walking, carefully following Ahmed's instructions until we came across a large store with a painted white front. An overhead sign proclaimed the name *Orange Skies*. It didn't look remotely dodgy, and I felt faintly disappointed.

'After you,' said Bella.

'No, after *you*,' said Caz, suddenly looking apprehensive.

'But I insist. After you,' said Bella again.

'For goodness' sake!' I huffed. 'The pair of you sound like Laurel and Hardy. Get out the way. I'm going in.'

'Wait for me,' squeaked Bella, catching hold of my arm just as Caz grabbed the other.

Suddenly it was three of us trying to get through the doorway at the same time. Exasperated, I shrugged them off.

'What are you both like? Let go! Now follow me.'

'Attagirl,' whispered Caz, giving me a little prod. 'Lead the way. And don't forget. Our contact is called Angus.'

'Angus,' I repeated, mentally rolling my eyes. Never a more Arab name. Not.

I made towards a counter at the rear of the shop – which wasn't easy with Bella and Caz hanging on to the back of my dress. A man was bent over a calculator, stabbing the buttons. He looked up. Dark watchful eyes took in the three conjoined white females shuffling across the shop floor.

We stopped before him, and he frowned. Now what?

Was I meant to speak in code? Ahmed hadn't given us any instructions.

'Hello,' I said woodenly. 'We seek' – I raised my eyebrows and waggled them meaningfully – '*Angus*.'

'Gordon Bennett,' muttered Caz.

The man's frown deepened.

'Gordon Bennett?' he repeated suspiciously. 'I don't know this person.'

'No, no, we want Angus,' squeaked Bella.

He glared at us, his eyes travelling from Bella, to me, to Caz and then back to me again. Nobody said anything. Nobody moved.

The silence stretched on. The left side of my dress began to vibrate telling me that the tension was getting to Bella. Still the man said nothing. My stomach chose that moment to loudly gurgle. The man's eyes bored into mine as my digestive system belatedly got to work on my earlier cheese sandwich. Now the right side of my dress was trembling. I deduced that Caz was also at breaking point. My guts continued to rumble on, now impersonating an emptying bathtub. The man's gaze dropped to my midriff as it mimicked water slurping down a plughole. His eyes flicked back to my face.

'Who sent you here?' he demanded.

I'd had enough. I wasn't grassing and giving Ahmed's name. For all I knew, this man could be an undercover cop, stationed to catch out tourists that were up to no good.

'That's classified information,' I said in my best

Detective Inspector Jane Tennison voice. 'Now are you going to tell us where Angus is, or not?'

'What's the password?' he barked.

Password? Ahmed hadn't said anything about that.

'Handbags,' I said, guessing wildly.

The man instantly doubled up with laughter. He staggered backwards, clutching his stomach, so consumed with mirth he couldn't speak. One hand began slapping his thigh as he convulsed, tears now running down his cheeks.

'Oh… oh…' he said feebly, still bent over and hanging on to his sides.

'Are you all right?' said Bella, letting go of my dress.

'Yes… yes… so funny…'

'Hilarious I'm sure,' said Caz primly.

'Sorry, ladies.' He straightened up, pulling a handkerchief from a hidden pocket to wipe his wet cheeks. 'Your faces were – as you say – a picture. Forgive me.' He took a deep breath and composed himself. 'I was just having a little joke at your expense. I am Angus. Presumably you want to see' – he lowered his voice – '*special* stock.'

This was more like it.

'Yes, please.'

'One moment. I will ask my son to mind the shop.'

He pressed a buzzer under the counter. Almost immediately a younger version of Angus appeared. There was some hushed conferring, then Angus turned back to us.

'Please, ladies. Follow me.'

I was expecting him to take us to one side. Perhaps

show us a discreet corner of the shop. A false wall or a secret cupboard. Him furtively looking about before whispering, "Quick! What do you want?"

Instead, he led us out of *Orange Skies* and through the marketplace. Down a side street. A left turn. Now a right. Left, right. Right, left. The shops petered out and became a maze of low-rise flats. Where were we? And where were we going? I'd completely lost my bearings.

'I'm not sure about this,' Caz hissed.

Angus must have heard her. 'Don't worry,' he assured. 'This is totally normal. You are safe.' He paused outside a block of flats that were a far cry from the glamour we'd seen so far in Dubai. 'We're here. Follow me, please. If anyone asks who you are, you are my dear friends from England visiting my home for a cup of tea.'

'Right,' said Caz faintly.

We followed Angus up three flights of uncarpeted stairs. Our footsteps echoed hollowly as we ascended, elbows occasionally grazing scuffed walls and peeling paint.

Our guide stopped outside a shabby door. It was overlaid with a heavy-duty security grill gate. As he quietly tapped on the inner door, Bella, Caz, and I regarded each other nervously.

Suddenly the door opened. A second man gave us a welcoming smile.

'Hello,' he said. 'I'm Hamish.' Of course he was. 'Are you here to enjoy a cup of tea?'

Caz and Bella were once again hanging on to the back of my dress.

'Yes, please,' I said, sounding far braver than I felt.

The grill gate opened, and Hamish signalled for us to go inside.

Stepping into the hallway, it immediately became apparent that this "flat" was, in fact, a warehouse. Boxes were stacked everywhere.

'This way,' said Hamish.

He led us into a room that momentarily took our breath away.

'Holy Moly,' whispered Bella.

'Flipping heck,' mumbled Caz.

'Flaming Nora,' I muttered. All we needed was Del Boy bringing up the rear and muttering, "Fromage Frais".

The room was lined from floor to ceiling with narrow shelves upon which were displayed all "brands" of handbags. They looked amazing.

'This is our budget range. Everything here is between twenty and fifty of your Great British Pounds.'

I was already reaching for my purse ready to buy three, even four, assorted beauties.

'Wait,' said Hamish. 'There is more. And better.' He smiled. 'You see everything first, then you decide what to buy.'

He indicated we move back out to the narrow hallway. This time we were taken into a second room similarly kitted out.

'Everything in here is between fifty and one hundred pounds.'

'Oooh, look,' I said to Bella and Caz. 'A Birkin.' I

stroked it lovingly. 'The darling of the Hermes brand.'

'The genuine article sells anywhere between ten thousand and a hundred and fifty thousand dollars,' Hamish pointed out. 'But in this room, you will pay one hundred and fifty pounds. But' – he held up a finger indicating we should still wait – 'again I urge you to think before you buy from this room. You have yet to see our superior range. Follow me.'

This time we were taken into a box room. The stock was limited to just a dozen items. A great deal of care and thought had gone into the display. Spotlights were trained upon each one. The brands were Yves Saint Laurent, Hermes, Gucci, Chanel, and Louis Vuitton, but I also spotted a couple of classic-looking Mulberrys which instantly had me drooling.

'Everything you see here is different to the previous two rooms,' Hamish said reverently. 'Why? Because they are *exact* copies. The price – depending which one you buy – ranges from three to five hundred pounds. The previous two rooms contain counterfeited products by Chinese manufacturers and are imported over here secreted amongst legal goods.'

'What happens if you get caught smuggling?' asked Bella.

'Sometimes it happens,' Hamish acknowledged. 'The illegal stock is immediately confiscated, and big fines are given. One of our colleagues was fined the equivalent of fifty thousand pounds.'

We collectively gasped. Was it worth taking a chance

and losing your investment as well as being hit with a crippling fine?

'Despite countless raids, airport interceptions, lawsuits by luxury brands and entire coalitions dedicated to curbing the distribution of these goods, the market is thriving,' he smiled happily. 'Recently there has been an explosion of "super fakes" – like these. They're made in the same factories as the authentic handbags.' He beamed as that piece of information sank in. 'Sometimes the factory will produce ten thousand products but make two thousand on the run and sell them off cheaply.'

I gulped. In other words, they were the real thing that accidentally-on-purpose went missing. I suddenly felt ill at ease. It was one thing to buy a twenty quid knock-off. It was another to be perusing the real deal that had found its way out of a factory's side door. It was obvious that Hamish hoped we would purchase something from this room.

'I don't think I have enough money,' I said, giving the girls a meaningful look.

Bella caught on immediately. 'Oh, what a shame. Me neither.'

'Let's go to a cashpoint,' suggested Caz.

I could tell from her expression that she'd sussed my doubts on the matter.

'Sure, sure,' said Hamish. 'You come back later. We're always here.'

'Thank you,' I said.

Suddenly I felt claustrophobic and wanted to get away

from the place.

Silently, we shuffled out into the narrow hallway, then back through the metal security door and out to the stark landing.

Angus led us back to the shop where we made our excuses about finding an ATM and popping back. Caz discreetly texted Ahmed to pick us up.

Minutes later we were back in the sunshine and waiting on the main thoroughfare for Ahmed's limo.

'Honestly, Annie,' Caz grumbled. 'What a time to go all virtuous on me. That Chanel bag was within my grasp.' She held up a thumb and forefinger. 'It was *this* close.'

'You can go back and buy it,' I reasoned.

'No. Not now. I'd feel guilty every time I used it.'

'We did the right thing walking away,' said Bella. 'Oh look. Here's Ahmed. Come on, girls. We'll go back to the hotel and drown our sorrows with a pot of tea.'

'And then have a nap,' said Caz.

'Living life in the fast lane,' I said dryly.

'We'll be doing that later, darling,' said Caz with a wink.

When I finally returned to my cupboard room for a snooze, there was no sign of Gerard. But there was a small, gift-wrapped package on my bunk with a note attached. In neat handwriting and written out ten times was the declaration, "I must not use things that don't belong to me".

I ripped off the gift wrap, then smiled. A small pot of face cream.

Chapter Forty-Nine

I'd only been snoozing for around forty-five minutes when the ring of my mobile disturbed me. The caller display informed it was my father.

'Dad?' I said, instantly feeling the familiar anxiety playing in the pit of my stomach. It was always like this if *he* called *me*, and not the other way around.

'Darling, how are you?' His voice was strained.

'I'm good. And you? You sound… a little stressed.'

'No more than usual.'

'I'll be home this weekend and will make sure you have some respite. I'm so sorry I went away, Dad, but–'

'Nonsense, Annie. No need to apologise. I want you to be free to do your own thing. The last thing your mother and I ever wanted was to be a burden.'

'I know, and you're not' – I hastily assured – 'but maybe it's time to think… to rethink…'

I stuttered over the words. But my father wasn't daft. He knew what I was trying to spit out.

'No care assistance.' His tone was adamant. 'Not yet. Your mother would go berserk.'

This was true. It was bad enough continually fielding Mum's accusations about Alison, their cleaning lady, supposedly lusting after Dad and stealing Mum's clothes. The introduction of a "companion" to befriend Mum and give Dad breathing space would instantly have her thinking he was planning to elope to Gretna Green.

'Anyway,' he continued. 'Your mother would like a word.'

'Okay.'

'And, er' – he lowered his voice – 'good luck.'

In other words *batten down the hatches, fasten your seat belt* and any other idiom that sprang to mind.

There was a pause as the phone exchanged hands.

'Annie,' said my mother. Her tone was distinctly frosty.

'Hello, Mum. How are you?'

'No better for your asking.'

'Jolly good.'

It was best to gloss over replies like this when she was in a mood.

'I have been reliably informed that you're currently in Dubai.'

'Yes, Mum. We've already had this conversation.'

'No we haven't. How *dare* you swan off abroad and not tell me.'

I lay back down on my mattress and stared at the underside of Gerard's bunk.

'But you *know* I'm in Dubai. You spoke to me about my desert pictures.'

'I did no such thing.' Her voice was indignant. 'Nobody tells me anything. So why have you gone to *Dubai*?' She said the word with incredulity – as if I'd gone to the North Pole and was sharing an icefloe with a polar bear. 'I mean, it's not normal.'

'There's nothing wrong with Dubai. Anyway, I needed a break and this place is warm and sunny.'

'I suppose you're spending Keith's money, now he's dead.'

'That's right,' I agreed. There was no point in correcting her. 'Would you like me to buy you a present? They have an amazing shopping mall here.'

'Is it bigger than Swanley market?'

'Yes, it's even bigger than Asda's car park.'

'That sounds impressive.'

'It is. What do you fancy? I was in Old Dubai earlier today and saw camel milk chocolate. There's only one company in the whole country who manufacture it. Apparently it's a delicacy. There are different flavours too, including macadamia and "Arabia" – which is meant to be quite spicey. Or what about some dates? Actually, forget that. You can buy those in the supermarket. I know! I saw something called *oudh*. It's a scent gift in the form of pure oil and mixed with rose and jasmine. It smells divine.'

'It all sounds lovely, dear.'

I blinked. Mum's attitude had switched in the blink of an eye. Such was the nature of dementia.

'If it's okay with you, I'll have the first option,' she said.

'The camel chocolates?'

'No, no, not the chocolates. Just the camel.'

Chapter Fifty

I met up with the girls for a late dinner wearing party make-up but dressed casual-smart. There was no point swanning into the restaurant practically dressed in a ballgown.

Afterwards we sat on the terrace sipping cocktails and getting pleasantly – but discreetly – tipsy.

'This is the life,' said Caz, hoovering up her third concoction. It was so brightly coloured it looked radioactive. 'I'm definitely getting in the party mood.'

'Me too,' giggled Bella.

After one cocktail I'd switched to vodka and tonic, preferring a drink that wasn't so stickily sweet. I picked up the tumbler and took a sip, enjoying the warm fuzzy feeling I was currently enveloped in.

'And you're absolutely sure the club's rules are for women to be in long dresses?' I said to Caz.

'Well, I presume so.' She waved a hand expansively. 'I mean, everywhere we've been so far, it's all been very conservative. I haven't seen anyone parading around in tiny shorts or vest-tops with shoe-string straps. I can't see that a club is going to be any different.'

'I'm going to wear my ankle-length cocktail dress,' said

Bella. 'It's long-sleeved, so I'll be properly covered if the club gets busted.'

'Busted?' I said, nearly spitting out my drink.

'The club is not going to get busted, Belles,' said Caz firmly. 'Nobody is doing anything wrong. It would be a different matter if we danced in the streets or a park, or even on the beach. That's forbidden. As is the music. It's classed as "indecent and provocative". I checked the Dubai Code of Conduct earlier, just to make sure there's no risk of us getting into trouble.'

'Wow.' I let out a low whistle. 'That explains why we didn't hear music on Jumeirah Beach. Back home we take so much for granted.'

'Indeed,' said Bella. 'Like nipping into Asda in your PJs. You couldn't do that in Dubai. Although surely that's a bit hypocritical considering the men here shop in their nightdresses.'

'Hush, Belles!' Caz chided. 'You'll end up getting your wrists smacked for being insulting. They're proper costumes – a *kandura* or a *dishdasha*.'

She shrugged carelessly, eyes bleary from the alcohol.

'When Carly was a teen, I once did a taxi run in my pyjamas. It was after she'd been to a concert and I was collecting her from the O2.'

'Yes, but you were in the car,' Caz pointed out. 'That's a bit different.'

'Except I got caught out. You see, as I approached the O2 from John Harrison Way, my car got a flat tyre. There were plenty of people that night who saw a woman out in her dressing gown and slippers fiddling with locking nuts and wondering how to use the jack. Then a patrol car came along. I was worried about getting into trouble for being indecently dressed. Fortunately, the cop saw the funny side. He said so long as there were no inappropriate holes, I could wear what I liked.' I chuckled. 'Those were the days. Back then Keith and I used to take it in turns to pick up Carly. Mind you, he never took a chance on going out in his jim-jams.' I sipped my drink. 'The silly fool took other chances instead. Now he wears his pyjamas in Pippa's bed. Or maybe he wears nothing at all.'

Blimey, where had *that* come from? One minute I'd been talking about taxi runs in nightwear, the next my subconscious had allowed Keith to sneak into the conversation.

'Sorry, girls.' With an unsteady hand, I set my glass down. 'That sounded rather bitter. Perhaps I'd better stop drinking until my brain can supervise what comes out of the mouth.'

'It doesn't matter a jot what you say,' said Bella loyally. She sucked on her straw. 'You can be as harsh as you like. I'd be bitter too if Colin had done the same to me.'

Caz suddenly had a gleam in her eye.

'There's a saying. Don't get mad. Get even.'

'What do you mean?' I asked.

'I mean, go out and do the same thing. Just think, Annie!' The eyeball gleam had turned into a messianic light. 'Tonight, we're going clubbing. There could be any number of eligible men there. If I were you, I'd be checking them out before making a serious play for one of them.'

'Oh, right.' I rolled my eyes. 'And let's, for a moment, hypothesise that I did this. Let's just say that I find a single guy and like what I see. More appropriately' – I gave them both a knowing look – 'that *he* likes what he sees. After all, girls. I'm no spring chicken.'

Bella flapped a hand. 'You never know, he might be an old cock.'

'Rude,' Caz snorted into her drink.

'You know what I mean.' Bella flapped her hand again.

'In which case' – Caz whispered conspiratorially – 'Annie should smuggle him into her cupboard room and then shag him senseless.'

'Just like that?' I raised my eyebrows.

'Just like that,' Caz confirmed.

'And what about the other guy that I'm already sharing a room with?'

'You make him wait outside,' she sniggered. 'Hey, that reminds me of a joke Andrew once told me.'

'And we all know what Andrew's jokes can be like,' said Bella, nudging me. 'Laddish.'

'Well keep your voice down,' I warned, picking up my drink again. So much for abstaining.

'I will,' Caz promised. 'So' – she stage-whispered – 'a husband bought a box of a condoms from the pharmacy and the cashier asked if he wanted a paper bag. The guy replied, "Nah, I'll just turn off the lights."'

She snorted down her nose and began to wheeze with

laughter.

'I don't get that,' said Bella, frowning.

'Don't worry your pretty head, Belles.' Caz patted Bella's arm. 'I must say, much as I love my hubby to bits, I'm not missing his wake-up calls. He's always after you-know-what first thing in the morning. Drives me mad. There's nothing like being snuggled up in bed, then having your husband spooning into you with a flagpole nudging your back.'

'How annoying,' Bella agreed.

'It is. The last time I protested and said I needed to come to, Andrew replied, "Yes, I need to come too."'

I promptly choked on my vodka.

'Too much information, Caz,' I spluttered, waiting for my oesophagus to recover. 'I think we're all bit drunk.'

'I think you're right,' Caz agreed. 'Come on.' She drained her glass before placing it on the table in front of us. 'It's half eleven. Time to get dressed in our bling-bling, then give Ahmed a ding-ding.'

Chapter Fifty-One

It was with both excitement and trepidation that the three of us stepped out of Ahmed's limo.

We were standing at the foot of a towering hotel. It was full of twinkling lights and overlooked a stretch of water. Upon it bobbed *super boats*. They reeked of money.

I gazed at them in awe and for a moment wished my old dad were here to see them too. In my childhood, Dad had owned a dinghy. We'd spent many a happy weekend pottering up and down the River Medway. If my father saw these floating palaces, he'd be in his element.

Caz smoothed down her dress. 'We look awesome, girls,' she declared. 'Like…'

She trailed off to have a think about who she could compare us to.

'Oooh, oooh, I know!' said Bella, grinning widely. 'Sarah Jessica Parker, Kim Cattrall and Kristin Davis.'

'Nope.' Caz shook her head. 'We're better than that.'

'Monica, Phoebe and Rachel?' I suggested. 'Albeit three decades later.'

'No.' Caz shook her head again. 'I think we're like the women in *Bridgerton*. You know. That Regency drama on the telly where the ladies swish about in gorgeous costumes.' She gathered up part of her skirts and, holding the fabric out, gave a twirl on her tiptoes by way of demonstration.

'Come on, Margot Fonteyn.' I took Caz by the hand. 'Remember what you told us about not dancing in public.'

In high spirits, we hastened towards the hotel's entrance. Just look at us! We were dressed from head to toe in all our finery. Smothered in fake jewellery. Sparkling like the Burj Khalifa.

In the foyer, we were directed to an elevator. Up, up, up we went. We could hear the throbbing bass before the lift had even bumped to a gentle standstill.

The doors swished open revealing a penthouse-type nightclub, albeit smaller than I'd anticipated. The lighting was dim and the air thick with cigarette smoke. By the time we were done here, we'd have probably passive-smoked a pack of twenty.

I gazed around, and two things were immediately apparent.

First – whilst we weren't the only oldies in the club, we were in the minority.

Two – we were ridiculously overdressed.

'Caz,' I shouted over the music. 'We look absurd.'

'What shall we do?' Bella wailed.

'Not much we can do.' Caz shrugged. 'Let's drown our sorrows. There's the bar. Follow me – and blend in,' she instructed, just as a woman effortlessly grooved past looking like one of Madonna's backing dancers.

We tried. Really we did. Although I had a sinking

feeling we looked more like female versions of *The Inbetweeners* doing their cringeworthy nightclub moves.

As we bopped, hopped, jerked and – in Caz's case – twerked towards the bar, I sent up a silent prayer that this was all a bad dream. Never had I felt so uncomfortable or self-conscious.

We were surrounded by youth with flawless flesh and perfect figures. The glamour of both sexes was off the radar. The women were mostly wearing barely-there outfits – oh, hello Towie girls sitting in the corner! It was all toned midriffs and bejewelled navels. And then there was us. In the thick of it but looking ludicrous on so many levels.

Oh to be back home, in damp and dreary England, sitting in front of the wood burner, wearing comfy joggers, my bobbly cardigan, and–

'Can I buy you a drink?'

I looked to my left. A man was staring at me, a smile playing about his lips.

'Are you talking to me?' I asked.

'I most certainly am.'

He was tall and thin with an accent I couldn't place. He was also about thirty-five years old.

'I… er…'

I spotted Bella nudging Caz. The two of them immediately set about conferring behind their hands. Caz gave me a lascivious wink, then whisked Bella away. Both were instantly swallowed by the heaving throng.

Cheers, Caz! She obviously thought she was doing me

a favour leaving me to chat with this dark stranger. No doubt I was expected to follow the idiotic advice she'd dished out earlier. The bit about selecting an eligible man and getting my leg over. Or under. Or whatever body-bending way was appropriate in the *World of Caz* when tipsy.

'I'll take that as consent to join me,' said the man, signalling the bartender. 'Let's see.' He gave me an appraising look. 'Champagne?'

'Um…'

I wasn't sure if champagne sat well with vodka and cocktails.

Moments later a flute was pressed into my hands.

'Thanks.' Oh well.

'What is your name?'

'Annie.'

This was daft. Why was he chatting me up?

'A beautiful name.'

'Thank you.'

'A beautiful… English name?'

'Yes, I'm English.'

'Excellent,' he purred. 'So you are a beautiful Englishwoman with a beautiful English name.'

Was he wearing beer goggles?

'And you are?' I ventured.

Gosh, such original chit-chat, Annie.

'Jahi.'

Now what? I hadn't a clue about making getting-to-know-you conversation. Not with a guy. I was badly out of practice. I sipped the champagne and pondered. Should I ask a question about music? Or if he had a favourite film? But I was spared asking anything further because Jahi was on a mission.

'Dearest Annie. I hope you don't mind me calling you that. I feel an affinity with you. Do you know everything about you is gorgeous?'

I felt flustered. What was going on here? There were some stunning women in this club, but I wasn't one of them. Despite the lighting being kind on mature skin, I was under no illusions about looking older than him and didn't doubt he knew this.

'Do you live in Dubai?' I asked, desperate to get off the subject of my apparent raving beauty and into more regular conversation.

'For now. But it's not my country. I come from' – he waved a vague hand towards the elevator – 'elsewhere. Currently I'm working here but have plans to make changes.'

'I see.'

I didn't.

'Finish your drink, Annie. We need to talk.'

'Do we?' I frowned, draining my champagne.

'Let us go somewhere quieter.'

I looked around. 'I don't think there is anywhere.'

'Yes, there is' – he gave me a look – 'if we go to my hotel.'

'Your–?'

What had he just said?

271

He grinned. 'Annie, from the moment you walked into this club you had a mesmerising effect upon me. So much so that all I could think was... one day I want to marry this woman.'

And then the penny dropped. I'd read about guys like Jahi. They were exotic younger men from overseas who promised older women eternal love. Except, once in England, they left their victims heartbroken and often financially poorer for the experience.

'Thanks, but no thanks. Apart from anything else, I'm already married.'

No need to tell Jahi that it wouldn't be for much longer. But I certainly wasn't planning on replacing Keith with a toy boy out for a visa.

I turned and quickly moved away, threading through the shifting crowd, feeling as conspicuous as a palm tree in the Arctic Circle. And then I spotted Caz and Bella on the dance floor. The music was House. Its trippy beat ensured everyone danced all night long.

Bella had hitched up her hemline and appeared to be doing moves in the vein of *Knees Up Mother Brown* while Caz looked like a twerking ballerina. The pair of them were also dancing with a man. That is, one man between the two of them. A man who was laughing his head off, trying and failing to twirl the pair of them around. A man I'd recognise anywhere.

It was Gerard.

Chapter Fifty-Two

'Here she is!' Caz bellowed. 'The woman who set a thousand male hearts racing the moment she stepped out of the elevator.'

'Give over,' I retorted, rolling my eyes.

'It's too exciting!' Bella giggled. 'You pulled, darling! Clever old you.'

'Less of the old,' I muttered. 'But the champagne he bought was delicious.'

'Congratulations, Madam,' said Gerard, joining in the conversation.

'Thank you, Mr Butler.' I inclined my head.

'And where is the man in question?' he asked.

'By the bar, likely preparing his "Love at First Sight" speech to the next older woman that crosses his path.'

'Ah. Can I assume that having caught a tiger you released him back into the wild?'

'Yes. He was after an English wife and a visa.'

Gerard clasped his heart theatrically. 'You mean, despite the champers, it wasn't genuinely love at first sight?'

'I'm a little long in the tooth to believe such fairy tales.'

'Spoken like a woman who has had the magic sucked

out of her life.'

Sometimes Gerard had the unwitting knack of saying things that were awfully close to the truth.

'Well here we all are,' said Bella squiffily. She was looking slightly cross-eyed. 'And I predict that tonight there is going to be magic' – she flung her arms wide – 'everywhere.'

'I need another drink,' Caz gasped. 'Dancing is thirsty work.'

'Make mine a G&T,' said Bella, launching into some moves that would have been spot on had *Rockin' All Over the World* been playing. Which it wasn't.

'Would either of you like a drink?' asked Caz.

Gerard and I shook our heads.

'Come on, Belles,' said Caz. 'Keep me company so I don't get accosted by young men wanting visas.'

They whooped off. Caz was punching one arm in the air in time to the music. Bella was doing the same, but with her elbows. It made her look like a flapping chicken.

'There go two ladies who know how to have fun,' said Gerard.

I suddenly felt ridiculously upset – as if Gerard were suggesting that only my mates knew how to relax and enjoy themselves.

'Are you implying that I don't?' I said tetchily.

It probably didn't help that I was still feeling snippy after the experience with Jahi. Or maybe I'd simply consumed too much alcohol in the last few hours.

Gerard looked at me in surprise.

'Most certainly not, Madam. I think it would be fair to say that everyone at the Blue Jade knows you're a laugh-a-minute. From the scolded restaurant server to the brow-beaten receptionist, and from the handyman repairing our shower rail to your roommate receiving a telling off for pinching your face cream.'

'I *am* a laugh a minute,' I insisted, trying to remember the last time I'd made anyone convulse.

'By the way, did you see what I left on your bunk?'

'Yes. And thank you,' I said, trying to muster some grace. 'Although there was no need to buy another pot.'

'But I wanted to.'

'Why?'

'So I can borrow more face cream,' he said with a straight face.

I didn't know whether Gerard was winding me up or being serious.

'Just so long as we're clear' – I growled – 'that misunderstandings aside, I *do* know how to have fun. *Fun* is my middle name.'

'In which case, Madam, I invite you to have some fun with me and dance.'

I glared at him. He was definitely taking the micky. And if he thought I was going to launch myself into some sort of whacky headbanging routine, he had another thing coming.

'Well?' he prompted.

And then I spotted Celine heading towards us. She looked quite the worse for wear. Mascara was smudged under bloodshot eyes and her up-do was lopsided. Her eyes locked on mine. If looks could kill I'd now be a goner. It was time for a quick decision.

'I accept your invitation, Mr Butler.'

Chapter Fifty-Three

As we began to move together, I was suddenly aware of an increasingly charged-up atmosphere. Whilst we didn't exactly do Ceroc, our steps were fluid enough to fit in well with the tempo. I avoided treading on Gerard's toes, he didn't trip over my swishing hemline, and Celine did a U-turn and went off to find the rest of the Towie girls.

As Gerard twirled me this way and that, zingers constantly shot up my arms and exploded in my head. It was baffling. Why did this guy have such an effect on me when all he did was wind me up?

There was no pause in the music. No obvious track changes. No comment from the DJ. Just a seamless, pulsing, endlessly throbbing melody. I lost all sense of time. At some point I noticed Caz and Bella had returned to the dance floor. Jahi was trailing the pair of them. All three were exchanging words.

'I didn't touch your bum,' Jahi protested to Caz. 'It was your lower back.'

'If you touch any part of her again' — Bella was wagging a finger — 'I will bop your fingers with my clutch bag.'

'In which case, babe, tell your friend to stop twerking.

277

If she's not intentionally flirting, she's sending out the wrong signals.'

'I am *not* sending out signals,' Caz objected, her bottom once again bobbing away.

'You're insane.'

'I am *not*.'

'You *so* are.'

Jahi stuck his nose in the air and stomped off. He wasn't having much luck finding that UK visa.

'Thirsty?' Gerard eventually enquired.

Possibly another hour had slipped away, faster than sand trickling through a glass timer.

'A bit,' I acknowledged. The thought of downing something ice-cold was suddenly appealing.

'Come on. Let's go and see if your girl gang need refreshments too.'

As he led me by the hand to Caz and Bella, I tried not to fizz and pop. While asking the girls what they wanted to drink, his fingers remained entwined with mine.

Caz shook her head. 'Thank you, but no thank you. Actually, I'm shattered. If it's all right with you, ladies, I'll text Ahmed to pick us up.' She peered at her watch. 'Flipping heck. It's nearly three in the morning. I do hope the Blue Jade are paying him handsomely to look after us twenty-four-seven.'

'I'm definitely ready for my bed,' Bella declared. 'After all that dancing, I have a horrible feeling I'm going to ache tomorrow. Well, it's already tomorrow, but you know what I mean.'

Gerard lightly squeezed my hand. 'Do you want to go back? Or shall we have that drink?'

I didn't hesitate. 'The drink, please.'

Caz and Bella gave me a surprised look. I blinked. Blimey, my mouth hadn't even consulted my brain before making that decision.

'If it's okay with you, ladies?' I added casually. 'It's just that I'm... thirsty.'

Absolutely nothing to do with keeping the company of a man I usually protested about.

'Fine by me,' said Caz, shrugging her shoulders. 'You're not in our room, so it's not like you'll be disturbing us when you come in.'

'Exactly,' I said carelessly. 'And anyway, I'm really enjoying myself. Who knows when I'll get the chance to do this again – if ever? You were right, Caz, about coming out tonight for a boogie.'

Oh God, Annie. Don't say *boogie*. It's probably a has-been word. One that totally flags up your ancientness. Like *bonk*. Oh no. What was going on with my thought processes? I looked at Gerard, hoping he hadn't noticed the boogie word. I could tell by his laughing eyes that he had. How embarrassing.

'Right,' I said hastily. 'Well, I'm totally parched and gagging for a bonk.'

Three stunned faces stared at me.

'Beer,' I hastily amended. 'I'm absolutely gagging for a *beer*.'

Chapter Fifty-Four

'See you later, darling,' said Caz, giving me a hug. She was hot and sweaty, but I hugged her back. 'And just remember' – she put her mouth to my ear – 'when we were twenty, all-nighters made us attractively wan. But now we're older, so will look hideously wrecked.'

'Yes, Mum,' I tutted, before turning to Bella and embracing her. 'See you in the morning, Belles. Well, *later* in the morning.'

Bella yawned widely and nodded. 'Toodle-oo, folks,' she replied, tottering after Caz.

Gerard took hold of my hand again. *Zingggg.*

'Remind me what you wanted?' His mouth twitched. 'Beer or, what was the other thing you said?'

I flushed. 'Actually, make it a bottle of water. I seriously need to rehydrate.'

'Good idea. I'll join you. Sometimes, it's the best drink of the day.'

'I thought that was meant to be tea.'

'That too,' he smiled. 'There's nothing quite like a decent brew.'

As we stood waiting at the bar, Celine staggered over.

'I'm tired and want to go back to the hotel,' she

pouted. '*Now*.'

'Don't let me stop you,' said Gerard lightly.

'Aren't you coming with me?' The pout was turning into a lip wobble.

'No, sweetheart. You have my driver's number. Give him a call.'

'But… but…' The lip wobble was going into overdrive. She turned to me, suddenly furious. 'I have no idea what you have that I don't, but congratulations,' she spat, before stalking off.

I stared after her, gobsmacked. 'What was that all about?'

'Take no notice. She's had too much to drink and is annoyed that I haven't succumbed to her charms. Celine thought hooking an older guy would be a doddle.'

'Oh dear. She's probably not used to rejection. I can't help thinking that most men wouldn't turn her down.'

'I'm not most men,' said Gerard. 'Oh, look. The door is open.' He pointed to a roof terrace I hadn't spotted before. 'Let's go outside and cool down. Also, it will be quieter and easier to talk.'

Outside, a warm breeze instantly lifted my hair, tickling the back of my neck and sending a rash of goosebumps across my skin. Despite it not being cold, I shivered. I wasn't sure if it was due to cooling down too quickly, or something else. Anticipation?

'Fabulous. There's a table straight ahead,' said Gerard. 'The last one, too. What a stroke of luck!'

As we walked over, I could see Dubai spread out far

below, lights twinkling away. All around us, other couples were dotted about. Sitting quietly. Heads together. Voices no more than a murmur. The vibe was so romantic. Magical. Suddenly I felt gauche and horribly anxious.

Get a grip, Annie. It's just your roommate.

And I *still* didn't know his name.

'You look sensational, by the way,' he said.

'Don't be daft.'

'Why do you always put yourself down?'

'I don't. I mean… I'm being realistic. *Sensational* is an amazing compliment, but it's not an accurate one. However, if you want to say I scrub up okay, then I'll accept that as a reasonable truth.'

He took a sip of water and regarded me over the rim of his glass.

'Okay.' He cradled the tumbler between his hands, appraising me. 'You scrub up sensationally.' He grinned. 'Is that better?'

I laughed. 'Why are you being nice to me?'

'I'm always nice,' he countered.

'I don't even know your name.'

Oh no. Somehow, the way those words had come out, I'd made it sound like we'd just had sex and was implying, "Wow, all that intimacy and I *still* don't know your name!". Not that I was thinking about bonking. Oooh nooo. Not the bonk word again. I could feel myself reddening.

Annie, stop. Just… settle down. This is one moment in time. In a *life*time. Enjoy the mood. The… whatever-is-going-on-here. Because come the weekend you'll be back in England, dealing with your holiday laundry and fretting about the binmen not coming while you were away.

'Is it a prerequisite that someone must know your name before they're nice to you?' he teased.

'Only if they want to borrow my face cream.'

'Good point,' he nodded. 'Perhaps we should rewind. Let's pretend we're meeting each other for the first time.'

'On the plane?'

'Sure.'

'Okay.' I could feel my mouth quirking into a grin. 'You go first.'

'Right.' He cleared his throat. 'Hi, there! I'm–'

'Do complete strangers instantly launch into, "Hi, there!"?'

'What do you mean?'

I wrinkled my nose. 'It just sounds like bad acting in a sit-com.'

'Oh, right. Let me try again.' He paused. 'Hey. How are you doing? I'm–'

'Now you sound like you're trying to be Joey Tribbiani from *Friends*.'

Gerard rolled his eyes. 'Excuse me. Is this your handbag on my seat?'

'That's more like it,' I murmured.

He mimed passing me the offending object. 'Just to say, I'm hoping to spend this flight sleeping. However, I have a feeling that you're the type who needs the loo every five minutes, or endlessly wants something from the overhead locker, or scatters the contents of your handbag over those sitting next to you, or–

'I did not scatter the contents of my handbag over you,' I protested. 'I dropped a biro and–'

'And' – he waggled a finger at me for interrupting – 'that you're partial to bolshy moments–'

'I do *not* have bolshy moments,' I said bolshily.

'In which case' – he swept on – 'would you please address me by my proper name and not call me Mr Butler.'

I opened my mouth to say something, then shut it again.

He looked at me in amusement. 'Why *do* you keep calling me Mr Butler?'

'Because' – I could feel myself growing hot – 'I, er, thought I once overheard someone else call you that.'

I was *not* going to tell him he looked like a certain film star. I just couldn't. He might think I fancied him. Which – I was appalled to acknowledge – I did. A bit. Okay, a lot. Okay, hugely. Because, by God, he was sexy. Sexy as hell sitting there looking at me across this small expanse of table. And so what if I was sixty? I could still fancy a guy, couldn't I? After all, it was only a bit of admiration. An oldie could surely appreciate a handsome man's looks without it being deemed as… you know… *yuckaroo*. It wasn't like I was going to launch myself at him, for heaven's sake. Or send that glass of water flying as I wrestled him to the ground… and glued my lips to his… as my dress rode up my thighs and… oh, hello! Was that a tingle at the top of my legs? Omigod. When had that last happened? I couldn't remember. But I had a feeling that tingles were a precursor to common sense doing a bunk.

'And why do you keep calling me *Madam*?' I gasped, desperate to shatter the soft-porn imagery that was now rampaging through my brain.

'Because you're uppity. An uppity madam.'

'I am not,' I protested. 'Well, not usually.' I was aware that Gerard provoked that trait in me.

'Actually,' he demurred. 'I know your name. But I thought it was fun to tease you. I've overheard your gal pals calling you Annie. And I know their names too. The bossy one is Caz and the giggly one is Belles. But I'll pretend I don't know all that so you can introduce yourself properly.'

'Well you *still* haven't told me *your* name,' I pointed out.

His eyes bored into mine and I found myself knowing exactly how a rabbit felt when caught in a car's headlights. I was completely unable to look away.

'Theo,' he said softly.

I felt my soul sigh. Theo. *Theo*. What a beautiful name. I realised that I'd also been holding my breath. I mean, what if he'd said *Malcolm*. Or *Nigel*. The spell would have been entirely broken. Not that there was anything wrong with being a Malcolm or a Nigel but, in my generation, if a guy was known by either name he was unfairly regarded as, well, a teeny bit boring. A bit of a Malcolm. A bit of a Nigel.

A bit like the name Keith.

I blinked. Blimey. Why had I never made that connection before? *Keith* was definitely up there with the Malcolms and Nigels. I tried to think of a hot celebrity called Keith and could only come up with Keith Lemon. A nice enough guy I'm sure, but it was hard to believe an army of females might be lusting after him. Aside from Mrs Lemon. But the gorgeous Gerard had now revealed himself to be the handsome Theo.

'Delighted to meet you, Theo,' I said, suddenly feeling a bit shy. I held out my hand to shake his. 'And my name is Annie Rosewood.'

For a moment, Theo went very still. Then in one smooth move he leant across the short expanse of tabletop and enfolded both my hands in his. For some reason, the gesture seemed unbearably poignant. There was something else going on here, although I couldn't work it out. His eyes were searching mine for... what? I didn't know. But in his I briefly saw pain. Then it was gone.

'Annie Rosewood,' he said, voice soft as silk. 'It's so good to meet you.'

Chapter Fifty-Five

The other couples on the roof terrace had, one by one, disappeared back inside.

Theo and I had been talking about everything and nothing for – it felt like five minutes – but I knew from the changing colour of the sky that time had shifted.

There were no longer stars in a blue-black sky. Instead, there was an overhead palette of smudgy grey. Night was signalling that soon it would be day.

We stood up and went back inside. Unsurprisingly, the place was almost deserted. Only die-hards and stragglers remained. Gerard started to guide me towards the lift.

'Hang on a mo,' I said hastily. 'After all that water, I need the rest room.'

'I'll wait here,' he said.

Inside the Ladies, I was shocked to catch sight of my reflection in the floor-to-ceiling mirrors. Caz had warned that only twenty-somethings could do all-nighters and still look great. She was wrong. The woman gazing back at me was glowing from the inside out. I stepped closer to the glass. Studied my eyes. No hint of eyebags. Where had they gone? The pupils were dilated and sparkling. Cheeks attractively flushed. Wow.

Humming to myself, I went into a cubicle. I'd have to do all-nighters more often. Maybe volunteer myself when my grandchild had 3 a.m. colic and Carly was exhausted.

I floated out of the cubicle feeling ridiculously happy. As I washed my hands, I caught sight of my reflection again. And winked.

'I'm not tired,' said Theo, as I joined him. 'How peculiar.'

'Me neither. That's weird.'

'Shall we go for a walk?'

'Yes, but' – I pointed to my feet – 'I have super-high heels on. It will be more of a totter on my part.'

'That's fine. We'll "totter" around the marina,' he grinned.

Theo had taken my hand again and it felt like the most natural thing in the world. A part of me wondered if anybody was watching and, if so, whether they'd protest. After all, this was Dubai. A different culture. Customs needed respecting. But I seemed to recall that handholding was permitted for married couples. Hopefully, nobody would ask to see a marriage certificate.

We found ourselves heading along Marina Walk, a palm-tree-lined pedestrian walkway. It went on for seven kilometres and bordered the emerald-hued waterway that was full of yachts. There were over three hundred shops along this stretch, and sixty-plus restaurants. Perhaps it was a bustling place during the day but, right now, it was quiet. The only sounds were that of lapping water.

In the last few hours I'd learnt quite a bit about the

man walking by my side. Many barriers had come down between us. Theo's divorce was now finalised. His job had contributed to the breakdown of the relationship. He'd worked long hours which had left his wife feeling neglected. Hindsight was a marvellous thing.

'All those lockdowns played havoc with so many businesses, Annie. Mine was no exception. Salvaging it became my number one priority, and eventually I succeeded. But my wife wanted out – not to mention demanding half of what I'd struggled to salvage. I agreed to her keeping the marital home in exchange for leaving my company alone. Those initial months were very dark ones.'

'I can imagine. I've yet to go through dividing up the marital assets. Fortunately, Keith seems anxious to keep things amicable.'

'I hope it stays that way. How's the heart barometer?'

I shrugged. 'In the first few days it was off the scale. But I have a lot of distractions to stop me getting maudlin. Like my parents. More specifically, my mother. She has dementia.'

'That's a toughie.'

'But on the upside I keep busy with work. I have my own business – nothing high-flying I hasten to add.'

'There you go again, doing yourself down. Be proud of what you've created, Annie. Celebrate it. It's a huge achievement.'

'Wow. Well, put like that, yes, I guess it is.' I nodded. 'Work aside, I have a married daughter. Carly. And my first grandchild is on the way.' I smiled at the thought of welcoming a new life into the world. It was impossible to be sad for long when a baby girl would soon be turning life upside down.

'I'm sure you'll be a really groovy grandma.'

I glanced at him. Groovy? Now *there* was a word! Hadn't it gone out of fashion ages ago? I wondered how old Theo really was. I'd initially thought him to be mid to late forties.

'Every now and again something triggers a memory that makes me sad,' I continued. 'But I guess that's the way things go.'

'Is that what happened at the dancing fountains?'

I looked at him blankly.

'You crashed into me,' Theo prompted. 'Then charged off before I could ask if you were okay.'

'Ah, yes.' I was rather hoping I'd got away with that. 'Sorry. It was the music. It reminded me of a long-ago moment, and I didn't want to have a public meltdown.' We walked on, still hand in hand. 'So where do you live?'

'Crowborough. That's in East Sussex.'

'I know it. A nice part of the world.'

It was about forty-five minutes from Little Waterlow.

'Look.' Theo pointed to the sky. 'The sun is coming up. A new day is dawning.'

'I can't believe it's gone six in the morning,' I whispered, shocked.

'Come on. Let's watch it together.'

We sat down on a low wall, side by side. I felt a moment of déjà vu. But instead of watching a sunset with this man, now I was watching a sunrise. We sat in companionable silence, caught up in the mesmerising display of colour.

'Time for a photo,' said Theo, holding his phone aloft. 'Smile.'

We inclined our heads, grinning into the lens. He sent the picture to me and this time I didn't hesitate. Within seconds it was uploaded to Facebook.

I didn't care who saw it or what conclusions they drew from it.

Chapter Fifty-Six

Having discovered that Theo had rescued his business, he went on to tell me that he'd landed a contract in Dubai and had even considered coming out here to work. He now had enough contacts to make that possible.

'Do you think you will?' I asked.

'No. Not now.'

'Oh,' I said, feeling inexplicably relieved. 'Why not?'

Theo gazed ahead. For a moment, he didn't speak. Then he turned to me.

'Because I've met you, Annie,' he said simply. 'For me, everything changed the moment an uppity madam on a flight to Dubai ended up sharing my cupboard room. And I don't know if it was when you wrecked the bathroom, or powered across the pool revealing – if you don't mind my saying – something Celine will never have no matter how many times she goes under the surgeon's knife, but something kept shifting in me until I realised I had feelings for you.'

Now it was my turn to be momentarily speechless.

'You live in Kent,' he continued. 'I live in Sussex. We're not a million miles from each other. I'd like to see you again, Annie. When we're back in the UK. That is, if *you* want to.'

I gazed at him incredulously. This divine-looking man wanted to see *me*?

'I… I…' I stared at him helplessly.

'If you don't want to, I'll totally understand. I'm not about to give you a hard time if you don't feel the same way.'

'Oh, but I do,' I gabbled. 'I do, I do feel the same way, I do, really, but—'

'I don't do "buts".'

'Theo, I have to be honest. There's something I haven't told you.'

'Let me brace myself.' He closed his eyes for a moment, apparently preparing to hear bad news. 'Is it that you've changed your mind about me borrowing your face cream?'

'All the face cream in the world isn't going to alter what I have to say.'

Theo nodded. 'Go on. I'm a big boy. I can take it on the chin – what you're about to say that is. Not the face cream. So spit it out.'

I took a deep breath. 'I'm older than you think.'

He nodded. 'Okay. I had you down for somewhere between forty-five and forty-seven. So, what are you? Fifty?'

I shook my head and looked at him fearfully. 'Sixty,' I whispered.

'And your point is?'

I blinked. 'My point is that I'm a lot older than you.'

'Annie, I'm fifty-three. Fifty-four soon.'

'What? You can't be.'

'Well I am. And thanks for thinking otherwise. I'm flattered.'

I stared at him. I was only *recently* sixty. And if Theo really was about to turn fifty-four, that made the age gap only a little over six years. Surely that wasn't too horrendous. Was it? And if things didn't work out between us… if he decided life would be more fun with a younger woman, at least our addresses weren't so close that we'd bump into each other. There would be no surprise encounters at the Tesco Express. No pretending we hadn't spotted each other as we ducked around parallel aisles and then suffered a head on trolley crash. No–

'So what do you say?' he said, interrupting my runaway thoughts.

'I say… yes. Yes, I'd love to see you when we're back in England.'

'Good.' He smiled, and his whole face lit up. 'I want to kiss you, Annie.'

'You can't. We might get arrested.'

'I happen to know' – he lowered his voice conspiratorially – 'a quaint little cupboard room where we won't be disturbed.'

Zinggggggggggggggg.

By the time we'd returned to the Blue Jade Hotel, it was almost seven in the morning. I thought I'd be knackered. Shattered. Instead, I'd never felt more alive.

As soon as we shut the door on the outside world,

Theo took me in his arms. His lips gently came down on mine. For a moment I was lost in the sweetest kiss that went on and on. We only broke apart when it became apparent both of us needed oxygen.

'There's something else I need to tell you,' I gasped, my heart hammering wildly.

'And I have something to confess too. But ladies first.'

'Okay. W-Well, the thing is,' – I stammered – 'the *thing* is…'

'Annie,' said Theo, sounding exasperated. 'Just say it how it is.'

'Okay.' I screwed up my eyes and let the words spill out in a hurry. 'I haven't done what we're about to do for an awfully long time.' I exhaled noisily. There. I'd been honest. 'Right. Your turn to confess.'

Theo gave me a lopsided grin. His eyes were twinkling again and full of mischief.

'Ditto. But it will probably be like getting back on a bike. Or a horse.'

'Or a pair of skis?' I suggested.

'Possibly. Although I've never been skiing. Why are we wasting time talking?'

'I don't know.'

And then he took me in his arms again.

Chapter Fifty-Seven

At some point we fell asleep in a tangle of sheets, but only for about three hours.

I was awoken by a gurgling sound followed by loud rumbling. I realised it was my stomach.

'Does your tummy always make that noise when you've rolled around in bed with a much younger man?' Theo teased.

'The younger the guy, the louder the noise,' I bantered back. 'Did my hunger pangs disturb you?'

'I've been awake for a little while,' he confessed, flicking on the side light.

I screwed up my eyes against the initial pale glow in our windowless room. 'I'm famished. Shall we have breakfast?'

'I think breakfast finished some time ago, but we might make lunch.'

'Bagsy I use the bathroom first.'

'Sure. And Annie' – Theo caught hold of my wrist as I made to sit up – 'we need to have another chat, darling.'

'Okay.' I mentally hugged myself. *Darling.* Such a lovely endearment.

When I came out of the shower, Theo had ordered a pot of coffee and a plate of mixed sandwiches.

'You tuck in,' he said. 'Give me five minutes to freshen up.'

I sighed happily and, sandwich in one hand, kindle in the other, flopped down on the lower bunk. This was the life. Who would have thought! Sex with a film star lookalike followed by slobbing around in bed at gone midday. And no worrying about crumbs in the sheets because somebody else would later change the linen.

Having stayed up all night, I felt mildly disorientated. Was it Wednesday or Thursday? Wednesday. I frowned. Thursday. I didn't have a scooby-doo. Where was my phone? A date and time check were required.

I'd had the sense to put the mobile on *do not disturb* before going to sleep. Checking it now, I was faintly horrified at what had been going on while I'd been otherwise engaged. Six missed calls. Four from Keith. Two from Carly. And... *how* many text messages?

Ten were from my husband, which I didn't bother to read. Six were from Carly and ditto. What was the matter with them both? Didn't they sleep during the night?

The last message was from Caz. I clicked on it.

Didn't want to disturb you. We're by the pool xx

PS – Belles and I have taken bets on whether you've had naughties xx

PPS – That's "bonk" in your language xx

I replied with an upside-down smiley face. That would have to suffice. I wasn't going into details about my new love life, by text or otherwise. Right now, I wanted to hug the events of the last few hours to myself. Like a delicious secret.

Meanwhile, my phone informed that it was Thursday, the seventh day of October, and twenty-seven minutes past one in the afternoon.

When Theo came out of the shower, he squeezed in beside me and we continued our picnic in bed.

'How are you feeling?' he asked, polishing off the rest of the sandwiches.

'Amazing.'

It was true. I felt so *alive*. And young. Yes, young. Even though the mirror would show me the truth of how the body looked, the inside – my heart? – seemed different. As if it had shed a heavy load. Carefree. Like how I used to feel when a teenager. Before marriage. Before motherhood. Before a thousand responsibilities. It was like being eighteen again and there was nobody to please except myself. Liberating!

'You feel amazing because you *are* amazing,' said Theo.

'You're pretty awesome too,' I grinned.

He inclined his head modestly. 'Can I assume from that comment that we both managed to find our way back onto that bike?'

'Yep – and the horse and the skis too.'

'It was that good, eh?'

'Definitely.'

He pulled me towards him and kissed me on the nose.

'While you were sleeping' – his face became serious – 'I had a text message from my new client. That's the one here, in Dubai. You may recall me telling you that I went straight from the airport to see him. That's why I was so late checking into the Blue Jade.'

I looked at him expectantly. 'It rings a distant bell. Is everything okay?'

'Yes. Couldn't be better. The only thing is, matters have progressed faster than I anticipated. I need to see him again.'

'Okie dokie. Shall we meet up afterwards?'

He didn't immediately answer, and I felt a wave of apprehension.

'I need to return to England. *With* the client. He wants to see my other stock.'

'Oh.' And then it dawned on me. Theo was leaving the Blue Jade today.

'He's already taken care of the flights on my behalf. So I won't be returning to England on Saturday, Annie. Instead, I'll be flying back this evening. However, I need to pack my suitcase shortly and check out.'

'Oh,' I said again. My eyes inexplicably filled with tears.

'Don't cry,' he said, hugging me tightly.

'I'm not,' I protested, as a tear rolled down my cheek. This was ridiculous. Get a grip, Annie. You're behaving like – oh yeah – behaving like the teenager you currently feel. Fair enough. But I couldn't help it. In the last few hours, I'd been in a romantic bubble with this man. Selfishly, I didn't want it to end.

'Listen to me.' He hooked a finger under my chin and

299

his expression was one of tenderness. 'You do know this isn't the end, right? It's the beginning. You and me. I think we could have something special together. I think we're *going* to have something special together,' he amended.

'Really?' I sniffed, as my stomach did a Red Arrows swoop–and–dive and rescued my sinking heart.

'Really,' he affirmed. 'It's going to be fun getting to know my Annie.'

I beamed at him. *His* Annie!

'Although, you may not believe this, but since we got properly chatting, I've discovered I know more about you than you do about me.'

I frowned. 'How do you mean?'

Theo sighed. 'It's a funny old world.' He shook his head imperceptibly, then gave me a look I couldn't fathom. 'There's something else I need to tell you, Annie. About me. I hope it won't alter anything between us.'

Oh Lord. That sounded ominous. What on earth could it be? Was Theo an ex-jailbird? Had he rubbed shoulders with bank robbers? Or – I gulped – was I currently propped up in bed with a murderer?

As he began to fill in the missing details about himself, something was revealed that didn't so much as make my eyes widen as bulge.

'So now you know,' he said, taking my hands.

'That's quite some… history,' I gasped.

He looked at me speculatively. 'I hope you don't feel things are weird because of it. I don't want you running for the hills.' He attempted to joke.

I looked at him, my mouth hanging open. 'It's… a bit of a bombshell,' I acknowledged. 'Something to… digest. The dynamics.'

'Yeah,' he agreed.

Wow. Talk about a flipping corker of a revelation. Right now, I felt too flummoxed to think straight. But maybe I was getting ahead of myself. One thing at a time.

'I'd like to think it won't change things between us,' he said cautiously.

I nodded. Smiled weakly.

'And now' – he looked sad, like he might have regretted telling me this latest development – 'I'm going to pack my suitcase.'

'I don't want to see you go,' I blurted, biting my lip. 'I'll go to the pool instead. Join Caz and Belles. They've already texted me.'

'Okay. Tell them I said good-bye and give them my best wishes.'

'I will.' My voice was barely a whisper.

I hugged him hard, then threw a sundress over my head. Grabbing my costume and towel, I shoved them in a tote along with my hat and sun cream. Then I left the cupboard room, shutting the door quietly behind me.

I couldn't decide if I felt sad or happy. Sad because suddenly I wasn't sure if what had happened had been a bit of romantic madness. Happy because Theo was adamant he wanted to see me when back in England.

The question was… could I still see him without upsetting one or two apple carts?

Chapter Fifty-Eight

'At last!' said Caz, as I approached her and Bella. 'We were going to send out a search party, weren't we, Belles.'

I was relieved to see there was no sign of the Towie girls around the pool. I wasn't sure I could deal with any dark looks from Celine.

My two besties were stretched out on sun loungers, sunglasses hiding bleary eyes.

'It's not fair,' said Bella, propping herself up on one elbow. She lifted her shades to study me. 'You look all glowy and sparkly-eyed. Like you've been plugged into Dubai's Sparkle Towers. How come? After all, the three of us went clubbing at the same time and drank at the same pace. And we all stayed up way past our usual bedtimes. What have you done that we didn't?'

'I think that's a censored question,' said Caz with a wry grin.

'I agree,' I said, tapping the side of my nose.

I flopped down on the lounger next to them.

'Oh come on.' Caz whipped off her sunnies, immediately revealing some spectacular eyebags. 'You can't keep us dangling. What happened? Actually, no need to say a word. It's written all over your face.'

'Really?'

'Yes,' she nodded. 'It says, "Annie stayed out for another two hours after Caz and Belles returned to the hotel. Then Annie went back to her cupboard room with a man who proceeded to become her lover." Am I right or am I right?'

'Omigod,' squeaked Bella. 'Did you and your roommate do it?'

'His name is Theo,' I replied.

As I said Theo's name, my insides seemed to melt like chocolate left in the sun.

'I think, darling' – Caz addressed Bella – 'that it's safe to presume from Annie's gooey-eyed expression that shenanigans under the sheets took place.'

'Actually it was on top of the sheets,' I corrected.

'I knew it,' Bella crowed. 'What was it like?'

'Nosy!'

'C'mon,' Caz wheedled. 'This is *us* you're talking to. And what happens in Dubai stays in Dubai.'

'Apart from when you post it to Facebook,' Bella muttered.

I paled slightly. The sunrise pic.

A moment of reckless bravado that had seemed like a good idea. Now I wasn't so sure. Not after what Theo had revealed. But, then again, it wasn't the first picture of the two of us. It was the second. Except previously I'd passed Theo off as a random stranger. No way would I get away with that twice, especially with our heads touching and our bodies snuggled into each other like two billing and cooing lovebirds. And I *still* hadn't read Carly and Keith's text messages or returned their calls.

'Annie?' Caz prompted.

'Sorry.' I hauled my mind back to the present. 'What can I say?' I shrugged.

'Just say it all!' Caz howled. 'Was it fun? How many times did you do it? How does he compare to Keith? Are you going to hook up when home? And actually, where *is* he?' Caz peered at my tote as if Theo might suddenly climb out of it.

'Yes. Twice. No comparison. Yes again. Heading back to the airport.'

Bella blinked. 'I think I got all that.'

'Heading back to the airport?' echoed Caz. 'I thought he was on the same return flight as us.'

'Business got in the way. Oh girls,' I said, putting my head in my hands. 'It's all shiny and brand new but there's something you just wouldn't believe. I'm not sure if it puts a spanner in the works.'

'What works?' said Bella.

'The *romantic* works,' said Caz patiently. 'Now hush, Belles. Let Annie tell us what the problem is.'

So I told them. Bella blinked rapidly throughout, and Caz said "hm" several times.

'What would you do?' I asked, rattling to a standstill.

'Do?' Caz questioned. 'I'd live my life, that's what I'd do. If you want to carry on seeing Theo, that is totally your prerogative. Let's put it this way, one reaps what one sows. I'm a firm believer in that. This isn't your problem, Annie.'

304

'So whose problem is it?' Bella looked from Caz to me and then back to Caz again.

'The sower's,' said Caz firmly.

Bella frowned. 'I'm so lost.'

Chapter Fifty-Nine

I spent the rest of the day deepening my suntan while feeling mentally and physically disembodied. I didn't know whether this was due to lack of sleep or falling in love.

What?

Rewind, Annie.

In love? Don't be daft! You can't fall in love with someone you met less than a week ago. But the fact was, I felt like I'd known Theo for a lifetime. And he'd said the same to me when we'd been out on the club's roof terrace under a sky full of stars.

Oh Lord. Put that thought aside for now, Annie. Just… press pause.

To distract myself, I settled back against the sun lounger and checked out all the messages from Carly and Keith.

Carly: *Hello, Mum. It's the early hours of the morning in England. I got up to answer a call of nature and, don't ask me why, but I felt compelled to look at my mother's Facebook page – and promptly had the shock of my life. WHAT are you doing posting lovey-dovey pictures of the SAME man you watched a sundown with, not to mention* getting up close and personal together to ride a camel? What else are you riding, Mum? And sorry to sound uncouth, but I'm deeply concerned. You're sixty, Mum. SIXTY! Can you hear the shriek in my voice? In the last few weeks, I've watched you morph from Thora Hird to Amber Heard. I've had Dad around here quizzing me, wanting to know if you went to Dubai with this guy. He suspects you're using Belles and Caz as a smokescreen and that this is some act of warped revenge. Meanwhile, do you know how I feel? Well, I'll tell you. Piggy in the middle. I can't stand it. My parents – my sensible, solid, predictable, no-nonsense mother and father – have not only gone off the rails, they've both taken a space rocket to Planet Lost-the-Plot. My grandpa-type father has abandoned straw hats and gardening for yoga mats and a gardening assistant, and my mother has reinvented herself as Princess Jasmine with her Aladdin. If you really must rub his magic lamp, could you refrain from posting the pictures all over Facebook? It's embarrassing. It's bad enough that I'm dealing with my parents breaking up when I'm about to become a parent myself, but it's truly upsetting when my mother's Facebook friends direct message me saying, "Oooh, Carly! WHAT is your mother up to? Who knew Annie was such a dark horse! And who's the silver fox nuzzling her earlobe?" And have you heeded ANY of my advice about protection?

Keith: *Annie. Woke up for a wee and checked my Facebook Notifications. As you do. How COULD you? I don't believe it.*

307

Carly: *Sorry, Mum. I'm hormonal. That was a really mean message. I want nothing more than for you to be happy. But not with a tourist gigolo. I love you very much xxx*

Keith: *I. Just. Do. Not. Believe. It.*

Carly: *Now I can't get back to sleep xxx*

Keith: *Now I can't get back to sleep.*

Carly: *Do you forgive me? Oh God, I'm such an awful daughter. Why am I such a horrible person? When you were pregnant with me, did you turn into a sniping bitch? Ryan was really cross with me earlier. He said the way I spoke to him was appalling. I snapped at him, but surely it was justified. I mean, he said he'd do the cooking to let me get off my swollen feet. However, he slopped baked beans across the worktop and a puddle of orange sauce on the floor. Nor did he toast the bread properly. Then he got loads of crumbs in the tub of spread and now the margarine looks yuck. And can beans on toast even be classified as a proper evening meal? Am I failing to properly nourish my unborn baby? If so, tonight's meal fail is down to Ryan. Why are men so useless? Why do they make such a mess? Why do they snap at you like a cornered stray dog? I only told him, for heaven's sake, that he was a messy slob and that his idea of cooking was rubbish and that he might have done one job, but he'd made me three more, and did he know that currently BENDING DOWN TO CLEAN IS TOTALLY IMPOSSIBLE? So, I told him to move in with his mother. I mean, that's hardly unreasonable, right? Xxx*

Keith: *It's not reasonable. You're my wife!*

Carly: *I've now disturbed Ryan. He's moaning about the screen's light in the bedroom. I told him I was texting you because it was a matter of life and death. Basically, he didn't believe me and asked if I'd woken him up out of revenge over the baked beans Xxx*

Keith: *Is this revenge?*

Keith: *Well?*

Keith: *Is it?*

Keith: *What are you doing right now?*

Keith: *Are you in bed with HIM?*

Carly: *Can you ring me, please? Xxx*

Keith: *Can you ring me, please?*

Oh God.

Chapter Sixty

Text to Carly:

Yes, it is quite normal to turn into Miss Bitch when pregnant.

Yes, I've had a holiday romance.

Re Amber Heard. I'm deeply flattered.

Love Mum xxx

PS No, darling, I will not be ringing you xxx

Text to Keith:

Sending sunshine and good wishes from Dubai.

From Annie (the wife YOU left).

PS No, I will not be ringing you.

Text from Theo to me:

Madam. I am missing you soooo much.

Love from Mr Butler xxxxxxxxxx

Chapter Sixty-One

When Friday rolled around, Caz's eyebags had retreated, and Bella's eyeballs were once again snow white.

Both my friends' equilibrium and looks were fully restored whereas I... well, everything had caught up big time.

As Caz had warned – the mirror now reflected a woman who was *hideously wrecked.* I gazed in dismay at the pleated eyelids and accessorised cheeks. Where was that face cream?

'I did warn you about doing an all-nighter,' Caz crowed, over breakfast.

'You can talk,' I protested, rattling my coffee cup into its saucer. 'You were there with me!'

'But not all the time,' she said smugly. 'Belles and I were sensible and hit our pillows before sunrise.'

'I'm going to do some shopping,' I announced. 'I still haven't properly seen the inside of the mall.'

'Been there, done that,' said Bella, biting into a croissant. 'It was a far saner experience' – she added, spraying crumbs everywhere – 'than touching the clouds at the Burj Khalifa.'

'Do either of you fancy another shopping session?' I

asked.

Bella wrinkled her nose and Caz shook her head.

'I'd rather make the most of the sunshine,' said Caz apologetically.

'Me too,' Bella nodded.

'Then if you neither of you mind me disappearing,' I said, gathering up my phone and handbag.

Frankly, I couldn't wait to get away. As we'd walked into the restaurant, Celine had been coming out. She'd paused to confront me, demanding to know if I'd seen "her man". I'd been tempted to say yes, all of him. Instead, I'd gently told her that Theo was no longer in Dubai. Her face had worked for a moment and then, without another word, she'd stalked off. I could see Celine now, through the restaurant's picture windows. She was stationed at the far end of the pool area, her mouth pursed like a cat's bum.

Celine aside, whilst it would have been nice to spend the day in my cozzie, I really did want to check out the mall. Maybe I'd catch a few rays later.

'Go on then, off you go,' said Caz. 'But remember, once you've seen one Louis Vuitton shop, you've seen them all,' she winked.

'Not that we bought anything,' Bella added. 'I wasn't even brave enough to step over the store's threshold. I was too worried by the shop assistants thinking, "Time waster alert! She's just pretending she can afford to buy, but we can spot the truth a mile off." However, I did enjoy peering in beyond the window display. Everything looked mouth-wateringly wonderful. I promise you'll salivate over every single shop.'

'In which case, girls, I'll see you both later. I'll be back in time for one last swim.'

There wouldn't be time to enjoy the sunshine or pool tomorrow. Saturday would see the three of us getting up, having breakfast, and then immediately heading off to the airport.

'Enjoy,' said Caz.

'And don't get swept off your feet by a good-looking sheikh,' Bella giggled.

'Annie isn't going to do that, Belles,' Caz tutted. 'She has her handsome Theo waiting for her in England.

My handsome Theo.

I grinned. 'Laters.'

Much as I loved Bella and Caz, I was a teensy bit grateful to be going off on my own. My head was crammed with so many thoughts. I wanted to be able to sift through them in peace and without interruption.

So much had changed since coming to Dubai. It was almost impossible to believe I was even the same person. I'd arrived in this country still nursing a broken heart over the antics of my estranged husband. In the beginning I'd done my best to come to terms with being alone, but it had devastated me. Keith's desire to dismantle our marriage and start again with Pippa Kipling had been shattering. The whole cliché of being traded in for a younger model had left me embarrassed, as if it were a shameful thing to grow older. I'd lost both my marriage and self-esteem, and my confidence had been left in shreds. Smashed. Wrecked. And

313

any other adjective you cared to slot into the blank space left in my newly single life.

But now, perversely, instead of Keith periodically invading my thoughts, it was a completely different man. Rather than Keith making my heart ache, now it was Theo squeezing my soul with an intense longing.

Was Carly right? Had I taken a trip to Planet Lost-The-Plot? Or could it be that Theo was the universe's way of sending me someone to assist with healing. To help with the whole new chapter of "moving on". To finally have confidence in myself and completely rebuild a new life. This wasn't so much about rebounding. It was more about knowing that – whatever happened with Theo – I should believe in myself. Believe that I was a strong, independent woman perfectly able to be her own sovereign self. Or alternatively, as Theo had put it, a resilient *uppity madam*.

Either way, my time in Dubai had made me realise I could and should have faith in the future and embrace all new potentials.

I texted Ahmed and, with a swing in my step, headed through the hotel lobby. Within half an hour I was inside the air-conditioned coolness of the shopping mall.

I stared around in awe and began walking. This was a city within a city. On the ride over, Ahmed had told me that the entire complex had cost twenty billion dollars to build. I couldn't begin to imagine such a sum of money.

I floated around in a dream, walking through an endless maze of shops and more shops as my thoughts frequently strayed to Theo.

I couldn't go mad spending. My pocket contained Zara dosh, not Emirati cash. I noticed there were sheikhs aplenty by the high-end stores, their wives trailing behind in full length black cloaks. Ahmed had told me such a garment was known as an *abaya.* One sheikh appeared to have three wives. They were all dressed in the traditional *burqa,* which covered their faces as well as their bodies. I watched in fascination as the women were shepherded into what looked like a giant golf buggy driven by a uniformed chauffeur. My goodness. No sore tootsies for them. After all, this was a place where achieving one's daily ten thousand steps had the potential to be done several times over.

My mind pinged back to Theo. I couldn't *wait* to see him again. The thought of our reunion filled me with both trepidation and excitement. Trepidation in case the initial spark might have spluttered out like a barbecue grill in a British downpour. Excitement because the memory of those zingers made me feel so alive.

My thoughts then strayed to Carly. I was so looking forward to giving her and Charlotte Bump a big hug.

And then there was Keith. Well, he was giving me a completely different vibe. I was nervous about seeing him again. Despite his adultery, he'd done his best to be kind and caring. But that had been before I'd met Theo. Now Keith was carrying on as if it were *me* who'd done the dirty on *him.* It didn't make sense. I certainly wasn't looking forward to the chat he wanted to have. Previously he'd made every effort to take the sting out of the divorce topic. But ever since my posting the sunrise pic to Facebook, I had an ominous feeling that Keith's Divorce Petition might cite Theo as Co-Respondent.

Oh God. Don't think about it, Annie. You're in Dubai. Not England. You're on your own and pleasing yourself in a mall where – I boggled – it was possible to not only shop uninterrupted, but also marvel at a spectacular indoor waterfall. I gazed in awe at the art installation that spanned three floors of the mall. It was more like a human waterfall because it featured fibreglass sculptures of men diving in unison. The overall effect was mesmerising.

Walking on, I found a gorgeous mother and baby shop and went inside intent on buying something special for Carly and my unborn granddaughter.

Armed with my purchases, I then went off to seek out the aquarium and underwater zoo. I found it at the second level – a walk-in place spread across a forty-eight-metre tunnel. Initial worries about feeling claustrophobic faded at the sight of over four hundred sharks and rays, including sand tiger sharks and giant groupers, in a tank that claimed to hold ten million litres of water. I smiled to myself. Only Dubai could pull off sharks in a shopping mall!

Four hours later, I was ready to admit defeat. A full weekend was required to cover this sort of vastness.

It would have been nice to have checked out the ice rink, or the VR Park with its fifteen rides and motion simulators, to watch a film in the twenty-two-screen cinema, or even stop for a coffee in the rainforest café with its emulated tropical ruins and light shows, but I was starting to feel overwhelmed by the sheer enormity of the place.

Instead, I opted to soak up the atmosphere. As I rode up an escalator, the harmonized call to prayer sounded throughout the mall, inviting Muslims to go to dedicated prayer rooms.

I imagined myself back home, visiting Bluewater, and popping over to the concierge's desk to ask if there was a room available where I could have a quick word with God. Thinking of the look I'd get in return made me smile.

However, it struck me that having a word with God about *the whole situation* might be helpful, although I'd have to make do with our tête-à-tête taking place on this escalator rather than a prayer room.

As I glided upwards, I mentally drafted God an email.

Dear Lord, please don't let Keith give me any further unwanted surprises.

But God's inbox must have been jammed with more pressing requests because my prayer went unanswered.

Chapter Sixty-Two

I awoke on Saturday morning in my cupboard room's top bunk. For a moment I just lay there, looking at the ceiling, thinking about the night before.

Theo had telephoned me on Friday evening, just as I was packing my suitcase. My longing for him had been so ridiculously intense I'd felt like a schoolgirl in the first grip of crush. As we'd chatted, I'd climbed into his empty bunk to try and feel closer to him.

We'd murmured sweet nothings for half an hour with him promising to take me out for dinner Sunday evening, providing I wasn't too jet-lagged. I'd assured him that, if need be, I'd prop my eyelids open with the hotel's cocktail swizzle sticks, because nothing was going to stop me from seeing him. After we'd said good-bye, I'd wondered if it had been foolish to appear so keen.

When I was nineteen and living with my then flatmate Gail, the pair of us had often sat by the phone willing our respective love interests to ring. When they had, we'd promptly answered the phone for each other. "You want Annie?" Gail had said. "I'm so sorry, she's out. Is that Simon? Oh, *Neal*. I do beg your pardon. She's so flipping popular I can't keep up with her admirers." But there hadn't really been anyone called Simon. The name had been plucked from the air. Back then the only man who'd persistently called was my frustrated bank manager. But that had been the philosophy of my generation. Play hard to get and a man would be spurred on to pursue you. But now? Well, now I didn't want to play that game. Been there, done that.

But was it normal for a sixty-year-old singleton to feel so lovestruck? I had no idea. Nor did I know anybody in my situation to ask. Instead of speaking to God, perhaps it would be more realistic to email an agony aunt. Did agony aunts even still exist?

After I'd finished speaking to Theo, I'd done a quick Google search. It had revealed a British national newspaper claiming to have a brilliant new agony aunt. I'd spent a minute or two studying the portrait of a woman with a razor-sharp bob streaked à la *Cruella de Vil*. Personally, I didn't think she looked like the cosy sort, but perhaps one shouldn't be quick to make judgements. How to begin?

Dear Aunty (might I be so bold as to say you don't look like anybody's aunt?),

I took the liberty of finding out your age. You're three years older than me. So here goes.

Do you still have sex at sixty-three?

You see, I'm newly single and want to know if having sex at sixty is a bit "bleurgh".

In the last twenty-four hours... actually, make that forty-eight... no, thirty-six... actually, I'm not sure... you see, I stayed up all night, had sex twice, and now I'm so tired I've kind of lost track of exactly when I last did it. But it was recently.

Before this, I hadn't had sex for a while. Months. Maybe a year. Maybe longer. Does this make sense? I mean, does what I've written so far make sense? If it doesn't, it's probably down to my hormones. You see, I didn't have any. But now I do. They're not real. They come in a sachet.

Anyway, my adult daughter is horrified. Not about the hormones. About the sex. She thinks I should be wearing grandma slippers and have a blanket over my legs while watching telly, and that any sexual activity should be between actors. And when I say "actors" obviously I'm talking about the ones in programmes. Not the ones that go in porn movies. Not that I watch porn movies, just in case you're wondering. That said, years ago I did once watch a porn video with my estranged husband. It was just for a laugh. Not that there were many laughs to be had. The storyline was ridiculously vague. I never did figure out why the leading guy thought it such a turn on when the car broke down in the middle of the night on a garage forecourt. Especially when the garage attendant was secretly watching from his kiosk. Weird.

Anyway, where was I?

Oh yes. Carly. That's my daughter. If you were to read between the lines of her recent text message, you'd understand EXACTLY what I'm talking about.

Yours sincerely

Anonymous of Little Waterlow

(Please disregard the name on this email. As I said, I'm very tired.)

Dear Anonymous of Little Waterlow

Apologies, but I didn't understand one word of your communication. Perhaps you could forward me your daughter's text message.

Best wishes

Aunty

(I have done my best to disregard the name on this email. Unfortunately, Annie, the computer system here automatically signs you up for my weekly newsletter which you will have to manually unsubscribe from.)

Perhaps I'd be better off writing to Madonna.

Dear Madge (do you mind if I call you that?)

Do you really have a twenty-seven-year-old lover? Or is it all a big publicity stunt?

If it's true, how often do you have sex?

And are you embarrassed that your children know you're still sexually active?

Best wishes

A Big Fan

Dear Big Fan

Yes, I really do have a twenty-seven-year-old lover.

We only have sex three times a day because my lover

can't keep up with me.

Why should I be embarrassed if my kids have figured this out? I'm an icon.

Best wishes

Madonna

PS I hate being called "Madge".

Chapter Sixty-Three

The plane rumbled down the runway and in no time at all we were airborne.

I felt a huge pang of sadness to be leaving Dubai. The country had stolen a little piece of my heart. But, as the seatbelt sign flicked off, I knew that a greater piece of it had been taken by someone else. And soon I'd be seeing him again.

The background chit-chat of passengers murmured in time to an internal voice. It spoke only one word, but on a loop. *Theo, Theo, Theo.* I took a deep breath to quell the excitement that kept threatening to explode like a shaken bottle of champagne. It was as much as I could do to resist the urge to shout aloud. *Squeeeeeeeee!*

The three of us were once again sitting in the same row as when we'd departed Heathrow. I regarded the empty seat to my right. My stuff was upon it. I imagined Theo suddenly turning up, grumpy, and wanting to sit down. "Your handbag is on my seat." Who knew that our subsequent pithy exchange would lead to us being thrown together until a thaw took place under the Dubai sun… sunset… sunrise.

I looked at the vacant seat and smiled. I was fully

expecting Carly to say that a holiday romance couldn't possibly be duplicated. That it was best to leave it in the sunshine with warm memories. But I'd felt a connection with Theo. Even when we'd initially annoyed each other, there had been chemistry. A bond. And then my brain reminded me of that final conversation. What he'd revealed. It was a bit of a bummer. But now that I'd slept on it, it didn't seem to matter so much. Now that I knew his secret, was it so awful? It was in the past. Everything was in the past. All I was interested in was the future.

'Annie?'

Caz leant across Bella to get my attention.

'Do you want a drink? The stewardess is talking to you.'

'Oh, sorry,' I apologised. 'I… no… actually, yes. Can we all have champagne, please?'

'Champagne?' said Bella. 'Are we celebrating something?'

'Yes,' I smiled. 'And the bubbly is on me.'

'That's very generous, darling,' said Caz. 'What's the occasion?'

I took the glasses and ice-cold mini bottles from the stewardess.

'To say thank you to my besties,' I said, pouring fizz into my airline flute. Proper glass, I noted with delight. No plastic beaker. 'You've always had my back, girls, but when my marriage went tits up–'

'Language, Annie,' murmured Bella. 'We're not back in England yet.'

324

'Apologies.' I lowered my voice. 'When my marriage went bosoms up – better? – the two of you were absolute rocks. You've seen me through a rough patch bumpier than the air turbulence we went through earlier. You are both my 2 a.m. friends. Someone I can ring at any time of the day or night. Besties who always provide tissues, tea, and support.'

'It's been our pleasure, hasn't it, Belles,' said Caz.

'Or course,' said Bella stoutly.

'Yes, but you both did something that went above and beyond friendship. You dropped everything. You left your husbands. Your family. Both of you put a line through an entire week on your calendar and whisked me off to Dubai. You made sure I celebrated my recent sixtieth in a way that I will never forget. And for that, I'm truly grateful.'

'Oh, Annie,' said Bella. 'That's such a lovely thing to say.' Her eyes filled up and she blinked rapidly. 'We know you'd do the same for us.'

'You bet.' I nodded. My own eyes were now a little bright.

'But, darling,' Caz drawled. 'You have to realise that accompanying you to Dubai wasn't really a hardship.' She winked. 'We've had a fabulous time. No cooking. No housework.'

'No laundry,' Bella added.

'Or bed duties,' Caz continued.

'I thought you liked' – I looked around furtively – '*sex*,' I mouthed.

'I do. But it's all very' – she wrinkled her nose –

325

'*predictable* when you've been married for so long. Seeing all the sizzling chemistry between you and the handsome Theo has just made me…'

'What?' Bella and I shrieked in unison.

'Don't look at me like that, girls. I'm not about to leave Andrew for a younger man. Although' – she gave me and Bella a sly look – 'I have been having a very exciting exchange of texts with someone.'

Bella and I were so gobsmacked, the air stewardess could have parked her drinks trolley in our gaping mouths.

'What are you talking about?' I hissed.

Oh dear God. The last thing I wanted was Andrew knocking on my door. "Cheers for that, Annie. I'm glad your broken heart is better. Meanwhile, mine has been smashed to pieces. If you hadn't appropriated Caz to go to Dubai, my marriage would still be intact."

'Keep your eyelashes on,' said Caz. 'It's only a bit of texting. Perfectly harmless. But incredibly thrilling.'

'With who?' said Bella.

'Remember those American guys by the pool? It's one of them. His name is Brad.'

'Don't tell me anything else,' I said. 'You know me. I'm hopeless at keeping secrets. The last thing I want is putting my foot in anything.'

'Very intuitive, Annie.' She laughed throatily. 'Because he likes feet. In fact, Brad has a bit of a thing about them. He wants me to send him pictures of my bare feet with my toenails painted in a rainbow of colours.'

'Too much information,' Bella squeaked. 'Now drink

your champagne, Caz, and don't tell us anything else. I'm like Annie. Not very good at secrets.'

'Okay, okay. Let's have our champers and drink to us. Girl power. And, more importantly, the fact that we're not yet past it.'

'Cheers,' we said in unison, clinking our glasses together.

I took a sip and, as the bubbles exploded on my tongue, gave silent gratitude that my world was now a happier place.

The remainder of the flight was uneventful. We watched films. Chatted. Snoozed. And steered clear of talking about Americans with a foot fetish.

There were no hold ups at Heathrow and in no time at all we were in the pre-booked taxi heading back to Little Waterlow.

It had been a long day. Now, as we set our watches back three hours, we felt travel weary. Leaning back against the cab's comfortable upholstery, I let the scenery wash over me. How beautifully green and verdant England was. As we passed under a bridge covered in graffiti, I realised how scruffy the place could be too. Why didn't local councils clean it off or, better still, get the "artists" to do it? Not that I could see anything artistic about large black letters proclaiming *DAN IS AN ARSEHOLE*.

Caz was the first to be dropped off, Bella next, and finally myself.

As I trolleyed my suitcase up to the front door, I frowned. How strange. A lamp was on in the lounge. I thought I'd turned all the lights off before leaving. Oh well. One electric light bulb left on for a week wouldn't break the bank.

But as I went into the hallway, the sound of soft music reached my ears. The hi-fi was playing. I froze. Had somebody broken in while I'd been away? Popped on some classical music whilst checking out each room? Hummed along to Vivaldi as they'd looked for jewellery here, or cash there? But then again, if a burglar had visited, wouldn't he have taken the hi-fi? Well, probably not. I had a feeling that the ancient equipment in the front room wasn't in huge demand. Even so, my internal radar warned me I wasn't alone.

Leaving the front door wide open in case a swift exit was required, I gripped the handle of my suitcase for support and cleared my throat.

'Hello?' I called out nervously.

Movement came from the lounge. The sound of sofa springs releasing as someone got to their feet. My heart sped up as, a second later, the visitor revealed himself.

'What on earth–?' One hand fluttered up to my mouth.

'Hello, Annie,' said Keith softly. 'Wow. Great tan. You look amazing.'

'Never mind that,' I spluttered. 'You nearly gave me heart failure. What are you *doing* here?'

'Isn't it obvious?' He gazed at me with an expression I couldn't quite read... or maybe didn't *want* to read. 'I've come home.'

Chapter Sixty-Four

'Can I give you a hug?' said Keith, coming towards me.

I backed away, and nearly fell over my suitcase.

'Careful, darling.' He caught hold of me in the nick of time, righting my balance. 'There.' He smiled down at me. 'Safe and sound. And back in my arms again, where you belong.'

I recoiled from Keith's touch. How bizarre. Before going to Dubai, I would have melted into his embrace. But now? It felt wrong. Horribly alien.

'What are you talking about?' I demanded.

I could feel myself getting slightly wild about the eyes. It had been a long day. I was tired. I wanted to make a cup of tea. Ring my parents. Chat to Carly. Speak to Theo. Put my feet up on the sofa and wiggle my tanned toes. Giggle to myself about an American with a foot fetish. Not have my estranged husband here in the marital home announcing he was back, and wasn't that just peachy, and perhaps we could have that nice cup of tea together. In fact – I was starting to feel really angry now – what a bloody cheek!

'Let's go into the lounge. We'll sit down and have a calm discussion,' he said.

His hands were still on my arms, and I shook them off.

'Annie, don't push me away,' he said, sounding hurt.

'Push you away?' I cried. 'Hellooooo? You're the one that did that. Even though it now seems like a lifetime ago, the reality is that only last month you calmly announced you'd fallen for a woman called Pippa Kipling and that you wanted to be with her. You can't just reappear in my life as if nothing ever happened.'

'I know, I know. Come into the sitting room and–'

'No,' I snapped. 'I'm going into the kitchen to have a cup of tea.'

'I'll make it for you,' he said, hastily moving ahead of me. Moments later a chair was courteously pulled out. 'Take a seat. Relax. I'll put the kettle on.' Seconds later there was a whirr of activity as cupboards were opened and mugs gathered. Keith peered into the fridge. 'Ah, no milk.'

'I've been away,' I pointed out. 'There's some long life in the larder.'

'Of course.' He gave me one of his gentle smiles. His expression was calm. It was one of the things that had first attracted me to Keith. His mild manner. The capacity to always be unruffled. It had led me to conclude that he was a rock upon which, in crisis, one could lean upon. But it had been an illusion. Because in that same calm voice he'd announced our marriage was over.

I suddenly had a moment of déjà vu. Suddenly it was me sitting at the kitchen table while Keith faffed about. In that first week of September, I'd been making toast and he'd been trying to talk to me. But I hadn't been listening.

I'd been fussing about. Looking for marmalade. I certainly hadn't been heeding my husband's body language as he'd sat where my bottom was now parked. Now there was a reversal. Keith was the one behaving like a butterfly, delaying a conversation that needed to be had.

I decided to keep quiet. Let him make the tea. Prolong things. Search for a packet of unopened biscuits. Break the cellophane. Arrange them oh-so-nicely on a plate. When it became obvious there were no further delaying tactics to occupy him, he pulled out a chair and sat down opposite me.

'I can't wait to hear all about your holiday,' was his opening line.

'And I can't wait to hear why you're back in this house.'

No more stalling.

Keith inhaled and then let out a loaded sigh.

'The night before you flew off with Caz and Bella...'

'Yes,' I prompted.

'I rang you.'

'And?'

'I told you that we needed to have a conversation.'

'Yes, I remember. I presumed it was to discuss solicitors.'

He looked at me blankly.

'*Divorce* solicitors.' For goodness' sake. What was the matter with the man?

His expression cleared. 'Ah. No. No, it was never about that. I nearly told you I wanted to come back to you that night, but I bottled out.'

'Why?' I cried.

'You'd been through enough.' He shrugged his shoulders. 'I thought it better to let the dust settle a while longer. For you to go away with your girlfriends. Recharge the batteries. And that you'd come home and' – he spread his hands – 'we'd have a chat and pick up where we left off.'

'Pick up...?' I stared at him. 'You mean, get back together as if nothing had ever happened?'

'Yes.' He nodded eagerly. 'That's it. Just put everything down to a blip.'

'A blip,' I repeated. Oh boy. Such an innocuous four-letter word.

'Look, darling...'

He tried to take my hands across the table but I picked up my mug, blocking his attempt at contact.

'I made a mistake,' he said simply. 'I was stupid.'

'And when did you have this epiphany?'

The question came out sarcastically, although I hadn't meant it to.

'That night in The Angel,' he explained.

I had to think for a moment what he was talking about.

'You were with Caz and Bella,' he reminded. 'On a girls' night out.'

'Girls' night out?' I echoed. 'Keith, I fell apart after you left me. Caz and Bella have spent the last few weeks propping me up. They took me out to cheer me up. To support me. You make it sound like that occasion was a tipsy night out. When Cathy – one of the biggest gossip mongers in Little Waterlow – came over to take our orders, she noticed the three of us looking at a holiday brochure. Caz laughingly told her we were going to have a girly break and leave our hubbies at home. Then you walked in with Pippa Kipling' – I rounded on Keith furiously – 'and do you know what Cathy said?'

'I have a feeling you're going to tell me.'

'Cathy gave me one of her *looks* before saying, "Seems like *your* husband has already made provisions for being looked after." Talk about feeling humiliated. And then, when Cathy tried to diplomatically ask you and your new lady to think about dining elsewhere, your girlfriend decided to publicly kick off. There's nothing like announcing one's marriage has ended in front of an audience.'

'Yes, I appreciate that.' Keith cleared his throat. 'And that was the moment when I realised Pippa wasn't for me.'

'Am I meant to be pleased?' I demanded. 'Is that supposed to be some sort of *whoopee* moment, because I'm not feeling it, Keith.'

'Look' – he spread his palms wide upon the tabletop – 'what more can I say? When Pippa started publicly ranting and raving, whether it was justifiable or not–'

'Definitely *not*.'

'–she showed me she had no finesse. In that moment there was a blinding realisation that everything about her was false. And I don't just mean her eyelashes and nails. I was stupid enough to have my head turned by some flattery and attention. But it wasn't just the episode in the pub. Warning bells were ringing when she said she couldn't stand kids. I knew she'd never had children and wrongly presumed it was because Mother Nature didn't deliver them. When I mentioned looking forward to holding Baby Charlotte, Pippa looked revolted. She told me that women who wanted children were mad. That they were consigning themselves to sleepless nights for something that produced snot one end and… well… something else the other. And there's our Carly due to give birth to our first precious grandchild. It just made me realise – like a massive thunderbolt – Keith, you idiot! What the HELL have you done? Thrown away your lovely wife. Jeopardised your relationship with your daughter. All for what? A woman who, when she found out you had a tidy sum in the bank, was all over you like a nettle rash.'

Ah. He'd mentioned money. I'd wondered when the topic would crop up.

'So Pippa wasn't entirely captivated by your dashing good looks. There were other factors. Your bank balance.'

Keith looked sheepish.

'Yes, I guess so. She made a beeline for me at the garden centre when she noticed how much I was spending. Loads of bedding plants. New patio furniture. Then, when I wanted to replace our old garden shed and asked about one of their gorgeous summerhouses, she jokingly asked me if I'd come into a bit of money. And I'd said yes. I'd thought nothing of it. I then told her my parents had passed away and there had been a small inheritance. I didn't suspect her of being so calculating. I'd barely parked my feet under *her* kitchen table when she started making plans for home improvements. We're talking… easily… fifty grand. Oh, and another fifty on a vast orangery. All to be paid for by Yours Truly. Anyway. Enough about Pippa Kipling. I regret everything, Annie. I am so sorry. But the good news is… I'm back.'

'You're back,' I said, without enthusiasm. 'And I'm sorry too. Because things have changed.'

'I know.' Keith put up his hands, as if to hush what I was about to say. 'I'm not stupid, Annie.' He looked wounded. 'You've had a holiday romance.'

'Yes.'

'Nor am I surprised,' he said gallantly. 'You look terrific. Beyond glamorous. It's like you're… I don't know… transformed. But I loved you just the way you were, Annie. The hair colour, your tan, the make-up' – he searched my face – 'it's all gorgeous. *You're* gorgeous. But I'd like the old Annie back.'

'Annie Frump?' I said, looking surprised. 'The Annie that won't turn another man's head? Who let herself go? Who slid waaay too early into bobbly cardigans and salt-and-pepper hair?' I made a harumphing noise. 'I don't know what I was thinking of. That wasn't me, Keith. Not the real me. I think I was like that to please you. To be the good little wife.'

'Pardon?'

'Well that's what you're *really* after, isn't it? Security. Back to good old Annie. She never makes a fuss, because

335

she thinks she doesn't deserve anything special in life because she's not so special herself.'

'I... I... I object!' said Keith, sounding like he was talking to a judge giving summary before passing sentence.

'If you'd told me all this before I'd left for Dubai, I'd have likely had you back with open arms. But not now. It's too late.'

'No, it isn't!' he cried. 'We can get back to the way we were.'

'You don't understand.' I shook my head. 'I don't want to. Sorry, Keith. But I've met someone else.'

'Yes, I know. But... look, if I can overlook your holiday romance, surely you can forgive my moment of madness over Pippa Kipling?'

'This isn't about tit-for-tat.'

'Well, what is it, then?' Keith cried.

'I have feelings for this person. And he says the same about me.'

For a moment Keith was silent. His face was pale.

'I saw his picture,' he said eventually. 'On your Facebook page. He looks younger than me. Is that what this is about, Annie? Just wanting a good time with a good looker?'

'No,' I said, determined to keep my cool. Not to rise. 'I've already told you, we have feelings for each other.'

'What's this guy's name?' he demanded.

It was almost the same question I'd asked Keith when he'd broken the news that he was leaving me. "What is her name?" I'd demanded. "Why?" Keith had responded.

336

"What purpose does it serve?"

I looked at Keith with sadness as I found myself almost parroting his words.

'Telling you doesn't serve any purpose.'

When he next spoke, his voice was harsh.

'I want to know.'

Here we go.

'Okay,' I said, taking a deep breath. 'His name is Theo. Theo Kipling.'

Chapter Sixty-Five

Keith stared at me in shock.

'Kipling? Theo *Kipling?*'

'He's Pippa's ex-husband,' I said quietly.

'Is this some sort of ridiculous joke?'

'I wish it were.' My voice was sombre. 'Did Pippa never talk about her ex-husband?'

Keith was still looking stunned.

'No,' he muttered. 'Well, now and again she mentioned them.'

'*Them*? I didn't realise she'd been married twice.'

'Actually, three times.'

Blimey.

'But' – Keith continued – 'Pippa never referred to them by name. On a couple of occasions her exes had come into conversation, but she'd simply referred to them as *Ex Number One, Ex Number Two* and *Ex Number Three.*'

'Well, she was certainly game for walking down the aisle,' I said, trying to lighten the mood.

Theo hadn't mentioned that his ex-wife had married before. He'd simply referred to "Pippa's men" in a general context. I'd lumped that term into a long line of admirers with whom she'd had numerous affairs, not realising that there had been two other long-suffering husbands along the way.

Theo had also explained that Pippa's last infidelity had been the one that had not just broken the camel's back, but finally severed any ability to forgive. He'd partially blamed himself for that particular dalliance, due to putting his struggling business first. However, deep down he'd known his wife was a narcissist with a track record of repeated adultery.

I cast my mind back to the moment when I'd been on that Dubai roof terrace and properly introduced myself. "Delighted to meet you, Theo. And my name is Annie Rosewood." He'd gone very still for a moment, and I'd caught an emotion flicker across his face. I'd thought it was pain. Instead, it had been recognition. Not just of who I really was, but an understanding of my marriage breakdown and being unwittingly caught up in his ex-wife's manipulations.

We'd continued chatting on the walk by the marina. By then, many barriers between us had come down. By that point I'd mentioned Keith's name several times, so Theo had silently pieced together the details of my private life. He'd been left with no doubt that the woman on his arm was the estranged wife of the man co-habiting with his ex. And later still, when we'd been in bed, and talked about seeing each other again, he'd then told me who he really was.

Despite his divorce from Pippa being finalised the year

before, she'd rung Theo at the start of September pleading poverty. "I'd known this to be untrue, Annie. Our speedy divorce settlement had been based upon her having everything – and I mean *everything* – except my business. Not that she'd wanted anything from the company at the time because there had been nothing left to take. But I knew I'd turn things around eventually, and that Pippa might be back. So I took preventative legal steps. When I refused to fall for her tale of woe, she angrily told me where to go. There was much flowery language which I won't burn your ears by repeating. She then tried to goad me with details of her latest man. She said *Keith* had an inheritance and had more money than I'd ever make. I'd asked if this chap was married – because they usually were – and whether she never tired of wrecking other people's lives? She'd gone on to say that she'd looked up his wife on Facebook and that anybody as dowdy as *Annie Rosewood* didn't deserve to keep their husband." My face had burned with embarrassment when Theo had told me that. "So" – Theo had continued – "when you introduced yourself as Annie Rosewood, I just thought – hang on a minute – what are the chances?"

He'd then gone on to deliver the bombshell about who he really was. Pippa Kipling's ex-husband. And yes, this discovery had made me anxious. Why? Because, if things *did* go well between me and Theo... if we became "an item" – and he'd assured me he wanted that – then our family dynamics would be, to say the least, *interesting*. At the time I hadn't known that Pippa and Keith were no longer together. Neither had Theo. Instead, we'd been trying to get our heads around our exes being together and how it might play out on family occasions. My brain had immediately scooted off to a New Year dinner with everyone around Carly's dining table.

"More sprouts, Pippa?"

"Why thank you, Annie. I'd pass them over to Theo but, unlike you and Keith, we ignore each other."

"No worries, Pippa. I'll offer them to Theo on your behalf. Anyway! How's it going with the home improvements? Have you managed to divest Keith of his inheritance yet? Oh, look. Gravy. Where would you like it? In your lap, or over your head?"

But ultimately Theo and I had decided to cross the bridge of *Meet the Exes* if and when it arose. After all, the only thing we were interested in was the immediate future with each other.

Keith's voice brought me back to the present.

'It won't last with this guy, Annie. There's an age gap.'

I instantly bristled.

'He is younger, but by a handful of years. Not' – my eyes flashed – 'a couple of decades.'

'So what happens next?' Keith demanded. He was getting feisty. Not quite so calm now. 'I can't just leave, Annie. I have nowhere else to go. This is my home.'

'And it's my home too,' I pointed out.

'Oh terrific,' he growled. 'Well don't expect me to welcome Theo bloody Kipling under *this* roof. Absolutely no way am I letting him over the threshold. Don't think he's walking upstairs with *my* wife leaving me to turn up the volume on the telly while you do all sorts in the bedroom.'

'Well, quite,' I conceded. 'And we wouldn't want that either.'

'I have to say, Annie' – Keith folded his arms across his chest – 'I really hadn't anticipated tonight ending like this.'

'Look, I'm sorry you're upset, but what's done is done. I didn't set out to deliberately hurt you. Meeting someone else wasn't an act of spite or a desire to get even. It just happened. Nobody was more surprised than me.'

'How ironic,' Keith muttered, almost to himself. 'My guilty conscience about me leaving my wife sees me paying for a holiday, whereupon she meets another man who's not only linked to the woman I left her for, but also wrecks any chance of reconciliation.'

I pushed back my chair and stood up.

'But unlike the woman you left me for, I'm not a gold digger. Regarding Dubai, I will repay every penny. You have my word.'

'It doesn't have to be like this, Annie. Why don't we go upstairs together and see what happens? You never know, there may be magic.'

'I don't think that's wise,' I said gently. 'Goodnight.'

And with that, I took myself off to bed. Alone.

Chapter Sixty-Six

Despite my body not yet adjusting to an English time zone, I was up on Sunday morning long before Keith.

His routine had always been to enjoy a weekend lie-in. The last thing I wanted was to fall into comfortable patterns, like our previous toast-and-marmalade ritual. Old habits die hard, and all that.

Instead I slipped out of the house and headed to Little Waterlow's old-fashioned high street. Chloe's Café was open seven days a week. I could sit, inconspicuously, at a table within. It would be peaceful to let the world go by. Listen to comforting background noises. The hiss of Chloe's coffee making machine. The spit-spat of frying bacon.

My kindle was still in my handbag. Twenty minutes later, it was propped against a pepper pot while I tucked into a full English. Right now, I was happy to lose myself in a fictitious world. One of the leading ladies was having a row with her cuckolded husband. She was trying to persuade him that a snog wasn't cheating because no lower body parts had been involved.

Sometimes, even in the world of make-believe, there was no getting away from complications. I wondered what

Andrew would say if he knew Caz was sending pictures of her feet to that American guy. Was that a form of infidelity? Or would it be in*foot*elity?

My mobile rang, distracting such musings.

'Darling!' I said, smiling into the handset, even though Carly couldn't see me.

'Hey, Mum. Where are you?'

'At Chloe's indulging my stomach – as if it hasn't had enough amazing food in the last week.'

'Oh, right. Only I rang the landline and Dad answered, which kind of had me reeling. Are you two' – I could hear the hope in her voice – 'back together?'

'Er, it's a bit of a story.'

'Yes, or no?' she said, quick to impatience and wanting an answer.

'Your dad has left Pippa. He gave me quite a shock when I arrived home last night.'

'Yayyy,' she crowed. 'So you *are* back together!'

She sounded so happy I almost didn't want to burst her bubble.

'Sweetheart' – my voice was gentle – 'if that ever happens, it won't be just yet.'

'But if he's left Pippa, surely that means he wants you back?'

'I think, right now, it's more a case of Dad not having anywhere else to go. It would be easy to pick up where we left off. And yes. Your father has said he'd like a reconciliation, but–'

'But nothing. What's the problem?' I could hear the

exasperation in her voice.

'–but if you'd let me finish what I was saying, I'm not prepared to be second best.'

'You're not second best, Mum. Why would you say such a thing?'

'Look,' I sighed. 'Think of a man owning – oh, I don't know – a Ford Fiesta. But one day his head is turned by a Ferrari. In a moment of madness, he throws everything he has at buying that Ferrari. For a while, the man is overjoyed, especially by others' envious looks as he zooms along. He feels young again and oh-so-vital. However, he soon realises something. The Ferrari might look amazing, but it's proving expensive to run and maintain. So he lets it go. After all, his trusty Ford Fiesta is still in the garage. It might have more miles on the clock and be rusty in places, but it's never let him down. Except, when he lowers himself into the driving seat, he discovers that his previously reliable car won't start.'

'Okay, okay. I'm getting the picture, Mum. You're saying that your battery has gone flat with Dad. The spark has gone.'

'That's exactly what I'm saying.'

'Well can't you recharge it?' she huffed. 'Stick on a couple of jump leads and fire things up again.'

'That would be forcing the issue. Anyway, there are other things to be considered, darling. Like trust. Trust isn't something that just falls back into place. Forgiving is one thing. Trusting again… that's something else.'

'I totally get that. But time heals. I mean, there's other

things to consider. Positive things. Like companionship. Having someone to potter about with in the garden. Someone to discuss the headlines with. Someone to make you a cup of tea if you're feeling poorly. Just because sparks aren't flying, don't dismiss companionship.'

'I hear what you're saying. Really, I do. But for now, I'm putting myself first.'

'How do you mean? Oh, wait. It's this guy, isn't it. The one on your Facebook page. Are you seeing him again?'

'Look,' I hesitated, not wanting to get into a deep conversation in a public place. 'How about I pop over? I have some gifts from Dubai for you. They're in the car. Put the kettle on and we'll have a proper chat.'

Chapter Sixty-Seven

By the time I'd seen Carly, brought her up to date with Theo and the whole *love quadrangle* situation, I'd drunk so much tea I thought my bladder might explode.

Ryan had tactfully removed himself, saying that he needed to pop to the garage for diesel and do some errands.

'I hope you know what you're doing, Mum,' said Carly eventually. Her tone was morose.

'Does it matter if I don't?' I shrugged.

We were sitting in her kitchen and, tea aside, we'd munched our way through an entire packet of chocolate digestives. What with Chloe's cooked breakfast and now eight hundred calories courtesy of Mr McVitie, at this rate I wouldn't have any room for dinner tonight.

'I can't believe this is my mother talking.' Carly rolled her eyes. 'You used to be so…'

'Boring?'

'Sensible!' she countered.

'You mean, predictable.'

'Well, okay, yes. Predictable. Is that so awful?'

She stood up, gathering our mugs. Charlotte Bump nudged against one of the biscuit plates, knocking it perilously close to the table's edge. I quickly grabbed it.

'Another cuppa?' she asked.

'No, thanks. I feel like my very veins are full of tea. In fact, excuse me for a minute. I need to use your loo.'

A minute or two later, as I washed my hands, there was a pinging sound from my handbag. I felt a moment of dread. Would it be Keith asking where I was? What I was doing? When I'd be home? So far, he'd texted Carly twice. The first message had been to ascertain if I was with her. The second had been more forthright. Keith had demanded to know if Carly was "in cahoots with your mother and acting as an alibi".

To say my feathers had been ruffled was an understatement. As far as I was concerned, we were separated. Which made me a free agent. I realised that living together under one roof, with Keith hoping I'd change my mind, wasn't going to work.

I patted my hands dry and removed the phone from my bag. My heart instantly did a few skippy beats. It was a text from Theo.

Shall I pick you up at 7? Table is booked for 8. Suggest you bring toothbrush. Don't forget face cream. And don't wreck my bathroom. Am fond of shower curtain xxx

I texted back almost immediately:

Lovely! Looking forward to seeing my Mr Butler xxx
PS Any bathroom wreckage will result in me making a clean getaway.

(Sorry, couldn't resist!) x

Smiling to myself, I joined Carly back in her kitchen. Her eyes instantly laser-beamed into mine.

'What are you grinning about?' The laser-beams narrowed with suspicion.

'Mind your own beeswax,' I retorted.

'I heard your phone ding while you were in the loo. Was it him? Has he been in touch?'

'*Him?*' I blinked. '*Him* has a name. Yes, it was Theo. He's taking me out for dinner tonight.'

'Is that appropriate?'

I frowned. 'What do you mean?'

'Well, let's face it. Anywhere in Little Waterlow will have people gossiping for days. When Dad wheeled Pippa into The Angel, it was the talk of the village. Apart from anything else, I seem to remember you being put out that Dad hadn't been more respectful and thought to wine and dine his fancy woman in *her* neck of the woods.'

'Oh, I see. No, we're not going public round here. Theo is taking me to a restaurant his way. He lives in Crowborough so there's no chance of bumping into anyone. Well, hopefully not.'

Never say never. After all, I'd travelled over four thousand miles to Dubai and ended up sharing a room with Pippa Kipling's ex-husband. What were the odds? But sometimes crazy stuff happened.

'Do you know Crowborough?'

'Not particularly. I'm familiar with Tunbridge Wells

because me and the girls have sometimes shopped at The Pantiles. Crowborough is about fifteen minutes further on.'

'Well make sure you program your satnav. There's nothing worse than ending up lost in the dark.'

'Oh, that won't happen,' I said airily. 'Theo is picking me up.'

There was a pregnant pause that was nothing to do with Charlotte Bump.

'Flaming Nora, Mum,' Carly exploded. 'That's bang out of order.'

'What do you mean?' I stared at my daughter, aghast at her outburst.

'What about Dad?'

'He can cook his own dinner,' I said indignantly.

For heaven's sake. I'd been back five minutes, and Carly expected me to slot back into servitude.

She rolled her eyes. 'I'm talking' – she enunciated – 'about Theo and Dad coming face to face. Or is Theo going to stay in his car while Dad waves you off. "Have a fabulous time, darling! Don't do anything I wouldn't!" Is that what you're assuming?'

I looked at my daughter and paled. Oh Lord. She was right. Thanks to jet lag and tiredness, I'd failed to properly think this through.

Chapter Sixty-Eight

Hugging Carly good-bye and trying not to notice the disapproval emanating from her, I jumped in the car and drove off.

The next stop was my parents' bungalow. When I'd telephoned earlier – from Carly's – Dad had said everything was fine, although he could never say otherwise. Mum always insisted the phone was switched to loudspeaker. This was so she could hear who was calling and what they were saying. The dementia had brought a deep mistrust about people. She was paranoid that "dolly birds" were ringing my father. Either that or a caller was spreading false rumours behind her back. To check if all really was well with Dad, I'd have to pay a visit. But that was no hardship. I wanted to see my parents.

On the drive over, I rang Theo.

'Are you phoning to say you'll bring along a spare shower curtain, just in case?' he teased.

'Ha! Very witty. Um, no. Nothing like that.'

'You sound a little stressed. Is everything okay?'

'Yes. As such. Just one small problem, but I can tweak it.'

'Is it something I can help with?'

'Erm, no. Well, yes. Change of plan. I'll drive to yours.'

There was a pause while Theo processed this. When he next spoke, his tone was guarded.

'Something has changed, hasn't it? Let me guess. Is it to do with your husband?'

I gasped at his astuteness, and knew he'd heard my sharp intake of breath. There was no lying my way out of this. Nor should I have to, really. It was no biggie, was it? Keith being under my roof was just a temporary situation, even if it did beggar the question *how long is a piece of string?*

'Yes,' I admitted. 'Keith has left Pippa. He's come back. Look, Theo–'

'It's okay, Annie. If you're ringing to tell me you've had a change of heart about us and want to do the decent thing and have a face-to-face, you really don't have to. A phone call is fine.'

'No!' I cried. 'It's nothing like that. Really it isn't. As far as I'm concerned, I'm a single woman. And Keith knows it.'

'Ah, but Annie, this is where things start to get messy. I don't want to be fraternising with a woman who strenuously insists she's single while her husband's car is permanently parked on the drive. That's not my style. I've spent the last few years living with a marriage-wrecker. I'm not about to become one myself.'

'But you're not,' I protested. 'Really. Please. Let me come over to you this evening. I want to see you,' I babbled. 'Just give me some time to put on my thinking cap. This situation has been totally sprung upon me. Keith is only at home because he has nowhere else to go.' I wasn't going to add that he wanted a reconciliation, because that nugget of information would see Theo disappearing faster than a participant in Wacky Races. He'd had enough insecurity with Pippa. The last thing he needed was starting a new relationship while Keith had his feet under the kitchen table. I knew exactly where Theo was coming from. He only had my word for it that Keith wasn't under my duvet too.

At the other end of the phone came a long silence. I could start to feel hope ebbing away. My heart grew heavy. Great. Theo wasn't buying my story. He was going to politely tell me not to bother coming over. To first sort out my private life. And that was fair enough. If the situation were reversed, I wouldn't want to ring Theo's doorbell and be confronted by a female wearing a hostile expression with arms folded across her chest. And yes. I knew that was exactly how Keith would behave if Theo rocked up. For one wild moment I wondered if I could persuade Keith to reassure Theo. To shake his hand and say, "We can be civilised, matey. Annie might still be my wife, but it's only a formality." Except Keith wouldn't do that because he *did* want me back.

'Are you still there?' I asked timorously. 'Listen to me, Theo. I'll move out. I'll ask Caz and Belles if I can do some sofa surfing until things are sorted.'

'Annie.' When Theo finally spoke, his voice was

tender. 'Sofa surfing is no fun. I've been there and done that and really don't recommend it. It puts strain on your friendships and, apart from anything else, it's really bad for your back.'

'Please can I come over this evening?' I quavered. 'I'll totally understand if you don't want to see me anymore, but…' I trailed off. I'd been going to add, "but I'd like closure." However, it sounded a bit ridiculous putting a label on something that had barely got off the ground.

'Okay, we'll keep the dinner date,' said Theo reluctantly. 'I'll text you the restaurant address.'

Oh. No witty mentions of bringing my face cream. From the sound of it, I wouldn't be going to his place. Just an impartial meal followed by a take-care-of-yourself send off.

I bit my lip. Oh well, Annie. Why did you think you were entitled to a new adventure? Or a fresh start? You're sixty. Too old for new beginnings. My eyes brimmed.

'See you at eight o'clock,' I whispered, before disconnecting the call.

Chapter Sixty-Nine

From the moment I hung up on Theo, I felt as if my mind had split in two.

One part of me was driving the car, heading on autopilot to my parents' house. The other was scrabbling around in a dark room desperately seeking a way out. There had to be an Exit door somewhere.

Even if Theo no longer wanted to see me, it made me even more certain that I didn't want to salvage things with Keith.

My husband was essentially a caring man. When he'd gone off with Pippa, he'd still treated me kindly. Okay, he'd been bogged down by a guilty conscience, but he could have easily growled, "I'm off. Tough. Get on with it." Now he was back, and it was me who wanted out. It wasn't just the trust that had gone. Love had evaporated too. Correction. I loved Keith, but in the same way I loved Caz and Bella. I was no longer *in* love with my husband. An important distinction.

Keith had taken it as a given that I'd welcome his return. Telling him there would be no reconciliation had resulted in him showing a different side. He was quite happy to be repaid for the Dubai holiday. I wouldn't be surprised if he subsequently asked for the return of the jewellery bought for my sixtieth.

I wondered what other hidden depths Keith would reveal. It was going to be a bumpy ride until the legalities were sorted. And in that moment, I knew that living under the same roof was not viable. I couldn't do it. Sofa surfing might not be the answer, but neither was sharing the marital home with a man I didn't want to be with.

I suddenly felt consumed with frustration and resentment. My fledgling romance with Theo might have come to an abrupt full stop, but the sooner I consulted a solicitor the better. How *dare* Keith just turn up as though nothing had ever happened. How *dare* he assume so much. How *dare* he not even give a courtesy phone call by way of warning. It was outrageous. And why couldn't *he* be the one to do the sofa surfing? After all, he was the one who'd brought this whole situation about. Let *him* find somewhere else to live in the interim.

But the more I thought about that, the more I knew Keith would dig his heels in. He wouldn't be the one to oblige. What? Give up his home comforts? Walk away from just the tiniest chance of me changing my mind? Knowing that he had the psychological upper hand here because, at our time of life, wasn't it easier to cave in and say, "Oh to hell with it. I'm too old and knackered to fight my corner. Let's agree to jog along nicely together."

Except I didn't want to jog along nicely together. I didn't want to be accountable for where I was going, who I was with or how long for. The fact that Keith had already telephoned Carly to check upon my movements didn't bode well. Why should I sneak around as if I were the one who had something to hide?

A blaring horn made me physically jump. Hell, I'd just driven through a red light. Omigod. Concentrate Annie.

I eventually pulled up on my parents' driveway, parking alongside Dad's car. A thick layer of wet leaves blanketed the car's wipers, and copious amounts of bird poo was splattered over the windscreen. Such signs told me my father hadn't been out for several days.

Guilt washed over me. I shouldn't have swanned off to Dubai leaving him with no respite. Carly had popped in once while I'd been away, but it wasn't enough to break the tedium for Dad. I'd held off asking Carly to visit them every day because she had her own life to oversee. A husband to look after. A home to run. Nesting. Making a nursery for a newborn. No, Mum and Dad were my responsibility.

I rang the doorbell. After waiting a full minute, I rang it again. Still no answer. This was usually the moment my brain kicked in with a list of worries:

Dad has dropped down dead, and my mother's mind is too addled to take it on board.

Or…

Dad failed to get the boiler serviced. He was too exhausted from looking after Mum to remember. Now the pair of them are dead in their beds from carbon monoxide poisoning.

Or…

Mum has wandered off and Dad is out looking for her.
Or…

Oh shut up you damn voice.

I rang the doorbell again. If I couldn't raise either of them in the next sixty seconds, I'd use the spare housekey on my fob.

Suddenly the door opened. My father stood there looking apologetic.

'Annie, darling.' He gave me a tired smile. 'Sorry to make you wait. I was' – he lowered his voice as if sharing a confidence – 'indisposed. I did call out to your mother to answer the door, but she wasn't willing to oblige. Today isn't such a good day.'

'I heard that, Michael Evans.' My mother's voice boomed from the lounge. 'I'm having a perfectly good day, thank you very much. Well, I would be, if you weren't such a problem.'

I leant in to peck my father on the cheek just as Mum appeared in the lounge doorway. She was bristling with hostility.

'What the hell do you think you're doing?' she demanded.

'Now then, Dorothy,' Dad cautioned.

'Get your paws off my husband, you hussy.'

I took a deep breath. Oh, joy. We were in one of those moods.

'It's Annie, Mum. Your daughter. I'm greeting Dad. Would you like a kiss too?'

She eyed me suspiciously, and then her eyes cleared.

'Hello, dear. How are you? You look wonderfully tanned. Got it out of a bottle, I suppose. You youngsters and your weird fads.'

I smiled at her description of me being a youngster and gave her a hug, exchanging a look with my father over her shoulder. He gave an imperceptible shrug. One that read, "It's just another day in La La Land."

'Let me put the kettle on,' I said, releasing Mum.

As I headed off to the kitchen, I inwardly groaned. I'd be looking like a teabag at this rate.

'I have a present for you both,' I said, as the kettle heated up.

'A present?' said Mum. 'Is it someone's birthday?'

'No, it's a gift. From Dubai.'

My mother sat down at the kitchen table, a frown upon her face.

'You went all the way to Dubai to buy a gift?'

'That's right,' I said. There was no point in explaining. It would be forgotten in moments.

'How was the holiday, love?' asked Dad, pulling out a chair. 'I can't wait to hear all about it.'

He was looking at me eagerly, and my heart did its familiar squeeze whenever I was talking to him. I knew exactly what he was thinking. That this was such a treat. Chatting to someone who could hold a sane conversation.

Another ton of guilt rolled over me for leaving him alone with Mum for so long. Not that a week was a huge amount of time ordinarily, but in my father's world it would have felt like a month.

I placed the teas before them, then sat down too.

'Let me start off by giving you both your prezzies.'

I dug in my handbag and pulled out the camel milk chocolate. I gave it to my father.

'Well, I never,' he said, looking at it in awe.

'And this is for you, Mum.' I passed her a small, gift-wrapped package. 'Unfortunately, I couldn't get a real camel, so I bought you the next best thing.'

She peeled back the paper, then hugged the small plush toy to her chest.

'I love him,' she beamed. 'I shall call him Pony.'

'Lovely,' I nodded. 'Pony the camel.'

And it was then, that I had the germ of an idea.

Chapter Seventy

After I'd told Dad all about the holiday – taking care to leave Theo out – I'd gone on to mention that Keith was back.

'That man' – spat Mum – 'has risen from the dead more times than Jesus. How the hell does he do it?'

'Er, quite,' I nodded. 'The thing is' – I addressed Dad – 'he's hoping for a reconciliation, but I don't want one. It's going to be awkward living under the same roof until things are finalised. It takes ages to get divorced.'

'I'm so sad for you, darling.' Dad put a gnarled hand over mine. 'It's not a time of life to be starting all over again.'

'I suspect that's what Keith hopes I'll think too. To leave things the way they are. Except I really can't be doing with that.'

'You need to give it careful consideration.'

'I have. I've thought of nothing else these last few hours, but I've had a brainwave.'

'Oh?'

'Well, you know I'm always trying to persuade the two of you to have care assistance? I was thinking–'

'Assistance?' interrupted my mother, sitting up straight.

'Your father doesn't need any help. He has me to look after him.'

I took a deep breath, told myself to stay calm, and use some psychology.

'And you do an amazing job, Mum. But sometimes it's nice to have an extra pair of hands, hm? I mean, look at your skirt. It's covered in spilt food. When was it last laundered?'

'It hasn't been cleaned because of that confounded woman.'

'You mean Alison, the girl who does your housework?'

'The girl who *pretends* to do housework. I daren't take off my skirt because she'll steal it. That's why I've been sleeping in it too.'

Oh for God's sake. When had my mother last washed? I looked at Dad, my eyebrows raised in silent question. He gave an imperceptible shake of the head.

'Mum, what about I run you a nice bath? While you're having a soak, I'll whiz that skirt through your machine's economy cycle. It will be ready for you to wear again in a jiffy. Alison isn't even here, so she won't steal it.'

My mother pursed her lips. 'Ha! You don't fool me, young lady. You're after my skirt too, right? Well, it's not on. Do you hear me?'

'Actually, it is on. It's been on too long, and that's why I want it off.'

'What?' she barked. 'Are you talking about the central heating? Turn the heating off, Michael.'

Give me strength. I turned my attention to Dad.

362

'I was thinking that perhaps I could move in here?'

'Move in?' said my mother. 'Whatever for?'

'Because' – I took a deep breath – 'I'm divorcing Keith and need somewhere to live.'

'Stop telling lies. Keith is dead.'

'Dad' – I turned to him in desperation – 'would you give it some thought, please? It would give you some assistance, and help me out enormously.'

'What's she talking about, Michael?'

My father ignored Mum and instead regarded me sadly.

'Annie, darling. I'd like to say yes, but it would be no life for you.'

'Please.'

'No, sweetheart. While we are coming to the end of our days, you still have some way to go. It wouldn't be fair.'

'But, Dad–'

'No.' His tone was resolute. Stubborn. He wasn't going to oblige. 'It might be tricky living alongside Keith, but essentially you'd keep your freedom – not to mention your work. There's no way you could hold down your job here.'

'Would you just sleep on the idea?'

'The subject is closed.'

For a moment, there was silence. My mother looked from me to Dad and then back to me again.

'How do you sleep on an idea? I sleep on a bed.'

Chapter Seventy-One

By the time I was ready to leave my parents' place, I felt emotionally drained. How the heck did my father do it? How did he stay sane?

I'd stayed out for several hours, and my brain felt frazzled. I knew, in my heart, that Dad's refusal about me moving in was his way of looking out for me. He knew that Mum would reduce me to a gibbering wreck before a week was out.

It was almost seven o'clock when I finally took my leave. Starting up the car, I took a deep calming breath. In the last few hours, I'd struggled to maintain patience, and taken so many deep breaths it was a wonder I wasn't hyperventilating. Still, there was plenty of time for that to happen because the next stop was Crowborough.

As I drove along, I felt bogged down with sadness. This time last week I'd been in Dubai, and about to check into the Blue Jade Hotel. Little had I known that my heart would soon be stolen by a Gerard Butler doppelgänger with a fine line in dry wit. There had been so much chemistry sparking between us it was a wonder our cupboard room hadn't burst into flames. Theo had turned my world upside down and pulled my heart inside out.

Just seven days ago.

A lifetime ago.

Indicating left, I joined the A21. Pulling into the middle lane, I silently prayed that Theo wouldn't take one look at me and wonder how I'd ever turned his head.

Earlier, when breakfasting at Chloe's Café, I'd been so looking forward to this moment. I'd also imagined it to be very different. Like – for starters – looking sophisticated and well-groomed. How stupid to have overlooked Keith's presence putting a spanner in the works.

I'd deliberately stayed out all day. Had I returned home, he would have shadowed me as I'd attempted to get myself ready for this evening. I could see him now, in my mind's eye, boggling at the skyscraper heels I'd planned on wearing. Frowning at the dress I'd earmarked – the one that hid underarm crepe but flattered the waist and bust. Not to mention him looking thoroughly put out when it came to me applying make-up and styling my hair. Things I'd never done in the last few years with him. There had never been any point. He'd always preferred me "natural". In other words, drab.

I hoped I wasn't currently looking too dowdy. I was still in this morning's jeans, with sensible flatties on my feet. At least I'd had the foresight to chuck a lipstick in my handbag. I reached across to the passenger side and, rummaging with one hand, extracted the gold tube. Carefully, one eye on the road, one on the car's internal mirror, I reapplied a top-up, then pinched my cheeks for some rosy colour. At least my face was tanned and gave it a healthy glow. Not that it really mattered how I looked. Nothing was going to persuade Theo to change his mind about "us".

It no longer mattered. It was irrelevant. I realised this wasn't so much about Keith, or even Theo. It was now about me. Striking out. Rediscovering who I was. As for this evening – well, it would an opportunity to thank Theo for giving me back the confidence to face my future. Alone.

Chapter Seventy-Two

Entering Crowborough, almost immediately I spotted the large old-fashioned pub Theo had described. It looked cosy and welcoming. The restaurant's windows twinkled from the inner candlelight, setting the tone for romance.

Ducking under the entrance's low beam, I spotted Theo immediately. He was standing at the bar. A teal-coloured shirt set off his eyes and colouring. He looked impossibly handsome, and my tummy instantly somersaulted.

He looked my way and raised a hand. A netful of butterflies bashed my ribs as I made my way over.

'Annie,' he said softly, stooping to drop a featherlight kiss on my cheek. It was exactly how one would greet an aunt. Gentle. Affectionate. And totally platonic.

'Theo.' I didn't get a chance to peck him back as he'd already straightened up and was now signalling the bartender. 'Prosecco?'

'Please.'

'How was the journey?'

'Fine. It took fifty minutes, which gave me time to do some... reflecting.'

He grimaced. 'Despite the circumstances, it's lovely to

see you.'

I gulped. 'And you.'

The bartender put my wine on the counter and Theo tapped his card against the terminal.

'Cheers,' I said gamely, picking up the glass.

I was determined that this last time together wouldn't be heavy. That said, now I was here, surely it wasn't such a good idea to sit down at a table-for-two. Somehow it didn't seem right to work our way through a candlelit dinner. Such an event was for lovers and married couples. It smacked of starry-eyes and sweet nothings. Murmured endearments with heads together. There wasn't going to be any of that.

'There's a table over there,' I pointed to an alcove in the bar, near an unlit woodburning stove. 'Shall we?'

'What about the restaurant? They'll probably call us through shortly.'

'I need to talk to you first, Theo. Perhaps you should cancel the reservation.'

'How about you tell me what you want to say first? After you.' He indicated I lead the way.

I threaded my way through standing patrons, then sank down on a hard wooden chair. Theo sat down opposite. I gazed across the table, committing every part of him to memory. His body. Face. Hands. They were on the table's surface, his fingers inches from mine. They might as well have been miles away.

I smiled hesitantly. 'Thank you for meeting me.'

'You don't need to thank me, Annie. It's a pleasure to

see you.' His face was sad. 'I just wish the circumstances were different.'

'It is what it is.' I waved a hand. 'Earlier, in the afternoon, I thought I'd cracked the situation. I visited my parents and offered to move in with them. You know, be their full-time carers.'

Theo went very still. He stared at me. 'Why would you do that?'

'Because I can't live under the same roof as Keith. I just can't. It's going to take months to get divorced. Then there's the sale of the house to organise, and we all know how conveyancing can drag on. Then there's all the palaver of buying a new place to live. More conveyancing. Realistically the whole dismantling process could take up to two years. Sharing the same space in the interim with Keith is too challenging. I've been nagging Mum and Dad to get help for ages, but they've both been so stubborn about it. My mother doesn't recognise she has dementia, and her temper is such that my father doesn't want to upset her. Her moods are something else. Some days she's a sweet little old lady. Other days she'll have – as my dad laughingly describes it – "your guts for garters". But the truth is, it's no laughing matter. My father was so happy to see me this afternoon. So overjoyed to have sensible conversation. Respite. That's what's required. Someone to share the load every day. That was when I had a lightbulb moment and suggested moving in with them both.'

'And are you?' asked Theo quietly.

'No.' For a moment I gazed at my Prosecco bubbles.

Pop. Pop. Just like those earlier bubbles of happiness. My eyes flicked back to Theo. 'Dad flatly refused to entertain the idea. He said it wasn't the life he wanted for me. That, under their roof, I'd never be able to concentrate on my clients. As you know, I have a little business and work from home. He advised me to tough it out with Keith. That while the situation would be fraught, it would be a hundred times more bearable than living with an old lady with such a challenging condition. I was initially devastated at his refusal, but it made me even more determined to be independent. So before leaving their place, I registered online with one of those property websites. It provides accommodation for people who don't mind sharing with others. You know, a bit like student digs. I can easily afford to rent a room. So I just need to wait for some availability in my area. Hopefully it won't be too many weeks and then I can be on my way.'

Theo was looking at me intently. 'You're really prepared to do that?'

I sighed. So much sighing today. 'Yes. And you know what?'

'Go on.'

'I feel relieved. Like a huge weight has been lifted from my shoulders. I'm going to properly be a free agent.' I smiled at him. 'Shortly I'll have a steppingstone to rest upon while the formalities are taken care of. So, Theo, I want to thank you.'

'Me?'

'Yes, because' – I paused for a moment, terrified I

370

might suddenly break down – 'even though nothing is now happening between us, your change of heart was the prod that I needed. The needle on the compass, swinging me around, making me change direction. After Keith left Pippa and let himself back into the marital home, if you hadn't mentioned your unwillingness to keep the company of' – I posted quotation marks in the air – '"a married woman", I'd have probably just lurched from one week to the next letting Keith set the pace – and on his terms. Now I'm the one in the driving seat. And my father is right. It would have been the wrong decision to live with him and Mum. But this way, I can still pop in on them. Still help. Still give him respite. But I won't be wearing myself into the ground in the process because I'll have my own space. And just think' – I attempted flippancy – 'the upside of renting a single room means hardly any housework.'

Theo didn't smile. Instead, he was looking at me intensely.

'You're really adamant that your marriage is over?'

I looked at him in surprise.

'Do you still not believe me? Yes, it's over. A hundred per cent.'

'I wanted to believe you.' His eyes held mine as he let out a shaky breath. 'But I was scared to. It didn't sit right with me dating a woman whose husband was still at home. But now…' He trailed off for a moment. 'Annie, I don't want to lose you.'

Now it was my turn to sit very still. I stared at him, hardly daring to breathe.

'You don't have to,' I whispered.

'Darling Annie,' he murmured. Suddenly his hands were taking mine across the table. For a moment I felt like we were back on that rooftop terrace in Dubai. 'Move in with me.'

I stared at him in shock. 'What?'

'I'm serious. Move in with me.'

'But... but...' I stammered.

'I mean it, Annie. What is there to lose? If it doesn't work out, so what? You'll eventually have your house proceeds and be able to buy your own place. You're not married to me, so you'd still have your independence. And who knows? Maybe this will work out. Maybe we will be ecstatically happy. Perhaps one day, we'll even end up buying a place together.' He was holding my hands tightly now, which was just as well because the zingers whizzing up my arms might have had them vibrating right off the tabletop. 'What do you say?'

'I... wow... I mean... oh wow... yes. Yes, I'll move in with you. Omigod!'

I wanted to lunge across the table and grab hold of him. This gorgeous man who wanted to take such an impulsive chance on us. I had no idea what the future would hold for the two of us, but I was prepared to take that chance too. We'd met in an exotic location. Plunged headfirst into a romance. And let's face it, I was perfectly aware of Theo's annoying habits after sharing a week in a cupboard room with him. Likewise, he about me.

'I have a horrible feeling I'm going to cry.' My lip was

wobbling violently.

'Me too,' he bantered. Except maybe he wasn't kidding. His eyes were very shiny. 'Move in now, Annie.'

'Tonight?' I gasped.

'Why not?' he smiled. 'No time like the present.'

We were interrupted by the head waiter coming into the bar.

'Mr Theo Kipling and guest. Your table is ready. Please come through to the restaurant.'

'Shall we?' said Theo, pushing back his chair.

Suddenly I was ravenously hungry. 'Yes, please,' I beamed.

I stood up and let him lead me by the hand into the restaurant. A second later he paused, pulled me into him and kissed me hard on the mouth.

'I've been wanting to do that from the moment you walked in.'

'Me too,' I said, my eyes shining. 'But Theo, there's just one problem.'

'What?' he said, suddenly looking anxious.

'I haven't brought my toothbrush.'

'It's okay. You can borrow mine.' His eyes twinkled mischievously. 'I even have face cream.'

THE END

Author's Note

Just to give my readers an update.

Carly went on to give birth to a beautiful little girl. Charlotte Dorothy weighed in at 7lbs 2oz. The midwife asked if new daddy Ryan would like to cut the umbilical cord. Ryan agreed, but was so overcome with emotion, he fainted, hit his head, and suffered concussion. Mother and baby left the hospital later that day while Ryan was admitted for overnight observation. Six months later, his mates still pull his leg for passing out in the delivery room. However, Ryan is sure he'll be fine if the experience ever arises again. Which is good to know because Carly has just this second done a pregnancy test. And it's positive.

Annie's parents are thrilled to be great-grandparents. Mother Evans spends her days knitting voraciously. So far, she's made eighty-nine tea cosies.

Theo and Annie remain together and are totally in love. Annie is so happy she periodically stops to pinch herself. Their relationship is full of laughter and sizzling chemistry, which Carly finds mildly embarrassing, although she's delighted her mum is so happy and has welcomed Theo into the family as a third grandpa.

Keith rues the day he fell for Pippa Kipling. He's since

met Theo. First over the Christmas period, and then again at Charlotte's christening. On both occasions he was polite to Theo, but frosty. Annie hopes that Keith will one day thaw out but, as Caz said, it's the sower's problem.

Caz has stopped sending pictures of her feet to the American. Andrew saw her photographing her toes and wanted to know what she was doing. Caz confided in Bella and Annie that she'd nearly been caught out. They were unanimous in their advice. It must stop. When Caz told the American there would be no more pics, he was upset. But she put her foot down. (Sorry, couldn't resist!)

Meanwhile, Pippa was annoyed that Keith dumped her before she could spend his inheritance. However, a new visitor to the garden centre has caught her eye. She's now giving warm smiles and coquettish looks to Little Waterlow's latest newcomer, The Honourable Sir Arthur Wilton-Smith. He's a seventy-year-old widower with a spring in his step and a lecherous gleam in the eye. More importantly he recently purchased the sizeable country mansion on the outskirts of the village. But that's another story...

A Letter from Debbie

Dubai was the last place I travelled to before first lockdown. And it was AMAZING! However, I'd like to point out that it's highly unlikely any Emirati hotel would ever have a situation where two strangers – much less male and female – ended up sharing a room (and a cupboard room at that!). But in the world of fiction, anything goes, plus I needed a situation that threw Annie and Theo together for the sparks to start flying. One of the joys of being an author is changing rules to suit a purpose!

The Blue Jade Hotel doesn't exist. Whilst it's fictional, the style and smartness is loosely based on the *Sheraton Jumeirah Beach Resort* which I can highly recommend.

Caz, Bella, and Annie visited a shop called *Orange Skies* in Al Karama. There *is* such a shop, but it isn't called that! If you go online and do a bit of digging, like asking Google where to find the most authentic looking fakes in Al Karama, you'll likely come across the shop I've written about. There's a small clue in the fictional name!

A little of my mum's character went into creating Mother Evans. For those who follow me on Facebook, you might have read my occasional posts regarding conversations between the two of us. Whilst dementia is absolutely terrible, it can also have terribly funny moments. As a coping mechanism, it's far easier to giggle than cry. When Mother Bryant was first diagnosed, she was most indignant and snippily told the consultant that she "still had all her facilities". When I have retold such stories to followers, I have always concluded with #TheLighterSideOfDementia so it's clear we look on the bright side rather than wallow in despair. I know my mum would much rather the family laugh than weep.

This is my fifteenth novel and sees a return to the fictional village of Little Waterlow, which was the setting for my last romcom, *Daisy's Dilemma*. Little Waterlow is a small Kent village not dissimilar to my own stomping ground.

I love to write books that make a reader occasionally giggle and provide pure escapism. After intermittent lockdowns, I hope this story will raise a few smiles.

There are several people involved in getting a book "out there" and I want to thank them from the bottom of my heart.

Firstly, the brilliant Rebecca Emin of *Gingersnap Books*, who knows exactly what to do with machine code and is a formatting genius.

Secondly, the fabulous Cathy Helms of *Avalon Graphics* for working her magic in transforming a rough sketch to a gorgeous book cover. Cathy always delivers exactly what I want and is a joy to work with.

Thirdly, the amazing Rachel Gilbey of *Rachel's Random Resources*, blog tour organiser extraordinaire. Immense gratitude also goes to each of the fantastic bloggers who took the time to read and review *Annie's Autumn Escape*. They are:

B for bookreview; Books and Bindings; Being Anne; Tizi's Book Review; From Under the Duvet; Ginger Book Geek; Two ladies and a book; Amy's Booket List; Bookshelves & Teacups; Ceri's Little Blog; @Curlygrannylovestoread; Satisfaction for Insatiable Readers; Books, Life and Everything; Imreadingmybook; Eatwell2015; Grace J Reviewerlady; Sadie's Spotlight; What Irin Reads; Nikipedia; Kirsty_Reviews_Books; Chonky Books Review; Jazzy Book Reviews; Snowphiethebookworm; Corinne Rodrigues; School_librarian_loves_books; pawsandpagesbyannie; Sometimes Leelynn Reads; Book Escapes With BabsW67; and Dash Fan Book Reviews.

Fourthly, my lovely daughter, Eleanor, for assisting with proof-reading.

Finally, I want to thank you, my reader. Without you, there is no book. If you enjoyed reading *Annie's Autumn Escape* I'd be over the moon if you wrote a review – just a quick one liner – on Amazon. It makes such a difference helping new readers discover one of my books for the first time.

Debbie xx

Enjoyed *Annie's Autumn Escape?*
Then you might also like *Willow's Wedding Vows.*
Check out the first three chapters on the next page!

One

'Did you have a good weekend?' Willow asked her superior as they stood together, huddled over the staff room kettle on a bleak Monday morning in early September.

'I've had better,' said Jean, pulling her cardigan around her ample bosom. 'Our Julie broke her wrist.'

'Oh no. How did that happen?' asked Willow, pouring boiling water over coffee granules.

'Believe it or not, she did it when trying to open a jar of jam. The lid wouldn't come off, so she gave it some welly and the wretched thing flew up sending Julie's wrist smacking into an overhead cupboard. She's now in plaster.'

'Oh dear,' said Willow, sympathising. 'Nothing worse than being in plaster.' Except, she thought privately, getting plastered. Which was exactly what she'd done on Saturday night. But it hadn't been in a jolly let's-get-tipsy kind of way. Instead it had been in a let's-blot-out-the-misery way.

It had been her thirtieth birthday and boyfriend Charlie had taken Willow out for a slap-up meal at the local pub. She'd almost stuffed herself to a standstill on the huge plate of tender slow-cooked lamb, green beans and divine buttery mash. Throughout, Charlie had entertained her with anecdotes about work, including some rather bitchy criticisms

380

of staff.

'It's about time everyone realised what a plank the MD is. *I* could do that job with my eyes shut.'

There'd also been a dig about the scatty new receptionist who Charlie had nick-named Ditzy Di on account of how she always cocked things up. Last week's faux pas had been booking the boardroom for twelve different clients... all at the same time.

'Gorgeous looking girl, and sweet enough, but nothing between the ears.'

Willow had privately tutted thinking that, much as she loved her clever accountant boyfriend, it wasn't a nice trait to be so quick to put people down.

Sometimes Charlie put Willow down too. Not nastily, but in such a way as to let her know that being a library assistant wasn't rocket science, and no matter how irritating or rude some members of the public could be, Willow's days were surely never as stressful as Charlie's. But she forgave him this flaw, and one or two other niggles because, after all, nobody was perfect.

Or quite so good looking, eh? the little voice in Willow's head had piped up.

Willow had quietly sighed in agreement. For there was no doubt about it, Charlie was a "babe". His rugged blond looks and come-to-bed blue eyes played havoc with her heart — and that of other women too. At times he was an unashamed flirt, but Willow told herself it was excusable given the amount of female attention Charlie received. He was like a particularly glorious golden sunflower that towered over everything — and everyone, in his case.

But flirting didn't mean anything, did it? After all, Willow's good-looking postman had winked at her last week. He'd made her smile and blush, but she hadn't run after him, scattered his letters in all directions and panted, "Quick, deliver me to Heaven", had she? And as far as she was aware, Charlie had never taken his flirting any further.

Are you sure about that? the little voice had sneered.

She'd ignored it. The little voice was always taunting her, probably because she had body issues and lacked self-confidence.

Willow was a curvy girl. Friends said she looked just like Amanda Seyfried but with hips and boobs, and a bum that meant she always needed the next size up in jeans which left the waistband gaping. She hated standing next to her bestie, Emma, who had a metabolism faster than Usain Bolt, and almost disappeared whenever she stood sideways. Emma had recently come out of a disastrous long-term relationship and was living back home with her mother. There had been many tears, with Emma sobbing that she felt like a failure.

Emma had been sure her boyfriend was going to pop the question. Instead he'd asked Emma if they could take a break. An indefinite one. It had been Emma's situation that had prompted Willow to start thinking about her own long-term relationship with Charlie. Wasn't it about time the two of *them* got married? When she'd opened her birthday cards and found every single one to be sporting the numbers "three" and "zero", it had set something off in her brain, as if to remind her she'd reached a significant landmark in her life.

The sneery little voice in her head hadn't wasted a second in pointing out that Willow's biological clock was now ticking. Whilst having a baby before marriage wasn't an issue, she was old-fashioned enough to want a wedding band and a loads-of-sex honeymoon before stretchmarks and nipple shields.

Sipping her birthday champagne while Charlie had chatted away, she'd quietly weighed things up. She and Charlie had lived together for almost a decade. It wasn't like they didn't know each other's little foibles. Okay, he drove her slightly mad with his habit of leaving clothes inside-out and dumped on the floor, but she irritated him by nicking his socks and borrowing his razor. Charlie's flirting had never got out of hand – other than when she'd gone on a girly night with Emma to a club where Charlie just happened to also be. He'd been snogging another girl. But Willow had mentally shaken the memory away. That was *waaaay* back, and not long after they'd met. They hadn't been living together. They hadn't even been "exclusive". And he'd never done it since, had he?

I wouldn't trust him, sniffed the little voice in her head.

Good, she'd silently replied, *because you're not the one who wants to marry him, so why don't you just bog off, eh?*

Willow had decided to broach the subject of getting hitched whilst out celebrating her birthday with Charlie. Finishing her lamb, Willow had put her knife and fork together. At that moment, Charlie had leant across the table and romantically taken her hand in his. As he'd smiled at her, the soft candlelight had flickered across his handsome face, bathing them both in a golden glow. It had seemed like the perfect moment.

'So,' she'd beamed, aware that birthday champagne had made everything deliciously fuzzy as well as emboldening her. 'Can I ask you a question?'

Charlie's smile had expanded. The last time Willow had used that very suggestive tone of voice, she'd been faintly drunk – like now – and feeling randy. She'd later gone on to initiate some mind-blowing sex which had been amazing, especially as most of the time their love life was not an earthmoving experience. He supposed they'd been together too long for her to stir his loins more than a perfunctory once-a-week coupling. He allowed himself a little daydream. Perhaps his girlfriend was going to suggest something outrageous, like... having a threesome. Wasn't that every man's fantasy? He knew that Willow's bestie was back on the dating market. Perhaps the girls had been gossiping behind his back while drinking a bottle of wine between them. Maybe Emma had tipsily confided that she'd always fancied Charlie, and what about they shared him for one night of no-strings passion? Charlie wouldn't mind that at all. Her boobs weren't as big as Willow's, but her lean and wiry body indicated a capacity to crawl all over a man's body like a spider on amphetamines. Willow was now squeezing his hand, her tongue flicking over her lips to wet them. How suggestive and delightful.

'What is it?' he'd murmured huskily. 'Tell me, darling.'

'How do you feel–?'

Willow had paused, suddenly looking awkward.

'Go on!' he'd smiled encouragingly.

'About getting married?' Willow had blurted.

Charlie had frozen. There'd been a moment of stunned silence and then he'd whipped his hand away from hers.

'Married?' he'd yelped, loud enough to have the couple at the next table turning to look at them speculatively.

'Y–Yes,' Willow had quavered, her bravado popping as quickly as the champagne bubbles in the ice-bucket on the table.

'I thought you were going to ask–'

'Yes?'

'If I fancied… dessert,' Charlie had blustered.

'I do,' Willow had said, the two words further unnerving Charlie. Help. Was she saying her wedding vows already?

'I don't.'

'Don't want dessert, or don't want to get married?'

'Neither,' he'd said, aghast.

Willow had promptly burst into tears. The ear-wigging couple at the next table had looked upset on Willow's behalf.

'Give him time, love,' the lady had said, leaning across and patting Willow's arm.

'I've already given him over nine years,' Willow had sobbed. She'd pushed her chair back and stood up, leaving Charlie frantically summoning the waitress for the bill.

She'd cried all the way home. Charlie had sat silently beside her as he'd steered the car. Once home, he'd feigned a headache and disappeared upstairs. Willow had stayed downstairs and popped the cork on a birthday bottle of Prosecco. She'd drowned her sorrows while watching old re-runs of *Friends*. Willow had known exactly how Rachel had felt about wanting to marry Ross, but not being able to have him.

At some point Willow had fallen asleep. Upon waking, cold and stiff on a Sunday morning, she'd discovered Charlie had gone out. There was a note next to her.

Sorry about last night. I've gone to Mum's. She's feeling down. See you later xx

Charlie's mum had recently been widowed. Grace was, understandably, grieving and sad. When Charlie didn't come home Sunday evening, Willow had tried not to mind. Nor did she text Charlie to ask if his mum was okay. Better to wrap her dignity around her like the duvet she was later huddled under, alone.

When Monday morning rolled around, she was surprised to discover that at some point Charlie had come home, showered and gone to work. She must have been out cold. Willow had crawled out of bed and into the shower before setting off to work at Mosley Library.

And now, as she stirred her first coffee of the day in the library's tiny kitchen, she briefly wished she was colleague Jean's daughter, recovering in plaster from a broken wrist. Because a broken wrist would heal far more swiftly than a broken heart.

Two

Charlie was behind his London desk long before any other staff began filtering into the trendy open-plan office block that overlooked the River Thames. A desire to distance himself from Willow before she was properly up and about had been his number one priority. The last thing he wanted was twenty questions on why he didn't want to get married.

He'd spent some of the remainder of the weekend at his childhood home where his widowed mother now lived alone. Grace had expressed surprise upon seeing her son on the doorstep without Willow. She knew it had been Willow's birthday, but Charlie had made an excuse about his girlfriend having a migraine and it being important she was left alone to quietly sleep it off. On Sunday, he'd taken his mother out to a carvery for lunch, and then announced that Willow had texted saying she was feeling much better, so he'd better get back.

As soon as Grace had waved him off, Charlie had taken advantage of his car's Bluetooth and rung a number saved on his mobile simply as "Kev". But Kev wasn't a man. Moments later, a woman's voice answered. It was the same woman he'd spent two hours with *prior* to turning up on his mother's doorstep to establish a cast-iron alibi. As he waited for the number to connect, Charlie told himself it was unlikely Willow would check up on his movements, but it was best not to take chances. The number began to ring. Almost immediately, it was answered.

'Hey, sexy lady,' he said, making his voice deliberately husky.

'Hey yourself,' said the woman, clearly pleased to hear from him.

'Fancy a re-run of last night?'

'If you insist,' the woman giggled.

'I do, I do,' Charlie murmured, and then blanched. God, those hideous words again.

'The coast is clear for the rest of the day and all of tonight,' she said.

'In that case, I'll stay over – as long as you don't mind me disappearing before the sun comes up. I'll try not to wake you in the morning.'

'Can't you go to work from mine?'

Charlie could imagine her lovely mouth pouting at the other end of the line, and he smiled.

'You are very demanding. In more ways than one.'

'I can't help it where you're concerned,' she said, voice teasing again.

'Good,' said Charlie smugly, 'but unfortunately I don't have a suit with me, so I have no choice but to get up with the dawn chorus.'

'Never mind. I'll take what I can of you,' she said happily.

'See you in ten minutes.'

Charlie had hung up and floored the accelerator. He hadn't meant to start an affair. He hadn't meant to start *anything*. Their paths had, from time to time, crossed over the years. And yes, there had always been banter. But Charlie bantered with all the ladies. Some women called it flirting. But most of the time it really was meaningless in Charlie's case. After all, he bantered with the old girl who sometimes vacuumed around his legs if he was working a little late on a report. Just because he made risqué comments about the sucking power of her nozzle didn't mean he was hinting at a blow job for God's sake. That was the trouble with females. They had a propensity to misunderstand things and muddle it out of proportion. If Charlie meant business with a woman, then he would leave her in no doubt of his intention. All it needed was a raised eyebrow, a loaded silence, and a few smoulders. There was no need to muck about wasting precious shagging time on meaningless banter if he was planning on going in for the kill.

Charlie had always been careful not to do the dirty on his own doorstep. Any extra-curricular sexual activity on his part had always been well away from home base – stag weekends abroad, hens looking for one last fling before saying "I do" – God, those words again – or business meetings at the sister company in Birmingham where the totty was hot even if the accent was not. This was the closest to home he'd ever got regarding messing about. It was also the longest he'd ever had another woman on the go. Usually he loved them and left them. One-night stands with no strings sex had been the rule. Except he'd broken his own rule. Somehow he'd let this woman become a lover. Charlie had been in her bed more times than he could now remember, and he didn't like that. It made him feel uneasy. It also thrilled him.

If someone had asked Charlie whether he'd cheated on Willow a lot, he'd have looked incredulous and said, "Most definitely not". But the fact remained that, in the years they'd been together, there had probably been as many women, which wasn't good as a track record. Charlie told himself that it was purely because he'd not had enough time to sow his wild oats before buying a house with Willow and "sort of" settling down.

He'd met Willow on a lad's holiday in Ibiza where the boys' collective plan had been to booze and bonk the night away and recover under a sunshade on the beach during the day. Charlie had spotted Willow two sun loungers along from his, laying on her back, her Rapunzel-gold hair sheeting out behind her and flowing down to the wet sand. She'd looked almost like a mermaid with her shell-coloured bikini struggling to contain two magnificent breasts that gently rose and fell as she snoozed. A pretty but not-so-ample brunette had been on the sun bed next to the blonde vision and caught Charlie looking. He'd smiled helplessly and the girl had got up and come over.

'I'll get straight to the point,' she'd said, doing exactly that. 'Is it me or my friend you're interested in?'

Charlie had been mildly amused at the brunette's frankness.

'You're very lovely,' he'd said, smiling disarmingly at

her, 'but I do rather favour curvy girls.'

'What you really mean is that you're a boob man,' she'd tutted.

'Yes,' he'd grinned. 'But you're definitely Stuart's type' – he'd pointed to his mate crashed out under the sunbrella to his right – 'so go and wake him up and tell him to buy us all some ice-cold beers.'

Charlie had later found out that the brunette was called Emma. As he'd predicted, Stuart had immediately hit it off with Emma and they'd ended up inseparable for the remainder of the holiday, just like Charlie and Willow. But, in Charlie's case, instead of the holiday romance coming to a natural end, he'd reconnected with Willow once home and been with her ever since. He should have taken a leaf out of Stu's book and waved good-bye to her at the airport but, at the time, Willow's golden hair and shapely figure had mesmerised him. Apart from anything else, he couldn't bring himself to hurt her. Willow was like a puppy. Very, very sweet.

Charlie wasn't prepared to risk his car being spotted by anyone who might – no matter how unlikely – know him, so he parked two streets away. The door was on the latch and he hastened towards it.

'Darling,' she purred, pulling him into the hallway. 'You came.'

'Not yet, but I will shortly,' he quipped, scooping her up into his arms and kicking the door shut behind them. And the rest was kiss-tory.

A lack of sleep had cast a pallor over Charlie's usually

glowing complexion. Poring over a merger and acquisitions report, he heard rather than saw Ben – a longstanding colleague and now long-time friend – pulling out his chair at the next cubicle along.

'Hello, hello,' said Ben with a grin as he flicked on his screen. 'You're in very early. Trouble at home?'

'Course not,' said Charlie, looking up and making sure his expression conveyed the right amount of incredulity. Ben might now be his best buddy, but there were some secrets you kept to yourself. Especially when they were so close to home. 'I should have done this wretched report on Brown & Humphrey before going home on Friday. Consequently, I spent the whole weekend worrying about it, so decided to set the alarm for five and get in before the phones started ringing.' Charlie added some figures to the on-screen spreadsheet. 'What's your excuse to be in so early, and with such enviably white eyeballs?'

Charlie was aware that a marathon sexy stint and lack of sleep had left his pretty blue eyes shot through with pink lines. Early night tonight. He'd give Willow a ring in a bit and make placatory noises and suggest spag bol in front of the telly. It would give him the chance to assess her mood, make peace if required, and practice dodging the "M" word if she brought it up again. Calling her at work also meant she wouldn't be able to have hysterics of the unfunny kind whilst dealing with the public.

'Ditto,' said Ben, interrupting Charlie's thoughts, 'and my eyeballs are always white, even if get bladdered.'

'It's not natural.'

'What, getting bladdered?'

'No, having such white eyeballs.'

'Here,' said Ben, reaching into his jacket pocket and extracting a small oblong box. He chucked it at Charlie. 'Eyedrops. White eyeballs guaranteed. Have them on me. I have more at home.'

'Cheers,' said Charlie, pocketing the box with a grin. He leant back and stretched. 'Go and get us both a coffee, mate.'

'Blimey, I've only been here two minutes and already you've whipped my eyedrops and started giving orders.'

'Yeah, but I've had a heavy weekend,' said Charlie, yawning.

'Thought so,' Ben murmured. 'Hope she's worth it.'

Charlie tutted, feigning annoyance. He watched Ben go off to the fancy kitchen at the far end of the floor where Beryl, coffee-maker extraordinaire, usually presided between the hours of nine and five. The hour was still too early for Beryl to make an appearance.

Charlie turned back to his screen with Ben's words echoing in his head. *Hope she's worth it.* The truth of it was, she wasn't. Not really. She might be ace in bed, but it was only because it was all new and fresh and fizzy. She wasn't even his type, dammit! So why did he find himself repeatedly risking everything he had with Willow? Did he subconsciously want Willow to find out and be the one to do the dumping, saving him the trouble of doing it? Not really, because he didn't want to end it with Willow. He might not want to marry her, but he didn't want to let her go either. So why did he behave like this? Because... because...

His mind struggled to find the reasons why.

Willow was pretty. She turned heads. *He* knew that, even if she didn't. His girlfriend was kind. She was also very efficient on the home front. The house always looked nice, she was a good cook *and* she ironed his shirts. Ben's girlfriend didn't do that. Usually it was Ben ironing *her* stuff. Was Charlie, perhaps, staying with Willow out of habit? Maybe. But, then again, he couldn't imagine life without her. His thoughts looped round and around in circles. He was too young to remember Prince Charles's embarrassingly awkward moment when asked if he was in love with Princess Diana, or the famous reply of "Whatever *in love* means", but like the future king, Charlie presumed that whatever love was it was *that* that kept him by Willow's side. He comforted himself with that thought whilst squirting some eyedrops in his tired eyes, then thanked Ben for the coffee. He took a noisy slurp as he mentally ran through what he'd say when he called Willow, preferably when Ben wouldn't be able to overhear.

Three

'For goodness' sake, Willow,' snapped Jean. 'Whatever is the matter with you this morning? That's the third time you've misdirected a member of the public. That lady was asking you to help her with IT access, not a tooth abscess.'

'Sorry,' Willow mumbled.

'We've got an author coming in shortly to give a talk to the public. Perhaps you could help her set up her display table without losing concentration.'

'Okay.'

'And try and look enthusiastic and smile.'

'Okay,' Willow repeated.

She must pull herself together. But it was hard when you'd wrecked your own birthday night mentioning the M word to a boyfriend with a bachelor mindset.

Willow had devoted hours to privately analysing the whole thing. She'd been too forward. She should have let Charlie do the talking. She'd emasculated him... been too presumptuous... frightened him... scared him off... made him feel trapped. And then she'd got angry and berated herself. She hadn't been forward enough... she should have grimly hung on to Charlie's hand therefore denying him escape whilst setting out the reasons to get hitched, like...

proving they were committed to each other… publicly celebrating their devotion in front of their family, friends and loved ones… because, dammit, it was also romantic and wonderful and gorgeous, and surely every girl's dream to feel – just for one day – like a fairy-tale princess in her Cinderella dress, a tiara glittering away in her hair as her very own Prince Charming promised to love her for ever.

Oh. My. God, sneered the little voice in her head. *You don't truly believe all that sexist rubbish, do you?*

'Excuse me–'

Do you think women burned their bras and fought for independence so that the likes of you could carry on playing the little woman? What century are you living in?

'Hello? Er, I wonder if–'

Geez, Willow, if Charlie wore slippers, you're the sort of idiotic female who'd have warmed them by the fire ready for him to step into when he was home from work. Man up, girl! Be indignant! Be strong! He turned you down. How DARE he!

'Um, can you hear me–?'

If he doesn't want to marry you, that's his loss, BUT for heaven's sake start having some respect for both yourself and the sisterhood and get HIM to iron YOUR stuff, occasionally walk the vacuum around the house, put a wash on, oversee the online shop, ask if he can run YOUR bath, and generally scamper after YOU! Do you hear me?

'Can you hear me–?'

'Oh give me a flipping break,' Willow snapped.

'O-Oh, I'm so sorry, I didn't mean–'

Willow turned scarlet as she realised that a little old lady had been trying to get her attention.

'Omigod, I'm so sorry,' she gabbled. 'I wasn't talking to you, I was talking to–'

A pair of cloudy blue eyes bored into hers, waiting for an answer.

'–Myself,' said Willow firmly. 'I'm in... amateur dramatics... just rehearsing my lines.'

'You're very believable,' said the little old lady.

'Good.' Willow gave a shaky laugh. Thank goodness Jean was busy talking to the other two members of staff, Fiona and Theresa. If Jean had overheard Willow snapping at a library visitor, there would have been hell to pay. 'How can I help?'

'I want to give a talk about my latest book. I can do it now, if that's okay.'

Ah. This must be the author Jean had mentioned.

'Fantastic,' said Willow, dredging up a smile. 'What's it called.'

'Free Willy.'

'Really? Hasn't that already been done? I'm sure a guy wrote it... now what was his name?' – she clicked her fingers, waiting for the info to drop into her brain – 'got it, Keith Walker.'

'Oh no, dear' – the little old lady shook her head – 'that became a movie and was about a whale. *My* book is about how to have a successful and rewarding sex life in your eighties if your partner can't perform, or if you're widowed and there isn't anyone there to perform, or you don't have

397

enough pension left in your purse to *pay* for someone to perform. Free willy. Literally.'

Willow blinked. Was this conversation really happening?

'I self-published the book,' said the little old lady proudly.

'W-Wow,' said Willow faintly. What the hell was Jean playing at not properly vetting who was coming in to promote their book?

'Where are your paperbacks?

'It's one of those new-fangled e-books. My granddaughter sorted out the techie side for me, but I've brought in some visual props for demonstration purposes,' she said, shaking a grocery in her right hand. Willow caught a glimpse of cucumbers, courgettes and aubergines.

'Um, could you just wait here a minute? I need to have a word with my superior.'

'Of course, dear,' said the little old lady, beaming.

Willow shot over to Jean who was manning the enquiries desk.

'Jean, can I have a quick word? You know that author you were talk–?'

The phone rang. Like a traffic cop, Jean's palm shot up.

'A member of the public is ringing this library,' she said reverently, for all the world as if it was Her Majesty on the line. 'Therefore that person takes priority.' She picked up the handset, chest swelling importantly. 'Mosley Library, good morning. How can I help you?'

'Excuse me?' said a pleasant looking middle-aged woman, tapping Willow's arm. 'I'm Mary Rogers. I'm giving

398

an author talk today about my book.'

Willow looked at the woman blankly. How many authors had Jean booked?

'Um, could I ask you to take a seat over there,' said Willow, pointing to a row of hard-backed chairs. 'My colleague will be with you shortly.' Willow turned back to Jean in time to see her face darkening with displeasure.

'This call is for you. It's Charlie.'

'Oh,' squeaked Willow, in both fear and delight.

'One moment, please,' said Jean to Charlie. She put down the handset and turned to Willow. 'Can I remind you,' she hissed, 'that personal calls are not permitted during working hours, especially on the library's phone.

'I-I'm sorry,' Willow stuttered. She really wasn't having a great Monday morning. 'It must be an emergency.'

'Let's hope so, otherwise I might have to consider giving you a verbal warning. Now what was the problem with the visiting author?'

'We seem to have two of them. The first is over there.'

Willow pointed to the little old lady who was now busily making a vegetable display on a side table. Jean's face instantly morphed into a bulldog chewing a wasp.

'What on earth–?'

She marched off leaving Willow to grab the handset and take Charlie's call.

'Hello?' Willow quavered.

What could possibly be so important for Charlie to call her in *his* working hours *and* on the library number. Her blood ran cold. Perhaps there had been some sort of family emergency. Or... now her blood was turning to ice... perhaps he couldn't stand the thought of going home to her tonight and wanted to give her fair warning? Could today get any worse? Perhaps, in the next five minutes, she'd have been sacked by both her boss and her boyfriend.

'Darling,' said Charlie, and Willow was so relieved at hearing the endearment she slumped over the enquiry desk's upper counter. 'I've behaved like a dick. Will you accept my apology?'

'Yes,' she said, without hesitation.

'Good,' he said, then lowered his voice. 'Can we have kiss-and-make-up-sex tonight?'

'Yes,' Willow repeated, wishing that her boyfriend was more romantic and had instead said he'd like to *make love* to her. Like the M word, the L word wasn't really part of Charlie's vocabulary. But she mustn't complain. A squawk from Jean briefly fragmented Willow's thoughts. Turning, she saw her boss firmly guiding the little old lady towards the exit, vegetable props back in the shopping .

'I shall look forward to ravishing you later, angel,' whispered Charlie.

'Me too,' Willow murmured. She'd pull out all the stops tonight and try and think of an added ingredient to really spice things up.

As if on cue, the little old lady shrieked, 'What am I going to do with all these cucumbers?'

Want to know what happens next?
Head over to Amazon

Also by Debbie Viggiano

Daisy's Dilemma

The Watchful Neighbour (debut psychological thriller)

Cappuccino and Chick-Chat (memoir)

Willow's Wedding Vows

Lucy's Last Straw

What Holly's Husband Did

Stockings and Cellulite

Lipstick and Lies

Flings and Arrows

The Perfect Marriage

Secrets

The Corner Shop of Whispers

The Woman Who Knew Everything

Mixed Emotions (short stories)

The Ex Factor (a family drama)

Lily's Pink Cloud ~ a child's fairytale

100 ~ the Author's experience of Chronic Myeloid Leukaemia

Printed in Great Britain
by Amazon